D0037090

NEW YORK TIMES BESTSELLING AUTHOR

DIANA PALMER

TEXAS DARE

Previously published as
The Rancher and *Passion Flower*

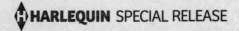

HARLEQUIN SPECIAL RELEASE

HARLEQUIN® SPECIAL RELEASE

ISBN-13: 978-1-335-93101-6

Texas Dare

Copyright © 2021 by Harlequin Books S.A.

The Rancher
First published in 2012. This edition published in 2021.
Copyright © 2012 by Diana Palmer

Passion Flower
First published in 1984. This edition published in 2021.
Copyright © 1984 by Diana Palmer

PLEASE RECYCLE
THIS PRODUCT IS RECYCLABLE

Recycling programs
for this product may
not exist in your area.

For questions and comments about the quality of this book, please contact us at CustomerService@Harlequin.com.

Harlequin Enterprises ULC
22 Adelaide St. West, 40th Floor
Toronto, Ontario M5H 4E3, Canada
www.Harlequin.com

Printed in U.S.A.

CONTENTS

A prolific author of more than one hundred books,
Diana Palmer got her start as a newspaper reporter.
A *New York Times* bestselling author and voted one of
the top ten romance writers in America, she has a gift
for telling the most sensual tales with charm and humor.
Diana lives with her family in Cornelia, Georgia. Visit her
website at www.dianapalmer.com.

Books by Diana Palmer

Long, Tall Texans

Fearless
Heartless
Dangerous
Merciless
Courageous
Protector
Invincible
Untamed
Defender
Undaunted

The Wyoming Men

Wyoming Tough
Wyoming Fierce
Wyoming Bold
Wyoming Strong
Wyoming Rugged
Wyoming Brave

Morcai Battalion

The Morcai Battalion
The Morcai Battalion: The Recruit
The Morcai Battalion: Invictus
The Morcai Battalion: The Rescue

Visit the Author Profile page
at Harlequin.com for more titles.

THE RANCHER

CHAPTER ONE

MADDIE LANE WAS WORRIED. She was standing in her big yard, looking at her chickens, and all she saw was a mixture of hens. There were red ones and white ones and gray speckled ones. But they were all hens. Someone was missing: her big Rhode Island Red rooster, Pumpkin.

She knew where he likely was. It made her grind her teeth together. There was going to be trouble, again, and she was going to be on the receiving end of it.

She pushed back her short, wavy blond hair and grimaced. Her wide gray eyes searched the yard, hoping against hope that she was mistaken, that Pumpkin had only gone in search of bugs, not cowboys.

"Pumpkin?" she called loudly.

Great-Aunt Sadie came to the door. She was slight and a little dumpy, with short, thin gray hair, wearing glasses and a worried look.

"I saw him go over toward the Brannt place, Maddie," she said as she moved out onto the porch. "I'm sorry."

Maddie groaned aloud. "I'll have to go after him. Cort will kill me!"

"Well, he hasn't so far," Sadie replied gently. "And he could have shot Pumpkin, but he didn't…"

"Only because he missed!" Maddie huffed. She sighed and put her hands on her slim hips. She had a boyish figure. She wasn't tall or short, just sort of in the middle. But she was graceful, for all that. And she could work on a ranch, which she did. Her father had taught her how to raise cattle, how to market them, how to plan and how to budget. Her little ranch wasn't anything big or special, but she made a little money. Things had been going fine until she decided she wanted to branch out her organic egg-laying business and bought Pumpkin after her other rooster was killed by a coyote, along with several hens. But now things weren't so great financially.

Maddie had worried about getting a new rooster. Her other one wasn't really vicious, but she did have to carry a tree branch around with her to keep from getting spurred. She didn't want another aggressive one.

"Oh, he's gentle as a lamb," the former owner assured her. "Great bloodlines, good breeder, you'll get along just fine with him!"

Sure, she thought when she put him in the chicken yard and his first act was to jump on her foreman, old Ben Harrison, when he started to gather eggs.

"Better get rid of him now," Ben had warned as she doctored the cuts on his arms the rooster had made even through the fabric.

"He'll settle down, he's just excited about being in a new place," Maddie assured him.

Looking back at that conversation now, she laughed. Ben had been right. She should have sent the rooster back to the vendor in a shoebox. But she'd gotten attached to the feathered assassin. Sadly, Cort Brannt hadn't.

Cort Matthew Brannt was every woman's dream of the perfect man. He was tall, muscular without making it obvious, cultured, and he could play a guitar like a professional. He had jet-black hair with a slight wave, large dark brown eyes and a sensuous mouth that Maddie often dreamed of kissing.

The problem was that Cort was in love with their other neighbor, Odalie Everett. Odalie was the daughter of big-time rancher Cole Everett and his wife, Heather, who was a former singer and songwriter. She had two brothers, John and Tanner. John still lived at home, but Tanner lived in Europe. Nobody talked about him.

Odalie loved grand opera. She had her mother's clear, beautiful voice and she wanted to be a professional soprano. That meant specialized training.

Cort wanted to marry Odalie, who couldn't see him for dust. She'd gone off to Italy to study with some famous voice trainer. Cort was distraught and it didn't help that Maddie's rooster kept showing up in his yard and attacking him without warning.

"I can't understand why he wants to go all the way over there to attack Cort," Maddie said aloud. "I mean, we've got cowboys here!"

"Cort threw a rake at him the last time he came over here to look at one of your yearling bulls," Sadie reminded her.

"I throw things at him all the time," Maddie pointed out.

"Yes, but Cort chased him around the yard, picked him up by his feet, and carried him out to the hen yard to show him to the hens. Hurt his pride," Sadie continued. "He's getting even."

"You think so?"

"Roosters are unpredictable. That particular one," she added with a bite in her voice that was very out of character, "should have been chicken soup!"

"Great-Aunt Sadie!"

"Just telling you the way it is," Sadie huffed. "My brother—your granddaddy—would have killed him the first time he spurred you."

Maddie smiled. "I guess he would. I don't like killing things. Not even mean roosters."

"Cort would kill him for you if he could shoot straight," Sadie said with veiled contempt. "You load that .28 gauge shotgun in the closet for me, and I'll do it."

"Great-Aunt Sadie!"

She made a face. "Stupid thing. I wanted to pet the hens and he ran me all the way into the house. Pitiful, when a chicken can terrorize a whole ranch. You go ask Ben how he feels about that red rooster. I dare you. If you'd let him, he'd run a truck over it!"

Maddie sighed. "I guess Pumpkin is a terror. Well, maybe Cort will deal with him once and for all and I can go get us a nice rooster."

"In my experience, no such thing," the older woman said. "And about Cort dealing with him…" She nodded toward the highway.

Maddie grimaced. A big black ranch truck turned off the highway and came careening down the road toward the house. It was obviously being driven by a maniac.

The truck screeched to a stop at the front porch, sending chickens running for cover in the hen yard because of the noise.

"Great," Maddie muttered. "Now they'll stop laying for two days because he's terrified them!"

"Better worry about yourself," Great-Aunt Sadie said. "Hello, Cort! Nice to see you," she added with a wave and ran back into the house, almost at a run.

Maddie bit off what she was going to say about traitors. She braced herself as a tall, lean, furious cowboy in jeans, boots, a chambray shirt and a black Stetson cocked over one eye came straight toward her. She knew what the set of that hat meant. He was out for blood.

"I'm sorry!" she said at once, raising her hands, palms out. "I'll do something about him, I promise!"

"Andy landed in a cow patty," he raged in his deep voice. "That's nothing compared to what happened to the others while we were chasing him. I went headfirst into the dipping tray!"

She wouldn't laugh, she wouldn't laugh, she wouldn't...

"Oh, hell, stop that!" he raged while she bent over double at the mental image of big, handsome Cort lying facedown in the stinky stuff they dipped cattle in to prevent disease.

"I'm sorry. Really!" She forced herself to stop laughing. She wiped her wet eyes and tried to look serious. "Go ahead, keep yelling at me. Really. It's okay."

"Your stupid rooster is going to feed my ranch hands if you don't keep him at home!" he said angrily.

"Oh, my, chance would be a fine thing, wouldn't it?" she asked wistfully. "I mean, I guess I could hire an off-duty army unit to come out here and spend the next week trying to run him down." She gave him a droll look. "If you and your men can't catch him, how do you expect me to catch him?"

"I caught him the first day he was here," he reminded her.

"Yes, but that was three months ago," she pointed out. "And he'd just arrived. Now he's learned evasion techniques." She frowned. "I wonder if they've ever thought of using roosters as attack animals for the military? I should suggest it to someone."

"I'd suggest you find some way to keep him at home before I resort to the courts."

"You'd sue me over a chicken?" she exclaimed. "Wow, what a headline that would be. Rich, Successful Rancher Sues Starving, Female Small-Rancher for Rooster Attack. Wouldn't your dad love reading that headline in the local paper?" she asked with a bland smile.

His expression was growing so hard that his high cheekbones stood out. "One more flying red feather attack and I'll risk it. I'm not kidding."

"Oh, me, neither." She crossed her heart. "I'll have the vet prescribe some tranquilizers for Pumpkin to calm him down," she said facetiously. She frowned. "Ever thought about asking your family doctor for some? You look very stressed."

"I'm stressed because your damned rooster keeps attacking me! On my own damned ranch!" he raged.

"Well, I can see that it's a stressful situation to be in," she sympathized. "With him attacking you, and all." She knew it would make him furious, but she had to know. "I hear Odalie Everett went to Italy."

The anger grew. Now it was cold and threatening. "Since when is Odalie of interest to you?"

"Just passing on the latest gossip." She peered at him through her lashes. "Maybe you should study opera…"

"You venomous little snake," he said furiously. "As if you could sing a note that wasn't flat!"

She colored. "I could sing if I wanted to!"

He looked her up and down. "Sure. And get suddenly beautiful with it?"

The color left her face.

"You're too thin, too flat-chested, too plain and too untalented to ever appeal to me, just in case you wondered," he added with unconcealed distaste.

She drew herself up to her full height, which only brought the top of her head to his chin, and stared at him with ragged dignity. "Thank you. I was wondering why men don't come around. It's nice to know the reason."

Her damaged pride hit him soundly, and he felt small. He shifted from one big booted foot to the other. "I didn't mean it like that," he said after a minute.

She turned away. She wasn't going to cry in front of him.

Her sudden vulnerability hurt him. He started after her. "Listen, Madeline," he began.

She whirled on her booted heel. Her pale eyes shot fire at him. Her exquisite complexion went ruddy. Beside her thighs, her hands were clenched. "You think you're God's gift to women, don't you? Well, let me tell you a thing or two! You've traded on your good looks for years to get you what you want, but it didn't get you Odalie, did it?"

His face went stony. "Odalie is none of your damned business," he said in a soft, dangerous tone.

"Looks like she's none of yours, either," she said spitefully. "Or she'd never have left you."

He turned around and stomped back to his truck.

"And don't you dare roar out of my driveway and scare my hens again!"

He slammed the door, started the truck and deliberately gunned the engine as he roared out toward the main highway.

"Three days they won't lay, now," Maddie said to herself. She turned, miserable, and went up the porch steps. Her pride was never going to heal from that attack. She'd had secret feelings for Cort since she was sixteen. He'd never noticed her, of course, not even to tease her as men sometimes did. He simply ignored her existence most of the time, when her rooster wasn't attacking him. Now she knew why. Now she knew what he really thought of her.

Great-Aunt Sadie was waiting by the porch screen door. She was frowning. "No call for him to say that about you," she muttered. "Conceited man!"

Maddie fought tears and lost.

Great-Aunt Sadie wrapped her up tight and hugged her. "Don't you believe what he said. He was just mad and looking for a way to hurt you because you mentioned his precious Odalie. She's too good for any cowboy. At least, she thinks she is."

"She's beautiful and rich and talented. But so is

Cort," Maddie choked out. "It really would have been a good match, to pair the Everett's Big Spur ranch with Skylance, the Brannt ranch. What a merger that would be."

"Except that Odalie doesn't love Cort and she probably never will."

"She may come home with changed feelings," Maddie replied, drawing away. "She might have a change of heart. He's always been around, sending her flowers, calling her. All that romantic stuff. The sudden stop might open her eyes to what a catch he is."

"You either love somebody or you don't," the older woman said quietly.

"You think?"

"I'll make you a nice pound cake. That will cheer you up."

"Thanks. That's sweet of you." She wiped her eyes. "Well, at least I've lost all my illusions. Now I can just deal with my ranch and stop mooning over a man who thinks he's too good for me."

"No man is too good for you, sweetheart," Great-Aunt Sadie said gently. "You're pure gold. Don't you ever let anyone tell you different."

She smiled.

WHEN SHE WENT out late in the afternoon to put her hens in their henhouse to protect them from overnight predators, Pumpkin was right where he should be—back in the yard.

"You're going to get me sued, you red-feathered problem child," she muttered. She was carrying a small tree branch and a metal garbage can lid as she herded her hens into the large chicken house. Pumpkin lowered his head and charged her, but he bounced off the lid.

"Get in there, you fowl assassin," she said, evading and turning on him.

He ran into the henhouse. She closed the door behind him and latched it, leaned back against it with a sigh.

"Need to get rid of that rooster, Miss Maddie," Ben murmured as he walked by. "Be delicious with some dumplings."

"I'm not eating Pumpkin!"

He shrugged. "That's okay. I'll eat him for you."

"I'm not feeding him to you, either, Ben."

He made a face and kept walking.

She went inside to wash her hands and put antibiotic cream on the places where her knuckles were scraped from using the garbage can lid. She looked at her hands under the running water. They weren't elegant hands. They had short nails and they were functional, not pretty. She remembered Odalie Everett's long, beautiful white fingers on the keyboard at church, because Odalie could play as well as she sang. The woman was gorgeous, except for her snobbish attitude. No wonder Cort was in love with her.

Maddie looked in the mirror on the medicine cabinet above the sink and winced. She really was plain, she thought. Of course, she never used makeup or perfume, because she worked from dawn to dusk on the ranch. Not that makeup would make her beautiful, or give her bigger breasts or anything like that. She was basically just pleasant to look at, and Cort wanted beauty, brains and talent.

"I guess you'll end up an old spinster with a rooster who terrorizes the countryside."

The thought made her laugh. She thought of photographing Pumpkin and making a giant Wanted poster, with the legend, Wanted: Dead or Alive. She could hardly contain herself at the image that presented itself if she offered some outlandish reward. Men would wander the land with shotguns, looking for a small red rooster.

"Now you're getting silly," she told her image, and went back to work.

CORT BRANNT SLAMMED out of his pickup truck and into the ranch house, flushed with anger and self-contempt.

His mother, beautiful Shelby Brannt, glanced up as he passed the living room.

"Wow," she murmured. "Cloudy and looking like rain."

He paused and glanced at her. He grimaced, retraced his steps, tossed his hat onto the sofa and sat down beside her. "Yeah."

"That rooster again, huh?" she teased.

His dark eyes widened. "How did you guess?"

She tried to suppress laughter and lost. "Your father came in here bent over double, laughing his head off. He said half the cowboys were ready to load rifles and go rooster-hunting about the time you drove off. He wondered if we might need to find legal representation for you…?"

"I didn't shoot her," he said. He shrugged his power-ful shoulders and let out a long sigh, his hands dangling between his splayed legs as he stared at the carpet. "But I said some really terrible things to her."

Shelby put down the European fashion magazine she'd been reading. In her younger days, she had been a world-class model before she married King Brannt. "Want to talk about it, Matt?" she asked gently.

"Cort," he corrected with a grin.

She sighed. "Cort. Listen, your dad and I were call-ing you Matt until you were teenager, so it's hard…"

"Yes, well, you were calling Morie 'Dana,' too, weren't you?"

Shelby laughed. "It was an inside-joke. I'll tell it to you one day." She smiled. "Come on. Talk to me."

His mother could always take the weight off his shoulders. He'd never been able to speak so comfort-ably about personal things to his father, although he loved the older man dearly. He and his mother were on the same wavelength. She could almost read his mind.

"I was pretty mad," he confessed. "And she was cracking jokes about that stupid rooster. Then she made a crack about Odalie and I just, well, I just lost it."

Odalie, she knew, was a sore spot with her son. "I'm sorry about the way things worked out, Cort," she said gently. "But there's always hope. Never lose sight of that."

"I sent her roses. Serenaded her. Called her just to talk. Listened to her problems." He looked up. "None of that mattered. That Italian voice trainer gave her an invitation and she got on the next plane to Rome."

"She wants to sing. You know that. You've always known it. Her mother has the voice of an angel, too."

"Yes, but Heather never wanted fame. She wanted Cole Everett," he pointed out with a faint smile.

"That was one hard case of a man," Shelby pointed out. "Like your father." She shook her head. "We had a very, very rocky road to the altar. And so did Heather and Cole."

She continued pensively. "You and Odalie's brother, John Everett, were good friends for a while. What happened there?"

"His sister happened," Cort replied. "She got tired of having me at their place all the time playing video games with John and was very vocal about it, so he stopped inviting me over. I invited him here, but he got into rodeo and then I never saw him much. We're still friends, in spite of everything."

"He's a good fellow."

"Yeah."

Shelby got up, ruffled his hair and grinned. "You're a good fellow, too."

He laughed softly. "Thanks."

"Try not to dwell so much on things," she advised. "Sit back and just let life happen for a while. You're so intense, Cort. Like your dad," she said affectionately, her dark eyes soft on his face. "One day Odalie may discover that you're the sun in her sky and come home. But you have to let her try her wings. She's traveled, but only with her parents. This is her first real taste of freedom. Let her enjoy it."

"Even if she messes up her life with that Italian guy?"

"Even then. It's her life," she reminded him gently. "You don't like people telling you what to do, even if it's for your own good, right?"

He glowered at her. "If you're going to mention that time you told me not to climb up the barn roof and I didn't listen…"

"Your first broken arm," she recalled, and pursed her lips. "And I didn't even say I told you so," she reminded him.

"No. You didn't." He stared at his linked fingers. "Maddie Lane sets me off. But I should never have said she was ugly and no man would want her."

"You said that?" she exclaimed, wincing. "Cort…!"

"I know." He sighed. "Not my finest moment. She's not a bad person. It's just she gets these goofy notions about animals. That rooster is going to hurt somebody bad one day, maybe put an eye out, and she thinks it's funny."

"She doesn't realize he's dangerous," she replied.

"She doesn't want to realize it. She's in over her head with these expansion projects. Cage-free eggs. She hasn't got the capital to go into that sort of operation, and she's probably already breaking half a dozen laws by selling them to restaurants."

"She's hurting for money," Shelby reminded somberly. "Most ranchers are, even us. The drought is killing us. But Maddie only has a few head of cattle and she can't buy feed for them if her corn crop dies. She'll have to sell at a loss. Her breeding program is already losing money." She shook her head. "Her father was a fine rancher. He taught your father things about breeding bulls. But Maddie just doesn't have the experience. She jumped in at the deep end when her father died, but it was by necessity, not choice. I'm sure she'd much rather be drawing pictures than trying to produce calves."

"Drawing." He said it with contempt.

She stared at him. "Cort, haven't you ever noticed that?" She indicated a beautiful rendering in pastels of a fairy in a patch of daisies in an exquisite frame on the wall.

He glanced at it. "Not bad. Didn't you get that at an art show last year?"

"I got it from Maddie last year. She drew it."

He frowned. He actually got up and went to look at the piece. "She drew that?" he asked.

"Yes. She was selling two pastel drawings at the art show. This was one of them. She sculpts, too—beautiful little fairies—but she doesn't like to show those to people. I told her she should draw professionally, perhaps in graphic design or even illustration. She laughed. She doesn't think she's good enough." She sighed. "Maddie is insecure. She has one of the poorest self-images of anyone I know."

Cort knew that. His lips made a thin line. He felt even worse after what he'd said to her. "I should probably call and apologize," he murmured.

"That's not a bad idea, son," she agreed.

"And then I should drive over there, hide in the grass and shoot that damned red-feathered son of a…!"

"Cort!"

He let out a harsh breath. "Okay. I'll call her."

"Roosters don't live that long," she called after him. "He'll die of old age before too much longer."

"With my luck, he'll hit fifteen and keep going. Animals that nasty never die!" he called back.

HE WANTED TO apologize to Maddie. But when he turned on his cell phone, he realized that he didn't even know her phone number. He tried to look it up on the internet, but couldn't find a listing.

He went back downstairs. His mother was in the kitchen.

"Do you know the Lanes' phone number?" he asked.

She blinked. "Well, no. I don't think I've ever tried to call them, not since Pierce Lane died last year, anyway."

"No number listed, anywhere," he said.

"You might drive by there later in the week," she suggested gently. "It's not that far."

He hesitated. "She'd lock the doors and hide inside when I drove up," he predicted.

His mother didn't know what to say. He was probably right.

"I need to get away," he said after a minute. "I'm wired like a piano. I need to get away from the rooster and Odalie and…everything."

"Why don't you go to Wyoming and visit your sister?" she suggested.

He sighed. "She's not expecting me until Thursday."

She laughed. "She won't care. Go early. It would do both of you good."

"It might at that."

"It won't take you long to fly up there," she added. "You can use the corporate jet. I'm sure your father wouldn't mind. He misses Morie. So do I."

"Yeah, I miss her, too," he said. He hugged his mother. "I'll go pack a bag. If that rooster shows up looking for me, put him on a plane to France, would you? I hear they love chicken over there. Get him a business-class ticket. If someone can ship a lobster from Maine," he added with a laugh, referring to a joke that had gone the rounds years before, "I can ship a chicken to France."

"I'll take it under advisement," she promised.

His mother was right, Cort thought that evening. He loved being with his sister. He and Morie were a lot alike, from their hot tempers to their very Puritan attitudes. They'd always been friends. When she was just five, she'd followed her big brother around everywhere, to the amusement of his friends. Cort was tolerant and he adored her. He never minded the kidding.

"I'm sorry about your rooster problems," Morie told him with a gentle laugh. "Believe me, we can understand. My poor sister-in-law has fits with ours."

"I like Bodie," he said, smiling. "Cane sure seems different these days."

"He is. He's back in therapy, he's stopped smashing bars and he seems to have settled down for good. Bodie's wonderful for him. She and Cane have had some problems, but they're mostly solved now," she said. She smiled secretly. "Actually, Bodie and I are going to have a lot more in common for the next few months."

Cort was quick. He glanced at her in the semidarkness of the front porch, with fireflies darting around. "A baby?"

She laughed with pure delight. "A baby," she said, and her voice was like velvet. "I only found out a little while ago. Bodie found out the day you showed up." She sighed. "So much happiness. It's almost too much to bear. Mal's over the moon."

"Is it a boy or a girl? Do you know yet?"

She shook her head. "Too early to tell. But we're not going to ask. We want it to be a surprise, however old-fashioned that might be."

He chuckled. "I'm going to be an uncle. Wow. That's super. Have you told Mom and Dad?"

"Not yet. I'll call Mom tonight, though."

"She'll be so excited. Her first grandchild."

Morie glanced at him. "You ever going to get married?" she asked.

"Sure, if Odalie ever says yes." He sighed. "She was warming up to me there just for a while. Then that Italian fellow came along and offered her voice training. He's something of a legend among opera stars. And that's what she wants, to sing at the Met." He grimaced. "Just my luck, to fall in love with a woman who only wants a career."

"I believe her mother was the same way, wasn't she?" Morie asked gently. "And then she and Cole Everett got really close. She gave up being a professional singer to come home and have kids. Although she still composes. That Wyoming group, Desperado, had a major hit from a song she wrote for them some years ago."

"I think she still composes. But she likes living on a ranch. Odalie hates it. She says she's never going to marry a man who smells like cow droppings." He looked at one of his big boots, where his ankle was resting on his other knee in the rocking chair. "I'm a rancher, damn it," he muttered. "I can't learn another trade. Dad's counting on me to take over when he can't do the work anymore."

"Yes, I know," she said sadly. "What else could you do?"

"Teach, I guess," he replied. "I have a degree in animal husbandry." He made a face. "I'd rather be shot. I'd rather let that red-feathered assassin loose on my nose. I hate the whole idea of routine."

"Me, too," Morie confessed. "I love ranching. I guess the drought is giving Dad problems, too, huh?"

"It's been pretty bad," Cort agreed. "People in Oklahoma and the other plains states are having it worse, though. No rain. It's like the Dust Bowl in the thirties, people are saying. So many disaster declarations."

"How are you getting around it?"

"Wells, mostly," he said. "We've drilled new ones and filled the tanks to the top. Irrigating our grain crops. Of course, we'll still have to buy some feed through the winter. But we're in better shape than a lot of other cattle producers. Damn, I hate how it's going to impact small ranchers and farmers. Those huge combines will be standing in the shadows, just waiting to pounce when the foreclosures come."

"Family ranches are going to be obsolete one day,

like family farms," Morie said sadly. "Except, maybe, for the big ones, like ours."

"True words. People don't realize how critical this really is."

She reached over and squeezed his hand. "That's why we have the National Cattleman's Association and the state organizations," she reminded him. "Now stop worrying. We're going fishing tomorrow!"

"Really?" he asked, delighted. "Trout?"

"Yes. The water's just cold enough, still. When it heats up too much, you can't eat them." She sighed. "This may be the last chance we'll get for a while, if this heat doesn't relent."

"Tell me about it. We hardly had winter at all in Texas. Spring was like summer, and it's gone downhill since. I'd love to stand in a trout stream, even if I don't catch a thing."

"Me, too."

"Does Bodie fish?"

"You know, I've never asked. We'll do that tomorrow. For now," she said, rising, "I'm for bed." She paused and hugged him. "It's nice to have you here for a while."

"For me, too, little sis." He hugged her back, and kissed her forehead. "See you in the morning."

CHAPTER TWO

MADDIE HADN'T THOUGHT about Cort for one whole hour. She laughed at herself while she fed her hens. Pumpkin was in the henhouse, locked in for the time being, so that she could feed the chickens without having to defend herself.

The laughter died away as she recalled the things Cort had said to her. She was ugly and flat-chested and he could never be attracted to her. She looked down at her slender body and frowned. She couldn't suddenly become beautiful. She didn't have the money to buy fancy clothes that flattered her, like Odalie did. In fact, her wardrobe was two years old.

When her father had been dying of cancer, every penny they had was tied up trying to keep up with doctor bills that the insurance didn't cover. Her father did carry life insurance, which was a lucky break because at his death, it was enough to pay back everybody.

But things were still hard. This year, they'd struggled to pay just the utility bills. It was going to come down to a hard choice, sell off cattle or sell off land. There was a developer who'd already been to see Maddie about selling the ranch. He wanted to build a huge hotel and amusement park complex. He was offering her over a million dollars, and he was persistent.

"You just run a few head of cattle here, don't you?" the tall man in the expensive suit said, but his smile didn't really reach his eyes. He was an opportunist, looking for a great deal. He thought Maddie would be a pushover once he pulled out a figure that would tempt a saint.

But Maddie's whole heritage was in that land. Her great-grandfather had started the ranch and suffered all sorts of deprivations to get it going. Her grandfather had taken over where he left off, improving both the cattle herd and the land. Her father had toiled for years to find just the right mix of grasses to pursue a purebred cattle breeding herd that was now the envy of several neighbors. All that would be gone. The cattle sold off, the productive grasslands torn up and paved for the complex, which would attract people passing by on the long, monotonous interstate highway that ran close to the border of the ranch.

"I'll have to think about it," she told him, nodding. Her smile didn't reach her eyes, either.

He pursed his lips. "You know, we're looking at other land in the area, too. You might get left out in the cold if we find someone who's more enthusiastic about the price we're offering."

Maddie didn't like threats. Even nice ones, that came with soft words and smiles.

"Whatever," she said. She smiled again. "I did say I'd have to think about it."

His smile faded, and his eyes narrowed. "You have

a prime location here, only one close neighbor and a nearby interstate. I really want this place. I want it a lot."

"Listen, I hate being pressured…!"

He held up both hands. "Okay! But you think about it. You think hard." His expression became dangerous-looking. "We know how to deal with reluctant buyers. That's not a threat, it's just a statement. Here's my card."

She took it gingerly, as if she thought it had germs.

He made a huffing sound and climbed back into his fantastically expensive foreign car. He roared out of the driveway, scattering chickens.

She glared after it. No more eggs for two more days, she thought irritably. She'd rather starve than sell the ranch. But money was getting very tight. The drought was going to be a major hit to their poor finances, she thought dismally.

"Miss Maddie, you got that rooster locked up?" Ben called at the fence, interrupting her depressing reverie.

She turned. "Yes, Ben, he's restrained." She laughed.

"Thanks." He grimaced. "Going to feed the live-stock and I'd just as soon not be mauled in the process."

"I know." She glanced at the wire door behind which Pumpkin was calling to the hens in that odd tone that roosters used when there was some special treat on the ground for them. It was actually a handful of meal-worms that Maddie had tossed in the henhouse to keep him occupied while she locked him in.

Two of the hens went running to the door.

"He's lying," Maddie told them solemnly. "He's al-ready eaten the mealworms, he just wants out."

"Cort left town, you hear?" Ben asked.

Her heart jumped. "Where did he go?" she asked miserably, waiting to hear that he'd flown to Italy to see Odalie.

"Wyoming, one of his cowboys said, to see his sister."

"Oh."

"Mooning over that Odalie girl, I guess," he muttered. "She said she hated men who smelled like cattle. I guess she hates her dad, then, because he made his fortune on the Big Spur raising cattle, and he still does!"

"She's just been spoiled," Maddie said quietly.

Ben glanced at her irritably. "She was mean to you when you were in school. Your dad actually went to the school to get it stopped. He went to see Cole Everett about it, too, didn't he?"

"Yes." She flushed. She didn't like remembering that situation, although Odalie had quickly stopped victimizing her after her father got involved.

"Had a nasty attitude, that one," Ben muttered. "Looked down her nose at every other girl and most of the boys. Thought she was too good to live in a hick town in Texas." His eyes narrowed. "She's going to come a cropper one day, you mark my words. What's that quote, 'pride goeth after a fall'? And she's got a lot farther to fall than some women."

"There's another quote, something about love your enemies?" she teased.

"Yes, well, she's given a lot of people reason to put that one into practice."

Maddie grimaced. "It must be nice, to have beauty

and talent. I'd settle for one or the other myself." She laughed.

"You ought to be selling them little fairy statues you make," he advised. "Prettiest little things I ever saw. That one you sent my granddaughter for her birthday sits in the living room, because her mother loves to look at it. One of her friends has an art gallery in San Antonio. She said," he emphasized, "that you could make a fortune with those things."

Maddie flushed. "Wow."

"Not that those pretty drawings are bad, either. Sold one to Shelby Brannt, didn't you?"

"Yes." She'd loved the idea of Cort having to see her artwork every day, because she knew that Shelby had mounted it on a wall in the dining room of her home. But he probably never even looked at it. Though cultured, Cort had little use for art or sculpture. Unless it was a sculpture of one of the ranch's prize bulls. They had one done in bronze. It sat on the mantel in the living room of the Brannt home.

"Ought to paint that rooster while he's still alive," Ben said darkly.

"Ben!"

He held up both hands. "Didn't say I was going to hurt him."

"Okay."

"But somebody else might." He pursed his lips. "You know, he could be the victim of a terrible traffic accident one day. He loves to run down that dirt road in front of the house."

"You bite your tongue," she admonished.

"Spoilsport."

"That visitor who came the other day, that developer, you see him again?" Ben asked curiously.

"No, but he left his name." She pulled his business card out of her pocket and held it up. "He's from Las Vegas. He wants to build a hotel and amusement park complex right here." She looked around wistfully. "Offered me a million dollars. Gosh, what I could do with that!"

"You could sell and throw away everything your family worked for here?" Ben asked sadly. "My great-grandfather started working here with your great-grandfather. Our families have been together all that time." He sighed. "Guess I could learn to use a computer and make a killing with a dot-com business," he mused facetiously.

"Aw, Ben," she said gently. "I don't want to sell up. I was just thinking out loud." She smiled, and this time it was genuine. "I'd put a lot of people out of work, and God knows what I'd do with all the animals who live here."

"Especially them fancy breeding bulls and cows," he replied. "Cort Brannt would love to get his hands on them. He's always over here buying our calves."

"So he is."

Ben hesitated. "Heard something about that developer, that Archie Lawson fellow."

"You did? What?"

"Just gossip, mind."

"So? Tell me!" she prodded.

He made a face. "Well, he wanted a piece of land

over around Cheyenne, on the interstate. The owner wouldn't sell. So cattle started dying of mysterious causes. So did the owner's dog, a big border collie he'd had for years. He hired a private investigator, and had the dog autopsied. It was poison. They could never prove it was Lawson, but they were pretty sure of it. See, he has a background in chemistry. Used to work at a big government lab, they say, before he started buying and selling land."

Her heart stopped. "Oh, dear." She bit her lip. "He said something about knowing how to force deals..."

"I'll get a couple of my pals to keep an eye on the cattle in the outer pastures," Ben said. "I'll tell them to shoot first and ask questions later if they see anybody prowling around here."

"Thanks, Ben," she said heavily. "Good heavens, as if we don't already have enough trouble here with no rain, for God knows how long."

"Everybody's praying for it." He cocked his head. "I know a Cheyenne medicine man. Been friends for a couple of years. They say he can make rain."

"Well!" She hesitated. "What does he charge?"

"He doesn't. He says he has these abilities that God gave him, and if he ever takes money for it, he'll lose it. Seems to believe it, and I hear he's made rain at least twice in the area. If things go from bad to worse, maybe we should talk to him."

She grinned. "Let's talk to him."

He chuckled. "I'll give him a call later."

Her eyebrows arched. "He has a telephone?"

"Miss Maddie," he scoffed, "do you think Native

American people still live in teepees and wear head-dresses?"

She flushed. "Of course not," she lied.

"He lives in a house just like ours, he wears jeans and T-shirts mostly and he's got a degree in anthropology. When he's not fossicking, they say he goes overseas with a group of mercs from Texas for top secret operations."

She was fascinated. "Really!"

"He's something of a local celebrity on the rez. He lives there."

"Could you call him and ask him to come over when he has time?"

He laughed. "I'll do that tonight."

"Even if he can't make rain, I'd love to meet him," she said. "He sounds very interesting."

"Take my word for it, he is. Doesn't talk much, but when he does, it's worth hearing. Well, I'll get back to work."

"Thanks, Ben."

He smiled. "My pleasure. And don't let that developer bully you," he said firmly. "Maybe you need to talk to Cort's dad and tell him what's going on. He's not going to like that, about the development. It's too close to his barns. In these hard times, even the Brannts couldn't afford to build new ones with all that high tech they use."

"Got a point. I'll talk to him."

Maddie went back to the house. She put the feed basket absently on the kitchen counter, mentally reviewing all the things she had planned for the week. She missed

Cort already. But at least it meant the rooster was likely to stay at home. He only went over to the Brannt ranch when Cort was in residence, to attack him.

"Better wash those eggs and put them in the refrigerator," Great-Aunt Sadie advised. "They're the ones for the restaurant, aren't they?"

"Yes. Old Mr. Bailey said his customers have been raving about the taste of his egg omelets lately." She laughed. "I'll have to give my girls a treat for that."

Great-Aunt Sadie was frowning. "Maddie, did you ever look up the law about selling raw products?"

Maddie shook her head. "I meant to. But I'm sure it's not illegal to sell eggs. My mother did it for years before she died...."

"That was a long time ago, honey. Don't you remember that raid a few years ago on those poor farmers who were selling raw milk?" She made a face. "What sort of country do we live in? Sending an armed raid team after helpless farmers for selling milk!"

Maddie felt uneasy. "I'd forgotten that."

"I hadn't. In my day we had homemade butter and we could drink all the raw milk we wanted—didn't have all this fancy stuff a hundred years ago and it seems to me people were a whole lot healthier."

"You weren't here a hundred years ago," Maddie pointed out with a grin. "Anyway, the government's not going to come out here and attack me for selling a few eggs!"

She did look on the internet for the law pertaining to egg production and found that she was in compliance. In fact, there were even places in the country licensed to sell raw milk. She'd have to tell Great-Aunt Sadie about that, she mused. Apparently armed teams weren't raiding farms out west.

MEANWHILE, A DAY LATER, she did call King Brannt. She was hesitant about it. Not only was he Cort's father, he had a reputation in the county for being one tough customer, and difficult to get along with. He had a fiery temper that he wasn't shy about using. But the developer's determination to get the Lane ranch could have repercussions. A lot of them.

She picked up the phone and dialed the ranch.

The housekeeper answered.

"Could I speak to King Brannt, please?" she asked. "It's Maddie Lane."

There was a skirl of laughter. "Yes, you've got a rooster named Pumpkin."

Maddie laughed. "Is he famous?"

"He is around here," the woman said. "Cort isn't laughing, but the rest of us are. Imagine having a personal devil in the form of a little red rooster! We've been teasing Cort that he must have done something terrible that we don't know about."

Maddie sighed. "I'm afraid Pumpkin has it in for Cort. See, he picked him up by the feet and showed him to my girls, my hens, I mean, and hurt his pride. That was when he started looking for Cort."

"Oh, I see. It's vengeance." She laughed again. "Nice talking to you, I'll go get Mr. Brannt. Take just a minute…"

Maddie held on. Her gaze fell on one of her little

fairy statues. It was delicate and beautiful; the tiny face perfect, lovely, with sculpted long blond hair, sitting on a stone with a butterfly in its hand. It was a new piece, one she'd just finished with the plastic sculpture mix that was the best on the market. Her egg money paid for the materials. She loved the little things and could never bear to sell one. But she did wonder if there was a market for such a specialized piece.

"Brannt," a deep voice said curtly.

She almost jumped. "Mr. Brannt? It's… I mean I'm Maddie Lane. I live on the little ranch next door to yours," she faltered.

"Hi, Maddie," he said, and his voice lost its curt edge and was pleasant. "What can I do for you?"

"I've got sort of a situation over here. I wanted to tell you about it."

"What's wrong? Can we help?"

"That's so nice of you." She didn't add that she'd been told some very scary things about his temper. "It's this developer. He's from Las Vegas…"

"Yes. Archie Lawson. I had him investigated."

"He's trying to get me to sell my ranch to him. I don't want to. This ranch has been in my family for generations. But he's very pushy and he made some threats."

"He's carried them out in the past," King said, very curtly. "But you can be sure I'm not going to let him hurt you or your cattle herd. I'll put on extra patrols on the land boundary we share, and station men at the cabin out there. We use it for roundup, but it's been vacant for a week or so. I'll make sure someone's there at all times, and we'll hook up cameras around your cattle herd and monitor them constantly."

"You'd do that for me?" she faltered. "Cameras. It's so expensive." She knew, because in desperation she'd looked at them and been shocked at the prices for even a cheap system.

"I'd do that for you," he replied. "You have one of the finest breeding herds I know of, which is why we buy so many of your young bulls."

"Why, thank you."

"You're welcome. You see, it's looking out for our interests as well as yours. I can't have a complex so close to my barns, or my purebred herd. The noise of construction would be bad enough, but the constant traffic would injure production."

"Yes, I know what you mean."

"Besides that, Lawson is unscrupulous. He's got his fingers in lots of dirty pies. He's had several brushes with the law, too."

"I'm not surprised. He was a little scary."

"Don't you worry. If he comes back and makes any threat at all, you call over here. If you can't find me, talk to Cort. He'll take care of it."

She hesitated. "Actually Cort isn't speaking to me right now."

There was a pause. "Because of the rooster?" His voice was almost smiling.

"Actually because I made a nasty crack about Odalie Everett," she confessed heavily. "I didn't mean to. He made me mad. I guess he was justified to complain. Pumpkin is really mean to him."

"So I heard. That rooster has had brushes with several of our cowboys." She could tell that he was trying not to laugh.

"The man who sold him to me said he was real gentle and wouldn't hurt a fly. That's sort of true. I've never seen Pumpkin hurt a fly." She laughed. "Just people."

"You need a gentle rooster, especially if you're going to be selling eggs and baby chicks."

"The baby chick operation is down the road, but I'm doing well with my egg business."

"Glad to hear it. Our housekeeper wants to get on your customer list, by the way."

"I'll talk to her, and thanks!"

He chuckled. "My pleasure."

"If Mr. Lawson comes back, I'll let you know."

"Please do. The man is trouble."

"I know. Thanks again, Mr. Brannt. I feel better now."

"Your dad was a friend of mine," he said quietly. "I miss him. I know you do, too."

"I miss him a lot," she said. "But Great-Aunt Sadie and I are coping. It's just this ranching thing," she added miserably. "Dad was good at it, he had charts in the barn, he knew which traits to breed for, all that technical stuff. He taught me well, but I'm not as good as he was at it. Not at all. I like to paint and sculpt." She hesitated. "Creative people shouldn't have to breed cattle!" she burst out.

He laughed. "I hear you. Listen, suppose I send Cort over there to help you with the genetics? He's even better at it than I am. And I'm good. No conceit, just fact."

She laughed, too. "You really are. We read about your bulls in the cattle journals." She paused. "I don't think Cort would come."

"He'll come." He sounded certain of it. "He needs something to take his mind off that woman. She's a sweet girl, in her way, but she's got some serious growing up to do. She thinks the world revolves around her. It doesn't."

"She's just been a little spoiled, I think." She tried to be gracious.

"Rotten," he replied. "My kids never were."

"You and Mrs. Brannt did a great job with yours. And John Everett is a really nice man. So the Everetts did a great job there, too." She didn't mention the second Everett son, Tanner. The Everetts never spoke about him. Neither did anyone else. He was something of a mystery man. But gossip was that he and his dad didn't get along.

"They did a great job on John, for sure." He let out a breath. "I just wish Cort would wake up. Odalie is never going to settle in a small community. She's meant for high society and big cities. Cort would die in a high-rise apartment. He's got too much country in him, although he'd jump at the chance if Odalie would offer him one. Just between us," he added quietly, "I hope she doesn't. If she makes it in opera, and I think she can, what would Cort do with himself while she trained and performed? He'd be bored out of his mind. He doesn't even like opera. He likes country-western."

"He plays it very well," Maddie said softly. "I loved coming to the barbecue at your place during the spring sale and hearing him sing. It was nice of you to invite all of us. Even old Ben. He was over the moon."

He laughed. "You're all neighbors. I know you think of Ben as more family than employee. His family has worked for your family for four generations."

"That's a long time," she agreed. "I'm not selling my place," she added firmly. "No matter what that fancy Las Vegas man does."

"Good for you. I'll help you make sure of that. I'll send Cort on over."

"He's back from visiting his sister?" she stammered.

"Yes. Got back yesterday. They went trout fishing."

She sighed. "I'd love to go trout fishing."

"Cort loves it. He said they did close the trout streams for fishing a couple of days after he and Dana—Morie, I mean, went. The heat makes it impossible."

"That's true." She hesitated. "Why do you call Morie Dana?" she blurted out.

He laughed. "When Shelby was carrying them, we called them Matt and Dana. Those were the names we picked out. Except that two of our friends used those names for theirs and we had to change ours. It got to be a habit, though, until the kids were adolescents.

"Hey, Cort," she heard King call, his hand covering the receiver so his voice was a little muffled.

"Yes, Dad?" came the reply.

"I want you to go over to the Lane place and give Maddie some help with her breeding program."

"The hell I will!" Cort burst out.

The hand over the phone seemed to close, because the rest of it was muffled. Angry voices, followed by more discussion, followed like what seemed a string of horrible curses from Cort.

King came back on the line. "He said he'd be pleased to come over and help," he lied. "But he did ask if you'd shut your rooster up first." He chuckled.

"I'll put him in the chicken house right now." She tried not to sound as miserable as she felt. She knew Cort didn't want to help her. He hated her. "And thank you again."

"You're very welcome. Call us if you need help with Lawson. Okay?"

"Okay."

TRUE TO HIS father's words, Cort drove up in front of the house less than an hour later. He wasn't slamming doors or scattering chickens this time, either. He looked almost pleasant. Apparently his father had talked to him very firmly.

Maddie had combed her hair and washed her face. She still wasn't going to win any beauty contests. She had on her nicest jeans and a pink T-shirt that said La Vie en Rose.

It called attention, unfortunately, to breasts that were small and pert instead of big and tempting. But Cort was looking at her shirt with his lips pursed.

"The world through rose-colored glasses?" he mused.

"You speak French."

"Of course. French, Spanish and enough German to get me arrested in Munich. We do cattle deals all over the world," he added.

"Yes, I remember." She swallowed, hard, recalling

the things he'd said at their last unfortunate meeting. "Your father said you could help me figure out Dad's breeding program."

"I think so. I helped him work up the new one before he passed away," he added quietly. "We were all shocked by how fast it happened."

"So were we," Maddie confessed. "Two months from the time he was diagnosed until he passed on." She drew in a long breath. "He hated tests, you know. He wouldn't go to the doctor about anything unless he was already at death's door. I think the doctor suspected something, but Dad just passed right over the lecture about tests being necessary and walked out. By the time they diagnosed the cancer, it was too late for anything except radiation. And somebody said that they only did that to help contain the pain." Her pale eyes grew sad. "It was terrible, the pain. At the last, he was so sedated that he hardly knew me. It was the only way he could cope."

"I'm sorry," he said. "I haven't lost parents, but I lost both my grandparents. They were wonderful people. It was hard to let them go."

"Life goes on," she said quietly. "Everybody dies. It's just a matter of how and when."

"True."

She swallowed. "Dad kept his chalkboard in the barn, and his books in the library, along with his journals. I've read them all, but I can't make sense of what he was doing. I'm not college educated, and I don't really know much about animal husbandry. I know what I do from watching Dad."

"I can explain it to you."

She nodded. "Thanks."

She turned and led the way to the house.

"Where's that...rooster?" he asked.

"Shut up in the henhouse with a fan."

"A fan?" he exclaimed and burst out laughing.

"It really isn't funny," she said softly. "I lost two of my girls to the heat. Found them dead in the henhouse, trying to lay. I had Ben go and get us a fan and install it there. It does help with the heat, a little at least."

"My grandmother used to keep hens," he recalled. "But we only have one or two now. Foxes got the rest." He glanced at her. "Andie, our housekeeper, wants to get on your egg customer list for two dozen a week."

She nodded. "Your dad mentioned that. I can do that. I've got pullets that should start laying soon. My flock is growing by leaps and bounds." She indicated the large fenced chicken yard, dotted with all sorts of chickens. The henhouse was huge, enough to accommodate them all, complete with perches and ladders and egg boxes and, now, a fan.

"Nice operation."

"I'm going to expand it next year, if I do enough business."

"Did you check the law on egg production?"

She laughed. "Yes, I did. I'm in compliance. I don't have a middleman, or I could be in trouble. I sell directly to the customer, so it's all okay."

"Good." He shrugged, his hands in his jean pockets. "I'd hate to have to bail you out of jail."

"You wouldn't," she sighed.

He stopped and looked down at her. She seemed so

dejected. "Yes, I would," he said, his deep voice quiet and almost tender as he studied her small frame, her short wavy blond hair, her wide, soft gray eyes. Her complexion was exquisite, not a blemish on it except for one small mole on her cheek. She had a pretty mouth, too. It looked tempting. Bow-shaped, soft, naturally pink...

"Cort?" she asked suddenly, her whole body tingling, her heart racing at the way he was staring at her mouth.

"What? Oh. Yes. The breeding books." He nodded. "We should get to it."

"Yes." She swallowed, tried to hide her blush and opened the front door.

CHAPTER THREE

MADDIE COULDN'T HELP but stare at Cort as he leaned over the desk to read the last page of her father's breeding journal. He was the handsomest man she'd ever seen. And that physique! He was long and lean, but also muscular. Broad-shouldered, narrow-hipped, and in the opening of his chambray shirt, thick curling black hair peeked out.

She'd never been overly interested in intimacy. Never having indulged, she had no idea how it felt, although she'd been reading romance novels since her early teens. She did know how things worked between men and women from health class. What she didn't know was why women gave in to men. She supposed it came naturally.

Cort felt her eyes on him and turned, so that he was looking directly into her wide, shocked gray eyes. His own dark ones narrowed. He knew that look, that expression. She was trying to hide it, but he wasn't fooled.

"Take a picture," he drawled, because her interest irritated him. She wasn't his type. Not at all.

Her reaction shamed him. She looked away, cleared her throat and went beet-red. "Sorry," she choked. "I was just thinking. You were sort of in the way. I was thinking about my fairies…"

He felt guilty. That made him even more irritable. "What fairies?"

She stumbled and had to catch herself as she went past him. She was so embarrassed she could hardly even walk.

She went to the shelf where she'd put the newest one. Taking it down very carefully, she carried it to the desk and put it in front of him.

He caught his breath. He picked it up, delicately for a man with such large, strong hands, and held it up to his eyes. He turned it. He was smiling. "This is really beautiful," he said, as if it surprised him. He glanced at her. "You did this by yourself?"

She moved uneasily. "Yes," she muttered. What did he think—that she had somebody come in and do the work so she could claim credit for it?

"I didn't mean it like that, Maddie," he said gently. The sound of her name on his lips made her tingle. She didn't dare look up, because her attraction to him would surely show. He knew a lot more about women than she knew about men. He could probably tell already that she liked him. It had made him mad. So she'd have to hide it.

"Okay," she said. But she still wouldn't look up.

He gave the beautiful little statuette another look before he put it down very gently on the desk. "You should be marketing those," he said firmly. "I've seen things half as lovely sell for thousands of dollars."

"Thousands?" she exclaimed.

"Yes. Sometimes five figures. I was staying at a hotel in Arizona during a cattlemen's conference and a doll show was exhibiting at the same hotel. I talked to some of the artists." He shook his head. "It's amazing how much collectors will pay for stuff like that." He indicated the fairy with his head. "You should look into it."

She was stunned. "I never dreamed people would pay so much for a little sculpture."

"Your paintings are nice, too," he admitted. "My mother loves the drawing you did. She bought it at that art show last year. She said you should be selling the sculptures, too."

"I would. It's just that they're like my children," she confessed, and flushed because that sounded nutty. "I mean…well, it's hard to explain."

"Each one is unique and you put a lot of yourself into it," he guessed. "So it would be hard to sell one."

"Yes." She did look up then, surprised that he was so perceptive.

"You have the talent. All you need is the drive."

"Drive." She sighed. She smiled faintly. "How about imminent starvation? Does that work for drive?"

He laughed. "We wouldn't let you starve. Your bull calves are too valuable to us," he added, just when she thought he might actually care.

"Thanks," she said shyly. "In that journal of Dad's—" she changed the subject "—he talks about heritability traits for lean meat with marbling to produce cuts that health-conscious consumers will buy. Can you explain to me how I go about producing herd sires that carry the traits we breed for?"

He smiled. "It's complicated. Want to take notes?"

She sighed. "Just like going back to school." Then she remembered school, and the agonies she went through in her junior and senior years because of Odalie Everett, and her face clenched.

"What's wrong?" he asked, frowning.

She swallowed. She almost said what was wrong. But she'd been down that road with him already, making comments she shouldn't have made about Odalie. She wasn't going to make him mad. Not now, when he was being pleasant and helpful.

"Nothing. Just a stray thought." She smiled. "I'll get some paper and a pencil."

AFTER A HALF hour she put down the pencil. "It's got to be like learning to speak Martian," she muttered.

He laughed out loud. "Listen, I didn't come into the world knowing how this stuff worked, either. I had to learn it, and if my dad hadn't been a patient man, I'd have jumped off a cliff."

"Your dad is patient?" she asked, and couldn't help sounding surprised.

"I know he's got a reputation for being just the opposite. But he really is patient. I had a hard time with algebra in high school. He'd take me into the office every night and go over problems with me until I understood how to do them. He never fussed, or yelled, or raised his voice. And I was a problem child." He shook his head. "I'm amazed I got through my childhood in one piece. I've broken half the bones in my body at some point, and I know my mother's gray hairs are all because of me. Morie was a little lady. She never caused anybody any trouble."

"I remember," Maddie said with a smile. "She was always kind to me. She was a couple of years ahead of me, but she was never snobby."

His dark eyes narrowed. "There's a hidden comment in there."

She flushed. "I didn't mention anybody else."

"You meant Odalie," he said. "She can't help being beautiful and rich and talented," he pointed out. "And it wasn't her fault that her parents put her in public school instead of private school, where she might have been better treated."

"Better treated." She glared at him. "Not one teacher or administrator ever had a bad word to say about her, even though she bullied younger girls mercilessly and spent most of her time bad-mouthing people she didn't like. One year she had a party for our whole class, at the ranch. She invited every single girl in the class—except me."

Cort's eyes narrowed. "I'm sure it wasn't intentional."

"My father went to see her father, that's how unintentional it was," she replied quietly. "When Cole Everett knew what she'd done to me, he grounded her for a month and took away her end-of-school trip as punishment."

"That seems extreme for not inviting someone to a party," he scoffed.

"I guess that's because you don't know about the other things she did to me," she replied.

"Let me guess—she didn't send you a Valentine's Day card, either," he drawled in a tone that dripped sarcasm.

She looked at him with open sadness. "Sure. That's it. I held a grudge because she didn't send me a holiday card and my father went to see the school principal and Odalie's father because he liked starting trouble."

Cort remembered her father. He was the mildest, most forgiving man anywhere around Branntville. He'd walk away from a fight if he could. The very fact that he got involved meant that he felt there was more than a slight problem.

But Cort loved Odalie, and here was this bad-tempered little frump making cracks about her, probably because she was jealous.

"I guess if you don't have a real talent and you aren't as pretty, it's hard to get along with someone who has it all," he commented.

Her face went beet-red. She stood up, took her father's journal, closed it and put it back in the desk drawer. She faced him across the width of the desk.

"Thank you for explaining the journal to me," she said in a formal tone. "I'll study the notes I took very carefully."

"Fine." He started to leave, hesitated. He turned and looked back at her. He could see an unusual brightness in her eyes. "Look, I didn't mean to hurt your feelings. It's just, well, you don't know Odalie. She's sweet and kind, she'd never hurt anybody on purpose."

"I don't have any talent, I'm ugly and I lie." She nodded. "Thanks."

"Hell, I never said you lied!"

She swallowed. Loud voices and curses made her nervous. She gripped the edge of the desk.

"Now what's wrong?" he asked angrily.

She shook her head. "Nothing," she said quickly.

He took a sudden, quick step toward her. She backed up, knocked over the desk chair and almost fell again getting it between him and herself. She was white in the face.

He stopped in his tracks. His lips fell open. In all his life, he'd never seen a woman react that way.

"What the hell is wrong with you?" he asked, but not in a loud or menacing tone.

She swallowed. "Nothing. Thanks for coming over."

He scowled. She looked scared to death.

Great-Aunt Sadie had heard a crash in the room. She opened the door gingerly and looked in. She glanced from Maddie's white face to Cort's drawn one. "Maddie, you okay?" she asked hesitantly, her eyes flicking back and forth to Cort's as if she, too, was uneasy.

"I'm fine. I just…knocked the chair over." She laughed, but it was a nervous, quick laugh. "Cort was just leaving. He gave me lots of information."

"Nice of him," Sadie agreed. She moved closer to Maddie, as if prepared to act as a human shield if Cort took another step toward the younger woman. "Good night, Cort."

He wanted to know what was wrong. It was true he'd said some mean things, but the fear in Maddie's eyes, and the looks he was getting, really disturbed him. He moved to the door, hesitated. "If you need any more help…" he began.

"I'll call. Sure. Thanks for offering." Maddie's voice sounded tight. She was standing very still. He was reminded forcibly of deer's eyes in headlights.

"Well, I'll get on home. Good night."

"Night," Maddie choked out.

He glanced from one woman to the other, turned and pulled the door closed behind him.

Maddie almost collapsed into the chair. Tears were running down her cheeks. Great-Aunt Sadie knelt beside the chair and pulled her close, rocking her. "There, there, it's all right. He's gone. What happened?"

"I mentioned about Odalie not inviting me to the party and he said I was just jealous of her. I said something, I don't…remember what, and he started toward me, all mad and impatient…" She closed her eyes, shivering. "I can't forget. All those years ago, and I still can't forget!"

"Nobody ever told Cort just what Odalie did to you, did they?"

"Apparently not," Maddie said heavily. She wiped her eyes. "Her dad made her apologize, but I know she never regretted it." She drew in a breath. "I told her that one day somebody was going to pay her back for all the mean things she did." She looked up. "Cort thinks she's a saint. If he only knew what she's really like…"

"It wouldn't matter," the older woman said sadly. "Men get hooked on a pretty face and they'd believe white was black if the woman told them it was. He's infatuated, baby. No cure for that but time."

"I thought he was so sexy." Maddie laughed. She brushed at her eyes again. "Then he lost his temper like that. He scared me," she said on a nervous smile.

"It's all right. Nobody's going to hurt you here. I promise."

She hugged the older woman tight. "Thanks."

"At the time, that boy did apologize, and he meant it," Sadie reminded her. "He was as much a victim as you were."

"Yes, but he got in trouble and he should have. No man, even an angry young one with justification, should ever do what he did to a girl. He didn't have nightmares for a month, either, did he, or carry emotional scars that never go away? Sad thing about him," she added quietly, "he died overseas when a roadside bomb blew up when he was serving in the Middle East. With a temper like that, I often wondered what he might do to a woman if he got even more upset than he was at me that time."

"No telling. And just as well we don't have to find out." Her face hardened. "But you're right about that Odalie girl. Got a bad attitude and no compassion for anybody. One of these days, life is going to pay her out in her own coin. She'll be sorry for the things she's done, but it will be too late. God forgives," she added. "But there's a price."

"What's that old saying, 'God's mill grinds slowly, but relentlessly'?"

"Something like that. Come on. I'll make you a nice cup of hot coffee."

"Make that a nice cup of hot chocolate instead,"

Maddie said. "I've had a rough day and I want to go to bed."

"I don't blame you. Not one bit."

CORT WAS THOUGHTFUL at breakfast the next morning. He was usually animated with his parents while he ate. But now he was quiet and retrospective.

"Something wrong?" his dad asked.

Cort glanced at him. He managed a smile. "Yeah. Something." He sipped coffee. "I went over her dad's journal with Maddie. We had sort of an argument and I started toward her while I was mad." He hesitated. "She knocked over a chair getting away from me. White in the face, shaking all over. It was an extreme reaction. We've argued before, but that's the first time she's been afraid of me."

"And you don't understand why." His father's expression was troubled.

"I don't." Cort's eyes narrowed. "But you do, don't you?"

He nodded.

"King, should you tell him?" Shelby asked worriedly.

"I think I should, honey," he said gently, and his dark eyes smiled with affection. "Somebody needs to."

"Okay then." She got up with her coffee. "You men talk. I'm going to phone Morie and see how she's doing."

"Give her my love," King called after her.

"Mine, too," Cort added.

She waved a hand and closed the door behind her. "Tell me," Cort asked his dad.

King put down his coffee cup. "In her senior year,

Maddie was Odalie's worst enemy. There was a boy, seemingly a nice boy, who liked Maddie. But Odalie liked him, and she was angry that Maddie, a younger girl who wasn't pretty or rich or talented, seemed to be winning in the affection sweepstakes."

"I told Maddie, Odalie's not like that," Cort began angrily.

King held up a hand. "Just hear me out. Don't interrupt."

Cort made a face, but he shut up.

"So Odalie and a girlfriend got on one of the social websites and started posting things that she said Maddie told her about the boy. She said Maddie thought he was a hick, that his mother was stupid, that both his parents couldn't even pass a basic IQ test."

"What? That's a lie…!"

"Sit down!" King's voice was soft, but the look in his eyes wasn't. Cort sat.

"The boy's mother was dying of cancer. He was outraged and furious at what Maddie had allegedly said about his family. His mother had just been taken to the hospital, not expected to live. She died that same day. He went to school just to find Maddie. She was in the library." He picked up his cup and sipped coffee. "He jerked her out of her chair, slapped her over a table and pulled her by her hair to the window. He was in the act of throwing her out—and it was on the second floor— when the librarian screamed for help and two big, stronger boys restrained him, in the nick of time."

Cort's face froze. "Maddie told you that?"

"Her father's lawyer told Cole Everett that," came

the terse reply. "There were at least five witnesses. The boy was arrested for assault. It was hushed up, because that's what's done in small communities to protect the families. Odalie was implicated, because the attorney hired a private investigator to find the source of the allegations. They traced the posts to her computer."

Cort felt uneasy. He was certain Odalie couldn't have done such a thing. "Maybe somebody used her computer," he began.

"She confessed," King said curtly.

Cort was even more uneasy now.

"Cole Everett had his own attorney speak to the one Maddie's father had hired. They worked out a compromise that wouldn't involve a trial. But Odalie had to toe the line from that time forward. They put her on probation, you see. She had first-offender status, so her record was wiped when she stayed out of trouble for the next two years. She had a girlfriend who'd egged her on. The girlfriend left town shortly thereafter."

"Yes," Cort replied, relaxing. "I see now. The girlfriend forced her to do it."

King made a curt sound deep in his throat. "Son, nobody forced her to do a damned thing. She was jealous of Maddie. She was lucky the boy didn't kill Maddie, or she'd have been an accessory to murder." He watched Cort's face pale. "That's right. And I don't think even Cole Everett could have kept her out of jail if that had happened."

Cort leaned back in his chair. "Poor Odalie."

"Funny," King said. "I would have said, 'Poor Maddie.'"

Cort flushed. "It must have been terrible for both of them, I suppose."

King just shook his head. He got up. "Blind as a bat," he mused. "Just like me, when I was giving your mother hell twice a day for being engaged to my little brother. God, I hated him. Hated them both. Never would admit why."

"Uncle Danny?" Cort exclaimed. "He was engaged to Mom?"

"He was. It was a fake engagement, however." He chuckled. "He was just trying to show me what my feelings for Shelby really were. I forgave him every minute's agony. She's the best thing that ever happened to me. I didn't realize how deeply a man could love a woman. All these years," he added in a soft tone, "and those feelings haven't lessened a bit. I hope you find that sort of happiness in your life. I wish it for you."

"Thanks," Cort said. He smiled. "If I can get Odalie to marry me, I promise you, I'll have it."

King started to speak, but thought better of it. "I've got some book work to do."

"I've got a new video game I'm dying to try." Cort chuckled. "It's been a long day."

"I appreciate you going over to talk to Maddie."

"No problem. She just needed a few pointers."

"She's no cattlewoman," King said worriedly. "She's swimming upstream. She doesn't even like cattle. She likes chickens."

"Don't say chickens," Cort pleaded with a groan.

"Your problem isn't with chickens, it's with a rooster."

"I'd dearly love to help him have a fatal heart attack," Cort said irritably.

"He'll die of old age one day." His dad laughed.

"Maddie said that developer had been putting pressure on her to sell," King added solemnly. "I've put on some extra help to keep an eye over that way, just to make sure her breeding stock doesn't start dying mysteriously."

"What?" Cort asked, shocked. "She didn't say anything about that."

"Probably wouldn't, to you. It smacks of weakness to mention such things to the enemy."

"I'm not the enemy."

King smiled. "Aren't you?"

He left his son sitting at the table, deep in thought.

Maddie was working in the yard when the developer drove up a week later. She leaned on the pitchfork she was using to put hay into a trough, and waited, miserable, for him to get out of his car and talk to her.

"I won't sell," she said when he came up to her. "And in case you feel like high pressure tactics, my neighbor has mounted cameras all over the ranch." She flushed at his fury.

"Well, how about that?" he drawled, and his eyes were blazing with anger. He forced a smile. "You did know that cameras can be disabled?" he asked.

"The cameras also have listening devices that can pick up a whisper."

He actually seemed to go pale. He looked at the poles that contained the outside lighting and mumbled a curse under his breath. There was some sort of electronic device up there.

"I'll come back again one day and ask you the same question," he promised, but he smiled and his voice was pleasant. "Maybe you'll change your mind."

"We also have cowboys in the line cabins on the borders of this ranch. Mr. Brannt is very protective of me since my father died. He buys many of our young breeding bulls," she added for good measure.

He was very still. "King Brannt?"

"Yes. You've heard of him, I gather."

He didn't reply. He turned on his heel and marched back to his car. But this time he didn't spin his wheels.

Maddie almost fell over with relief.

Just as the developer left, another car drove up, a sleek Jaguar, black with silver trim. Maddie didn't recognize it. Oh, dear, didn't some hit men drive fancy cars…?

The door opened and big John Everett climbed out of the low-slung luxury car, holding on to his white Stetson so that it wouldn't be dislodged from his thick head of blond hair. Maddie almost laughed with relief.

John grinned as he approached her. He had pale blue eyes, almost silver-colored, like his dad's, and he was a real dish. He and Odalie both had their mother's blond fairness, instead of Cole Everett's dark hair and olive complexion.

"What the hell's wrong with you?" he drawled. "Black cars make you twitchy or something?"

"I think hit men drive them, is all."

He burst out laughing. "I've never shot one single

person. A deer or two, maybe, in season." He moved toward her and stopped, towering over her. His pale eyes were dancing on her flushed face. "I ran into King Brannt at a cattlemen's association meeting last night. He said you were having some problems trying to work out your father's breeding program. He said Cort explained it to you."

"Uh, well, yes, sort of." It was hard to admit that even taking notes, she hadn't understood much of what Cort had told her.

"Cort tried to tutor me in biology in high school. I got a D on the test. He's good at genetics, lousy at trying to explain them." He shoved his hat back on his head and grinned. "So I thought, maybe I'll come over and have a try at helping you understand it."

"You're a nice guy, John," she said gently. And he was. At the height of his sister's intimidation, John had been on Maddie's side.

He shrugged. "I'm the flower of my family." His face hardened. "Even if she is my sister, Odalie makes me ashamed sometimes. I haven't forgotten the things she did to you."

"We all make mistakes when we're young," she faltered, trying to be fair.

"You have a gentle nature," he observed. "Like Cort's mother. And mine," he added with a smile. "Mom can't bear to see anything hurt. She cried for days when your father's lawyer came over and told her and Dad what Odalie had done to you."

"I know. She called me. Your dad did, too. They're good people."

"Odalie might be a better person if she had a few dis-advantages," John said coldly. "As things stand, she'll give in to Cort's persuasion one day and marry him. He'll be in hell for the rest of his life. The only person she's ever really loved is herself."

"That's harsh, John," she chided gently.

"It's the truth, Maddie." He swung his pointing fin-ger at her nose. "You're like my mother…she'd find one nice thing to say about the devil." He smiled. "I'm in the mood to do some tutoring today. But I require pay-ment. Your great-aunt makes a mean cup of coffee, and I'm partial to French vanilla."

"That's my favorite."

He chuckled. "Mine, too." He went back to the car, opened the passenger seat, took out a big box and a bag. "So since I drink a lot of it, I brought my own."

She caught her breath. It was one of those European coffee machines that used pods. Maddie had always wanted one, but the price was prohibitive.

"Sad thing is it only brews one cup at a time, but we'll compensate." He grinned. "So lead the way to the kitchen and I'll show you how to use it."

Two cups of mouthwatering coffee later, they were sit-ting in Maddie's father's office, going over breeding charts. John found the blackboard her father had used to map out the genetics. He was able to explain it so simply that Maddie understood almost at once which herd sires to breed to which cows.

"You make it sound so simple!" she exclaimed. "You're a wonder, John!"

He laughed. "It's all a matter of simplification," he drawled. He leaned back in the chair and sketched Maddie's radiant face with narrowed pale blue eyes. "You sell yourself short. It's not that you can't understand. You just have to have things explained. Cort's too impatient."

She averted her eyes. Mention of Cort made her uneasy.

"Yes, he loses his temper," John said thoughtfully. "But he's not dangerous. Not like that boy."

She paled. "I can't talk about it."

"You can, and you should," he replied solemnly. "Your father was advised to get some counseling for you, but he didn't believe in such things. That boy had a record for domestic assault, did you ever know? He beat his grandmother almost to death one day. She refused to press charges, or he would have gone to jail. His parents jumped in and got a fancy lawyer and convinced the authorities that he wasn't dangerous. I believe they contributed to the reelection campaign of the man who was police chief at the time as well."

"That's a harsh accusation," she said, shocked.

"It's a harsh world, and politics is the dirtiest business in town. Corruption doesn't stop at criminals, you know. Rich people have a way of subverting justice from time to time."

"You're rich, and you don't do those types of things."

"Yes, I am rich," he replied honestly. "And I'm honest. I have my own business, but I didn't get where I am by depending on my dad to support me."

She searched his eyes curiously. "Is that a dig at Cort?"

"It is," he replied quietly. "He stays at home, works on the ranch and does what King tells him to do. I told him some time ago that he's hurting himself by doing no more than wait to inherit Skylance, but he just nods and walks off."

"Somebody will have to take over the ranch when King is too old to manage it," she pointed out reasonably. "There isn't anybody else."

John grimaced. "I suppose that's true. But it's the same with me. Can you really see Odalie running a ranch?" He burst out laughing. "God, she might chip a fingernail!"

She grinned from ear to ear.

"Anyway, I was a maverick. I wanted my own business. I have a farm-equipment business and I also specialize in marketing native grasses for pasture improvement."

"You're an entrepreneur," she said with a chuckle.

"Something like that, I guess." He cocked his head and studied her. "You know I don't date much."

"Yes. Sort of like me. I'm not modern enough for most men."

"I'm not modern enough for most women," he replied, and smiled. "Uh, there's going to be a dressy party over at the Hancock place to introduce a new rancher in the area. I wondered if you might like to go with me?"

"A party?" she asked. She did have one good dress. She'd bought it for a special occasion a while ago, and she couldn't really afford another one with the ranch having financial issues. But it was a nice dress. Her eyes brightened. "I haven't been to a party in a long time. I went with Dad to a conference in Denver before he got sick."

"I remember. You looked very nice."

"Well, I'd be wearing the same dress I had on then," she pointed out.

He laughed. "I don't follow the current fashions for women," he mused. "I'm inviting you, not the dress."

"In that case," she said with a pert smile, "I'd be delighted!"

CHAPTER FOUR

SOME MEN DRAGGED their feet around the room and called it dancing. John Everett could actually dance! He knew all the Latin dances and how to waltz, although he was uncomfortable with some of the newer ways to display on a dance floor. Fortunately the organizers of the party were older people and they liked older music.

Only a minute into an enthusiastic samba, John and Maddie found themselves in the middle of the dance floor with the other guests clapping as they marked the fast rhythm.

"We should take this show on the road." John chuckled as they danced.

"I'm game. I'll give up ranching and become a professional samba performer, if you'll come, too," she suggested.

"Maybe only part of the year," he mused. "We can't let our businesses go to pot."

"Spoilsport."

He grinned.

While the two were dancing, oblivious to the other guests, a tall, dark man in a suit walked in and found himself a flute of champagne. He tasted it, nodding to other guests. Everyone was gathered around the dance floor of the ballroom in the Victorian mansion. He wandered to the fringes and caught his breath. There, on the dance floor, was Maddie Lane.

She was wearing a dress, a sheath of black slinky material that dipped in front to display just a hint of the lovely curve of her breasts and display her long elegant neck and rounded arms. Her pale blond hair shone like gold in the light from the chandeliers. She was wearing makeup, just enough to enhance what seemed to be a rather pretty face, and the pretty calves of her legs were displayed to their best advantage from the arch of her spiked high-heel shoes. He'd rarely seen her dressed up. Not that he'd been interested in her or anything.

But there she was, decked out like a Christmas tree, dancing with his best friend. John didn't date anybody. Until now.

Cort Brannt felt irritation rise in him like bile. He scowled at the display they were making of themselves. Had they no modesty at all? And people were clapping like idiots.

He glared at Maddie. He remembered the last time he'd seen her. She backed away from Cort, but she was dancing with John as if she really liked him. Her face was radiant. She was smiling. Cort had rarely seen her smile at all. Of course, usually he was yelling at her or making hurtful remarks. Not much incentive for smiles.

He sipped champagne. Someone spoke to him. He just nodded. He was intent on the dancing couple, focused and furious.

Suddenly he noticed that the flute was empty. He turned and went back to the hors d'oeuvres table and had them refill it. But he didn't go back to the dance floor. Instead he found a fellow cattleman to talk to about the drought and selling off cattle.

A few minutes later he was aware of two people helping themselves to punch and cake.

"Oh, hi, Cort," John greeted him with a smile. "I didn't think you were coming."

"Hadn't planned to," Cort said in a cool tone. "My dad had an emergency on the ranch, so I'm filling in. One of the officers of the cattlemen's association is here." He indicated the man with a nod of his head. "Dad wanted me to ask him about any pending legislation that might help us through the drought. We've heard rumors, but nothing substantial."

"My dad was wondering the same." John frowned. "You okay?"

"I'm fine," Cort said, making sure that he enunciated as plainly as possible. He stood taller, although he still wasn't as tall, or as big, as his friend. "Why do you ask?"

"Because that's your second glass of champagne and you don't drink," John said flatly.

Cort held the flute up and looked at it. It was empty. "Where did that go?" he murmured.

"Just a guess, but maybe you drank it?" John replied.

Cort set the flute on the spotless white tablecloth and looked down at Maddie. "You're keeping expensive company these days."

She was shocked at the implication.

"Hold it right there," John said, and his deep tone was menacing. "I invited her."

"Got plans, have you?" Cort replied coldly.

"Why shouldn't I?" came the droll reply. "Oh, by the way, Odalie says her Italian voice teacher is an idiot. He doesn't know beans about how to sing, and he isn't teaching her anything. So she thinks she may come home soon."

Maddie felt her heart sink. Cort's expression lightened. "You think she might?"

"It's possible. You should lay off that stuff."

Cort glanced at the flute. "I suppose so."

"Hey, John, can I talk to you for a minute?" a man called to him. "I need a new combine!"

"I need a new sale," John teased. He glanced at Maddie. "I won't be a minute, okay?"

"Okay," she said. But she was clutching her small evening bag as if she was afraid that it might escape. She started looking around for someone, anyone, to talk to besides Cort Brannt.

While she was thinking about running, he slid his big hand into her small one and pulled her onto the dance floor. He didn't even ask. He folded her into his arms and led her to the lazy, slow rhythm.

He smelled of spicy, rich cologne. He was much taller than she was, so she couldn't see his face. She felt his cheek against the big wave of blond hair at her temple and her body began to do odd things. She felt uneasy, nervous. She felt...safe, excited.

"Your hand is like ice," he murmured as he danced with her around the room.

"They get cold all the time," she lied.

He laughed deep in his throat. "Really."

She wondered why he was doing this. Surely he should be pleased about Odalie's imminent reappearance in his life. He hated Maddie. Why was he dancing with her?

"I've never raised my hand to a woman," he said at her ear. "I never would, no matter how angry I was."

She swallowed and stopped dancing. She didn't want to talk about that.

He coaxed her eyes up. His were dark, narrow, intent. He was remembering what his father had told him, about the boy who tried to throw Maddie out a second-story window because of Odalie's lies. He didn't want to believe that Odalie had meant that to happen. Surely her female friend had talked her into putting those nasty things about the boy and his family on the internet. But however it had happened, the thought of someone manhandling Maddie made him angry. It upset him.

He didn't really understand why. He'd never thought of her in any romantic way. She was just Pierce Lane's daughter. He'd known her since she was a child, watched her follow her dad around the ranch. She was always petting a calf or a dog, or carrying chickens around because she liked the sounds they made.

"Why are you watching me like that?" she faltered.

"You love animals, don't you?" he asked, and there was an odd, soft glow about his dark eyes. "I remember you carrying Mom's chickens around like cuddly toys when you'd come over to the ranch with your dad. You were very small then. I had to rescue you from one of the herding dogs. You tried to pet him, and he wasn't a pet."

"His name was Rowdy," she recalled. "He was so pretty."

"We never let anybody touch those dogs except the man who trains and uses them. They have to be focused. You didn't know." He smiled. "You were a cute little kid. Always asking questions, always curious about everything."

She shifted uncomfortably. He wasn't dancing and they were drawing attention.

He looked around, cocked an eyebrow and moved her back around the room in his arms. "Sorry."

She didn't know what to think. She was tingling all over. She wanted him to hold her so close that she could feel every inch of his powerful frame against her. She wanted him to bend his head and kiss her so hard that her lips would sting. She wanted…something. Something more. She didn't understand these new and unexpected longings. It was getting hard to breathe and her heartbeat was almost shaking her. She couldn't bear it if he noticed.

He did notice. She was like melting ice in his arms. He felt her shiver when he drew her even closer, so that her soft, pert little breasts were hard against his chest through the thin suit jacket he was wearing. He liked the way she smelled, of wildflowers in the sun.

He drank in that scent. It made his head swim. His arm contracted. He was feeling sensations that he'd almost forgotten. Odalie didn't like him close to her, so his longing for her had been stifled. But Maddie was soft and warm and receptive. Too receptive.

His mouth touched her ear. "You make me hungry," he whispered roughly.

"Ex-excuse me?" she stammered.

"I want to lay you down on the carpet and kiss your breasts until my body stops hurting."

She caught her breath and stopped dancing. She pushed back from him, her eyes blazing, her face red with embarrassment. She wanted to kick him in the shin, but that would cause more problems.

She turned away from him, almost shivering with the emotions he'd kindled in her, shocked at the things he'd said to her. She almost ran toward John, who was walking toward her, frowning.

"What is it?" he asked suddenly, putting his arm around her.

She hid her face against him.

He glared at Cort, who was approaching them with more conflicting emotions than he'd ever felt in his life.

"You need to go home," John told Cort in a patient tone that was belied by his expression. "You've had too much to drink and you're going to make a spectacle of yourself and us if you keep this up."

"I want to dance with her," Cort muttered stubbornly.

"Well, it's pretty obvious that she doesn't want to dance with you." John leaned closer. "I can pick you up over my shoulder and carry you out of here, and I will."

"I'd like to see you try it," Cort replied, and his eyes blazed with anger.

Another cattleman, seeing a confrontation building, came strolling over and deliberately got between the two men.

"Hey, Cort," he said pleasantly, "I need to ask you about those new calves your dad's going to put up at the fall production sale. Can I ride home with you and see them?"

Cort blinked. "It's the middle of the night."

"The barn doesn't have lights?" the older man asked, raising an eyebrow.

Cort was torn. He knew the man. He was from up around the Frio river. He had a huge ranch, and Cort's dad was hungry for new customers.

"The barn has lights. I guess we could…go look at the calves." He was feeling very light-headed. He wasn't used to alcohol. Not at all.

"I'll drive you home," the rancher said gently. "You can have one of your cowboys fetch your car, can't you?"

"Yeah. I guess so."

"Thanks," John told the man.

He shrugged and smiled. "No problem."

He indicated the door. Cort hesitated for just a minute. He looked back at Maddie with dark, stormy eyes, long enough that she dropped her own like hot bricks. He gave John a smug glance and followed the visiting cattleman out the door.

"Oh, boy," John said to himself. "Now we get to the complications."

"Complications?" Maddie was only half listening. Her eyes were on Cort's long, elegant back. She couldn't remember ever being so confused.

AFTER THE PARTY was over, John drove her to her front door and cut off the engine.

"What happened?" he asked her gently, because she was still visibly upset.

"Cort was out of line," she murmured without lifting her eyes.

"Not surprising. He doesn't drink. I can't imagine what got him started."

"I guess he's missing your sister," she replied with a sigh. She looked up at him. "She's really coming home?"

"She says she is," he told her. He made a face. "That's Odalie. She always knows more than anybody else about any subject. My parents let her get away with being sassy because she was pretty and talented." He laughed shortly. "My dad let me have it if I was ever rude or impolite or spoke out of turn. My brother had it even rougher."

She cocked her head. "You never talk about Tanner."

He grimaced. "I can't. It's a family thing. Maybe I'll tell you one day. Anyway, Dad pulled me up short if I didn't toe the line at home." He shook his head. "You wouldn't believe how many times I had to clean the horse stalls when I made him mad."

"Odalie is beautiful," Maddie conceded, but in a subdued tone.

"Only a very few people know what she did to you," John said quietly. "It shamed the family. Odalie was only sorry she got caught. I think she finally realized how tragic the results could have been, though."

"How so?"

"For one thing, she never spoke again to the girl-friend who put her up to it," he said. "After she got out of school, she stopped posting on her social page and threw herself into studying music."

"The girlfriend moved away, didn't she, though?"

"She moved because threats were made. Legal ones," John confided. "My dad sent his attorneys after her. He was pretty sure that Odalie didn't know how to link internet sites and post simultaneously, which is what was done about you." He touched her short hair gently. "Odalie is spoiled and snobbish and she thinks she's the center of the universe. But she isn't cruel."

"Isn't she?"

"Well, not anymore," he added. "Not since the lawyers got involved. You weren't the only girl she victimized. Several others came forward and talked to my dad when they heard about what happened to you in the library. He was absolutely dumbfounded. So was my mother." He shook his head. "Odalie never got over what they said to her. She started making a real effort to consider the feelings of other people. Years too late, of course, and she's still got that bad attitude."

"It's a shame she isn't more like your mother," Maddie said gently, and she smiled. "Mrs. Everett is a sweet woman."

"Yes. Mom has an amazing voice and is not conceited. She was offered a career in opera but she turned it down. She liked singing the blues, she said. Now, she just plays and sings for us, and composes. There's still the occasional journalist who shows up at the door when one of her songs is a big hit, like Desperado's."

"Do they still perform… I mean Desperado?" she qualified.

"Yes, but not so much. They've all got kids now. It makes it tough to go on the road, except during summer holidays."

She laughed. "I love their music."

"Me, too." He studied her. "Odd."

"What is?"

"You're so easy to talk to. I don't get along with most women. I'm strung up and nervous and the aggressive ones make me uncomfortable. I sort of gave up dating after my last bad experience." He laughed. "I don't like women making crude remarks to me."

"Isn't it funny how things have changed?" she wondered aloud. "Not that I'm making fun of you. It's just that women used to get hassled. They still do, but it's turned around somewhat—now men get it, too."

"Yes, life is much more complicated now."

"I really enjoyed the party. Especially the dancing."

"Me, too. We might do that again one day."

She raised both eyebrows. "We might?"

He chuckled. "I'll call you."

"That would be nice."

He smiled, got out, went around and opened the door for her. He seemed to be debating whether or not to kiss her. She liked that lack of aggression in him. She smiled, went on tiptoe and kissed him right beside his chiseled mouth.

"Thanks again," she said. "See you!"

She went up the steps and into the house. John Everett stood looking after her wistfully. She thought he was nice. She liked him. But when she'd come off the dance floor trailing Cort Brannt, she'd been radiating like a furnace. Whether she knew it or not, she was in love with Cort. Shame, he thought as he drove off. She was just the sort of woman he'd like to settle down with. Not much chance of that, now.

Maddie didn't sleep at all. She stared at the ceiling. Her body tingled from the long contact with Cort's. She could feel his breath on her forehead, his lips in her hair. She could hear what he'd whispered.

She flushed at the memory. It had evoked incredible hunger. She didn't understand why she had these feelings now, when she hadn't had them for that boy who'd tried to hurt her so badly. She'd really thought she was crazy about him. But it was nothing like this.

Since her bad experience, she hadn't dated much. She'd seen her father get mad, but it was always quick and never physical. She hadn't been exposed to men who hit women. Now she knew they existed. It had been a worrying discovery.

Cort had frightened her when he'd lost his temper so violently in her father's office. She didn't think he'd attack her. But she'd been wary of him, until they danced together. Even if he was drunk, it had been the experience of a lifetime. She thought she could live on it forever, even if Odalie came home and Cort married her. He was never going to be happy with her, though. Odalie loved herself so much that there was no room in her life for a man.

If only the other woman had fallen in love with the Italian voice trainer and married him. Then Cort would have to let go of his unrequited feelings for Odalie, and maybe look in another direction. Maybe look in Maddie's direction.

On the other hand, he'd only been teasing at the dance. He wasn't himself.

Cold sober, he'd never have anything to do with Maddie. Probably, he'd just been missing Odalie and wanted a warm body to hold. Yes. That was probably it.

JUST BEFORE DAWN she fell asleep, but all too soon it was time to get up and start doing the chores around the ranch.

She went to feed her flock of hens, clutching the metal garbage can lid and the leafy limb to fend off Pumpkin. Somewhere in the back of her mind, she realized that it was going to come down to a hard decision one day. Pumpkin protected her hens, yes; he would be the bane of predators everywhere. But he was equally dangerous to people. What if he flew up and got one of her cowboys in the eye? She'd been reading up on rooster behavior, and she'd read some horror stories.

There had been all sorts of helpful advice, like giving him special treats and being nice to him. That had resulted in more gouges on her legs, even through her slacks, where his spurs had landed. Then there was the advice about having his spurs trimmed. Good advice, but who was going to catch and hold him while someone did that? None of her cowboys were lining up to volunteer.

"You problem child," she told Pumpkin as he chased her toward the gate. "One day, I'll have to do something about you!"

She got through the gate in the nick of time and shut it, hard. At least he wasn't going to get out of there, she told herself. She'd had Ben go around the perimeter of the large fenced area that surrounded the henhouse and plug any openings where that sneaky feathered fiend could possibly get out. If she kept him shut up, he couldn't hurt anybody, and the fence was seven feet high. No way he was jumping that!

She said so to Ben as she made her way to the barn to check on a calf they were nursing; it had dropped late and its mother had been killed by predators. They found it far on the outskirts of the ranch. They couldn't figure how it had wandered so far, but then, cattle did that. It was why you brought pregnant cows up close to the barn, so that you'd know when they were calving. It was especially important to do that in winter, just before the spring calves were due.

She looked over the gate at the little calf in the stall and smiled. "Pretty boy," she teased.

He was a purebred Santa Gertrudis bull. Some were culled and castrated and became steers, if they had poor conformation or were less than robust. But the best ones were treated like cattle royalty, spoiled rotten and watched over. This little guy would one day bring a handsome price as a breeding bull.

She heard a car door slam and turned just as Cort came into the barn.

She felt her heartbeat shoot off like a rocket.

He tilted his hat back and moved to the stall, peering over it. "That's a nice young one," he remarked.

"His mother was killed, so we're nursing him," she faltered.

He frowned. "Killed?"

"Predators, we think," she replied. "She was pretty torn up. We found her almost at the highway, out near your line cabin. Odd, that she wandered so far."

"Very odd," he agreed.

Ben came walking in with a bottle. "'Day, Cort," he said pleasantly.

"How's it going, Ben?" the younger man replied.

"So far so good."

Maddie smiled as Ben settled down in the hay and fed the bottle to the hungry calf.

"Poor little guy," Maddie said.

"He'll make it," Ben promised, smiling up at her.

"Well, I'll leave you to it," Maddie said. She was reluctant to be alone with Cort after the night before, but she couldn't see any way around it.

"You're up early," she said, fishing for a safe topic.

"I didn't sleep." He stuck his hands into his pockets as he strolled along with her toward the house.

"Oh?"

He stopped, so that she had to. His eyes were bloodshot and they had dark circles under them. "I drank too much," he said. "I wanted to apologize for the way I behaved with you."

"Oh." She looked around for anything more than one syllable that she could reply with. "That's…that's okay."

He stared down at her with curiously intent eyes. "You're incredibly naive."

She averted her eyes and her jaw clenched. "Yes,

well, with my background, you'd probably be the same way. I haven't been anxious to repeat the mistakes of the past with some other man who wasn't what he seemed to be."

"I'm sorry. About what happened to you."

"Everybody was sorry," she replied heavily. "But nobody else has to live with the emotional baggage I'm carrying around."

"How did you end up at the party with John?"

She blinked. "Well, he came over to show me some things about animal husbandry, and he asked me to go with him. It was sort of surprising, really. He doesn't date anybody."

"He's had a few bad experiences with women. So have I."

She'd heard about Cort's, but she wasn't opening that topic with him. "Would you like coffee?" she asked. "Great-Aunt Sadie went shopping, but she left a nice coffee cake baking in the oven. It should be about ready."

"Thanks. I could use a second cup," he added with a smile.

But the smile faded when he saw the fancy European coffee machine on the counter. "Where the hell did you buy that?" he asked.

She flushed. "I didn't. John likes European coffee, so he brought the machine and the pods over with him."

He lifted his chin. "Did he, now? I gather he thinks he'll be having coffee here often, then?"

She frowned. "He didn't say anything about that."

He made a huffing sound in his throat, just as the

stove timer rang. Maddie went to take the coffee cake out of the oven. She was feeling so rattled, it was a good thing she'd remembered that it was baking. She placed it on a trivet. It smelled of cinnamon and butter.

"My great-aunt can really cook," she remarked as she took off the oven mitts she'd used to lift it out.

"She can, can't she?"

She turned and walked right into Cort. She hadn't realized he was so close. He caught her small waist in his big hands and lifted her right onto the counter next to the coffee cake, so that she was even with his dark, probing eyes.

"You looked lovely last night," he said in a strange, deep tone. "I've never really seen you dressed up before."

"I… I don't dress up," she stammered. He was tracing her collarbone and the sensations it aroused were delicious and unsettling. "Just occasionally."

"I didn't know you could do those complicated Latin dances, either," he continued.

"I learned them from watching television," she said.

His head was lower now. She could feel his breath on her lips; feel the heat from his body as he moved closer, in between her legs so that he was right up against her.

"I'm not in John Everett's class as a dancer," he drawled, tilting her chin up. "But, then, he's not in my class…at this…"

His mouth slowly covered hers, teasing gently, so that he didn't startle her. He tilted her head just a little more, so that her mouth was at just the right angle. His firm lips pushed hers apart, easing them back, so that he had access to the soft, warm depths of her mouth.

He kissed her with muted hunger, so slowly that she didn't realize until too late how much a trap it was. He grew insistent then, one lean hand at the back of her head, holding it still, as his mouth devoured her soft lips.

"Sweet," he whispered huskily. "You taste like honey...."

His arms went under hers and around her, lifting her, so that her breasts were flattened against his broad, strong chest.

Involuntarily her cold hands snaked around his neck. She'd never felt hunger like this. She hadn't known it was possible. She let him open her mouth with his, let him grind her breasts against him. She moaned softly as sensations she'd never experienced left her helpless, vulnerable.

She felt his hand in her hair, tangling in it, while he kissed her in the soft silence of the kitchen. It was a moment out of time when she wished it could never end, that she could go on kissing him forever.

But just when he lifted his head, and looked into her eyes, and started to speak...

A car pulled up at the front porch and a door slammed.

Maddie looked into Cort's eyes with shock. He seemed almost as unsettled as she did. He moved back, helping her off the counter and onto her feet. He backed up just as Great-Aunt Sadie walked in with two bags of groceries.

"Didn't even have fresh mushrooms, can you believe it?" she was moaning, her mind on the door that was trying to close in her face rather than the two dazed people in the kitchen.

"Here, let me have those," Cort said politely, and he took the bags and put them on the counter. "Are there more in the car?" he asked.

"No, but thank you, Cort," Sadie said with a warm smile.

He grinned. "No problem." He glanced at Maddie, who still looked rattled. "I have to go. Thanks for the offer of coffee. Rain check?" he added, and his eyes were almost black with feeling.

"Oh, yes," Maddie managed breathlessly. "Rain check."

He smiled at her and left her standing there, vibrating with new hope.

CHAPTER FIVE

MADDIE STILL COULDN'T believe what had happened right there in her kitchen. Cort had kissed her, and as if he really did feel something for her. Besides that, he was very obviously jealous of John Everett. She felt as if she could actually walk on air.

"You look happier than I've seen you in years, sweetie," Great-Aunt Sadie said with a smile.

"I am."

Sadie grinned. "It's that John Everett, isn't it?" she teased. She indicated the coffeemaker. "Thought he was pretty interested. I mean, those things cost the earth. Not every man would start out courting a girl with a present like that!"

"Oh. Well, of course, I like John," Maddie stammered. And then she realized that she couldn't very well tell her great-aunt what was going on. Sadie might start gossiping. Maddie's ranch hands had friends who worked for the Brannts. She didn't want Cort to think she was telling tales about him, even in an innocent way. After all, it might have been a fluke. He could be missing Odalie and just reacted to Maddie in unexpected ways.

"He's a dish," Sadie continued as she peeled potatoes in the kitchen. "Handsome young man, just like his dad." She grimaced. "I'm not too fond of his sister, but, then, no family is perfect."

"No." She hesitated. "Sadie, do you know why nobody talks about the oldest brother, Tanner?"

Sadie smiled. "Just gossip. They said he and his dad had a major falling out over his choice of careers and he packed up and went to Europe. That was when he was in his late teens. As far as I know, he's never contacted the family since. It's a sore spot with the Everetts, so they don't talk about him anymore. Too painful, I expect."

"That's sad."

"Yes, it is. There was a rumor that he was hanging out with some dangerous people as well. But you know what rumors are."

"Yes," Maddie said.

"What was Cort doing over here earlier in the week?" Sadie asked suddenly.

"Oh, he was just…giving me some more pointers on dad's breeding program," Maddie lied.

"Scared you to death, too," Sadie said irritably. "I don't think he'd hurt you, but he's got a bad temper, sweetie."

Maddie had forgotten that, in the new relationship she seemed to be building with Cort. "People say his father was like that, when he was young. But Shelby married him and tamed him," she added with a secret smile.

Sadie glanced at her curiously. "I guess that can happen. A good woman can be the salvation of a man. But just…be careful."

"I will," she promised. "Cort isn't a mean person."

Sadie gave her a careful look. "So that's how it is."

Maddie flushed. "I don't know what you mean."

"John likes you, a lot," she replied.

Maddie sighed. "John's got a barracuda for a sister, too," she reminded the older woman. "No way in the world am I having her for a sister-in-law, no matter how nice John is."

Sadie grimaced. "Should have thought of that, shouldn't I?"

"I did."

She laughed. "I guess so. But just a suggestion, if you stick your neck out with Cort," she added very seriously. "Make him mad. Make him really mad, someplace where you can get help if you need to. Don't wait and find out when it's too late if he can't control his temper."

"I remember that boy in high school," Maddie reminded her. "He didn't stop. Cort frightened me, yes, but when he saw I was afraid, he started apologizing. If he couldn't control his temper, he'd never have been able to stop."

Sadie looked calmer. "No. I don't think he would."

"He's still apologizing for it, in fact," Maddie added.

Sadie smiled and her eyes were kind. "All right, then. I won't harp on it. He's a lot like his father, and his dad is a good man."

"They're all nice people. Morie was wonderful to me in school. She stuck up for me when Odalie and her girlfriend were making my life a daily purgatory."

"Pity Odalie never really gets paid back for the things she does," Sadie muttered.

Maddie hugged her. "That mill grinds slowly but relentlessly," she reminded her. She grinned. "One day..."

Sadie laughed. "One day."

Maddie let her go with a sigh. "I hope I can learn enough of this stuff not to sink dad's cattle operation," she moaned. "I wasn't really faced with having to deal with the breeding aspect until now, with roundup ahead and fall breeding standing on the line in front of me. Which bull do I put on which cows? Gosh! It's enough to drive you nuts!"

"Getting a lot of help in that, though, aren't you?" Sadie teased. "Did you tell Cort that John had been coaching you, too?"

"Yes." She sighed. "Cort wasn't overjoyed about it, either. But John makes it understandable." She threw up her hands. "I'm just slow. I don't understand cattle. I love to paint and sculpt. But Dad never expected to go so soon and have to leave me in charge of things. We're going in the hole because I don't know what I'm doing." She glanced at the older woman. "In about two years, we're going to start losing customers. It terrifies me. I don't want to lose the ranch, but it's going to go downhill without dad to run it." She toyed with a bag on the counter. "I've been thinking about that developer..."

"Don't you dare," Sadie said firmly. "Darlin', do you realize what he'd do to this place if he got his hands on it?" she exclaimed. "He'd sell off all the livestock to anybody who wanted it, even for slaughter, and he'd rip the land to pieces. All that prime farmland, gone, all the native grasses your dad planted and nurtured, gone. This house—" she indicated it "—where your father and your grandfather and I were born! Gone!"

Maddie felt sick. "Oh, dear."

"You're not going to run the ranch into the ground. Not when you have people, like King Brannt, who want to help you get it going again," she said firmly. "If you ever want to sell up, you talk to him. I'll bet he'd offer for it and put in a manager. We could probably even stay on and pay rent."

"With what?" Maddie asked reasonably. "Your social security check and my egg money?" She sighed. "I can't sell enough paintings or enough eggs to pay for lunch in town," she added miserably. "I should have gone to school and learned a trade or something." She grimaced. "I don't know what to do."

"Give it a little time," the older woman said gently. "I know it's overwhelming, but you can learn. Ask John to make you a chart and have Ben in on the conversation. Your dad trusted Ben with everything, even the finances. I daresay he knows as much as you do about things."

"That's an idea." She smiled sadly. "I don't really want to sell that developer anything. He's got a shady look about him."

"You're telling me."

"I guess I'll wait a bit."

"Meanwhile, you might look in that bag I brought home yesterday."

"Isn't it groceries…dry goods?"

"Look."

She peered in the big brown bag and caught her

breath. "Sculpting material. Paint! Great-Aunt Sadie!" she exclaimed, and ran and hugged the other woman. "That's so sweet of you!"

"Looking out for you, darling," she teased. "I want you to be famous so those big TV people will want to interview me on account of we're related!" She stood up and struck a pose. "Don't you think I'd be a hit?"

Maddie hugged her even tighter. "I think you're already a hit. Okay. I can take a hint. I'll get to work right now!"

Sadie chortled as she rushed from the room.

CORT CAME IN several days later while she was retouching one of the four new fairies she'd created, working where the light was best, in a corner of her father's old office. She looked up, startled, when Great-Aunt Sadie let him in.

She froze. "Pumpkin came after you again?" she asked, worried.

"What?" He looked around, as if expecting the big red rooster to appear. "Oh, Pumpkin." He chuckled. "No. He was in the hen yard giving me mean looks, but he seems to be well contained."

"Thank goodness!"

He moved to the table and looked at her handiwork. "What a group," he mused, smiling. "They're all beautiful."

"Thanks." She wished she didn't sound so breathless, and that she didn't have paint dabbed all over her face from her day's efforts. She probably looked like a painting herself.

"Going to sell them?"

"Oh, I couldn't," she said hesitantly. "I mean, I... well, I just couldn't."

"Can't you imagine what joy they'd bring to other people?" he asked, thinking out loud. "Why do you think doll collectors pay so much for one-of-a-kind creations like those? They build special cabinets for them, take them out and talk to them..."

"You're kidding!" she exclaimed, laughing. "Really?"

"This one guy I met at the conference said he had about ten really rare dolls. He sat them around the dining room table every night and talked to them while he ate. He was very rich and very eccentric, but you get the idea. He loved his dolls. He goes to all the doll collector conventions. In fact, there's one coming up in Denver, where they're holding a cattlemen's workshop." He smiled. "Anyway, your fairies wouldn't be sitting collecting dust on the shelf of a collector like that. They'd be loved."

"Wow." She looked back at the little statuettes. "I never thought of it like that."

"Maybe you should."

She managed a shy smile. He looked delicious in a pair of beige slacks and a yellow, very expensive pullover shirt with an emblem on the pocket. Thick black hair peeked out where the top buttons were undone. She wondered how his bare chest would feel against her hands. She blushed. "What can I do for you?" she asked quickly, trying to hide her interest.

Her reaction to him was amusing. He found it really

touching. Flattering. He hadn't been able to get her out of his mind since he'd kissed her so hungrily in her kitchen. He'd wanted to come back sooner than this, but business had overwhelmed him.

"I have to drive down to Jacobsville, Texas, to see a rancher about some livestock," he said. "I thought you might like to ride with me."

She stared at him as if she'd won the lottery. "Me?"

"You." He smiled. "I'll buy you lunch on the way. I know this little tearoom off the beaten path. We can have high tea and buttermilk pie."

She caught her breath. "I used to hear my mother talk about that one. I've never had high tea. I'm not even sure what it is, exactly."

"Come with me and find out."

She grinned. "Okay! Just let me wash up first."

"Take your time. I'm not in any hurry."

"I'll just be a few minutes."

She almost ran up the staircase to her room.

Cort picked up one of the delicate little fairies and stared at it with utter fascination. It was ethereal, beautiful, stunning. He'd seen such things before, but never anything so small with such personality. The little fairy had short blond hair, like Maddie's, and pale eyes. It amused him that she could paint something so tiny. He noted the magnifying glass standing on the table, and realized that she must use it for the more detailed work. Still, it was like magic, making something so small look so realistic.

He put it down, very carefully, and went into the

kitchen to talk to Sadie while he waited for Maddie to get ready.

"Those little fairies she makes are amazing," he commented, lounging against the counter.

Sadie smiled at him. "They really are. I don't know how she does all that tiny detailed work without going blind. The little faces are so realistic. She has a gift."

"She does. I wish she'd do something with it."

"Me, too," Sadie replied. "But she doesn't want to sell her babies, as she calls them."

"She's sitting on a gold mine here." Cort sighed. "You know, breeding herd sires is hard work, even for people who've done it for generations and love it."

She glanced at him and she looked worried. "I know. She doesn't really want to do it. My nephew had to toss her in at the deep end when he knew his cancer was fatal." She shook her head. "I hate it for her. You shouldn't be locked into a job you don't want to do. But she's had no training. She really can't do anything else."

"She can paint. And she can sculpt."

"Yes, but there's still the ranch," Sadie emphasized.

"Any problem has a solution. It's just a question of finding it." He sighed. "Ben said you'd had another cow go missing."

"Yes." She frowned. "Odd thing, too, she was in a pasture with several other cows, all of them healthier than her. I can't think somebody would steal her."

"I know what you mean. They do wander off. It's just that it looks suspicious, having two go missing in the same month."

"Could it be that developer man?"

Cort shook his head. "I wouldn't think so. We've got armed patrols and cameras mounted everywhere. If anything like that was going on, we'd see it."

"I suppose so."

There was the clatter of footsteps almost leaping down the staircase.

"Okay, I'm ready," Maddie said, breathless. She was wearing jeans and boots and a pretty pink button-up blouse. She looked radiant.

"Where are you off to?" Sadie asked, laughing.

"I'm going to Jacobsville with Cort to look at livestock."

"Oh." Sadie forced a smile. "Well, have fun, then."

Cort started the sleek two-seater Jaguar. He glanced at Maddie, who was looking at everything with utter fascination.

"Not quite like your little Volkswagen, huh?" he teased.

"No! It's like a spaceship or something."

"Watch this."

As he started the car, the air vents suddenly opened up and the Jaguar symbol lit up on a touch screen between the steering wheel and the glove compartment. At the same time, the gearshift rose up from the console, where it had been lying flat.

"Oh, gosh!" she exclaimed. "That's amazing!"

He chuckled. "I like high-tech gadgets."

"John has one of these," she recalled.

His eyes narrowed. "So he does. I rode him around in mine and he found a dealership the next day. His is more sedate."

"I just think they're incredible."

He smiled. "Fasten your seat belt."

"Oops, sorry, wasn't thinking." She reached up and drew it between her breasts, to fasten it beside her hip.

"I always wear my seat belt," he said. "Dad refused to drive the car until we were all strapped in. He was in a wreck once. He said he never forgot that he'd be dead except for the seat belt."

"My dad wasn't in a wreck, but he was always careful about them, too." She put her strappy purse on the floorboard. "Did Odalie come home?" she asked, trying not to sound too interested.

"Not yet," he said. He had to hide a smile, because the question lacked any subtlety.

"Oh."

He was beginning to realize that Odalie had been a major infatuation for him. Someone unreachable that he'd dreamed about, much as young boys dreamed about movie stars. He knew somewhere in the back of his mind that he and Odalie were as different as night and day. She wanted an operatic career and wasn't interested in fitting him into that picture. Would he be forever hanging around opera houses where she performed, carrying bags and organizing fans? Or would he be in Texas, waiting for her rare visits? She couldn't have a family and be a performer, not in the early stages of her career, maybe never. Cort wanted a family. He wanted children.

Funny, he'd never thought of himself as a parent before. But when he'd listened to Maddie talk about her little fairy sculptures and spoke of them as her children, he'd pictured her with a baby in her arms. It had shocked him how much he wanted to see that for real.

"You like kids, don't you?" he asked suddenly.

"What brought that on?" She laughed.

"What you said, about your little fairy sculptures. They're beautiful kids."

"Thanks." She looked out the window at the dry, parched grasslands they were passing through. "Yes, I love kids. Oh, Cort, look at the poor corn crops! That's old Mr. Raines's land, isn't it?" she added. "He's already holding on to his place by his fingernails I guess he'll have to sell if it doesn't rain."

"My sister said they're having the same issues up in Wyoming." He glanced at her. "Her husband knows a medicine man from one of the plains tribes. She said that he actually did make it rain a few times. Nobody understands how, and most people think it's fake, but I wonder."

"Ben was talking about a Cheyenne medicine man who can make rain. He's friends with him. I've known people who could douse for water," she said.

"Now, there's a rare talent indeed," he commented. He pursed his lips. "Can't Ben do that?"

"Shh," she said, laughing. "He doesn't want people to think he's odd, so he doesn't want us to tell anybody."

"Still, you might ask him to go see if he could find water. If he does, we could send a well-borer over to do the job for him."

She looked at him with new eyes. "That's really nice of you."

He shrugged. "I'm nice enough. From time to time."

He glanced at her pointedly. "When women aren't driving me to drink."

"What? I didn't drive you to drink!"

"The hell you didn't," he mused, his eyes on the road so that he missed her blush. "Dancing with John Everett. Fancy dancing. Latin dancing." He sighed. "I can't even do a waltz."

"Oh, but that doesn't matter," she faltered, trying to deal with the fact that he was jealous. Was he? That was how it sounded! "I mean, I think you dance very nicely."

"I said some crude things to you," he said heavily. "I'm really sorry. I don't drink, you see. When I do..." He let the sentence trail off. "Anyway, I apologize."

"You already apologized."

"Yes, but it weighs on my conscience." He stopped at a traffic light. He glanced at her with dark, soft eyes. "John's my friend. I think a lot of him. But I don't like him taking you out on dates and hanging around you."

She went beet-red. She didn't even know what to say.

"I thought it might come as a shock," he said softly. He reached a big hand across the console and caught hers in it. He linked her fingers with his and looked into her eyes while he waited for the lights to change. "I thought we might take in a movie Friday night. There's that new Batman one."

"There's that new Ice Age one," she said at the same time.

He gave her a long, amused look. "You like cartoon movies?"

She flushed. "Well..."

He burst out laughing. "So do I. Dad thinks I'm nuts."

"Oh, I don't!"

His fingers contracted around hers. "Well, in that case, we'll see the Ice Age one."

"Great!"

The light changed and he drove on. But he didn't let go of her hand.

High tea was amazing! There were several kinds of tea, china cups and saucers to contain it, and little cucumber sandwiches, chicken salad sandwiches, little cakes and other nibbles. Maddie had never seen anything like it. The tearoom was full, too, with tourists almost overflowing out of the building, which also housed an antique shop.

"This is awesome!" she exclaimed as she sampled one thing after another.

"Why, thank you." The owner laughed, pausing by their table. "We hoped it would be a success." She shook her head. "Everybody thought we were crazy. We're from Charleston, South Carolina. We came out here when my husband was stationed in the air force base at San Antonio, and stayed. We'd seen another tearoom, way north, almost in Dallas, and we were so impressed with it that we thought we might try one of our own. Neither of us knew a thing about restaurants, but we learned, with help from our staff." She shook her head. "Never dreamed we'd have this kind of success," she added, looking around. "It's quite a dream come true."

"That cameo," Maddie said hesitantly, nodding toward a display case close by. "Does it have a story?"

"A sad one. The lady who owned it said it was handed down in her family for five generations. Finally there was nobody to leave it to. She fell on hard times and asked me to sell it for her." She sighed. "She died a month ago." She opened the case with a key and pulled out the cameo, handing it to Maddie. It was black lacquer with a beautiful black-haired Spanish lady painted on it. She had laughing black eyes and a sweet smile. "She was so beautiful."

"It was the great-great-grandmother of the owner. They said a visiting artist made it and gave it to her. She and her husband owned a huge ranch, from one of those Spanish land grants. Pity there's nobody to keep the legend going."

"Oh, but there is." Cort took it from the woman and handed it to Maddie. "Put it on the tab, if you will," he told the owner. "I can't think of anyone who'll take better care of her."

"No, you can't," Maddie protested, because she saw the price tag.

"I can," Cort said firmly. "It was a family legacy. It still is." His dark eyes stared meaningfully into hers. "It can be handed down, to your own children. You might have a daughter who'd love it one day."

Maddie's heart ran wild. She looked into Cort's dark eyes and couldn't turn away.

"I'll put the ticket with lunch," the owner said with a soft laugh. "I'm glad she'll have a home," she added gently.

"Can you write down the woman's name who sold it to you?" Maddie asked. "I want to remember her, too."

"That I can. How about some buttermilk pie? It's the house specialty," she added with a grin.

"I'd love some."

"Me, too," Cort said.

Maddie touched the beautiful cheek of the cameo's subject. "I should sculpt a fairy who looks like her."

"Yes, you should," Cort agreed at once. "And show it with the cameo."

She nodded. "How sad," she said, "to be the last of your family."

"I can almost guarantee that you won't be the last of yours," he said in a breathlessly tender tone.

She looked up into his face and her whole heart was in her eyes.

He had to fight his first impulse, which was to drag her across the table into his arms and kiss the breath out of her.

She saw that hunger in him and was fascinated that she seemed to have inspired it. He'd said that she was plain and uninteresting. But he was looking at her as if he thought her the most beautiful woman on earth.

"Dangerous," he teased softly, "looking at me like that in a public place."

"Huh?" She caught her breath as she realized what he was saying. She laughed nervously, put the beautiful cameo beside her plate and smiled at him. "Thank you, for the cameo."

"My pleasure. Eat up. We've still got a long drive ahead of us!"

Jacobsville, Texas, was a place Maddie had heard of all her life, but she'd never seen it before. In the town square, there was a towering statue of Big John Jacobs, the founder of Jacobsville, for whom Jacobs County was named. Legend had it that he came to Texas from Georgia after the Civil War, with a wagonload of black sharecroppers. He also had a couple of Comanche men who helped him on the ranch. It was a fascinating story, how he'd married the spunky but not so pretty daughter of a multimillionaire and started a dynasty in Texas.

Maddie shared the history with Cort as they drove down a long dirt road to the ranch, which was owned by Cy Parks. He was an odd sort of person, very reticent, with jet-black hair sprinkled with silver and piercing green eyes. He favored one of his arms, and Maddie could tell that it had been badly burned at some point. His wife was a plain little blonde woman who wore glasses and obviously adored her husband. The feeling seemed to be mutual. They had two sons who were in school, Lisa explained shyly. She was sorry she couldn't introduce them to the visitors.

Cy Parks showed them around his ranch in a huge SUV. He stopped at one pasture and then another, grimacing at the dry grass.

"We're having to use up our winter hay to feed them," he said with a sigh. "It's going to make it a very hard winter if we have to buy extra feed to carry us through." He glanced at Cort and laughed. "You'll make my situation a bit easier if you want to carry a couple of my young bulls home with you."

Cort grinned, too. "I think I might manage that. Although we're in the same situation you are. Even my sister's husband, who runs purebred cattle in Wyoming, is having it rough. This drought is out of anybody's experience. People are likening it to the famous Dust Bowl of the thirties."

"There was another bad drought in the fifties," Parks added. "When we live on the land, we always have issues with weather, even in good years. This one has been a disaster, though. It will put a lot of the family farms and ranches out of business." He made a face. "They'll be bought up by those damned great combines, corporate ranching, I call it. Animals pumped up with drugs, genetically altered—damned shame. Pardon the language," he added, smiling apologetically at Maddie.

"She's lived around cattlemen all her life," Cort said affectionately, smiling over the back of the seat at her.

"Yes, I have." Maddie laughed. She looked into Cort's dark eyes and blushed. He grinned.

They stopped at the big barn on the way back and Cy led them through it to a stall in the rear. It connected to a huge paddock with plenty of feed and fresh water.

"Now this is my pride and joy," he said, indicating a sleek, exquisite young Santa Gertrudis bull.

"That is some conformation," Cort said, whistling. "He's out of Red Irony, isn't he?" he added.

Cy chuckled. "So you read the cattle journals, do you?"

"All of them. Your ranch has some of the best breeding stock in Texas. In the country, in fact."

"So does Skylance," Parks replied. "I've bought your own bulls over the years. And your father's," he added to Maddie. "Good stock."

"Thanks," she said.

"Same here," Cort replied. He drew in a breath. "Well, if this little fellow's up for bids, I'll put ours in."

"No bids. He's yours if you want him." He named a price that made Maddie feel faint, but Cort just smiled.

"Done," he said, and they shook hands.

On the way back home, Maddie was still astonished at the price. "That's a fortune," she exclaimed.

"Worth every penny, though," Cort assured her. "Healthy genetics make healthy progeny. We have to put new bulls on our cows every couple of years to avoid any defects. Too much inbreeding can be dangerous to the cattle and disastrous for us."

"I guess so. Mr. Parks seems like a very nice man," she mused.

He chuckled. "You don't know his history, do you? He led one of the most respected groups of mercenaries in the world into small wars overseas. His friend Eb Scott still runs a world-class counterterrorism school on his ranch. He was part of the merc group, along with a couple of other citizens of Jacobsville."

"I didn't know!"

"He's a good guy. Dad's known him for years."

"What a dangerous way to make a living, though."

"No more dangerous than dealing with livestock," Cort returned.

That was true. There were many pitfalls of working with cattle, the least of which was broken bones. Concussions could be, and sometimes were, fatal. You could drown in a river or be trampled...the list went on and on.

"You're very thoughtful," Cort remarked.

She smiled. "I was just thinking."

"Me, too." He turned off onto a side road that led to a park. "I want to stretch my legs for a bit. You game?"

"Of course."

He pulled into the car park and led the way down a small bank to the nearby river. The water level was down, but flowing beautifully over mossy rocks, with mesquite trees drooping a little in the heat, but still pretty enough to catch the eye.

"It's lovely here."

"Yes." He turned and pulled her into his arms, looking down into her wide eyes. "It's very lovely here." He bent his head and kissed her.

CHAPTER SIX

Maddie's head was swimming. She felt the blood rush to her heart as Cort riveted her to his long, hard body and kissed her as if he might never see her again. She pressed closer, wrapping her arms around him, holding on for dear life.

His mouth tasted of coffee. It was warm and hard, insistent as it ground into hers. She thought if she died now, it would be all right. She'd never been so happy.

She heard a soft groan from his mouth. One lean hand swept down her back and pressed her hips firmly into his. She stiffened a little. She didn't know much about men, but she was a great reader. The contours of his body had changed quite suddenly.

"Nothing to worry about," he whispered into her mouth. "Just relax…"

She did. It was intoxicating. His free hand went under her blouse and expertly unclasped her bra to give free rein to his searching fingers. They found her breast and teased the nipple until it went hard. He groaned and bent his head, putting his mouth right over it, over the cloth. She arched up to him, so entranced that she couldn't even find means to protest.

"Yes," he groaned. "Yes, yes…!"

Her hands tangled in his thick black hair, tugging it closer. She arched backward, held by his strong arms as he fed on the softness of her breast under his demanding mouth. His hand at her back was more insistent now, grinding her against the growing hardness of his body.

She was melting, dying, starving to death. She wanted him to take off her clothes; she wanted to lie down with him and she wanted something, anything that would ease the terrible ache in her young body.

And just when she was certain that it would happen, that he wasn't going to stop, a noisy car pulled into the car park above and a car door slammed.

She jerked back from him, tugging down her blouse, shivering at the interruption. His eyes were almost black with hunger. He cursed under his breath, biting his lip as he fought down the need that almost bent him over double.

From above there were children's voices, laughing and calling to each other. Maddie stood with her back to him, her arms wrapped around her body, while she struggled with wild excitement, embarrassment and confusion. He didn't like her. He thought she was ugly. But he'd kissed her as if he were dying for her mouth. It was one big puzzle...

She felt his big, warm hands on her shoulders. "Don't sweat it," he said in a deep, soft tone. "Things happen."

She swallowed and forced a smile. "Right."

He turned her around, tipping her red face up to his eyes. He searched them in a silence punctuated with the screams and laughter of children. She was very pretty like that, her mouth swollen from his kisses, her face shy, timid. He was used to women who demanded. Aggressive women. Even Odalie, when he'd kissed her once, had been very outspoken about what she liked and didn't like. Maddie simply…accepted.

"Don't be embarrassed," he said softly. "Everything's all right. But we should probably go now. It's getting late."

She nodded. He took her small hand in his, curled his fingers into hers and drew her with him along the dirt path that led back up to the parking lot.

Two bedraggled parents were trying to put out food in plastic containers on a picnic table, fighting the wind, which was blowing like crazy in the sweltering heat. They glanced at the couple and grinned.

Cort grinned back. There were three children, all under school age, one in his father's arms. They looked happy, even though they were driving a car that looked as if it wouldn't make it out of the parking lot.

"Nice day for a picnic," Cort remarked.

The father made a face. "Not so much, but we've got a long drive ahead of us and it's hard to sit in a fast-food joint with this company." He indicated the leaping, running toddlers. He laughed. "Tomorrow, they'll be hijacking my car," he added with an ear-to-ear smile, "so we're enjoying it while we can."

"Nothing like kids to make a home a home," the mother commented.

"Nice looking kids, too," Cort said.

"Very nice," Maddie said, finally finding her voice.

"Thanks," the mother said. "They're a handful, but we don't mind."

She went back to her food containers, and the father went running after the toddlers, who were about to climb down the bank.

"Nice family," Cort remarked as they reached his car.

"Yes. They seemed so happy."

He glanced down at her as he stopped to open the passenger door. He was thoughtful. He didn't say anything, but his eyes were soft and full of secrets. "In you go."

She got in, fastened her seat belt without any prompting and smiled all the way back home.

Things were going great, until they got out of the car in front of Maddie's house. Pumpkin had found a way out of the hen enclosure. He spotted Cort and broke into a halting run, with his head down and his feathers ruffled.

"No!" Maddie yelled. "Pumpkin, no!"

She tried to head him off, but he jumped at her and she turned away just in time to avoid spurs in her face. "Cort, run! It's okay, just run!" she called when he hesitated.

He threw his hands up and darted toward his car. "You have to do something about that damned rooster, Maddie!" he called back.

"I know," she wailed. "I will, honest! I had fun. Thanks so much!"

He threw up his hands and dived into the car. He started it and drove off just before Pumpkin reached him.

"You stupid chicken! I'm going to let Ben eat you, I swear I am!" she raged.

But when he started toward her, she ran up the steps, into the house and slammed the door.

She opened her cell phone and called her foreman.

"Ben, can you please get Pumpkin back into the hen lot and try to see where he got out? Be sure to wear your chaps and carry a shield," she added.

"Need to eat that rooster, Maddie," he drawled.

"I know." She groaned. "Please?"

There was a long sigh. "All right. One more time…" He hung up.

Great-Aunt Sadie gave her a long look. "Pumpkin got out again?"

"Yes. There must be a hole in the fence or something," she moaned. "I don't know how in the world he does it!"

"Ben will find a way to shut him in, don't worry. But you are going to have to do something, you know. He's dangerous."

"I love him," Maddie said miserably.

"Well, sometimes things we love don't love us back and should be made into chicken and dumplings," Sadie mused with pursed lips.

Maddie made a face at her. She opened her shoulder bag and pulled out a box. "I want to show you something. Cort bought it for me."

"Cort's buying you presents?" Sadie exclaimed.

"It's some present, too," Maddie said with a flushed smile.

She opened the box. There, inside, was the hand-painted cameo of the little Spanish lady, with a card that gave all the information about the woman, now deceased, who left it with the antiques dealer.

"She's lovely," Sadie said, tracing the face with a forefinger very gently.

"Read the card." Maddie showed it to her.

When Sadie finished reading it, she was almost in tears. "How sad, to be the last one in your family."

"Yes. But this will be handed down someday." She was remembering the family at the picnic tables and Cort's strange smile, holding hands with him, kissing him. "Someday," she said again, and she sounded as breathless as she felt.

Sadie didn't ask any questions. But she didn't have to. Maddie's bemused expression told her everything she needed to know. Apparently Maddie and Cort were getting along very well, all of a sudden.

CORT WALKED INTO the house muttering about the rooster.

"Trouble again?" Shelby asked. She was curled up on the sofa watching the news, but she turned off the television when she saw her son. She smiled, dark-eyed and still beautiful.

"The rooster," he sighed. He tossed his hat into a chair and dropped down into his father's big recliner. "I bought us a bull. He's very nice."

"From Cy Parks?"

He nodded. "He's quite a character."

"So I've heard."

"I bought Maddie a cameo," he added. "In that tea-room halfway between here and Jacobsville. It's got an antiques store in with it." He shook his head. "Beautiful thing. It's hand-painted…a pretty Spanish lady with a fan, enameled. She had a fit over it. The seller died recently and had no family."

"Sad. But it was nice of you to buy it for Maddie."

He pursed his lips. "When you met Dad, you said you didn't get along."

She shivered dramatically. "That's putting it mildly. He hated me. Or he seemed to. But when my mother, your grandmother, died, I was alone in a media circus. They think she committed suicide and she was a big-name movie star, you see. So there was a lot of publicity. I was almost in hysterics when your father showed up out of nowhere and managed everything."

"Well!"

"I was shocked. He'd sent me home, told me he had a girlfriend and broke me up with Danny. Not that I needed breaking-up, Danny was only pretending to be engaged to me to make King face how he really felt. But it was fireworks from the start." She peered at him through her thick black eyelashes. "Sort of the way it was with you and Maddie, I think."

"It's fireworks, now, too. But of a different sort," he added very slowly.

"Oh?" She didn't want to pry, but she was curious.

"I'm confused. Maddie isn't pretty. She can't sing or play anything. But she can paint and sculpt and she's sharp about people." He grimaced. "Odalie is beautiful, like the rising sun, and she can play any instrument and sing like an angel."

"Accomplishments and education don't matter as much as personality and character," his mother replied quietly. "I'm not an educated person, although I've taken online courses. I made my living modeling. Do you think I'm less valuable to your father than a woman with a college degree and greater beauty?"

"Goodness, no!" he exclaimed at once.

She smiled gently. "See what I mean?"

"I think I'm beginning to." He leaned back. "It was a good day."

"I'm glad."

"Except for that damned rooster," he muttered. "One of these days…!"

She laughed.

He was about to call Maddie, just to talk, when his cell phone rang.

He didn't recognize the number. He put it up to his ear. "Hello?"

"Hello, Cort," Odalie's voice purred in his ear. "Guess what, I'm home! Want to come over for supper tonight?"

He hesitated. Things had just gotten complicated.

MADDIE HALF EXPECTED Cort to phone her, after their lovely day together, but he didn't. The next morning, she heard a car pull up in the driveway and went running out. But it wasn't Cort. It was John Everett.

She tried not to let her disappointment show. "Hi!" she said. "Would you like a cup of very nice European coffee from a fancy European coffeemaker?" she added, grinning.

He burst out laughing. "I would. Thanks. It's been a hectic day and night."

"Has it? Why?" she asked as they walked up the steps.

"I had to drive up to Dallas-Fort Worth airport to pick up Odalie yesterday."

Her heart did a nosedive. She'd hoped against hope that the other woman would stay in Italy, marry her voice teacher, get a job at the opera house, anything but come home, and especially right now! She and Cort were only just beginning to get to know each other. It wasn't fair!

"How is she?" she asked, her heart shattering.

"Good," he said heavily. "She and the voice teacher disagreed, so she's going to find someone in this country to take over from him." He grimaced. "I don't know who. Since she knows more than the voice trainers do, I don't really see the point in it. She can't take criticism."

She swallowed, hard, as she went to work at the coffee machine. "Has Cort seen her?"

"Oh, yes," he said, sitting down at the little kitchen table. "He came over for supper last night. They went driving."

She froze at the counter. She didn't let him see her face, but her stiff back was a good indication of how she'd received the news.

"I'm really sorry," he said gently. "But I thought you should know before you heard gossip."

She nodded. Tears were stinging her eyes, but she hid them. "Thanks, John."

He drew in a long breath. "She doesn't love him," he said. "He's just a habit she can't give up. I don't think he loves her, either, really. It's like those crushes we get on movie stars. Odalie is an image, not someone real who wants to settle down and have kids and live on a ranch. She can't stand cattle!"

She started the coffee machine, collected herself, smiled and turned around. "Good thing your parents don't mind them," she said.

"And I've told her so. Repeatedly." He studied her through narrowed eyes. His thick blond hair shone like pale yellow diamonds in the overhead light. He was so good-looking, she thought. She wished she could feel for him what she felt for Cort.

"People can't help being who they are," she replied quietly.

"You're wise for your years," he teased.

She laughed. "Not so wise, or I'd get out of the cattle business." She chuckled. "After we have coffee, want to have another go at explaining genetics to me? I'm a lost cause, but we can try."

"You're not a lost cause, and I'd love to try."

ODALIE WAS IRRITABLE and not trying to hide it. "What's the matter with you?" she snapped at Cort. "You haven't heard a word I've said."

He glanced at her and grimaced. "Sorry. We've got a new bull coming. I'm distracted."

Her pale blue eyes narrowed. "More than distracted, I think. What's this I hear about you taking that Lane girl with you to buy the new bull?"

He gave her a long look and didn't reply.

She cleared her throat. Cort was usually running after her, doing everything he could to make her happy, make her smile. She'd come home to find a stranger, a man she didn't know. Her beauty hadn't interested the voice trainer; her voice hadn't really impressed him. She'd come home with a damaged ego and wanted Cort to fix it by catering to her. That hadn't happened. She'd invited him over today for lunch and he'd eaten it in a fog. He actually seemed to not want to be with her, and that was new and scary.

"Well, she's plain as toast," Odalie said haughtily. "She has no talent and she's not educated."

He cocked his head. "And you think those are the most important character traits?"

She didn't like the way he was looking at her. "None of my friends had anything to do with her in school," she muttered.

"You had plenty to do with that, didn't you?" Cort asked with a cold smile. "I believe attorneys were involved...?"

"Cort!" She went flaming red. She turned her head. "That was a terrible misunderstanding. And it was Millie who put me up to it. That's the truth. I didn't like Maddie, but I'd never have done it if I'd realized what that boy might do." She bit her lip. She'd thought about that a lot in recent weeks, she didn't know why. "He could have killed her. I'd have had it on my conscience forever," she added in a strange, absent tone.

Cort was not impressed. This was the first time he'd heard Odalie say anything about the other woman that didn't have a barb in it, and even this comment was self-centered. Though it was small, he still took her words as a sign that maybe she was changing and becoming more tolerant...

"Deep thoughts," he told her.

She glanced at him and smiled. "Yes. I've become introspective. Enjoy it while it lasts." She laughed, and she was so beautiful that he was really confused.

"I love your car," she said, glancing out the window. "Would you let me drive it?"

He hesitated. She was the worst driver he'd ever known. "As long as I'm in it," he said firmly.

She laughed. "I didn't mean I wanted to go alone," she teased.

She knew where she wanted to drive it, too. Right past Maddie Lane's house, so that she'd see Odalie with Cort. So she'd know that he was no longer available. Odalie seemed to have lost her chance at a career in opera, but here was Cort, who'd always loved her. Maybe she'd settle down, maybe she wouldn't, but Cort was hers. She wanted Maddie to know it.

She'd never driven a Jaguar before. This was a very fast, very powerful, very expensive two-seater. Cort handed her the key.

She clicked it to open the door. She frowned. "Where's the key?" she asked.

"You don't need a key. It's a smart key. You just keep it in your pocket or lay it in the cup holder."

"Oh."

She climbed into the car and put the smart key in the cup holder.

"Seat belt," he emphasized.

She glared at him. "It will wrinkle my dress," she said fussily, because it was delicate silk, pink and very pretty.

"Seat belt or the car doesn't move," he repeated.

She sighed. He was very forceful. She liked that. She smiled at him prettily. "Okay."

She put it on, grimacing as it wrinkled the delicate fabric. Oh, well, the dry cleaners could fix it. She didn't want to make Cort mad. She pushed the button Cort showed her, the button that would start the car, but nothing happened.

"Brake," he said.

She glared at him. "I'm not going fast enough to brake!"

"You have to put your foot on the brake or it won't start," he explained patiently.

"Oh."

She put her foot on the brake and it started. The air vents opened and the touch screen came on. "It's like something out of a science-fiction movie," she said, impressed.

"Isn't it, though?" He chuckled.

She glanced at him, her face radiant. "I have got to have Daddy get me one of these!" she exclaimed.

Cort hoped her father wouldn't murder him when he saw what they cost.

Odalie pulled the car out of the driveway in short jerks. She grimaced. "I haven't driven in a while, but it will come back to me, honest."

"Okay. I'm not worried." He was petrified, but he wasn't showing it. He hoped he could grab the wheel if he had to.

She smoothed out the motions when she got onto the highway. "There, better?" she teased, looking at him.

"Eyes on the road," he cautioned.

She sighed. "Cort, you're no fun."

"It's a powerful machine. You have to respect it. That means keeping your eyes on the road and paying attention to your surroundings."

"I'm doing that," she argued, looking at him again.

He prayed silently that they'd get home again.

She pulled off on a side road and he began to worry.

"Why are we going this way?" he asked suspiciously.

"Isn't this the way to Catelow?" she asked in all innocence.

"No, it's not," he said. "It's the road that leads to the Lane ranch."

"Oh, dear, I don't want to go there. But there's no place to turn off," she worried. "Anyway, the ranch is just ahead, I'll turn around there."

Cort had to bite his lip to keep from saying something.

Maddie was out in the yard with her garbage can lid. This time Pumpkin had gotten out of the pen when she was looking. He'd jumped a seven-foot-high fence. If she hadn't seen it with her own eyes, she'd never have believed it.

"Pumpkin, you fool!" she yelled at him. "Why can't you stay where I put you? Get back in there!"

But he ran around her. This time he wasn't even trying to spur her. He ran toward the road. It was his favorite place, for some reason, despite the heat that made the ribbon of black asphalt hotter than a frying pan.

"You come back here!" she yelled.

Just as she started after him, Odalie's foot hit the accelerator pedal too hard, Cort called out, Odalie looked at him instead of the road…

MADDIE HEARD SCREAMING. She was numb. She opened her eyes and there was Cort, his face contorted with horror. Beside him, Odalie was screaming and crying.

"Just lie still," Cort said hoarsely. "The ambulance is on the way. Just lie still, baby."

"I hit her, I hit her!" Odalie screamed. "I didn't see her until it was too late! I hit her!"

"Odalie, you have to calm down. You're not helping!" Cort snapped at her. "Find something to cover her. Hurry!"

"Yes…there's a blanket…in the backseat, isn't there…?"

Odalie fetched it with cold, shaking hands. She drew it over Maddie's prone body. There was blood. So much blood. She felt as if she were going to faint, or throw up. Then she saw Maddie's face and tears ran down her cheeks. "Oh, Maddie," she sobbed, "I'm so sorry!"

"Find something to prop her head, in case her spine is injured," Cort gritted. He was terrified. He brushed back Maddie's blond hair, listened to her ragged breathing, saw her face go even paler. "Please hurry!" he groaned.

There wasn't anything. Odalie put her beautiful white leather purse on one side of Maddie's head without a single word, knowing it would ruin the leather and not caring at all. She put her knit overblouse on the other, crumpled up. She knelt in the dirt road beside Maddie and sat down, tears in her eyes. She touched

Maddie's arm. "Help is coming," she whispered brokenly. "You hold on, Maddie. Hold on!"

Maddie couldn't believe it. Her worst enemy was sitting beside her in a vision of a horrifically expensive pink silk dress that was going to be absolutely ruined, and apparently didn't mind at all.

She tried to speak. "Pum… Pumpkin?" she rasped.

Cort looked past her and grimaced. He didn't say anything. He didn't have to.

Maddie started to cry, great heaving sobs.

"We'll get you another rooster," Cort said at once. "I'll train him to attack me. Anything. You just have to…hold on, baby," he pleaded. "Hold on!"

She couldn't breathe. "Hurts," she whispered as sensation rushed back in and she began to shudder.

Cort was in hell. There was no other word that would express what he felt as he saw her lying there in bloody clothing, maybe dying, and he couldn't do one damned thing to help her. He was sick to his soul.

He brushed back her hair, trying to remember anything else, anything that would help her until the ambulance arrived.

"Call them again!" Odalie said firmly.

He did. The operator assured them that the ambulance was almost there. She began asking questions, which Cort did his best to answer.

"Where's your great-aunt?" he asked Maddie softly.

"Store," she choked out.

"It's okay, I'll call her," he said when she looked upset.

Odalie had come out of her stupor and she was checking for injuries while Cort talked to the 911 operator. "I don't see anything that looks dangerous, but I'm afraid to move her," she said, ignoring the blood in her efforts to give aid. "There are some abrasions, pretty raw ones. Maddie, can you move your arms and legs?" she asked in a voice so tender that Maddie thought maybe she really was just dreaming all this.

She moved. "Yes," she said. "But…it hurts…"

"Move your ankles."

"Okay."

Odalie looked at Cort with horror.

"I moved…them," Maddie said, wincing. "Hurts!"

"Please, ask them to hurry," Cort groaned into the phone.

"No need," Odalie said, noting the red-and-white vehicle that was speeding toward them.

"No sirens?" Cort asked blankly.

"They don't run the sirens or lights unless they have to," the operator explained kindly. "It scares people to death and can cause wrecks. They'll use them to get the victim to the hospital, though, you bet," she reassured him.

"Thanks so much," Cort said.

"I hope she does well."

"Me, too," he replied huskily and hung up.

Odalie took one of the EMTs aside. "She can't move her feet," she whispered.

He nodded. "We won't let her know."

They went to the patient.

MADDIE WASN'T AWARE of anything after they loaded her into the ambulance on a backboard. They talked to someone on the radio and stuck a needle into her arm. She slept.

When she woke again, she was in a hospital bed with two people hovering. Cort and Odalie. Odalie's dress was dirty and bloodstained.

"Your...beautiful dress," Maddie whispered, wincing.

Odalie went to the bed. She felt very strange. Her whole life she'd lived as if there was nobody else around. She'd never been in the position of nursing anybody—her parents and brother had never even sprained a hand. She'd been petted, spoiled, praised, but never depended upon.

Now here was this woman, this enemy, whom her actions had placed almost at death's door. And suddenly she was needed. Really needed.

Maddie's great-aunt had been called. She was in the waiting room, but in no condition to be let near the patient. The hospital staff had to calm her down, she was so terrified.

They hadn't told Maddie yet. When Sadie was calmer, they'd let her in to see the injured woman.

"Your great-aunt is here, too," Odalie said gently. "You're going to be fine."

"Fine." Maddie felt tears run down her cheeks. "So much...to be done at the ranch, and I'm stove up...!"

"I'll handle it," Cort said firmly. "No worries there."

"Pumpkin," she sobbed. "He was horrible. Just horrible. But I loved him." She cried harder.

Odalie leaned down and kissed her unkempt hair. "We'll find you another horrible rooster. Honest."

Maddie sobbed. "You hate me."

"No," Odalie said softly. "No, I don't. And I'm so sorry that I put you in here. I was driving." She bit her lip. "I wasn't watching the road," she said stiffly. "God, I'm sorry!"

Maddie reached out a lacerated hand and touched Odalie's. "I ran into the road after Pumpkin… I wasn't looking. Not your fault. My fault."

Odalie was crying, too. "Okay. Both our faults. Now we have to get you well."

"Both of us," Cort agreed, touching Maddie's bruised cheek.

Maddie swallowed, hard. She wanted to say something else, but they'd given her drugs to make her comfortable, apparently. She opened her mouth to speak and went right to sleep.

CHAPTER SEVEN

"IS SHE GOING to be all right?" Great-Aunt Sadie asked when Odalie and Cort dropped into chairs in the waiting room while Maddie was sleeping.

"Yes, but it's going to be a long recovery," Cort said heavily.

"You can't tell her," Odalie said gently, "but there seems to be some paralysis in her legs. No, it's all right," she interrupted when Sadie looked as if she might start crying. "We've called one of the foremost orthopedic surgeons in the country at the Mayo Clinic. We're flying him down here to see her. We'll go from there, once he's examined her."

"But the expense," Sadie exclaimed.

"No expense. None. This is my fault and I'm paying for it," Odalie said firmly.

"It's my car, I'm helping," Cort added.

She started crying again. "It's so nice of you, both of you."

Odalie hugged her. "I'm so sorry," she said sadly. "I didn't mean to hit her. I wasn't looking, and I should have been."

Sadie hugged her back. "Accidents happen," she sobbed. "It was that stupid rooster, wasn't it?"

"It was." Cort sighed. "He ran right into the road and Maddie ran after him. The road was clear and then, seconds later, she was in the middle of it."

Odalie couldn't confess that she'd gone that way deliberately to show Maddie she was with Cort. She was too ashamed. "She'll be all right," she promised.

"Oh, my poor little girl," Sadie said miserably. "She'll give up, if she knows she might not be able to walk again. She won't fight!"

"She will. Because we'll make her," Odalie said quietly.

Sadie looked at her with new eyes. Her gaze fell to Odalie's dress. "Oh, your dress," she exclaimed.

Odalie just smiled. "I can get another dress. It's Maddie I'm worried about." It sounded like a glib reply, but it wasn't. In the past few hours, Odalie's outlook had totally shifted from herself to someone who needed her. She knew that her life would never be the same again.

A sheriff's deputy came into the waiting room, spotted Odalie and Cort and approached them, shaking his head.

"I know," Odalie said. "It's my fault. I was driving his car—" she indicated Cort "—and not looking where I was going. Maddie ran out into the road after her stupid rooster, trying to save him. She's like that."

The deputy smiled. "We know all that from the recreation of the scene that we did," he said. "It's very scientific," he added. "How is she?"

"Bad," Odalie said heavily. "They think she may lose the use of her legs. But we've called in a world-famous surgeon. If anything can be done, it will be. We're going to take care of her."

The deputy looked at the beautiful woman, at her bloodstained, dirty, expensive dress, with kind eyes. "I know some women who would be much more concerned with the state of their clothing than the state of the victim. Your parents must be very proud of you, young lady. If you were my daughter, I would be."

Odalie flushed and smiled. "I feel pretty guilty right now. So thanks for making me feel better."

"You going to charge her?" Cort asked.

The deputy shook his head. "Probably not, as long as she survives. In the law, everything is intent. You didn't mean to do it, and the young lady ran into the road by her own admission." He didn't add that having to watch the results of the accident day after day would probably be a worse punishment than anything the law could prescribe. But he was thinking it.

"That doesn't preclude the young lady pressing charges, however," the deputy added.

Odalie smiled wanly. "I wouldn't blame her if she did."

He smiled back. "I hope she does well."

"So do we," Odalie agreed. "Thanks."

He nodded and went back out again.

"Tell me what the doctor said about her legs," Sadie said sadly, leaning toward them.

Odalie took a long breath. She was very tired and she had no plans to go home that night. She'd have to call her family and tell them what was happening here. She hadn't had time to do that yet, nor had Cort.

"He said that there's a great deal of bruising, with inflammation and swelling. That can cause partial paralysis, apparently. He's started her on anti-inflammatories and when she's able, he'll have her in rehab to help get her moving," she added gently.

"But she was in so much pain…surely they won't make her get up!" Sadie was astonished.

"The longer she stays there, the stronger the possibility that she won't ever get up, Sadie," Odalie said gently. She patted the other woman's hands, which were resting clenched in her lap. "He's a very good doctor."

"Yes," Sadie said absently. "He treated my nephew when he had cancer. Sent him to some of the best oncologists in Texas." She looked up. "So maybe it isn't going to be permanent?"

"A good chance. So you stop worrying. We all have to be strong so that we can make her look ahead instead of behind, so that we can keep her from brooding." She bit her lower lip. "It's going to be very depressing for her, and it's going to be a long haul, even if it has a good result."

"I don't care. I'm just so happy she's still alive," the older woman cried.

"Oh, so am I," Odalie said heavily. "I can't remember ever feeling quite so bad in all my life. I took my eyes off the road, just for a minute." Her eyes closed and she shuddered. "I'll be able to hear that horrible sound when I'm an old lady…"

Cort put his arm around her. "Stop that. I shouldn't have let you drive the car until you were familiar with it. My fault, too. I feel as bad as you do. But we're going to get Maddie back on her feet."

"Yes," Odalie agreed, forcing a smile. "Yes, we are."

Sadie wiped her eyes and looked from one young determined face to the other. Funny how things worked out, she was thinking. Here was Odalie, Maddie's worst enemy, being protective of her, and Cort just as determined to make her walk again when he'd been yelling at her only a week or so earlier. What odd companions they were going to be for her young great-niece. But what a blessing.

She considered how it could have worked out, if Maddie had chased that stupid red rooster out into the road and been hit by someone else, maybe someone who ran and left her there to die. It did happen. The newspapers were full of such cases.

"What are you thinking so hard about?" Cort asked with a faint smile.

Sadie laughed self-consciously. "That if she had to get run over, it was by such nice people who stopped and rendered aid."

"I know what you mean," Cort replied. "A man was killed just a couple of weeks ago by a hit-and-run driver who was drunk and took off. The pedestrian died. I wondered at the time if his life might have been spared, if the man had just stopped to call an ambulance before he ran." He shook his head. "So many cases like that."

"Well, you didn't run, either of you." Sadie smiled. "Thanks, for saving my baby."

Odalie hugged her again, impulsively. "For the foreseeable future, she's my baby, too," she said with a laugh. "Now, how about some coffee? I don't know about you, but I'm about to go to sleep out here and I have no intention of leaving the hospital."

"Nor do I," Cort agreed. He stood up. "Let's go down to the cafeteria and see what we can find to eat, too. I just realized I'm starving."

The women smiled, as they were meant to.

MADDIE CAME AROUND a long time later, or so it seemed. A dignified man with black wavy hair was standing over her with a nurse. He was wearing a white lab coat with a stethoscope draped around his neck.

"Miss Lane?" the nurse asked gently. She smiled. "This is Dr. Parker from the Mayo Clinic. He's an orthopedic specialist, and we'd like him to have a look at your back. If you don't mind."

Maddie cleared her throat. She didn't seem to be in pain, which was odd. She felt very drowsy. "Of course," she said, puzzled as to why they would have such a famous man at such a small rural hospital.

"Just a few questions first," he said in a deep, pleasant tone, "and then I'll examine you." He smiled down at her.

"Okay."

The pain came back as the examination progressed, but he said it was a good sign. Especially the pain she felt in one leg. He pressed and poked and asked questions while he did it. After a few minutes she was allowed to lie down in the bed, which she did with a grimace of pure relief.

"There's a great deal of edema—swelling," he

translated quietly. "Bruising of the spinal column, inflammation, all to be expected from the trauma you experienced."

"I can't feel my legs. I can't move them," Maddie said with anguish in her wan face.

He dropped down elegantly into the chair by her bed, crossed his legs and picked up her chart. "Yes, I know. But you mustn't give up hope. I have every confidence that you'll start to regain feeling in a couple of weeks, three at the outside. You have to believe that as well." He made notations and read what her attending physician had written in the forms on the clipboard, very intent on every word. "He's started you on anti-inflammatories," he murmured. "Good, good, just what I would have advised. Getting fluids into you intravenously, antibiotics…" He stopped and made another notation. "And then, physical therapy."

"Physical therapy." She laughed and almost cried. "I can't stand up!"

"It's much more than just exercise," he said and smiled gently. "Heat, massage, gentle movements, you'll see. You've never had physical therapy I see."

She shook her head. "I've never really had an injury that required it."

"You're very lucky, then," he said.

"You think I'll walk again?" she prompted, her eyes wide and full of fear.

"I think so," he said. "I won't lie to you, there's a possibility that the injury may result in permanent disability." He held up a hand when she seemed distraught. "If that happens, you have a wonderful support group here. Your family. They'll make sure you have everything you need. You'll cope. You'll learn how to adapt. I've seen some miraculous things in my career, Miss Lane," he added. "One of my newest patients lost a leg overseas in a bombing. We repaired the damage, got him a prosthesis and now he's playing basketball."

She caught her breath. "Basketball?"

He grinned, looking much younger. "You'd be amazed at the advances science has made in such things. Right now, they're working on an interface that will allow quadriplegics to use a computer with just thought. Sounds like science fiction, doesn't it? But it's real. I watched a video of a researcher who linked a man's mind electronically to a computer screen, and he was able to move a curser just with the power of his thoughts." He shook his head. "Give those guys ten years and they'll build something that can read minds."

"Truly fascinating," she agreed.

"But right now, what I want from you is a promise that you'll do what your doctor tells you and work hard at getting back on your feet," he said. "No brooding. No pessimism. You have to believe you'll walk again."

She swallowed. She was bruised and broken and miserable. She drew in a breath. "I'll try," she said.

He stood up and handed the chart to the nurse with a smile. "I'll settle for that, as long as it's your very best try," he promised. He shook hands with her. "I'm going to stay in touch with your doctor and be available for consultation. If I'm needed, I can fly back down here. Your friends out there sent a private jet for me." He chuckled. "I felt like a rock star."

She laughed, then, for the first time since her ordeal had begun.

"That's more like it," he said. "Ninety-nine percent of recovery is in the mind. You remember that."

"I'll remember," she promised. "Thanks for coming all this way."

He threw up a hand. "Don't apologize for that. It got me out of a board meeting," he said. "I hate board meetings."

She grinned.

LATER, AFTER SHE'D been given her medicines and fed, Odalie and Cort came into the private room she'd been moved to.

"Dr. Parker is very nice," she told them. "He came all the way from the Mayo Clinic, though…!"

"Whatever it takes is what you'll get," Odalie said with a smile.

Maddie grimaced as she looked at Odalie's beautiful pink dress, creased and stained with blood and dirt. "Your dress," she moaned.

"I've got a dozen pretty much just like it," Odalie told her. "I won't even miss it." She sighed. "But I really should go home and change."

"Go home and go to bed," Maddie said softly. "You've done more than I ever expected already…"

"No," Odalie replied. "I'm staying with you. I got permission."

"But there's no bed," Maddie exclaimed. "You can't sleep in a chair…!"

"There's a rollaway bed. They're bringing it in." She

glanced at Cort with a wicked smile. "Cort gets to sleep in the chair."

He made a face. "Don't rub it in."

"But you don't have to stay," Maddie tried to reason with them. "I have nurses. I'll be fine, honest I will."

Odalie moved to the bed and brushed Maddie's unkempt hair away from her wan face. "You'll brood if we leave you alone," she said reasonably. "It's not as if I've got a full social calendar these days, and I'm not much for cocktail parties. I'd just as soon be here with you. We can talk about art. I majored in it at college."

"I remember," Maddie said slowly. "I don't go to college," she began.

"I'll wager you know more about it than I do," Odalie returned. "You had to learn something of anatomy to make those sculptures so accurate."

"Well, yes, I did," Maddie faltered. "I went on the internet and read everything I could find."

"I have all sorts of books on medieval legends and romances, I'll bring them over for you to read when they let you go home. Right now you have to rest," Odalie said.

Maddie flushed. "That would be so nice of you."

Odalie's eyes were sad. "I've been not so nice to you for most of the time we've known one another," she replied. "You can't imagine how I felt, after what happened because I let an idiot girl talk me into telling lies about you online. I've had to live with that, just as you have. I never even said I was sorry for it. But I am," she added.

Maddie drew in a breath. She was feeling drowsy. "Thanks," she said. "It means a lot."

"Don't you worry about a thing," Odalie added. "I'll take care of you."

Maddie flushed. She'd never even really had a girl-friend, and here was Odalie turning out to be one.

Odalie smiled. "Now go to sleep. Things will look brighter tomorrow. Sometimes a day can make all the difference in how we look at life."

"I'll try."

"Good girl." She glanced at Cort. "Can you drive me home and bring me back?"

"Sure," he said. "I need a change of clothes, too. I'll drop you off at Big Spur, go home and clean up and we'll both come back. We need to tell our parents what's going on, too."

"John will be beside himself," Odalie said without thinking. "All I've heard since I got home is how sweet Maddie is," she added with a smile.

She didn't see Cort's expression, and she couldn't understand why Maddie suddenly looked so miserable at the mention of her brother's name.

"Well, don't worry about that right now," Odalie said quickly. "But I'm sure he'll be in to see you as soon as he knows what happened."

Maddie nodded.

"I'll be right out," Cort said, smiling at Odalie.

"Sure. Sleep tight," she told Maddie. She hesitated. "I'm sorry about your rooster, too. Really sorry," she stammered, and left quickly.

Maddie felt tears running down her cheeks.

Cort picked a tissue out of the box by the bed, bent down and dabbed at both her eyes. "Stop that," he said softly. "They'll think I'm pinching you and throw me out."

She smiled sadly. "Nobody would ever think you were mean."

"Don't you believe it."

"You and Odalie…you've both been so kind," she said hesitantly. "Thank you."

"We feel terrible," he replied, resting his hand beside her tousled hair on the pillow. "It could have been a worse tragedy than it is. And Pumpkin…" He grimaced and dabbed at more tears on her face. "As much as I hated him, I really am sorry. I know you loved him."

She sniffed, and he dabbed at her nose, too. "He was so mean," she choked out. "But I really did love him."

"We'll get you a new rooster. I'll train him to attack me," he promised.

She laughed through her tears.

"That's better. The way you looked just now was breaking my heart."

She searched his eyes. He wasn't joking. He meant it.

He brushed back her hair. "God, I don't know what I would have done if you'd died," he whispered hoarsely. He bent and crushed his mouth down over hers, ground into it with helpless need. After a few seconds, he forced himself to pull back. "Sorry," he said huskily. "Couldn't help myself. I was terrified when I saw you lying there so still."

"You were?" She looked fascinated.

He shook his head and forced a smile. "Clueless," he

murmured. "I guess that's not such a bad thing. Not for the moment anyway." He bent and brushed his mouth tenderly over hers. "I'll be back. Don't go anywhere."

"If I tried to, three nurses would tackle me, and a doctor would sit on me while they sent for a gurney," she assured him, her eyes twinkling.

He wrinkled his nose and kissed her again. "Okay." He stood up. "Anything you want me to bring you?"

"A steak dinner, two strawberry milkshakes, a large order of fries…"

"For that, they'd drag me out the front door and pin me to a wall with scalpels," he assured her.

She sighed. "Oh, well. It was worth a try. They fed me green gelatin." She made a face.

"When we get you out of here, I'll buy you the tastiest steak in Texas, and that's a promise. With fries."

"Ooooh," she murmured.

He grinned. "Incentive to get better. Yes?"

She nodded. "Yes." The smile faded. "You don't have to come back. Odalie, either. I'll be okay."

"We're coming back, just the same. We'll drop Great-Aunt Sadie off at the house, but she can stay at Skylance if she's nervous about being there alone. She's been a real trooper, but she's very upset."

"Can I see her?"

"For just a minute. I'll bring her in. You be good."

She nodded.

Great-Aunt Sadie was still crying when she went to the bed and very carefully bent down to hug Maddie. "I'm so glad you're going to be all right," she sobbed.

Maddie touched her gray hair gently. "Can't kill a weed." She laughed.

"You're no weed, my baby." She smoothed back her hair. "You keep getting better. I'll bring your gown and robe and slippers and some cash when I come back. Here. This is for the machines if you want them to get you anything…"

"Put that back," Cort said, "Maddie won't need cash."

"Oh, but—" Sadie started to argue.

"It won't do any good," Cort interrupted with a grin. "Ask my dad."

"He's right," Maddie said drowsily. "I heard one of his cowboys say that it's easier to argue with a signpost, and you'll get further."

"Stop bad-mouthing me. Bad girl," he teased.

She grinned sleepily.

"You go to sleep," he told her. "Odalie and I will be back later, and we'll bring Sadie in the morning."

"You're a nice boy, Cort," Sadie said tearfully.

He hugged her. "You're a nice girl," he teased. "Good night, honey," he told Maddie, and didn't miss the faint blush in her cheeks as she registered the endearment.

"Good night," she replied.

She drifted off to sleep before they got out of the hospital. In her mind, she could still hear that soft, deep voice drawling "honey."

The next morning, Maddie opened her eyes when she heard a commotion.

"I can't bathe her with you sitting there," the nurse was saying reasonably.

Cort frowned as he stood up. "I know, I know. Sorry.

I only fell asleep about four," he added with a sheepish smile.

The nurse smiled back. "It's all right. A lot of patients don't have anybody who even cares if they live or die. Your friend's very fortunate that the two of you care so much."

"She's a sweet girl," Odalie said gently.

"So are you," Cort said, and smiled warmly at her. She flushed a little.

Maddie, watching, felt her heart sink. They'd both been so caring and attentive that she'd actually forgotten how Cort felt about Odalie. And now it seemed that Odalie was seeing him with new eyes.

Cort turned, but Maddie closed her eyes. She couldn't deal with this. Not now.

"Tell her we went to have breakfast and we'll be back," Cort said, studying Maddie's relaxed face.

"I will," the nurse promised.

Cort let Odalie go out before him and closed the door as he left.

"Time to wake up, sweetie," the nurse told Maddie. "I'm going to give you your bath and then you can have breakfast."

"Oh, is it morning?" Maddie asked, and pretended to yawn. "I slept very well."

"Good. Your friends went to have breakfast. That handsome man said they'd be back," she added with a laugh. "And that woman. What I wouldn't give to be that beautiful!"

"She sings like an angel, too," Maddie said.

"My, my, as handsome as he is, can you imagine

what beautiful children they'd have?" the nurse murmured as she got her things together to bathe Maddie.

"Yes, wouldn't they?" Maddie echoed.

Something in her tone made the other woman look at her curiously.

But Maddie just smiled wanly. "They've both been very kind," she said. "They're my neighbors."

"I see."

No, she didn't, but Maddie changed the subject to a popular television series that she watched. The nurse watched it, too, which gave them a talking point.

LATER, SADIE CAME in with a small overnight bag.

"I brought all your stuff," she told Maddie. "You look better," she lied, because Maddie was pale and lethargic and obviously fighting pain.

"It's a little worse today," she replied heavily. "You know what they say about injuries, they're worse until the third day and then they start getting better."

"Who said that?" Sadie wondered.

"Beats me, but I've heard it all my life. Did you bring me anything to read?" she added curiously.

"I didn't. But somebody else did." She glanced at the door. Odalie came in with three beautifully illustrated fairy-tale books. After breakfast, both Odalie and Cort had gone home to change, and then picked up Great-Aunt Sadie when returning to the hospital.

"I bought these while I was in college," Odalie said, handing one to Maddie. "I thought they had some of the most exquisite plates I'd ever seen."

And by plates, she meant paintings. Maddie caught

her breath as she opened the book and saw fairies, like the ones she made, depicted in a fantasy forest with a shimmering lake.

"Oh, this is…it's beyond words," she exclaimed, breathlessly turning pages.

"Yes. I thought you'd like them." She beamed. "These are updated versions of the ones I have. I bought these for you."

"For me?" Maddie looked as if she'd won the lottery. "You mean it?"

"I mean it. I'm so glad you like them."

"They're beautiful," she whispered reverently. She traced one of the fairies. "I have my own ideas about faces and expressions, but these are absolutely inspiring!"

"Fantasy art is my favorite."

"Mine, too." She looked up, flushing a little. "How can I ever thank you enough?"

"You can get better so that my conscience will stop killing me," Odalie said gently.

Maddie smiled. "Okay. I promise to try."

"I'll settle for that."

"I put your best gowns and slippers in the bag," Sadie told her. "And Cort brought you something, too."

"Cort?"

She looked toward the door. He was smiling and nodding at the nurses, backing into the room. Behind his back was a strange, bottom-heavy bear with a big grin and bushy eyebrows.

He turned into the room and handed it to Maddie. "I don't know if they'll let you keep it, but if they won't,

I'll let Sadie take him home and put him in your room. His name's Bubba."

"Bubba?" She burst out laughing as she took the bear from him. It was the cutest stuffed bear she'd ever seen. "Oh, he's so cute!"

"I'm glad you like him. I wanted to smuggle in a steak, but they'd have smelled it at the door."

"Thanks for the thought," she said shyly.

"You're welcome."

"Bears and books." She sighed. "I feel spoiled."

"I should hope so," Odalie said with a grin. "We're doing our best."

"When we get you out of here, we're taking you up to Dallas and we'll hit all the major museums and art galleries," Cort said, dropping into a chair. "Culture. Might give you some new ideas for your paintings and sculptures."

"Plus we bought out an art supply store for you," Odalie said with twinkling eyes. "You'll have enough to make all sorts of creations when you get home."

"Home." Maddie looked from one of them to the other. "When? When can I go home?"

"In a few days." Cort spoke for the others. "First they have to get you stabilized. Then you'll be on a regimen of medicine and physical therapy. We'll go from there."

Maddie drew in a long breath. It sounded like an ordeal. She wasn't looking forward to it. And afterward, what if she could never walk again? What if...?

"No pessimistic thoughts." Odalie spoke for the visitors. "You're going to get well. You're going to walk. Period."

"Absolutely," Sadie said.

"Amen," Cort added.

Maddie managed a sheepish smile. With a cheering section like that, she thought, perhaps she could, after all.

CHAPTER EIGHT

THE THIRD DAY was definitely the worst. Maddie was in incredible pain from all the bruising. It was agony to move at all, and her legs were still numb. They kept her sedated most of the day. And at night, as usual, Cort and Odalie stayed with her.

"How are you getting away with this?" Maddie asked Odalie when Cort left to get them both a cup of coffee.

"With this?" Odalie asked gently.

"Staying in the room with me," she replied drowsily. "I thought hospitals made people leave at eight-thirty."

"Well, they mostly do," Odalie said sheepishly. "But, you see, Cort's dad endowed the new pediatric unit, and mine paid for the equipment in the physical therapy unit. So, they sort of made an exception for us."

Maddie laughed in spite of the pain. "Oh, my."

"As my dad explained it, you can do a lot of good for other people and help defray your own taxes, all at once. But, just between us, my dad would give away money even if it didn't help his tax bill. So would Cort's. It's just the sort of people they are."

"It's very nice of them." She shifted and grimaced. "How are things at my ranch, do you know?" she asked worriedly.

"Great. Not that the boys don't miss you. But Cort's been over there every day getting roundup organized and deciding on your breeding program. I hope you don't mind."

"Are you kidding? I make fairies… I don't know anything about creating bloodlines." She sighed. "My dad knew all that stuff. He was great at it. But he should have had a boy who'd have loved running a ranch. I just got stuck with it because there was nobody else he could leave it to."

"Your father must have known that you'd do the best you could to keep it going," Odalie said gently.

"I am. It's just I have no aptitude for it, that's all."

"I think…"

"Finally!" John Everett said as he walked in, frowning at his sister. "There was such a conspiracy of silence. I couldn't get Cort to tell me where you were. I called every hospital in Dallas…"

"I left you seven emails and ten text messages!" Odalie gasped. "Don't tell me you never read them?"

He glowered at her. "I don't read my personal email because it's always advertisements, and I hate text messages. I disabled them from coming to my phone. You couldn't have called me in Denver and told me what happened?"

Odalie would have told him that Cort talked her out of it, but he was mad, and John in a temper would discourage most people from confessing that.

"Sorry," she said instead.

He turned his attention to Maddie and grimaced. The bruises were visible around the short-sleeved gown she was wearing. "Poor little thing," he said gently. "I brought you flowers."

He opened the door and nodded to a lady standing outside with a huge square vase full of every flower known to man—or so it seemed. "Right over there looks like a good place," he said, indicating a side table.

The lady, probably from the gift shop, smiled at Maddie and placed the flowers on the table. "I hope you feel better soon," she told her.

"The flowers are just lovely," Maddie exclaimed.

"Thanks," the lady replied, smiled at John and left them to it.

"Oh, how beautiful. Thanks, John!" she exclaimed.

Odalie looked very uncomfortable. John didn't even look at her. He went to the bedside, removed his Stetson and sat down in the chair by the bed, grasping one of Maddie's hands in his. "I've been beside myself since I knew what happened. I wanted to fly right home, but I was in the middle of negotiations for Dad and I couldn't. I did try to call your house, but nobody answered, and I didn't have your cell phone number." He glared at his sister again. "Nobody would even tell me which hospital you were in!"

"I sent you emails," Odalie said again.

"The telephone has a voice mode," he drawled sarcastically.

Odalie swallowed hard and got to her feet. "Maybe I should help Cort carry the coffee," she said. "Do you want some?"

"Don't be mean to her," Maddie said firmly. "She's been wonderful to me."

John blinked. He glanced at Odalie with wide-eyed surprise. "Her?"

"Yes, her," Maddie replied. "She hasn't left me since I've been in here. She brought me books…"

"Her?" John exclaimed again.

Odalie glared at him. "I am not totally beyond re-demption," she said haughtily.

"Maybe I have a fever," John mused, touching his forehead as he looked back down into Maddie's eyes. "I thought you said she stayed with you in the hospital. She hates hospitals."

"She's been here all night every night," Maddie said softly. She smiled at Odalie. "She's been amazing."

Odalie went beet-red. She didn't know how to han-dle the compliment. She'd had so many, all her life, about her beauty and her talent. But nobody had ever said she was amazing for exhibiting compassion. It felt really good.

"It was my fault, what happened," Odalie said qui-etly. "I was driving."

"Who the hell let you drive a car?" John exclaimed.

"I did," Cort said heavily as he joined them. He looked at John's hand holding Maddie's and his dark eyes began to burn with irritation. "Don't hold her hand, it's bruised," he blurted out before he thought.

John's blue eyes twinkled suddenly. "It is?" He turned it over and looked at it. "Doesn't look bruised. That hurt?" he asked Maddie.

"Well, no," she answered. The way Cort was look-ing at John was very odd.

"Yes, he let me drive because I badgered him into

it," Odalie broke in. "Poor Maddie tried to save her rooster and ran out into the road. I didn't see her until it was too late."

"Oh, no," John said, concerned. "Will you be all right?" he asked Maddie.

"I'm going to be fine," she assured him with more confidence than she really felt.

"Yes, she is," Odalie said, smiling. "We're all going to make sure of it."

"What about Pumpkin?" John asked.

Odalie tried to stop him from asking, but she was too late.

"It's all right," Maddie said gently. "I'm getting used to it. Pumpkin…didn't make it."

Sadie had told her that Ben had buried the awful rooster under a mesquite tree and even made a little headstone to go on the grave. Considering how many scars Ben had, it was quite a feat of compassion.

"I'll get you a new rooster," John said firmly.

"Already taken care of," Cort replied. "You're in my seat, bro."

John gave him a strange look. "Excuse me?"

"That's my seat. I've got it just the way I like it, from sleeping in it for two nights."

John was getting the picture. He laughed inside. Amazing how determined Cort was to get him away from Maddie. He glanced at his sister, who should be fuming. But she wasn't. Her eyes were smiling. She didn't even seem to be jealous.

Maddie was so out of it that she barely noticed the

byplay. The sedative was working on her. She could barely keep her eyes open.

As she drifted off, Cort was saying something about a rooster with feathers on his feet....

A WEEK AFTER the accident, Maddie began to feel her back again. It was agonizing pain. Dr. Brooks came in to examine her, his face impassive as he had her grip his fingers. He used a pin on the bottom of her feet, and actually grinned when she flinched.

"I'm not going to be paralyzed?" she asked, excited and hopeful.

"We can't say that for sure," Dr. Brooks said gently. "Once the swelling and edema are reduced, there may be additional injuries that become apparent. But I will say it's a good sign."

She let out a breath. "I'd have coped," she assured him. "But I'm hoping I won't have to."

He smiled and patted her on the shoulder. "One step at a time, young lady. Recovery first, then rehabilitation with physiotherapy. Meanwhile I'm going to consult with your orthopedic surgeon and put in a call to a friend of mine, a neurologist. We want to cover all our bases."

"You're being very cautious," she murmured.

"I have to be. The fact that you got excellent immediate care at the scene is greatly in your favor, however. Cort knew exactly what to do, and the paramedics followed up in textbook perfection. However," he added with a smile, "my personal opinion is your condition comes from bad bruising and it is not a permanent injury. We saw nothing on the tests that indicated a tearing of the spinal cord or critical damage to any of your lumbar vertebrae."

"You didn't say," she replied.

"Until the swelling goes down, we can't be absolutely sure of anything, which is why I'm reluctant to go all bright-eyed over a cheery prognosis," he explained. "But on the evidence of what I see, I think you're going to make a complete recovery."

She beamed. "Thank you!"

He held up a hand. "We'll still wait and see."

"When can I go home?" she asked.

"Ask me next week."

She made a face. "I'm tired of colored gelatin," she complained. "They're force feeding me water and stuff with fiber in it."

"To keep your kidney and bowel function within acceptable levels," he said. "Don't fuss. Do what they tell you."

She sighed. "Okay. Thanks for letting Cort and Odalie stay with me at night. One of the nurses said you spoke to the administrator himself."

He shrugged. "He and I were at med school together. I beat him at chess regularly."

She laughed. "Can you thank him for me? You don't know what it meant, that they wanted to stay."

"Yes, I do," he replied solemnly. "I've never seen anybody do a greater turnaround than your friend Odalie." He was the doctor who'd treated Maddie after the boy tried to throw her out of the window at school. He'd given a statement to the attorneys who went to see

Cole Everett, as well. He shook his head. "I've known your families since you were children. I know more about Odalie than most people do. I must say, she's impressed me. And I'm hard to impress."

Maddie smiled. "She's impressed me, too. I never expected her to be so compassionate. Of course, it could be guilt," she said hesitantly. She didn't add that Odalie could be trying to win back Cort. She made a face. "I'm ashamed that I said that."

"Don't be. It's natural to be suspicious of someone who's been nothing short of an enemy. But this time, I believe her motives are quite sincere."

"Thanks. That helps."

He smiled. "You keep improving. I'll be back to see you from time to time. But I'm pleased with the progress I see."

"Thanks more for that."

He chuckled. "I love my job," he said at the door.

LATE AT NIGHT, Maddie was prey to her secret fears of losing the use of her legs. Despite Dr. Brooks's assurances, she knew that the prognosis could change. The traumatic nature of her injury made it unpredictable.

"Hey," Cort said softly, holding her hand when she moved restlessly in bed. "Don't think about tomorrow. Just get through one day at a time."

She rolled her head on the pillow and looked at him with tormented eyes. Odalie was sound asleep on the rollaway bed nearby, oblivious. But last night, it had been the other woman who'd been awake while Cort slept, to make sure Maddie had anything she needed.

"It's hard not to think about it," she said worriedly. "I'm letting everybody at the ranch down...."

"Baloney," he mused, smiling. "I've got Ben and the others organized. We're making progress on your breeding program." He made a face. "John went over there today to oversee things while I was here with you."

"John's your best friend," she reminded him.

He didn't want to tell her that he was jealous of his friend. He'd wanted to thump John when he walked in and found him holding Maddie's hand. But he was trying to be reasonable. He couldn't be here and at the ranch. And John was talented with breeding livestock. He'd learned from Cole Everett, whose skills were at least equal with King Brannt's and, some people said, just a tad more scientific.

"That's nice of John," she remarked.

He forced a smile. "Yeah. He's a good guy."

She searched his eyes.

"Oh, hell," he muttered, "he's got an honors degree in animal husbandry. I've got an associate's."

She brightened. "Doesn't experience count for something?" she teased lightly.

He chuckled deep in his throat. "Nice of you, to make me feel better, when I've landed you in that hospital bed," he added with guilt in his eyes.

She squeezed his hand. "My dad used to say," she said softly, "that God sends people into our lives at various times, sometimes to help, sometimes as instruments to test us. He said that you should never blame people who cause things to happen to you, because that might be a test to teach you something you needed to know."

She glanced at Odalie. "I can't be the only person who's noticed how much she's changed," she added in a low tone. "She's been my rock through all this. You have, too, but…"

"I understand." He squeezed her hand back, turning it over to look at the neat, clean fingernails tipping her small, capable fingers. "I've been very proud of her."

"Me, too," Maddie confessed. "Honestly this whole experience has changed the way I look at the world, at people."

"Your dad," he replied, "was a very smart man. And not just with cattle."

She smiled. "I always thought so. I do miss him."

He nodded. "I know you do."

He put her hand back on the bed. "You try to go back to sleep. Want me to call the nurse and see if she can give you something else for pain?"

She laughed softly and indicated the patch on her arm. "It's automatic. Isn't science incredible?"

"Gets more incredible every day," he agreed. He got up. "I'm going for more coffee. I won't be long."

"Thanks. For all you're doing," she said seriously.

He stared down at her with quiet, guilty eyes. "It will never be enough to make up for what happened."

"That's not true," she began.

"I'll be back in a bit." He left her brooding.

"YOU HAVE TO try to make Cort stop blaming himself," Maddie told Odalie the next day after she'd had breakfast and Cort had gone to the ranch for a shower and change of clothes. Odalie would go when he returned, they'd decided.

"That's going to be a tall order," the other woman said with a gentle smile.

"If there was a fault, it was Pumpkin's and mine," Maddie said doggedly. "He ran out into the road and I chased after him without paying any attention to traffic."

Odalie sat down in the seat beside the bed, her face covered in guilt. "I have a confession," she said heavily. "You're going to hate me when you hear it."

"I couldn't hate you after all you've done," came the soft reply. "It isn't possible."

Odalie flushed. "Thanks," she said in a subdued tone. She drew in a deep breath. "I drove by your place deliberately. Cort had been talking about you when I got home. I was jealous. I wanted you to see me with him." She averted her eyes. "I swear to God, if I'd had any idea what misery and grief I was going to cause, I'd never have gotten in the car at all!"

"Oh, goodness," Maddie said unsteadily. But she was much more unsettled by Odalie's jealousy than she was of her actions. It meant that Odalie cared for Cort. And everybody knew how he felt about her; he'd never made any secret of it.

But Maddie had been hurt, and Cort felt responsible. So he was paying attention to Maddie instead of Odalie out of guilt.

Everything became clear. Maddie felt her heart break. But it wasn't Odalie's fault. She couldn't force Cort not to care about her.

Odalie's clear blue eyes lifted and looked into Maddie's gray ones. "You care for him, don't you?" she asked heavily. "I'm so sorry!"

Maddie reached out a hand and touched hers. "One thing I've learned in my life is that you can't make people love you," she said softly. She drew in a long breath and stared at the ceiling. "Life just doesn't work that way."

"So it seems…" Odalie said, and her voice trailed away. "But you see the accident really was my fault."

Maddie shook her head. She wasn't vindictive. She smiled. "It was Pumpkin's."

Odalie felt tears streaming down her cheeks. "All this time, all I could think about is the things I did to you when we were in school. I'm so ashamed, Maddie."

Maddie was stunned.

"I put on a great act for the adults. I was shy and sweet and everybody's idea of the perfect child. But when they weren't looking, I was horrible. My parents didn't know how horrible until your father came to the house with an attorney, and laid it out for them." She grimaced. "I didn't know what happened to you. There was gossip, but it was hushed up. And gossip is usually exaggerated, you know." She picked at her fingernail, her head lowered. "I pretended that I didn't care. But I did." She looked up. "It wasn't until the accident that I really faced up to the person I'd become." She shook her own head. "I didn't like what I saw."

Maddie didn't speak. She just listened.

Odalie smiled sadly. "You know, I've spent my life listening to people rave about how pretty I was, how talented I was. But until now, nobody ever liked me because I was kind to someone." She flushed red. "You needed me. That's new, having somebody need me." She grinned. "I really like it."

Maddie burst out laughing.

Odalie laughed, too, wiping at tears. "Anyway, I apologize wholeheartedly for all the misery I've caused you, and I'm going to work really hard at being the person I hope I can be."

"I don't know what I would have done without you," Maddie said with genuine feeling. "Nobody could have been kinder."

"Some of that was guilt. But I really like you," she said, and laughed again sheepishly. "I never knew what beautiful little creatures you could create from clay and paint."

"My hobby." She laughed.

"It's going to be a life-changing hobby. You wait."

Maddie only smiled. She didn't really believe that. But she wanted to.

CORT CAME BACK later and Odalie went home to freshen up.

Cort dropped into the chair beside Maddie's bed with a sigh. "I saw your doctor outside, doing rounds. He thinks you're progressing nicely."

She smiled. "Yes, he told me so. He said I might be able to go home in a few days. I'll still have to have physical therapy, though."

"Odalie and I will take turns bringing you here for it," he said, answering one of her fears that her car wouldn't stand up to the demands of daily trips, much less her gas budget.

"But, Cort," she protested automatically.

He held up a hand. "It won't do any good," he assured her.

She sighed. "Okay. Thanks, then." She studied his worn face. "Odalie's been amazing, hasn't she?"

He laughed. "Oh, I could think of better words. She really shocked me. I wouldn't have believed her capable of it."

"I know."

"I'm very proud of her," he said, smiling wistfully. He was thinking what a blessing it was that Odalie hadn't shown that side of herself to him when he thought he was in love with her. Because with hindsight, he realized that it was only an infatuation. He'd had a crush on Odalie that he'd mistaken for true love.

Maddie couldn't hear his thoughts. She saw that wistful smile and thought he was seeing Odalie as he'd always hoped she could be, and that he was more in love with her than ever before.

"So am I," she replied.

He noted the odd look in her eyes and started to question it when his mother came in with Heather Everett. Both women had been visiting every day. This time they had something with them. It was a beautiful arrangement of orchids.

"We worked on it together," Heather said, smiling. She was Odalie, aged, still beautiful with blue eyes and platinum blond hair. A knockout, like dark-eyed, dark-haired Shelby Brannt, even with a sprinkle of gray hairs.

"Yes, and we're not florists, but we wanted to do something personal," Shelby added.

Heather put it on the far table, by the window, where it caught the light and looked exotic and lush.

"It's so beautiful! Thank you both," Maddie enthused.

"How are you feeling, sweetheart?" Shelby asked, hovering.

"The pain is easing, and I have feeling in my legs," she said, the excitement in her gray eyes. "The doctor thinks I'll walk again."

"That's wonderful news," Shelby said heavily. "We've been so worried."

"All of us," Heather agreed. She smiled. "It's worse for us, because Odalie was driving."

"Odalie has been my rock in a storm," Maddie said gently. "She hasn't left me, except to freshen up, since they brought me in here. I honestly don't know how I would have made it without her. Or without Cort," she added, smiling at him. "They've stopped me from brooding, cheered me up, cheered me on…they've been wonderful."

Shelby hugged her tall son. "Well, of course, I think so." She laughed. "Still, it's been hard on all three families," she added quietly. "It could have been even more of a tragedy if—"

"I'm going to be fine," Maddie interrupted her.

"Yes, she is," Cort agreed. He smiled at Maddie. His dark eyes were like velvet. There was an expression in them that she'd never noticed before. Affection. Real affection.

She smiled back, shyly, and averted her eyes.

"Odalie wants you to talk to one of our friends, who has an art gallery in Dallas," Heather said. "She thinks your talent is quite incredible."

"It's not, but she's nice to say so..." Maddie began.

"They're her kids," Cort explained to the women, and Maddie's eyes widened. "Don't deny it, you told me so," he added, making a face at her. "She puts so much of herself into them that she can't bear to think of selling one."

"Well, I know it sounds odd, but it's like that with me and the songs I compose," Heather confessed, and flushed a little when they stared at her. "I really do put my whole heart into them. And I hesitate to share that with other people."

"Desperado owes you a lot for those wonderful songs." Shelby chuckled. "And not just money. They've made an international reputation with them."

"Thanks," Heather said. "I don't know where they come from. It's a gift. Truly a gift."

"Like Odalie's voice," Maddie replied. "She really does sing like an angel."

Heather smiled. "Thank you. I've always thought so. I wanted her to realize her dream, to sing at the Met, at the Italian opera houses." She looked introspective. "But it doesn't look like she's going to do that at all."

"Why not?" Shelby asked, curious.

Heather smiled. "I think she's hungry for a home of

her own and a family. She's been talking about children lately."

"Has she?" Cort asked, amused.

He didn't seem to realize that Maddie immediately connected Heather's statement with Odalie's changed nature and Cort's pride in her. She added those facts together and came up with Cort and Odalie getting married.

It was so depressing that she had to force herself to smile and pretend that she didn't care.

"Can you imagine what beautiful children she'll have?" Maddie asked with a wistful smile.

"Well, yours aren't going to be ugly," Cort retorted. Then he remembered that he'd called Maddie that, during one of their arguments, and his face paled with shame.

Maddie averted her eyes and tried not to show what she was feeling. "Not like Odalie's," she said. "Is she thinking about getting married?" she asked Heather.

"She says she is," she replied. "I don't know if she's really given it enough thought, though," she added with sadness in her tone. "Very often, we mistake infatuation for the real thing."

"You didn't," Shelby teased before anyone could react to Heather's statement. "You knew you wanted to marry Cole before you were even an adult."

Heather saw Maddie's curious glance. "Cole's mother married my father," she explained. "There was some terrible gossip spread, to the effect that we were related by blood. It broke my heart. I gave up on life. And then the truth came out, and I realized that Cole didn't hate me at all. He'd only been shoving me out of his life because he thought I was totally off-limits, and his pride wouldn't let him admit how thoroughly he'd accepted the gossip for truth."

"You made a good match." Shelby smiled.

"So did you, my friend." Heather laughed. "Your road to the altar was even more precarious than mine."

Shelby beamed. "Yes, but it was worth every tear." She hugged her son. "Look at my consolation prize!"

BUT WHEN THE women left, and Cort walked them out to the parking lot, Maddie was left with her fears and insecurities.

Odalie wanted to marry and raise a family. She'd seen how mature and caring Cort was, and she wanted to drive him by Maddie's house because she was jealous of her. She'd wanted Maddie to see her with Cort.

She could have cried. Once, Odalie's feelings wouldn't have mattered. But since she'd been in the hospital, Maddie had learned things about the other woman. She genuinely liked her. She was like the sister Maddie had never had.

What was she going to do? Cort seemed to like Maddie now, but she'd been hurt and it was his car that had hit her. Certainly he felt guilty. And nobody could deny how much he'd loved Odalie. He'd grieved for weeks after she left for Italy.

Surely his love for her hadn't died just because Maddie had been in an accident. He'd told Maddie that she was ugly and that she didn't appeal to him as a man, long before the wreck. That had been honest; she'd seen it in his dark eyes.

Now he was trying to make up for what had happened. He was trying to sacrifice himself to Maddie in a vain attempt to atone for her injuries. He was denying himself Odalie out of guilt.

Maddie closed her eyes. She couldn't have that. She wanted him to be happy. In fact, she wanted Odalie to be happy. Cort would be miserable if he forced himself into a relationship with Maddie that he didn't feel.

So that wasn't going to be allowed to happen. Maddie was going to make sure of it.

CHAPTER NINE

BY THE END of the second week after the accident, Maddie was back home, with a high-tech wheelchair to get around the house in.

Odalie and Cort had insisted on buying her one to use while she was recuperating, because she still couldn't walk, even though the feeling had come back into her legs. She was exhilarated with the doctor's cautious prognosis that she would probably heal completely after several months.

But she'd made her friends promise to get her an inexpensive manual wheelchair. Of course, they'd said, smiling.

Then they walked in with a salesman who asked questions, measured her and asked about her choice of colors. Oh, bright yellow, she'd teased, because she was sure they didn't make a bright yellow wheelchair. The only ones she'd seen were black and ugly and plain, and they all looked alike. She'd dreaded the thought of having to sit in one.

A few days later, the wheelchair was delivered. It came from Europe. It was the most advanced wheelchair of its type, fully motorized, able to turn in its own circumference, able to lift the user up to eye level with other people, and all-terrain. Oh, and also, bright yellow in color.

"This must have cost a fortune!" Maddie almost screamed when she saw it. "I said something inexpensive!"

Cort gave her a patient smile. "You said inexpensive. This is inexpensive," he added, glancing at Odalie.

"Cheap," the blonde girl nodded. She grinned unrepentantly. "When you get out of it, you can donate it to someone in need."

"Oh. Well." The thought that she would get out of it eventually sustained her. "I can donate it?"

Odalie nodded. She smiled.

Cort smiled, too.

"Barracudas," she concluded, looking from one to the other. "I can't get around either one of you!"

They both grinned.

She laughed. "Okay. Thanks. Really. Thanks."

"You might try it out," Odalie coaxed.

"Yes, in the direction of the hen yard," Cort added.

She looked from one of them to the other. They had very suspicious expressions. "Okay."

She was still learning to drive it, but the controls were straightforward, and it didn't take long to learn them. The salesman had come out with it, to further explain its operation.

It had big tires, and it went down steps. That was a revelation. It didn't even bump very much. She followed Cort and Odalie over the sandy yard to the huge enclosure where her hens lived. It was grassy, despite the tendency of chickens to scratch and eat the grass, with trees on one side. The other contained multiple feeders and hanging waterers. The enormous henhouse had individual nests and cowboys cleaned it out daily. There was almost no odor, and the hens were clean and beautiful.

"My girls look very happy," Maddie said, laughing.

"They have a good reason to be happy." Cort went into the enclosure, and a minute later, he came back out, carrying a large red rooster with a big comb and immaculate feathers.

He brought him to Maddie. The rooster looked sort of like Pumpkin, but he was much bigger. He didn't seem at all bothered to be carried under someone's arm. He handed the rooster to Maddie.

She perched him on her jean-clad lap and stared at him. He cocked his head and looked at her and made a sort of purring sound.

She was aghast. She looked up at Cort wide-eyed.

"His name's Percival," Cort told her with a chuckle. "He has impeccable bloodlines."

She looked at the feathery pet again. "I've never seen a rooster this tame," she remarked.

"That's from those impeccable bloodlines." Odalie giggled. "All their roosters are like this. They're even guaranteed to be tame, or your money back. So he's sort of returnable. But you won't need to return him. He's been here for a week and he hasn't attacked anybody yet. Considering his age, he's not likely to do it."

"His age?" Maddie prompted.

"He's two," Cort said. "Never attacked anybody on the farm for all that time. The owners' kids carry the roosters around with them all the time. They're gentled. But they're also bred for temperament. They have exceptions from time to time. But Percy's no exception. He's just sweet."

"Yes, he is." She hugged the big rooster, careful not to hug him too closely, because chickens have no diaphragm and they can be smothered if their chests are compressed for too long. "Percy, you're gorgeous!"

He made that purring sound again. Almost as if he were laughing. She handed him back to Cort. "You've got him separate from the girls?"

He nodded. "If you want biddies, we can put him with them in time for spring chicks. But they know he's nearby, and so will predators. He likes people. He hates predators. The owner says there's a fox who'll never trouble a henhouse again after the drubbing Percy gave him."

Maddie laughed with pure joy. "It will be such a relief not to have to carry a limb with me to gather eggs," she said. The smile faded. "I'll always miss Pumpkin," she said softly, "but even I knew that something had to give eventually. He was dangerous. I just didn't have the heart to do anything about him."

"Providence did that for you," Cort replied. He smiled warmly. Maddie smiled back but she avoided his eyes.

That bothered him. He put Percy back in the enclosure in his own fenced area, very thoughtful. Maddie was polite, but she'd been backing away from him for days now. He felt insecure. He wanted to ask her what was wrong. Probably, he was going to have to do that pretty soon.

MADDIE WENT TO work on her sculptures with a vengeance, now that she had enough materials to produce anything she liked.

Her first work, though, was a tribute to her new friend. She made a fairy who looked just like Odalie, perched on a lily pad, holding a firefly. She kept it hidden when Cort and Odalie came to see her, which was pretty much every single day. It was her secret project.

She was so thrilled with it that at first she didn't even want to share it with them. Of all the pieces she'd done, this was her best effort. It had been costly, too. Sitting in one position for a long time, even in her cushy imported wheelchair, was uncomfortable and took a toll on her back.

"You mustn't stress your back muscles like this," the therapist fussed when she went in for therapy, which she did every other day. "It's too much strain so early in your recovery."

She smiled while the woman used a heat lamp and massage on her taut back. "I know. I like to sculpt things. I got overenthusiastic."

"Take frequent breaks," the therapist advised.

"I'll do that. I promise."

SHE WAS WALKING NOW, just a little at a time, but steadily. Cort had bought a unit for her bathtub that created a Jacuzzi-like effect in the water. It felt wonderful on her sore and bruised back. He'd had a bar installed, too, so that she could ease herself up out of the water and not have to worry about slipping.

Odalie brought her exotic cheeses and crackers to

eat them with, having found out that cheese was pretty much Maddie's favorite food. She brought more art books, and classical music that Maddie loved.

Cort brought his guitar and sang to her. That was the hardest thing to bear. Because Maddie knew he was only doing it because he thought Maddie had feelings for him. It was humiliating that she couldn't hide them, especially since she knew that he loved Odalie and always would.

But she couldn't help but be entranced by it. She loved his deep, rich voice, loved the sound of the guitar, with its mix of nylon and steel strings. It was a classical guitar. He'd ordered it from Spain. He played as wonderfully as he sang.

When he'd played *"Recuerdos de la Alhambra"* for her, one of the most beautiful classical guitar compositions ever conceived, she wept like a baby.

"It is beautiful, isn't it?" he asked, drying her tears with a handkerchief. "It was composed by a Spaniard, Francisco Tárrega, in 1896." He smiled. "It's my favorite piece."

"Mine, too," she said. "I had a recording of guitar solos on my iPod with it. But you play it just as beautifully as that performer did. Even better than he did."

"Thanks." He put the guitar back into its case, very carefully. "From the time I was ten, there was never any other instrument I wanted to play. I worried my folks to death until they bought me one. And Morie used to go sit outside while I practiced, with earplugs in." He chuckled, referring to his sister.

"Poor Morie," she teased.

"She loves to hear me play, now. She said it was worth the pain while I learned."

She grinned. "You know, you could sing professionally."

He waved that thought away. "I'm a cattleman," he replied. "Never wanted to be anything else. The guitar is a nice hobby. But I don't think I'd enjoy playing and singing as much if I had to do it all the time."

"Good point."

"How's that sculpture coming along?"

Her eyes twinkled. "Come see."

She turned on the wheelchair and motored herself into the makeshift studio they'd furnished for her in her father's old bedroom. It had just the right airy, lighted accommodation that made it a great place to work. Besides that, she could almost feel her father's presence when she was in it.

"Don't tell her," she cautioned as she uncovered a mound on her worktable. "It's going to be a surprise."

"I promise."

She pulled off the handkerchief she'd used to conceal the little fairy sculpture. The paint was dry and the glossy finish she'd used over it gave the beautiful creature an ethereal glow.

"It looks just like her!" Cort exclaimed as he gently picked it up.

She grinned. "Do you think so? I did, but I'm too close to my work to be objective about it."

"It's the most beautiful thing you've done yet, and that's saying something." He looked down at her with an odd expression. "You really have the talent."

She flushed. "Thanks, Cort."

He put the sculpture down and bent, brushing his mouth tenderly over hers. "I have to be so careful with you," he whispered at her lips. "It's frustrating, in more ways than one."

She caught her breath. She couldn't resist him. But it was tearing her apart, to think that he might be caught in a web of deception laced by guilt. She looked up into his eyes with real pain.

He traced her lips with his forefinger. "When you're back on your feet," he whispered, "we have to talk."

She managed a smile. "Okay." Because she knew that, by then, she'd find a way to ease his guilt, and Odalie's, and step out of the picture. She wasn't going to let them sacrifice their happiness for her. That was far too much.

He kissed her again and stood up, smiling. "So when are you going to give it to her?"

"Tomorrow," she decided.

"I'll make sure she comes over."

"Thanks."

He shrugged and then smiled. "She's going to be over the moon when she sees it."

THAT WAS AN UNDERSTATEMENT. Odalie cried. She turned the little fairy around and around in her elegant hands, gasping at the level of detail in the features that were so exactly like her own.

"It's the most beautiful gift I've ever been given."

She put it down, very gently, and hugged Maddie as

carefully as she could. "You sweetie!" she exclaimed. "I'll never be able to thank you. It looks just like me!"

Maddie chuckled. "I'm glad you like it."

"You have to let me talk to my friend at the art gallery," Odalie said.

Maddie hesitated. "Maybe someday," she faltered. "Maybe."

"But you have so much talent, Maddie. It's such a gift."

Maddie flushed. "Thanks."

Odalie kept trying, but she couldn't move the other girl. Not at all.

"Okay," she relented. "You know your own mind. Oh, goodness, what is that?" she exclaimed, indicating a cameo lying beside another fairy, a black-haired one sitting on a riverbank holding a book.

Maddie told her the story of the antique dealer and the cameo that had no family to inherit.

"What an incredible story," Odalie said, impressed. "She's quite beautiful. You can do that, from a picture?"

Maddie laughed. "I did yours from the one in our school yearbook," she said, and this time she didn't flinch remembering the past.

Odalie looked uncomfortable, but she didn't refer to it. Perhaps in time she and Maddie could both let go of that terrible memory. "Maddie, could you do one of my great-grandmother if I brought you a picture of her? It's a commission, now…"

Maddie held up a hand. "No. I'd love to do it. It's just a hobby, you know, not a job. Just bring me a picture."

Odalie's eyes were unusually bright. "Okay. I'll bring it tomorrow!"

Maddie laughed at her enthusiasm. "I'll get started as soon as I have it."

THE PICTURE WAS SURPRISING. "This is your grand-mother?" Maddie asked, because it didn't look any-thing like Odalie. The subject of the painting had red hair and pale green eyes.

"My great-grandmother," Odalie assured her, but she averted her eyes to another sculpture while she said it.

"Oh. That explains it. Yes, I can do it."

"That's so sweet of you, Maddie."

"It's nothing at all."

IT TOOK TWO WEEKS. Maddie still had periods of discom-fort that kept her in bed, but she made sure she walked and moved around, as the therapist and her doctor had told her to do. It was amazing that, considering the impact of the car, she hadn't suffered a permanent dis-ability. The swelling and inflammation had been pretty bad, as was the bruising, but she wasn't going to lose the use of her legs. The doctor was still being cautious about that prognosis. But Maddie could tell from the way she was healing that she was going to be all right. She'd never been more certain of anything.

She finished the little fairy sculpture on a Friday. She was very pleased with the result. It looked just like the photograph, but with exquisite detail. This fairy was sitting on a tree stump, with a small green frog perched on her palm. She was laughing. Maddie loved the way it had turned out. But now it was going to be hard to part with it. She did put part of herself into her sculptures. It was like giving herself away with the art.

She'd promised Odalie, though, so she had to come to terms with it.

Odalie was overwhelmed with the result. She stared at it and just shook her head. "I can't believe how skilled you are," she said, smiling at Maddie. "This is so beautiful. She'll, I mean my mother, will love it!"

"Oh, it's her grandmother," Maddie recalled.

"Yes." Odalie still wouldn't meet her eyes, but she laughed. "What a treat this is going to be! Can I take it with me?" she asked.

Maddie only hesitated for a second. She smiled. "Of course you can."

"Wonderful!"

She bent and hugged Maddie gently. "Still doing okay?" she asked worriedly.

Maddie nodded. "Getting better all the time, thanks to a small pharmacy of meds on my bedside table," she quipped.

"I'm so glad. I mean that," she said solemnly. "The day you can walk to your car and drive it, I'll dance in the yard."

Maddie laughed. "Okay. I'll hold you to that!"

Odalie just grinned.

CORT CAME OVER every day. Saturday morning he went to the barn to study the charts he and John Everett had made. John had just come over to bring Maddie flowers. She was sitting on the porch with Great-Aunt Sadie.

As soon as John arrived, Cort came back from the barn and joined the group on the porch. The way Cort glared at him was surprising.

"They'll give her allergies," Cort muttered.

John gave him a stunned look, and waved around the yard at the blooming crepe myrtle and jasmine and sunflowers and sultanas and zinnias. "Are you nuts?" he asked, wide-eyed. "Look around you! Who do you think planted all these?"

Cort's dark eyes narrowed. He jammed his hands into his jean pockets. "Well, they're not in the house, are they?" he persisted.

John just laughed. He handed the pot of flowers to Great-Aunt Sadie, who was trying not to laugh. "Can you put those inside?" he asked her with a smile. "I want to check the board in the barn and see how the breeding program needs to go."

"I sure can," Sadie replied, and she went into the house.

Maddie was still staring at John with mixed feelings. "Uh, thanks for the flowers," she said haltingly. Cort was looking irritated.

"You're very welcome," John said. He studied her for a long moment. "You look better."

"I feel a lot better," she said. "In fact, I think I might try to walk to the barn."

"In your dreams, honey," Cort said softly. He picked her up, tenderly, and cradled her against his chest. "But I'll walk you there."

John stared at him intently. "Should you be picking her up like that?" he asked.

Cort wasn't listening. His dark eyes were probing Maddie's gray ones with deep tenderness. Neither of them was looking at John, who suddenly seemed to understand what was going on around him.

"Darn, I left my notes in the car," he said, hiding a smile. "I'll be right back."

He strode off. Cort bent his head. "I thought he'd never leave," he whispered, and brought his mouth down, hard, on Maddie's.

"Cort…"

"Shh," he whispered against her lips. "Don't fuss. Open your mouth…!"

The kiss grew hotter by the second. Maddie was clinging to his neck for dear life while he crushed her breasts into the softness of his blue-checked shirt and devoured her soft lips.

He groaned harshly, but suddenly he remembered where they were. He lifted his head, grateful that his back was to the house, and John's car. He drew in a long breath.

"I wish you weren't so fragile," he whispered. He kissed her shocked eyes shut. "I'm starving."

Her fingers teased the hair at the back of his head. "I could feed you a biscuit," she whispered.

He smiled. "I don't want biscuits." He looked at her mouth. "I want you."

Her face flamed with a combination of embarrassment and sheer delight.

"But we can talk about that later, after I've disposed of John's body," he added, turning to watch the other man approach, his eyes buried in a black notebook.

"Wh-h-hat?" she stammered, and burst out laughing at his expression.

He sighed. "I suppose no war is ever won without a few uncomfortable battles," he said under his breath.

"I found them," John said with a grin, waving the notebook. "Let's have a look at the breeding strategy you've mapped out, then."

"I put it all on the board," Cort replied. He carried Maddie into the barn and set her on her feet very carefully, so as not to jar her spine. "It's right there," he told John, nodding toward the large board where he'd indicated which bulls were to be bred to which heifers and cows.

John studied it for a long moment. He turned and looked at Cort curiously. "This is remarkable," he said. "I would have gone a different way, but yours is better."

Cort seemed surprised. "You've got a four-year degree in animal husbandry," he said. "Mine is only an associate's degree."

"Yes, but you've got a lifetime of watching your father do this." He indicated the board. "I've been busy studying and traveling. I haven't really spent that much time observing. It's rather like an internship, and I don't have the experience, even if I have the education."

"Thanks," Cort said. He was touchy about his two-year degree. He smiled. "Took courses in diplomacy, too, did you?" he teased.

John bumped shoulders with him. "You're my best friend," he murmured. "I'd never be the one to try to put you down."

Cort punched his shoulder gently. "Same here."

Maddie had both hands on her slender hips as she

stared at the breeding chart. "Would either of you like to try to translate this for me?" She waved one hand at the blackboard. "Because it looks like Martian to me!"

Both men burst out laughing.

Cort had to go out of town. He was worried when he called Maddie to tell her, apologizing for his absence.

"Mom and Dad will look out for you while I'm gone," he promised. "If you need anything, you call them. I'll phone you when I get to Denver."

Her heart raced. "Okay."

"Will you miss me?" he teased.

She drew in a breath. "Of course," she said.

There was a pause. "I'll miss you more," he said quietly. His deep voice was like velvet. "What do you want me to bring you from Denver?"

"Yourself."

There was a soft chuckle. "That's a deal. Talk to you later."

"Have a safe trip."

He sighed. "At least Dad isn't flying me. He flies like he drives. But we'll get there."

The plural went right over her head. She laughed. She'd heard stories about King Brannt's driving. "It's safer than driving, everybody says so."

"In my dad's case, it's actually true. He flies a lot better than he drives."

"I heard that!" came a deep voice from beside him.

"Sorry, Dad," Cort replied. "See you, Maddie."

He hung up. She held the cell phone to her ear for an extra minute, just drinking in the sound of his voice promising to miss her.

WHILE CORT WAS AWAY, Odalie didn't come, either. But even though she called, Maddie missed her daily visits. She apologized over the phone. She was actually out of town, but her mother had volunteered to do any running-around that Maddie needed if Sadie couldn't go.

Maddie thanked her warmly. But when she hung up she couldn't help but wonder at the fact that Cort and Odalie were out of town at the same time. Had Odalie gone to Denver with Cort and they didn't want to tell her? It was worrying.

She rode her wheelchair out to the hen enclosure. Ben was just coming out of it with the first of many egg baskets. There were a lot of hens, and her customer list for her fresh eggs was growing by the week.

"That's a lot of eggs," she ventured.

He chuckled. "Ya, and I still have to wash 'em and check 'em for cracks."

"I like Percy," she remarked.

"I love Percy," Ben replied. "Never saw such a gentle rooster."

"Thanks. For what you did for Pumpkin's grave," she said, averting her eyes. She still cried easily when she talked about him.

"It was no problem at all, Miss Maddie," he said gently.

She looked over her hens with proud eyes. "My girls look good."

"They do, don't they?" he agreed, then added, "Well, I should get to work."

"Ben, do you know where Odalie went?" she asked suddenly.

He bit his lip.

"Come on," she prodded. "Tell me."

He looked sad. "She went to Denver, Miss Maddie. Heard it from her dad when I went to pick up feed in town."

Maddie's heart fell to her feet. But she smiled. "She and Cort make a beautiful couple," she remarked, and tried to hide the fact that she was dying inside.

"Guess they do," he said. He tried to say something else, but he couldn't get the words to come out right. "I'll just go get these eggs cleaned."

She nodded. The eyes he couldn't see were wet with tears.

IT SEEMED THAT disaster followed disaster. While Cort and Odalie were away, bills flooded the mailbox. Maddie almost passed out when she saw the hospital bill. Even the minimum payment was more than she had in the bank.

"What are we going to do?" she wailed.

Sadie winced at her expression. "Well, we'll just manage," she said firmly. "There's got to be something we can sell that will help pay those bills." She didn't add that Cort and Odalie had promised they were taking care of all that. But they were out of town, and Sadie knew that Maddie's pride would stand in the way of asking them for money. She'd never do it.

"There is something," Maddie said heavily. She looked up at Sadie.

"No," Sadie said shortly. "No, you can't!"

"Look at these bills, Sadie," she replied, and spread

them out on the table. "There's nothing I can hock, nothing I can do that will make enough money fast enough to cover all this. There just isn't anything else to do."

"You aren't going to talk to that developer fellow?"

"Heavens, no!" Maddie assured her. "I'll call a real estate agent in town."

"I think that's…"

Just as she spoke, a car pulled up in the yard.

"Well, speak of the devil," Maddie muttered.

The developer climbed out of his car, looked around and started for the front porch.

"Do you suppose we could lock the door and pretend to be gone?" Sadie wondered aloud.

"No. We're not hiding. Let him in," Maddie said firmly.

"Don't you give in to his fancy talk," Sadie advised.

"Never in a million years. Let him in."

The developer, Arthur Lawson, came in the door with a smug look on his face. "Miss Lane," he greeted. He smiled like a crocodile. "Bad news does travel fast. I heard you were in an accident and that your bills are piling up. I believe I can help you."

Maddie looked at Sadie. Her expression was eloquent.

Archie Lawson grinned like the barracuda he was.

"I heard that your neighbors have gone away together," he said with mock sympathy. "Just left you with all those medical bills to pay, did they?"

Maddie felt terrible. She didn't want to say anything unkind about Odalie and Cort. They'd done more than most people could have expected of them. But Maddie was left with the bills, and she had no money to pay them with. She'd read about people who didn't pay their hospital bill on time and had to deal with collectors' agencies. She was terrified.

"They don't say I have to pay them at once," Maddie began.

"Yes, but the longer you wait, the higher the interest they charge," he pointed out.

"Interest?"

"It's such and such a percent," he continued. He sat down without being asked in her father's old easy chair. "Let me spell it out for you. I can write you a check that will cover all those medical bills, the hospital bill, everything. All you have to do is sign over the property to me. I'll even take care of the livestock. I'll make sure they're sold to people who will take good care of them."

"I don't know," Maddie faltered. She was torn. It was so quick…

"Maddie, can I talk to you for a minute?" Sadie asked tersely. "It's about supper," she lied.

"Okay."

She excused herself and followed Sadie into the kitchen.

Sadie closed the door. "Listen to me, don't you do that until you talk to Mr. Brannt," Sadie said firmly. "Don't you dare!"

"But, Sadie," she said in anguish, "we can't pay the bills, and we can't expect the Brannts and the Everetts to keep paying them forever!"

"Cort said he'd take care of the hospital bill, at least," Sadie reminded her.

"Miss Lane?" Lawson called. "I have to leave soon!"

"Don't let him push you into this," Sadie cautioned. "Make him wait. Tell him you have to make sure the estate's not entailed before you can sell, you'll have to talk to your lawyer!"

Maddie bit her lower lip.

"Tell him!" Sadie said, gesturing her toward the porch.

Maddie took a deep breath and Sadie opened the door for her to motor through.

"Sadie was reminding me that we had a couple of outstanding liens on the property after Dad died," Maddie lied. "I'll have to talk to our attorney and make sure they've been lifted before I can legally sell it to you."

"Oh." He stood up. "Well." He glared. "You didn't mention that earlier."

"I didn't think you thought I was going to sell the ranch today," Maddie said, and with a bland smile. "That's all. You wouldn't want to find out later that you didn't actually own it...?"

"No. Of course not." He made a face. "All right, I'll be back in, say, two days? Will that give you enough time?"

"Yes," Maddie said.

He picked up his briefcase and looked around the living room. "This house will have to be torn down. But if you want some pictures and stuff, I can let you have it after we wrap up the sale. The furniture's no loss." He laughed coldly. "I'll be in touch. And if your answer is no—well, don't be surprised if your cattle suddenly come down with unusual diseases. Anthrax always comes to mind… And if federal agencies have to be called in, your operation will be closed down immediately."

He left and Maddie had to bite back curses. "The furniture's no loss," she muttered. "These are antiques! And anthrax! What kind of horrible person would infect defenseless animals!" Maddie went inside, a chill settling in her heart.

"NASTY MAN. You can't let him have our house!" Sadie glared out the window as the developer drove off.

Maddie leaned back in her chair. "I wish I didn't," she said heavily. "But I don't know what else to do." She felt sick to her soul at the man's threats. "Cort is going to marry Odalie, you know."

Sadie wanted to argue, but she didn't know how to. It seemed pretty obvious that if he hadn't told Maddie he was leaving with Odalie, he had a guilty conscience and was trying to shield her from the truth.

"Should have just told you, instead of sneaking off together," Sadie muttered.

"They didn't want to hurt me," Maddie said heavily. "It's pretty obvious how I feel about Cort, you know."

"Still…"

Maddie looked at the bills lying open on the table. She leaned forward with her face in her hands. Her heart was breaking. At least she might be able to walk eventually. But that still left the problem of how she was going to walk herself out of this financial mess. The ranch was all she had left for collateral.

Collateral! She turned to Sadie. "We can take out a mortgage, can't we?" she asked Sadie.

Sadie frowned. "I don't know. Best you should call the lawyer and find out."

"I'll do that right now!"

She did at least have hope that there were options. A few options, at least.

BUT THE LIE she'd told Lawson turned out to be the truth.

"I'm really sorry, Maddie," Burt Davies told her. "But your dad did take out a lien on the property when he bought that last seed bull. I've been keeping up the payments out of the ranch revenues when I did the bills for you the past few months."

"You mean, I can't sell or even borrow on the ranch."

"You could sell," he admitted. "If you got enough for it that would pay off the lien… But, Maddie, that land's been in your family for generations. You can't mean to sell it."

She swallowed. "Burt, I've got medical bills I can't begin to pay."

"Odalie and Cort are taking care of those," he reminded her. "Legally, even if not morally, they're obligated to."

"Yes, but, they're getting married, don't you see?" she burst out. "I can't tie them up with my bills."

"You can and you will, if I have to go to court for you," Burt said firmly. "The accident wasn't your fault."

"Yes, it was," she said in a wan tone. "I ran out in the road to save my stupid rooster, who died anyway. As for guilt, Odalie and Cort have done everything humanly possible for me since the wreck. Nobody could fault them for that."

"I know, but…"

"If I sell the ranch," she argued gently, "I can pay off all my debts and I won't owe anyone anything."

"That's bad legal advice. You should never try to act as your own attorney."

She laughed. "Yes, I know. Okay, I'll think about it for a couple of days," she said.

"You think about it hard," he replied. "No sense in letting yourself be forced into a decision you don't want to make."

"All right. Thanks, Burt."

She hung up. "Life," she told the room at large, "is just not fair."

THE NEXT DAY, Ben came walking in with a sad expression. "Got bad news," he said.

"What now?" Maddie asked with a faint smile.

"Lost two more purebred cows. They wandered off."

"All right, that's more than coincidence," she muttered. She moved to the phone, picked it up and called King Brannt.

"How many cows does that make?" King asked, aghast.

"Four, in the past few weeks," she said. "Something's not right."

"I agree. I'll get our computer expert to check those recordings and see if he can find anything."

"Thanks, Mr. Brannt."

He hesitated. "How are things over there?"

She hesitated, too. "Just fine," she lied. "Fine."

"Cort's coming home day after tomorrow," he added.

"I hope he and Odalie have had a good time," she said, and tried not to sound as hurt as she felt. "They've both been very kind to me. I owe them a lot."

"Maddie," he began slowly, "about that trip they took—"

"They're my friends," she interrupted. "I want them to be happy. Look I have to go, okay? But if you find out anything about my cows, can you call me?"

"Sure."

"Thanks, Mr. Brannt."

She hung up. She didn't think she'd ever felt so miserable in her whole young life. She loved Cort. But he was never going to be hers. She realized now that he'd been pretending, to keep her spirits up so that she wouldn't despair. But he'd always loved Odalie, and she'd always known it. She couldn't expect him to give up everything he loved just to placate an injured woman, out of guilt. She wasn't going to let him do it.

And Odalie might have been her enemy once, but that was certainly no longer the case. Odalie had become a friend. She couldn't have hard feelings toward her....

Oh, what a bunch of bull, she told herself angrily. Of course she had hard feelings. She loved Cort. She wanted him! But he loved Odalie and that was never going to change. How would it feel, to let a man hang around just because he felt guilty that you'd been hurt? Knowing every day that he was smiling and pretending to care, when he really wanted that beautiful golden girl, Odalie Everett, and always would?

No. That would cheat all three of them. She had to let him go. He belonged to Odalie, and Maddie had always known it. She was going to sell the ranch to that terrible developer and make herself homeless out of pride, because she didn't want her friends to sacrifice any more than they already had for her.

That developer, could he have been responsible for her lost cows? But why would he hurt the livestock when he was hoping to buy the ranch? No. It made no sense. None at all.

LATER, WITH HER door closed, she cried herself to sleep. She couldn't stop thinking about Cort, about how tender he'd been to her, how kind. Surely he hadn't been able to pretend the passion she felt in his long, hard, insistent kisses? Could men pretend to want a woman?

She wished she knew. She wanted to believe that his hints at a shared future had been honest and real. But she didn't dare trust her instincts. Not when Cort had taken Odalie with him to Denver and hidden it from Maddie.

He hadn't wanted her to know. That meant he knew it would hurt her feelings and he couldn't bear to do it, not after all she'd been through.

She wiped her eyes. Crying wasn't going to solve anything. After all, what did she have to be sad about? There was a good chance that she would be able to walk normally again, when she was through recuperating. She'd still have Great-Aunt Sadie, and the developer said that he'd let her have her odds and ends out of the house.

The developer. She hated him. He was willing to set her up, to let her whole herd of cattle be destroyed, her breeding stock, just to get his hands on the ranch. She could tell someone, Mr. Brannt, maybe. But it would be her word against Lawson's. She had so much to lose. What if he could actually infect her cattle? Better to let her cattle be sold at auction to someone than risk having them destroyed. She couldn't bear to step on a spider, much less watch her prize cattle, her father's prize cattle, be exterminated.

No, she really didn't have a choice. She was going to lose the ranch one way or another, to the developer or to bill collectors.

She got up and went to the kitchen to make coffee. It was two in the morning, but it didn't matter. She was never going to sleep anyway.

She heard a sound out in the yard. She wished she kept a dog. She'd had one, but it had died not long after her father did. There was nothing to alert her to an intruder's presence anymore. She turned out the lights and motored to the window, hoping the sound of the wheelchair wouldn't be heard outside.

She saw something shadowy near the barn. That was where the surveillance equipment was set up.

She turned on all the outside lights, opened the door and yelled, "Who's out there?!" The best defense was offense, she told herself.

There was startled movement, a dark blur going out

behind the barn. Without a second thought, she got her cell phone and called the sheriff.

THE SHERIFF'S DEPARTMENT CAME, and so did King Brannt. He climbed out of his ranch pickup with another man about two steps behind the tall deputy.

Maddie rolled onto the porch. She'd been afraid to go outside until help arrived. She was no match, even with two good legs, for someone bent upon mischief.

"Miss Lane?" the deputy asked.

"Yes, sir," she said. "Someone was out here. I turned on the outside lights and yelled. Whoever it was ran."

The deputy's lips made a thin line.

"Yes, I know," she said heavily. "Stupid thing to do, opening the door. But I didn't go outside, and the screen was latched."

He didn't mention that any intruder could have gone through that latched screen like it was tissue paper.

"Miss Lane's had some threats," King commented. "This is Blair, my computer expert. We set up surveillance cameras on the ranch at cross fences to see if we could head off trouble." He smiled. "Looks like we might have succeeded."

"Have you noticed anything suspicious?" the deputy asked.

She grimaced. "Well, I've had a couple of cows found dead. Predators," she said, averting her eyes.

"Anyone prowling around the house, any break-ins?" he persisted.

"No, sir."

The deputy turned to King. "Mr. Brannt, I'd like to see what those cameras of yours picked up, if anything."

"Sure. Come on, Blair." He turned to Maddie. "You should go back inside, honey," he said gently. "Just in case."

"Okay." She went very quickly. She didn't want any of the men to ask her more questions. She was afraid of what Lawson might do if he was backed into a corner. She didn't want the government to come over and shut her cattle operation down, even if it meant giving away the ranch.

LATER, THE DEPUTY came inside, asked more questions and had her write out a report for him in her own words. He took that, and statements from King and Blair and told Maddie to call if she heard anything else.

"Did you find anything?" she asked worriedly.

"No," the deputy said. "But my guess is that someone meant to disable that surveillance equipment."

"Mine, too," King replied. "Which is why I've just sent several of my cowboys out to ride fence lines and watch for anything suspicious."

"That's very nice of you," she commented.

He shrugged. "We're neighbors and I like your breeding bulls," he told her.

"Well, thanks, just the same."

"If you think of anything else that would help us, please get in touch with me," the deputy said, handing her a card.

"I'll do that," she promised. "And thanks again."

King didn't leave when the deputy did. Sadie was making coffee in the kitchen, her face lined with worry.

"It will be all right," she assured the older woman.

"No, it won't," Sadie muttered. She glanced at Maddie. "You should tell him the truth. He's the one person who could help you!"

"Sadie!" Maddie groaned.

King pulled Blair aside, spoke to him in whispers, and sent him off. He moved into the kitchen, straddled a chair at the table and perched his Stetson on a free chair.

"Okay," he said. "No witnesses. Let's have it."

Maddie went pale.

King laughed softly. "I'm not an ogre. If you want my word that I won't tell anyone what you say, you have it."

Maddie bit her lower lip. "That developer," she said after a minute. "He said that he could bring in a federal agency and prove that my cattle had anthrax."

"Only if he put it there to begin with," King said, his dark eyes flashing with anger.

"That's what I think he means to do," she said. "I don't know what to do. The bills are just burying me…"

He held up a hand. "Cort and Odalie are taking care of those," he said.

"Yes, but they've done too much already, I'm not a charity case!" she burst out.

"It was an accident that they caused, Maddie," he said gently.

"I caused it, by running into the road," she said miserably.

"Accidents are things that don't happen on purpose," he said with a faint grin. "Now, listen, whatever trouble you're in, that developer has no right to make threats to do harm to your cattle."

"It would be my word against his," she sighed.

"I'd take your word against anyone else's, in a heartbeat," he replied. "You let me handle this. I know how to deal with people like Lawson."

"He's really vindictive."

"He won't get a chance to be vindictive. I promise." He got up. "I won't stay for coffee, Sadie, I've got a lot of phone calls to make."

"Thanks, Mr. Brannt," Maddie said gently. "Thanks a lot."

He put a hand on her shoulder. "We take care of our own," he said. "Cort will be back day after tomorrow."

"So will that developer," she said worriedly. So many complications, she was thinking. Poor Cort, he'd feel even more guilty.

"He won't stay long," King drawled, and he grinned. "Cort will make sure of that, believe me."

CHAPTER TEN

MADDIE WAS ON pins and needles Saturday morning.
It was worrying enough to know that Cort and Odalie
were coming back. She'd have to smile and pretend to
be happy for them, even though her heart was breaking.

But also she was going to have to face the developer.
She didn't know what King Brannt had in mind to save
her from him. She might have to go through with sign-
ing the contracts to ensure that her poor cattle weren't
infected. She hadn't slept a wink.

She and Sadie had coffee and then Maddie wandered
around the house in her wheelchair, making ruts.

"Will you relax?" Sadie said. "I know it's going to
be all right. You have to trust that Mr. Brannt knows
what to do."

"I hope so. My poor cattle!"

"Is that a car?"

Even as she spoke a car drove up in front of the house
and stopped. "Mr. Lawson, no doubt. I hope he's wearing body armor," she muttered, and she wheeled her
chair to the front porch.

But it wasn't the developer. It was Odalie and Cort.
They were grinning from ear to ear as they climbed out
of his Jaguar and came to the porch.

Just what I need right now, Maddie thought miserably. But she put on a happy face. "You're both home again. And I guess you have news?" she added. "I'm so happy for you."

"For us?" Cort looked at Odalie and back at Maddie blankly. "Why?"

They followed her into the house. She turned the chair around and swallowed. "Well," she began uneasily.

Odalie knew at once what she thought. She came forward. "No, it's not like that," she said quickly. "There was a doll collectors' convention at the hotel where the cattlemen were meeting. I want you to see this." She pulled a check out of her purse and handed it to Maddie.

It was a good thing she was sitting down. The check was for five figures. Five high figures. She looked at Odalie blankly.

"The fairy," she said, smiling. "I'm sorry I wasn't honest with you. It wasn't my great-grandmother's picture. It was a collector's. He wanted a fairy who looked like her to add to his collection, and I said I knew someone who would do the perfect one. So I flew to Denver to take him the one you made from the photograph." Odalie's blue eyes were soft. "He cried. He said the old lady was the light of his life… She was the only person in his family who didn't laugh and disown him when he said he wanted to go into the business of doll collecting. She encouraged him to follow his dream. He's worth millions now and all because he followed his dream." She nodded at the check. "He owns a doll boutique in Los Angeles. He ships all over the world. He said he'd pay that—" she indicated the check again "—for every fairy you made for him. And he wants to discuss licensing and branding. He thinks you can make a fortune with these. He said so."

Maddie couldn't even find words. The check would pay her medical bills, buy feed and pay taxes. It would save the ranch. She was sobbing and she didn't even realize it until Odalie took the check back and motioned to Cort.

Cort lifted her out of the wheelchair and cradled her against him. "You'll blot the ink off the check with those tears, sweetheart." He chuckled, and kissed them away. "And just for the record, Odalie and I aren't getting married."

"You aren't?" she asked with wet eyes.

"We aren't." Odalie giggled. "He's my friend. I love him. But not like that," she added softly.

"And she's my friend," Cort added. He smiled down at Maddie. "I went a little goofy over her, but, then, I got over it."

"Gee, thanks," Odalie said with amused sarcasm.

"You know what I mean." He laughed. "You're beautiful and talented."

"Not as talented as *our* friend over there." She indicated Maddie, with a warm smile. "She has magic in her hands."

"And other places," Cort mused, looking pointedly at her mouth.

She hid her face against him. He cuddled her close.

"Oh, dear," Sadie said from the doorway. "Maddie, he's back! What are you going to tell him?"

"Tell who?" Cort asked. He turned. His face grew hard. "Oh. Him. My dad gave me an earful about him when I got home."

He put Maddie gently back down into the wheelchair.

"You didn't encourage him?" he asked her.

She grimaced. "The medical bills and doctor bills and feed bills all came in at once," she began miserably. "I couldn't even pay taxes. He offered me a fortune…"

"We're paying the medical bills," Odalie told her firmly. "We even said so."

"It's not right to ask you," Maddie said stubbornly.

"That's okay. You're not asking. We're telling," Odalie said.

"Exactly." Cort was looking more dangerous by the second as the developer got out of his car with a brief-case. "My dad said you've had more cows killed over here, too."

"Yes." She was so miserable she could hardly talk.

"Dad found out a lot more than that about him. He was arrested up in Billings, Montana, on charges of intimidation and poisoning in another land deal," Cort added. "He's out on bond, but apparently it didn't teach him a thing."

"Well, he threatened to plant anthrax in my herd and have the feds come out and destroy them," she said sadly. "He says if I don't sell to him, he'll do it. I think he will."

"He might have," Cort said mysteriously. "Good thing my dad has a real suspicious nature and watches a lot of spy films."

"Excuse me?" Maddie inquired.

He grinned. "Wait and see, honey." He bent and kissed the tip of her nose.

Odalie laughed softly. "One fried developer, coming right up," she teased, and it was obvious that she wasn't jealous of Maddie at all.

THERE WAS A tap at the door and the developer walked right in. He was so intent on his contracts that he must not have noticed the other car in the driveway. "Miss Lane, I've brought the paper...work—" He stopped dead when he saw her companions.

"You can take your paperwork and shove it," Cort said pleasantly. He tilted his Stetson over one eye and put both hands on his narrow hips. "Or you can argue. Personally, I'd love it if you argued."

"She said she wanted to sell," the developer shot back. But he didn't move a step closer.

"She changed her mind," Cort replied.

"You changed it for her," the developer snarled. "Well, she can just change it right back. Things happen sometimes when people don't make the right decisions."

"You mean diseases can be planted in cattle?" Odalie asked sweetly.

The older man gave her a wary look. "What do you mean?"

"Maddie told us how you threatened her," Cort said evenly.

Lawson hesitated. "You can't prove that."

Cort smiled. "I don't have to." He pulled out a DVD in a plastic sleeve and held it up. "You're very trusting, Lawson. I mean, you knew there was surveillance equipment all over the ranch, but you didn't guess the house and porch were wired as well?"

Lawson looked a lot less confident. "You're bluffing."

Cort didn't look like he was bluffing. "My dad has a call in to the district attorney up in Billings, Montana. I believe you're facing indictment there for the destruction of a purebred herd of Herefords because of suspected anthrax?"

"They can't prove that!"

"I'm afraid they can," Cort replied. "There are two witnesses, one of whom used to work with you," he added easily. "He's willing to testify to save his butt." He held up the DVD. "This may not be admissible in court, but it will certainly help to encourage charges against you here for the loss of Miss Lane's purebred stock."

"You wouldn't dare!" the developer said harshly.

"I would dare," Cort replied.

The developer gripped his briefcase tighter. "On second thought," he said, looking around with disdain, "I've decided I don't want this property. It's not good enough for the sort of development I have in mind, and the location is terrible for business. Sorry," he spat at Maddie. "I guess you'll have to manage some other way to pay your medical bills."

"Speaking of medical bills," Cort said angrily, and stepped forward.

"Now, Cort," Maddie exclaimed.

The developer turned and almost ran out of the house to his car. He fumbled to start it and managed to get it in gear just before Cort got to him. He sped out the driveway, fishtailing all the way.

Cort was almost bent over double laughing when he went back into the house. He stopped when three wide-eyed females gaped at him worriedly.

"Oh, I wasn't going to kill him," he said, still laughing. "But I didn't mind letting him think I might. What do you want to bet that he's out of town by tonight and can't be reached by telephone?"

"I wouldn't bet against that," Odalie agreed.

"Me, neither," Sadie said.

"Dad said that Lawson's in more trouble than he can manage up in Billings already. I don't expect he'll wait around for more charges to be filed here."

"Are you going to turn that DVD over to the district attorney?" she asked, nodding toward the jacketed disc.

He glanced at her. "And give up my best performance of 'Recuerdos de la Alhambra?'" he exclaimed. "I'll never get this good a recording again!"

Maddie's eyes brightened. "You were bluffing!"

"For all I was worth." He chuckled.

"Cort, you're wonderful!"

He pursed his lips. "Am I, now?"

"We could take a vote," Odalie suggested. "You've got mine."

"And mine!" Sadie agreed. "Oh, Maddie, you'll have a way to make a living now," she exclaimed, indicating the little fairy. "You won't have to sell our ranch!"

"No, but we still have the problem of running it," Maddie said heavily. "If I'm going to be spending my life sculpting, and thanks to you two, I probably will—" she grinned "—who's going to manage the ranch?"

"I think we can work something out about that," Cort told her, and his dark eyes were flashing with amusement. "We'll talk about it later."

"Okay," she said. "Maybe Ben could manage it?"

Cort nodded. "He's a good man, with a good business head. We'll see."

We'll see? She stared at him as if she'd never seen him before. It was an odd statement. But before she could question it, Sadie went into the kitchen.

"Who wants chocolate pound cake?" she asked.

Three hands went up, and all discussion about the ranch went away.

MADDIE WANTED TO know all about the doll collector. He was a man in his fifties, very distinguished and he had a collection that was famous all over the world.

"There are magazines devoted to collectors," Odalie said excitedly. "They showcased his collection last year. I met him when we were at the Met last year during opera season. We spoke and he said that he loved small, very intricate work. When I saw your sculptures, I remembered him. I looked him up on his website and phoned him. He said he was always looking for new talent, but he wanted to see what you could do. So I asked him for a photo of someone he'd like made into a sculpture and he faxed me the one I gave you."

"I will never be able to repay you for this," Maddie said fervently.

"Maddie, you already have, over and over," Odalie

said softly. "Most especially with that little fairy statue that looks just like me." She shook her head. "I've never owned anything so beautiful."

"Thanks."

"Besides, you're my best friend," Odalie said with a gamine grin. "I have to take care of you."

Maddie felt all warm inside. "I'll take care of you, if you ever need me to," she promised.

Odalie flushed. "Thanks."

"This is great cake," Cort murmured. "Can you cook?" he asked Maddie.

"Yes, but not so much right now." She indicated the wheelchair with a grimace.

"Give it time," he said gently. He smiled, and his whole face grew radiant as he looked at her. "You'll be out of that thing before you know it."

"You think so?" she asked.

He nodded. "Yes, I do."

She smiled. He smiled back. Odalie smiled into her cake and pretended not to notice that they couldn't take their eyes off each other.

ODALIE SAID HER goodbyes and gave Maddie the collector's telephone number so that she could thank him personally for giving her fairy a good home. But Cort lingered.

He bent over the wheelchair, his hands on the arms, and looked into Maddie's eyes. "Later we'll talk about going behind my back to do business with a crook."

"I was scared. And not just that he might poison my cattle. There were so many bills!"

He brushed his mouth over her lips. "I told you I'd take care of all those bills."

"But they all came due, and you've done so much… I couldn't ask…"

He was kissing her. It made talking hard.

She reached up with cold, nervous hands and framed his face in them. She looked into his eyes and saw secrets revealed there. Her breath caught. "It isn't Odalie," she stammered. "It's me."

He nodded. And he didn't smile. "It was always you. I just didn't know it until there was a good chance that I was going to lose you." He smiled tightly then. "Couldn't do that. Couldn't live, if you didn't."

She bit her lip, fighting tears.

He kissed them away. "I don't have a life without you," he whispered at her nose. "So we have to make plans."

"When?" she asked, bursting with happiness.

"When you're out of that wheelchair," he said. He gave her a wicked smile. "Because when we start talking, things are apt to get, well, physical." He wiggled his eyebrows.

She laughed.

He laughed.

He kissed her affectionately and stood back up. "I'll drive Odalie home. I'll call you later. And I'll see you tomorrow. And the day after. And the day after. And the day after that…"

"And the day after that?" she prompted.

"Don't get pushy," he teased.

He threw up a hand and went out to the car. This

time, when he drove off with Odalie, Maddie didn't go through pangs of jealousy. The look in his eyes had been as sweet as a promise.

EPILOGUE

PHYSICAL THERAPY SEEMED to go on forever. The days turned to weeks, the leaves began to fall. The cows grew big with calves. Rain had come in time for some of the grain crops to come to harvest, and there would be enough hay, hopefully, to get them through the winter.

Maddie's legs were growing stronger. Little by little, she made progress.

Odalie and Cort were still around, prodding her, keeping her spirits up during the long mending process. She didn't let herself get discouraged. She created new fairies and Odalie shipped them off, carefully packed, to a man named Angus Moore, who acted as Maddie's agent and sold her dainty little creations for what amounted to a small fortune for the artist.

The developer, sure enough, left town and left no forwarding address. Gossip was that the authorities wanted to talk to him about several cases of dead cattle on properties he'd tried to buy in several states. Maddie hoped they caught up with him one day.

MEANWHILE, CORT CAME over every night for supper. He brought his guitar most nights, and serenaded Maddie on the porch until the nights got too cold for that. Then he serenaded her in the living room, by the fireplace with its leaping flames while she curled up under a blanket on the sofa.

From time to time, when Sadie was occupied in the kitchen, he curled up under the blanket with her.

She loved his big hands smoothing her bare skin under her shirt, the warmth and strength of them arousing sensations that grew sweeter by the day. He was familiar to her now. She had no fear of his temper. He didn't lose it with her, although he'd been volatile about a man who left a gate open and cattle poured through it onto the highway. At least none of the cattle was injured, and no cars were wrecked.

"He was just a kid," Cort murmured against her collarbone. "He works for us after school. Usually does a pretty good job, too, cleaning out the stables."

She arched her back and winced.

"Damn." He lifted his head and his hands stilled on her body. "Too soon."

She looked miserable.

He laughed. He peered toward the doorway before he slid the hem of her T-shirt up under her chin and looked at the pert little breasts he'd uncovered. "Buried treasure," he whispered, "and I'm a pirate…"

She moaned.

"Stop that. She'll hear you."

She bit her lip and gave him an anguished look. He grinned before he bent his head again, producing even more eloquent sounds that were, thankfully, soon muffled by his mouth.

But things between them were heating up more every

day. She had his shirt unbuttoned just before he eased over her. Her hard-tipped breasts nestled into the thick hair on his muscular chest and one long, powerful leg eased between both of hers. He levered himself down very gently while he was kissing her, but she felt the quick, hard swell of him as he began to move helplessly on her, grinding his hips into hers.

"Oh, God," he bit off. He jerked himself back and up, to sit beside her on the sofa with his head bent, shuddering.

"I'm sorry," she whispered shakily.

He drew in short, harsh breaths while his hands worked at buttoning up the shirt. "Well, I'm not," he murmured, glancing down at her. He groaned. "Honey, you have to cover those up or we're going to be back at first base all over again!"

She looked down and flushed a little as she pulled her shirt down and fumbled behind her to do up the bra again. "First base."

He laughed softly. "First base."

She beamed at him. "I'm getting better every day. It won't be long."

"It had better not be," he sighed. "I think I'll die of it pretty soon."

"No!"

"Just kidding." He turned on the sofa and looked down at her with warm, dark, possessive eyes. "I talked to a minister."

"You did? What did he have to say?"

He traced her nose. "We have to have a marriage license first."

Her heart jumped. They'd been kissing and petting for quite a long time, and he'd insinuated, but he'd never actually asked.

"I thought we might get one with flowers and stuff. You know. So it would look nice framed on the wall."

"Framed."

He nodded. His eyes were steady on her face. "Madeline Edith Lane, will you do me the honor of becoming my wife?" he asked softly.

She fought tears. "Yes," she whispered. "Yes!"

He brushed the tears away, his eyes so dark they seemed black. "I'll love you all my life," he whispered. "I'll love you until the sun burns out."

"I'll love you longer," she whispered back, and it was all there, in her eyes and his.

He smiled slowly. "And we'll have beautiful kids," he said softly. He pushed back her hair. "Absolutely beautiful. Like you."

Now she was really bawling.

He pulled her gently into his arms and across his lap, and rocked her and kissed away the tears.

Sadie came walking in with coffee and stopped dead. "Oh, goodness, what's wrong?"

"I told her we were going to have beautiful kids," he said with a chuckle. "She's very emotional."

"Beautiful kids? You're going to get married?" Sadie exclaimed.

"Yes." Maddie smiled.

"Whoopee!"

"Oh, dear!" Maddie exclaimed.

Sadie looked down at the remains of the glass coffeepot and two ceramic mugs. "Oh, dear," she echoed.

Cort just laughed. But then, like the gentleman he was, he went to help Sadie clean up the mess.

THEY WERE MARRIED at Christmas. Maddie was able to wear an exquisite designer gown that Odalie had insisted on buying for her, as her "something new." It was an A-line gown of white satin with cap sleeves and a lacy bodice that went up to encase her throat like a high-necked Victorian dress.

There was a train, also of delicate white lace, and a fingertip veil with lace and appliquéd roses. She wore lace gloves and carried a bouquet of white roses. There was a single red rose in the center of the bouquet. One red rose for true love, Cort had insisted, and white ones for purity because in a modern age of easy virtue, Maddie was a throwback to Victorian times. She went to her marriage a virgin, and never apologized once for not following the crowd.

She walked down the aisle on the arm of Cole Everett, who had volunteered to give her away. Odalie was her maid of honor. Heather Everett and Shelby Brannt were her matrons of honor. Four local girls she'd known all her life were bridesmaids, and John Everett was Cort's best man.

At an altar with pots of white and red roses they were married in the local Methodist church, where all three families were members. The minister had preached the funeral of most of their deceased kin. He was elderly and kind, and beloved by the community.

When he pronounced Cort and Maddie man and wife, Cort lifted the veil, ignoring the flash from the professional photographer's camera, and closed in to kiss his new bride.

Nobody heard him when he bent, very low, and whispered, "First base."

Nobody heard the soft, mischievous laughter the comment provoked from the bride. There was a huge reception. John Everett stopped by the table where Cort and Maddie were cutting the wedding cake.

"So, tell me, Cort," John said when the photographer finished shooting the cake-eating segment, "if I'm really the best man, why are you married to my girl?"

"Now, a remark like that could get you punched," Cort teased, catching the other man around the neck, "even at a wedding."

John chuckled, embracing him in a bear hug. "I was just kidding. No doubt in my mind from the beginning where her heart was." He indicated a beaming Maddie.

Cort glanced at her and smiled. "What an idiot I was," he said, shaking his head. "I almost lost her."

"Crazy, the way things turn out," John mused, his eyes on Odalie as she paused to speak to Maddie. "My sister, Attila the Hun, is ending up as Maddie's best friend. Go figure."

"I wouldn't have believed it myself. Odalie's quite a girl."

John smiled. "I thought it would be you and Odalie, eventually."

Cort shook his head. "We're too different. Neither of us would fit in the other's world. It took me a long time to realize that. But I saw my future in Maddie's eyes. I always will. I hope Odalie finds someone who can make her half as happy as I am today. She deserves it."

John nodded. "I'm very proud of her. She's matured a lot in the past few months." He turned back to Cort. "Christmas is next week. You guys coming home for it or not?"

"Oh, we have to…my folks would kill us, to say nothing of Sadie." He indicated the older woman in her pretty blue dress talking to some other people. "Maddie's like the daughter she never had. They can't have Christmas without us," he stated. "We're just going down to Panama City for a couple of days. Maybe later I can take Maddie to Europe and show her the sights. Right now, even a short plane trip is going to make her uncomfortable, much less a long one to somewhere exotic."

"I don't think Maddie will mind where you go, as long as she's with you," John said. "I wish you all the best. You know that."

"Thanks, bro."

"And when you come home, maybe we can crack open some new video games, now that my sister won't complain about my having you over," he added with a sigh.

Cort just grinned.

THE HOTEL WAS right on the beach. It was cold in Panama City, but not so cold that they couldn't sit on the patio beyond the glass sliding doors and look at the cold moonlight on the ocean.

Predictably, they'd barely made it into the hotel room when all the months of pent-up anguished desire were taken off the bridle for the first time.

He tried to be gentle, he really did, but his body was shivering with need long before he could do what he wanted to do: to show his love for Maddie.

Not that she noticed. She was with him every step of the way, even when the first encounter stung and made her cry out.

"This is part of it," he gritted, trying to slow down. "I'm so sorry!"

"Don't…sweat it," she panted, moving up to meet the furious downward motion of his hips. "You can hang out…the bedsheet in the morning…to prove I was a virgin…!"

"Wha-a-at?" he yelped, and burst out laughing even as his body shuddered with the beginning of ecstasy.

"First…base," she choked out, and bit him.

It was the most glorious high he'd ever experienced. He groaned and groaned as his body shuddered over hers. The pleasure was exquisite. He felt it in every cell of his body, with every beat of his heart. He could hear his own heartbeat, the passion was so violent.

Under him, her soft body was rising and falling like a piston as she kept pace with his need, encouraged it, fanned the flames and, finally, glued itself to his in an absolute epiphany of satisfaction that convulsed both of them as they almost passed out from the climax.

She clung to him, shivering with pleasure in the aftermath. Neither of them could stop moving, savoring the dregs of passion until they drained the cup dry.

"Wow," she whispered as she looked into his eyes.

"Wow," he whispered back. He looked down their bodies to where they were joined. They hadn't even thought of turning out the lights. He was glad. Looking at her, like this, was a joy he hadn't expected.

"Beautiful," he breathed.

She smiled slowly. "And to think I was nervous about the first time," she said.

"Obviously unnecessary, since I have skills far beyond those of most mortal men…*oof!*"

She'd hit him. She grinned, though. And then she wiggled her eyebrows and moved her hips ever so slowly. Despite the sting, and the discomfort, pleasure welled up like water above a dam in a flood.

"Oh, yes," she whispered as he began to move, looking straight into her eyes. "Yes. Do that."

He smiled. "This," he murmured, "is going to be indescribable."

And it was.

WHEN THEY GOT BACK, in time for the Christmas celebrations at Skylance, nobody could understand why, when Cort whispered, "first base," Maddie almost fell down laughing. But that was one secret neither one of them ever shared with another living soul.

* * * * *

PASSION FLOWER

CHAPTER ONE

JENNIFER KING EYED the closed hotel room door nervously. She hadn't wanted this assignment, but she hadn't had much choice, either. Her recent illness had left her savings account bare, and this job was all she had to hold on to. It was a long way from the brilliant career in interior decorating she'd left behind in New York. But it was a living.

She pushed back a loose strand of blond hair and hoped she looked sedate enough for the cattleman behind the door. The kind of clothes she'd favored in New York were too expensive for her budget in Atlanta.

She knocked at the door and waited. It seemed to take forever for the man inside to get there. Finally, without warning, the door swung open.

"Miss King?" he asked, smiling pleasantly.

She smiled back. He was much younger than she'd expected him to be. Tall and fair and pleasant. "Yes," she said. "You rang for a temporary secretary?"

"Just need a few letters done, actually," he said, taking the heavy portable typewriter from her hand. "I'm buying some cattle for my brother."

"Yes, Miss James at the agency told me it had to do with cattle." She sat down quickly. She was pale and wan, still feeling the after-effects of a terrible bout with pneumonia.

"Say, are you all right?" he asked, frowning.

"Fine, thank you, Mr. Culhane," she said, remembering his name from Miss James's description of the job. "I'm just getting over pneumonia, and I'm a little weak."

He sat down across from her on the sofa, lean and rangy, and smiled. "I guess it does take the whip out of you. I've never had it myself, but Everett nearly died on us one year. He smokes too much," he confided.

"Your brother?" she asked with polite interest as she got her steno pad and pen from her large purse.

"My brother. The senior partner. Everett runs the show." He sounded just a little jealous. She glanced up. Jennifer was twenty-three, and he couldn't have been much older. She felt a kinship with him. Until their deaths three years back, her parents had pretty much nudged her into the job they thought she wanted. By the sound of it, Everett Culhane had done the same with this young man.

She dug out her pad and pen and crossed her thin legs. All of her was thin. Back in New York, before the frantic pace threatened her health, she'd been slender and poised and pretty enough to draw any man's eye. But now she was only a pale wraith, a ghost of the woman she'd been. Her blond hair was brittle and lusterless, her pale green eyes were dull, without their old sparkle. She looked bad, and that fact registered in the young man's eyes.

"Are you sure you feel up to this?" he asked gently. "You don't look well."

"I'm a little frail, that's all," she replied proudly. "I'm only just out of the hospital, you see."

"I guess that's why," he muttered. He got up, pacing the room, and found some notes scribbled on lined white paper. "Well, this first letter goes to Everett Culhane, Circle C Ranch, Big Spur, Texas."

"Texas?" Her pale eyes lit up. "Really?"

His eyebrows lifted, and he grinned. "Really. The town is named after a king-size ranch nearby—the Big Spur. It's owned by Cole Everett and his wife Heather, and their three sons. Our ranch isn't a patch on that one, but big brother has high hopes."

"I've always wanted to see a real cattle ranch," she confided. "My grandfather went cowboying out to Texas as a boy. He used to talk about it all the time, about the places he'd seen, and the history..." She sat up straight, poising her pen over the pad. "Sorry. I didn't mean to get off the track."

"That's all right. Funny, you don't look like a girl who'd care for the outdoors," he commented as he sat back down with the sheaf of papers in his hand.

"I love it," she said quietly. "I lived in a small town until I was ten and my parents moved to Atlanta. I missed it terribly. I still do."

"Can't you go back?" he asked.

She shook her head sadly. "It's too late. I have no family left. My parents are dead. There are a few scattered relatives, but none close enough to visit."

"That's rough. Kind of like me and Everett," he added. "We got raised by our aunt and uncle. At least, I did. Everett wasn't so lucky. Our dad was still alive while he was a boy." His face clouded, as if with an unpleasant memory. He cleared his throat. "Well, anyway, back to the letter…"

He began to dictate, and she kept up with him easily. He thought out the sentences before he gave them to her, so there were few mistakes or changes. She wondered why he didn't just call his brother, but she didn't ask the question. She took down several pages of description about bulls and pedigrees and bloodlines. There was a second letter, to a bank executive in Big Spur, detailing the method the Culhane brothers had devised to pay back a sizeable loan. The third letter was to a breeder in Carrollton, outlining transport for a bull the man had evidently purchased from the Culhanes.

"Confused?" he murmured dryly when he stopped.

"It's not my business…" she began gently.

"We're selling off one of our best bulls," he said, "to give us enough down payment on another top breeding bull. Everett is trying for a purebred Hereford herd. But we don't have the cash, so I've come down here to do some fancy trading. I sold the bull we had. Now I'm trying to get a potential seller to come down on his price."

"Wouldn't a phone call to your brother be quicker?" she asked.

"Sure. And Everett would skin my head. I came out here on a bus, for God's sake, instead of a plane. We're just about mortgaged to the hilt, you see. Everett says we can't afford not to pinch pennies." His eyes twinkled. "We've got Highland Scots in our ancestry, you see."

She smiled. "Yes, I suppose so. I can see his point. Phone calls are expensive."

"Especially the kind it would take to relay this much information," he agreed, nodding toward what he'd dictated. "If I get it off today, he'll have it in a day or two. Then, if he thinks it's worth giving what the man wants, he can call me and just say a word or two. In the meantime, I've got other business to attend to."

"Shrewd idea," she murmured.

"Just a couple more," he continued. He leaned back and studied a magazine. "Okay, this one goes to…" He gave her a name and address in north Georgia, and dictated a letter asking if the breeder could give him a call at the hotel on Friday at 1:00 p.m. Then he dictated a second letter to a breeder in south Georgia, making the same request for 2:00 p.m. He grinned at her faint smile.

"Saving money," he assured her. "Although why Everett wants to do it the hard way is beyond me. There's a geologist who swears we've got one hell of a lot of oil on our western boundary, but Everett dug in his heels and refused to sell off the drilling rights. Even for a percentage. Can you beat that? We could be millionaires, and here I sit writing letters asking people to call me, just to save money."

"Why won't he sell?" she asked, curious.

"Because he's a purist," he grumbled. "He doesn't want to spoil the land. He'd rather struggle to make the cattle pay. Fat chance. The way things have been going, we're going to wind up eating those damned purebreds, paper and all."

She laughed helplessly at his phrasing and hid her face in her hand. "Sorry," she mumbled. "I didn't mean to laugh."

"It is kind of funny," he confessed. "But not when you're cutting corners like we are."

She got up and started to lift the typewriter onto the desk by the window, struggling with it.

"Here, let me do that," he said, and put it onto the flat surface for her. "You're pretty weak, little lady."

"I'm getting back on my feet," she assured him. "Just a little wobbly, that's all."

"Well, I'll leave you to it. I'm going down to get a sandwich. Can I bring you something?"

She'd have loved a sandwich, but she wasn't going to put any further drain on his resources. "No, thank you," she said, politely and with a smile. "I just had lunch before I came over here."

"Okay, then. See you in a half hour or so."

He jammed a straw cowboy hat on his head and went out the door, closing it softly behind him.

Jennifer typed the letters quickly and efficiently, even down to the cattle's pedigrees. It was a good thing she'd taken that typing course when she was going through the school of interior design in New York, she thought. It had come in handy when the pressure of competition laid her out. She wasn't ready to handle that competitive rat race again yet. She needed to rest, and by comparison typing letters for out-of-town businessmen was a piece of cake.

She felt oddly sorry for this businessman, and faintly sympathetic with his brother, who'd rather go spare than sell out on his principles. She wondered if he looked like his younger brother.

Her eyes fell on the name she was typing at the bottom of the letter. Robert G. Culhane. That must be the man who'd dictated them. He seemed to know cattle, from his meticulous description of them. Her eyes wandered over what looked like a production record for a herd sire, and she sighed. Texas and cattle. She wondered what the Circle C Ranch was like and while she finished up the letters, lost herself in dreams of riding horseback over flat plains. Pipe dreams, she thought, smiling as she stacked the neat letters with their accompanying envelopes. She'd never see Texas.

Just as she rose from the typewriter, the door opened, and Robert Culhane was back. He smiled at her.

"Taking a break?" he asked as he swept off his hat and whirled it onto a table.

"No, I'm finished," she said, astounding him.

"Already?" He grabbed up the letters and bent over the desk, proofreading them one by one and shaking his head. "Damn, you're fast."

"I do around a hundred words a minute," she replied. "It's one of my few talents."

"You'd be a godsend at the ranch," he sighed. "It takes Everett an hour to type one letter. He cusses a blue streak when he has to write anything on that infernal old machine. And there are all the production records we have to keep, and the tax records, and the payroll…" His head lifted and he frowned. "I don't suppose you'd like a job?"

She caught her breath. "In Texas?"

"You make it sound like a religious experience," he murmured on a laugh.

"You can't imagine how much I hate the city," she replied, brushing back a strand of dull hair. "I still cough all the time because of the pollution, and the apartment where I live has no space at all. I'd almost work for free just to be out in the country."

He cocked his head at her and pursed his boyish lips. "It wouldn't be easy, working for Everett," he said. "And you'd have to manage your own fare to Big Spur. You see, I'll need a little time to convince him. You'd barely get minimum wage. And knowing Everett, you'd wind up doing a lot of things besides typing. We don't have a housekeeper..."

Her face lit up. "I can make curtains and cook."

"Do you have a telephone?"

She sighed. "No."

"Kind of in the same boat we are in, aren't you?" he said with a sympathetic smile. "I'm Robert Culhane, by the way."

"Jennifer King," she said for the second time that day, and extended her hand.

"Nice to meet you, Jenny. How can I reach you?"

"The agency will take a message for me," she said.

"Fine. I'll be in town for several more days. I'll be in touch with you before I go back to Texas. Okay?"

She beamed. "You're really serious?"

"I'm really serious. And this is great work," he added, gesturing toward the letters. "Jenny, it won't be an easy life on the Circle C. It's nothing like those fancy ranches you see on the television."

"I'm not expecting it to be," she said honestly, and was picturing a ramshackle house that needed paint and curtains and overhauling, and two lonely men living in it. She smiled. "I'm just expecting to be needed."

"You'll be that," he sighed, staring at her critically. "But are you up to hard work?"

"I'll manage," she promised. "Being out in the open, in fresh air, will make me strong. Besides, it'll be dry air out there, and it's summer."

"You'll burn up in the heat," he promised.

"I burn up in the heat here," she said. "Atlanta is a southern city. We get hundred-degree temperatures here."

"Just like home," he murmured with a smile.

"I'd like to come," she said as she got her purse and closed up the typewriter. "But I don't want to get you into any trouble with your brother."

"Everett and I hardly ever have anything except trouble," he said easily. "Don't worry about me. You'd be doing us a big favor. I'll talk Everett into it."

"Should I write you another letter?" She hesitated.

He shook his head. "I'll have it out with him when I get home," he said. "No sweat. Thanks for doing my letters. I'll send the agency a check, you tell them."

"I will. And thank you!"

She hardly felt the weight of the typewriter on her way back to the agency. She was floating on a cloud.

Miss James gave her a hard look when she came back in. "You're late," she said. "We had to refuse a call."

"I'm sorry. There were several letters…" she began.

"You've another assignment. Here's the address. A politician. Wants several copies of a speech he's giving, to hand out to the press. You're to type the speech and get it photostatted for him."

She took the outstretched address and sighed. "The typewriter…?"

"He has his own, an electric one. Leave that one here, if you please." Miss James buried her silver head in paperwork. "You may go home when you finish. I'll see you in the morning. Good night."

"Good night," Jennifer said quietly, sighing as she went out onto the street. It would be well after quitting time when she finished, and Miss James knew it. But perhaps the politician would be generous enough to tip her. If only the Texas job worked out! Jennifer was a scrapper when she was at her peak, but she was weary and sick and dragged out. It wasn't a good time to get into an argument with the only employer she'd been able to find. All the other agencies were overstaffed with out-of-work people begging for any kind of job.

The politician was a city councilman, in a good mood and very generous. Jennifer treated herself to three hamburgers and two cups of coffee on the way back to her small apartment. It was in a private home, and dirt cheap. The landlady wasn't overly friendly, but it was a roof over her head and the price was right.

She slept fitfully, dreaming about the life she'd left behind in New York. It all seemed like something out of a fantasy. The competition for the plum jobs, the cocktail parties to make contacts, the deadlines, the endless fighting to land the best accounts, the agonizing perfecting of color schemes and coordinating pieces to fit fussy tastes… Her nerves had given out, and then her body.

It hadn't been her choice to go to New York. She'd have been happy in Atlanta. But the best schools were up north, and her parents had insisted. They wanted her to have the finest training available, so she let herself be gently pushed. Two years after she graduated, they were dead. She'd never truly gotten over their deaths in the plane crash. They'd been on their way to a party on Christmas Eve. The plane went down in the dark, in a lake, and it had been hours before they were missed.

In the two years since her graduation, Jennifer had landed a job at one of the top interior-decoration businesses in the city. She'd pushed herself over the limit to get clients, going to impossible lengths to please them. The outcome had been inevitable. Pneumonia landed her in the hospital for several days in March, and she was too drained to go back to work immediately after. An up-and-coming young designer had stepped neatly into her place, and she had found herself suddenly without work.

Everything had to go, of course. The luxury apartment, the furs, the designer clothes. She'd sold them all and headed south. Only to find that the job market was overloaded and she couldn't find a job that wouldn't finish killing her. Except at a temporary agency, where she could put her typing skills to work. She started working for Miss James, and trying to recover. But so far she'd failed miserably. And now the only bright spot in her future was Texas.

She prayed as she never had before, struggling from one assignment to the next and hoping beyond hope that the phone call would come. Late one Friday afternoon, it did. And she happened to be in the office when it came.

"Miss King?" Robert Culhane asked on a laugh. "Still want to go to Texas?"

"Oh, yes!" she said fervently, holding tightly to the telephone cord.

"Then pack a bag and be at the ranch bright and early a week from Monday morning. Got a pencil? Okay, here's how to get there."

She was so excited she could barely scribble. She got down the directions. "I can't believe it, it's like a dream!" she said enthusiastically. "I'll do a good job, really I will. I won't be any trouble, and the pay doesn't matter!"

"I'll tell Everett," he chuckled. "Don't forget. You needn't call. Just come on out to the ranch. I'll be there to smooth things over with old Everett, okay?"

"Okay. Thank you!"

"Thank *you*, Miss King," he said. "See you a week from Monday."

"Yes, sir!" She hung up, her face bright with hope. She was actually going to Texas!

"Miss King?" Miss James asked suspiciously.

"Oh! I won't be back in after today, Miss James," she said politely. "Thank you for letting me work with you. I've enjoyed it very much."

Miss James looked angry. "You can't just walk out like this," she said.

"But I can," Jennifer said, with some of her old spirit. She picked up her purse. "I didn't sign a contract, Miss James. And if you were to push the point, I'd tell you that I worked a great deal of overtime for which I wasn't paid," she added with a pointed stare. "How would you explain that to the people down at the state labor department?"

Miss James stiffened. "You're ungrateful."

"No, I'm not. I'm very grateful. But I'm leaving, all the same. Good day." She nodded politely just before she went out, and closed the door firmly behind her.

CHAPTER TWO

IT WAS BLAZING hot for a spring day in Texas. Jennifer
stopped in the middle of the ranch road to rest for a
minute and set her burdens down on the dusty, graveled
ground. She wished for the tenth time in as many minutes that she'd let the cab driver take her all the way to
the Culhanes' front door. But she'd wanted to walk. It
hadn't seemed a long way from the main road. And it
was so beautiful, with the wildflowers strewn across the
endless meadows toward the flat horizon. Bluebonnets,
which she'd only read about until then, and Mexican hat
and Indian paintbrush. Even the names of the flowers
were poetic. But her enthusiasm had outweighed her
common sense. And her strength.

She'd tried to call the ranch from town—apparently
Everett and Robert Culhane did have the luxury of a
telephone. But it rang and rang with no answer. Well, it
was Monday, and she'd been promised a job. She hefted
her portable typewriter and her suitcase and started
out again.

Her pale eyes lifted to the house in the distance. It
was a two-story white frame building, with badly peeling paint and a long front porch. Towering live oaks
protected it from the sun, trees bigger than anything

Jennifer had seen in Georgia. And the feathery green trees with the crooked trunks had to be mesquite. She'd never seen it, but she'd done her share of reading about it.

On either side of the long, graveled driveway were fences, gray with weathering and strung with rusting barbed wire. Red-coated cattle grazed behind the fences, and her eyes lingered on the wide horizon. She'd always thought Georgia was big—until now. Texas was just unreal. In a separate pasture, a mare and her colt frolicked in the hot sun.

Jennifer pushed back a strand of dull blond hair that had escaped from her bun. In a white shirtwaist dress and high heels, she was a strange sight to be walking up the driveway of a cattle ranch. But she'd wanted to make a good impression.

Her eyes glanced down ruefully at the red dust on the hem of her dress, and the scuff marks on her last good pair of white sling pumps. She could have cried. One of her stockings had a run, and she was sweating. She could hardly have looked worse if she'd planned it.

She couldn't help being a little nervous about the older brother. She had Everett Culhane pictured as a staid old rancher with a mean temper. She'd met businessmen like that before, and dealt with them. She wasn't afraid of him. But she hoped that he'd be glad of her help. It would make things easier all around.

Her footsteps echoed along the porch as she walked up the worn steps. She would have looked around more carefully weeks ago, but now she was tired and run-down and just too exhausted to care what her new surroundings looked like.

She paused at the screen door, and her slender fingers brushed the dust from her dress. She put the suitcase and the typewriter down, took a steadying breath, and knocked.

There was no sound from inside the house. The wooden door was standing open, and she thought she heard the whir of a fan. She knocked again. Maybe it would be the nice young man she'd met in Atlanta who would answer the door. She only hoped she was welcome.

The sound of quick, hard footsteps made her heart quicken. Someone was home, at least. Maybe she could sit down. She was feeling a little faint.

"Who the hell are you?" came a harsh masculine voice from behind the screen door, and Jennifer looked up into the hardest face and the coldest dark eyes she'd ever seen.

She couldn't even find her voice. Her immediate reaction was to turn around and run for it. But she'd come too far, and she was too tired.

"I'm Jennifer King," she said as professionally as she could. "Is Robert Culhane home, please?"

She was aware of the sudden tautening of his big body, a harsh intake of breath, before she looked up and saw the fury in his dark eyes.

"What the hell kind of game are you playing, lady?" he demanded.

She stared at him. It had been a long walk, and now it looked as if she might have made a mistake and come to the wrong ranch. Her usual confidence faltered. "Is this the Circle C Ranch?" she asked.

"Yes, it is."

He wasn't forthcoming, and she wondered if he might be one of the hired hands. "Is this where Robert Culhane lives?" she persisted, trying to peek past him—there was a lot of him, all hard muscle and blue denim.

"Bobby was killed in a bus wreck a week ago," he said harshly.

Jennifer was aware of a numb feeling in her legs. The long trip on the bus, the heavy suitcase, the effects of her recent illness—all of it added up to exhaustion. And those cold words were the final blow. With a pitiful little sound, she sank down onto the porch, her head whirling, nausea running up into her throat like warm water.

The screen door flew open and a pair of hard, impatient arms reached down to lift her. She felt herself effortlessly carried, like a sack of flour, into the cool house. She was unceremoniously dumped down onto a worn brocade sofa and left there while booted feet stomped off into another room. There were muttered words that she was glad she couldn't understand, and clinking sounds. Then, a minute later, a glass of dark amber liquid was held to her numb lips and a hard hand raised her head.

She sipped at the cold, sweet iced tea like a runner on the desert when confronted with wet salvation. She struggled to catch her breath and sat up, gently nudging the dark, lean hand holding the glass to one side. She breathed in deeply, trying to get her whirling mind to slow down. She was still trying to take it all in. She'd been promised a job, she'd come hundreds of miles at her own expense to work for minimum wage, and now the man who'd offered it to her was dead. That was the worst part, imagining such a nice young man dead.

"You look like a bleached handkerchief," the deep, harsh voice observed.

She sighed. "You ought to write for television. You sure do have a gift for prose."

His dark eyes narrowed. "Walking in this heat without a hat. My God, how many stupid city women are there in the world? And what landed you on my doorstep?"

She lifted her eyes then, to look at him properly. He was darkly tanned, and there were deep lines in his face, from the hatchet nose down to the wide, chiseled mouth. His eyes were deep-set, unblinking under heavy dark brows and a wide forehead. His hair was jet-black, straight and thick and a little shaggy. He was wearing what had to be work clothes: faded denim jeans that emphasized long, powerfully muscled legs, and a matching shirt whose open neck revealed a brown chest thick with short, curling hair. He had the look of a man who was all business, all the time. All at once she realized that this man wasn't the hired hand she'd mistaken him for.

"You're Everett Culhane," she said hesitantly.

His face didn't move. Not a muscle in it changed position, but she had the distinct feeling that the sound of his name on her lips had shocked him.

She took another long sip of the tea and sighed at the pleasure of the icy liquid going down her parched throat.

"How far did you walk?" he asked.

"Just from the end of your driveway," she admitted, looking down at her ruined shoes. "Distance is deceptive out here."

"Haven't you ever heard of sunstroke?"

She nodded. "It just didn't occur to me."

She put the glass down on the napkin he'd brought with it. Well, this was Texas. How sad that she wouldn't see anything more of it.

"I'm very sorry about your brother, Mr. Culhane," she said with dignity. "I didn't know him very well, but he seemed like a nice man." She got up with an odd kind of grace despite the unsteadiness of her legs. "I won't take up any more of your time."

"Why did you come, Miss King?"

She shook her head. "It doesn't matter now in the least." She turned and went out the screen door, lifting her suitcase and typewriter from where they'd fallen when she fainted. It was going to be a long walk back to town, but she'd just have to manage it. She had bus fare back home and a little more. A cab was a luxury now, with no job at the end of her long ride.

"Where do you think you're going?" Everett Culhane asked from behind her, his tone like a whiplash.

"Back to town," she said without turning. "Goodbye, Mr. Culhane."

"Walking?" he mused. "In this heat, without a hat?"

"Got here, didn't I?" she drawled as she walked down the steps.

"You'll never make it back. Wait a minute. I'll drive you."

"No, thanks," she said proudly. "I get around all right by myself, Mr. Culhane. I don't need any handouts."

"You'll need a doctor if you try that walk," he said, and turned back into the house.

She thought the matter was settled, until a battered red pickup truck roared up beside her and stopped. The passenger door flew open.

"Get in," he said curtly, in a tone that made it clear he expected instant obedience.

"I said…" she began irritatedly.

His dark eyes narrowed. "I don't mind lifting you in and holding you down until we get to town," he said quietly.

With a grimace, she climbed in, putting the typewriter and suitcase on the floorboard.

There was a marked lack of conversation. Everett smoked his cigarette with sharp glances in her direction when she began coughing. Her lungs were still sensitive, and he seemed to be smoking shucks or something equally potent. Eventually he crushed out the cigarette and cracked a window.

"You don't sound well," he said suddenly.

"I'm getting over pneumonia," she said, staring lovingly at the horizon. "Texas sure is big."

"It sure is." He glanced at her. "Which part of it do you call home?"

"I don't."

The truck lurched as he slammed on the brakes. "What did you say?"

"I'm not a Texan," she confessed. "I'm from Atlanta."

"Georgia?"

"Is there another one?"

He let out a heavy breath. "What the hell did you mean, coming this distance just to see a man you hardly knew?" he burst out. "Surely to God, it wasn't love at first sight?"

"Love?" She blinked. "Heavens, no. I only did some typing for your brother."

He cut off the engine. "Start over. Start at the beginning. You're giving me one hell of a headache. How did you wind up out here?"

"Your brother offered me a job," she said quietly. "Typing. Of course, he said there'd be other duties as well. Cooking, cleaning, things like that. And a very small salary," she added with a tiny smile.

"He was honest with you, at least," he growled. "But then why did you come? Didn't you believe him?"

"Yes, of course," she said hesitantly. "Why wouldn't I want to come?"

He started to light another cigarette, stared hard at her, and put the pack back in his shirt pocket. "Keep talking."

He was an odd man, she thought. "Well, I'd lost my old job, because once I got over the pneumonia I was too weak to keep up the pace. I got a job in Atlanta with one of the temporary talent agencies doing typing. My speed is quite good, and it was something that didn't wring me out, you see. Mr. Culhane wanted some letters typed. We started talking," she smiled, remembering how kind he'd been, "and when I found out he was from Texas, from a real ranch, I guess I just went crazy. I've spent my whole life listening to my grandfather relive his youth in Texas, Mr. Culhane. I've read everything Zane Grey and Louis L'Amour ever wrote, and it was the dream of my life to come out here. The end of the rainbow. I figured that a low salary on open land would be worth a lot more than a big salary in the city, where I was choking to death on smog and civilization. He offered me the job and I said yes on the spot." She glanced at him ruefully. "I'm not usually so slow. But I was feeling so bad, and it sounded so wonderful… I didn't even think about checking with you first. Mr. Culhane said he'd have it all worked out, and that I was just to get on a bus and come on out today." Her eyes clouded. "I'm so sorry about him. Losing the job isn't nearly as bad as hearing that he…was killed. I liked him."

Everett's fingers were tapping an angry pattern on the steering wheel. "A job." He laughed mirthlessly, then sighed. "Well, maybe he had a point. I'm so behind on my production records and tax records, it isn't funny. I'm choking to death on my own cooking, the house hasn't been swept in a month…" He glanced at her narrowly. "You aren't pregnant?"

Her pale eyes flashed at him. "That, sir, would make medical history."

One dark eyebrow lifted and he glanced at her studiously before he smiled. "Little Southern lady, are you really that innocent?"

"Call me Scarlett and, unemployment or no unemployment, I'll paste you one, cowboy," she returned with a glimmer of her old spirit. It was too bad that the outburst triggered a coughing spree.

"Damn," he muttered, passing her his handkerchief. "All right, I'll stop baiting you. Do you want the job, or don't you? Robert was right about the wages. You'll get bed and board free, but it's going to be a frugal existence. Interested?"

"If it means getting to stay in Texas, yes, I am."

He smiled. "How old are you, schoolgirl?"

"I haven't been a schoolgirl for years, Mr. Culhane," she told him. "I'm twenty-three, in fact." She glared at him. "How old are you?"

"Make a guess," he invited.

Her eyes went from his thick hair down the hawk-like features to his massive chest, which tapered to narrow hips, long powerful legs, and large, booted feet. "Thirty," she said.

He chuckled softly. It was the first time she'd heard the deep, pleasant sound, and it surprised her to find that he was capable of laughter. He didn't seem like the kind of man who laughed very often.

His eyes wandered over her thin body with amused indifference, and she regretted for a minute that she was such a shadow of her former self. "Try again, honey," he said.

She noticed then the deep lines in his darkly tanned face, the sprinkling of gray hair at his temples. In the open neck of his shirt, she could see threads of silver among the curling dark hair. No, he wasn't as young as she'd first thought.

"Thirty-four," she guessed.

"Add a year and you've got it."

She smiled. "Poor old man," she said with gentle humor.

He chuckled again. "That's no way to talk to your new boss," he cautioned.

"I won't forget again, honestly." She stared at him. "Do you have other people working for you?"

"Just Eddie and Bib," he said. "They're married." He nodded as he watched her eyes become wide and apprehensive. "That's right. We'll be alone. I'm a bachelor and there's no staff in the house."

"Well…"

"There'll be a lock on your door," he said after a minute. "When you know me better, you'll see that I'm pretty conventional in my outlook. It's a big house. We'll rattle around like two peas in a pod. It's only on rare occasions that I'm in before bedtime." His dark eyes held hers. "And for the record, my taste doesn't run to city girls."

That sounded as if there was a good reason for his taste in women, but she didn't pry. "I'll work hard, Mr. Culhane."

"My name is Everett," he said, watching her. "Or Rett, if you prefer. You can cook meals and do the laundry and housekeeping. And when you have time, you can work in what passes for my office. Wages won't be much. I can pay the bills, and that's about it."

"I don't care about getting rich." Meanwhile she was thinking fast, sorely tempted to accept the offer, but afraid of the big, angry man at her side. There were worse things than being alone and without money, and she didn't really know him at all.

He saw the thoughts in her mind. "Jenny Wren," he said softly, "do I look like a mad rapist?"

Hearing her name that way on his lips sent a surge of warmth through her. No one had called her by a pet name since the death of her parents.

"No," she said quietly. "Of course you don't. I'll work for you, Mr. Culhane."

He didn't answer her. He only scanned her face and nodded. Then he started the truck, turned it around, and headed back to the Circle C Ranch.

CHAPTER THREE

Two HOURS LATER, Jennifer was well and truly in residence, to the evident amusement of Everett's two ranch hands. They apparently knew better than to make any snide comments about her presence, but they did seem to find something fascinating about having a young woman around the place.

Jennifer had her own room, with peeling wallpaper, worn blue gingham curtains at the windows, and a faded quilt on the bed. Most of the house was like that. Even the rugs on the floor were faded and worn from use. She'd have given anything to be robust and healthy and have a free hand to redecorate the place. It had such wonderful potential with its long history and simple, uncluttered architecture.

The next morning she slept late, rising to bright sunlight and a strange sense that she belonged there. She hadn't felt that way since her childhood, and couldn't help wondering why. Everett had been polite, but not much more. He wasn't really a welcoming kind of man. But, then, he'd just lost his brother. That must account for his taciturn aloofness.

He was long gone when she went downstairs. She fixed herself a cup of coffee and two pieces of toast and then went to the small room that doubled as his office. As he'd promised the day before, he'd laid out a stack of production records and budget information that needed typing. He'd even put her electric typewriter on a table and plugged it in. There was a stack of white paper beside it, and a note.

"Don't feel obliged to work yourself into a coma the first day," it read. And his bold signature was slashed under the terse sentence. She smiled at the flowing handwriting and the perfect spelling. He was a literate man, at least.

She sat down in her cool blue shirtwaist dress and got to work. Two hours later, she'd made great inroads into the paperwork and was starting a new sheet when Everett's heavy footsteps resounded throughout the house. The door swung open and his dark eyebrows shot straight up.

"Aren't you going to eat lunch?" he asked.

More to the point, wasn't she going to feed him, she thought, and grinned.

"Something funny, Miss King?" he asked.

"Oh, no, boss," she said, leaving the typewriter behind. He was expecting that she'd forgotten his noon meal, but she had a surprise in store for him.

She led him into the kitchen, where two places were set. He stood there staring at the table, scowling, while she put out bread, mayonnaise, some thick ham she'd found in the refrigerator, and a small salad she'd made with a bottled dressing.

"Coffee?" she asked, poised with the pot in her hand.

He nodded, sliding into the place at the head of the table.

She poured it into his thick white mug and then filled her own.

"How did you know I wanted coffee instead of tea?" he asked with a narrow gaze as she seated herself beside him.

"Because the coffee cannister was half empty and the tea had hardly been touched," she replied with a smile.

He chuckled softly as he sipped the black liquid. "Not bad," he murmured, glancing at her.

"I'm sorry about breakfast," she said. "I usually wake up around six, but this morning I was kind of tired."

"No problem," he told her, reaching for bread. "I'm used to getting my own breakfast."

"What do you have?"

"Coffee."

She gaped at him. "Coffee?"

He shrugged. "Eggs bounce, bacon's half raw, and the toast hides under some black stuff. Coffee's better."

Her eyes danced as he put some salad on her plate. "I guess so. I'll try to wake up on time tomorrow."

"Don't rush it," he said, glancing at her with a slight frown. "You look puny to me."

"Most people would look puny compared to you," she replied.

"Have you always been that thin?" he persisted.

"No. Not until I got pneumonia," she said. "I just went straight downhill. I suppose I just kept pushing too hard. It caught up with me."

"How's the paperwork coming along?"

"Oh, I'm doing fine," she said. "Your handwriting is very clear. I've had some correspondence to type for doctors that required translation."

"Who did you get to translate?"

She grinned. "The nearest pharmacist. They have experience, you see."

He smiled at her briefly before he bit into his sandwich. He made a second one, but she noticed that he ignored the salad.

"Don't you want some of this?" she asked, indicating the salad bowl.

"I'm not a rabbit," he informed her.

"It's very good for you."

"So is liver, I'm told, but I won't eat that either." He finished his sandwich and got up to pour himself another cup of coffee.

"Then why do you keep lettuce and tomatoes?"

He glanced at her. "I like it on sandwiches."

This was a great time to tell her, after she'd used it all up in the salad. Just like a man...

"You could have dug it out of here," she said weakly.

He cocked an eyebrow. "With salad dressing all over it?"

"You could scrape it off..."

"I don't like broccoli or cauliflower, and never fix creamed beef," he added. "I'm more or less a meat and potatoes man."

"I'll sure remember that from now on, Mr. Culhane," she promised. "I'll be careful to use potatoes instead of apples in the pie I'm fixing for supper."

He glared at her. "Funny girl. Why don't you go on the stage?"

"Because you'd starve to death and weigh heavily on my conscience," she promised. "Some man named Brickmayer called and asked did you have a farrier's hammer he could borrow." She glanced up. "What's a farrier?"

He burst out laughing. "A farrier is a man who shoes horses."

"I'd like a horse," she sighed. "I'd put him in saddle oxfords."

"Go back to work. But slowly," he added from the doorway. "I don't want you knocking yourself into a sickbed on my account."

"You can count on me, sir," she promised, with a wry glance. "I'm much too afraid of your cooking to ever be at the mercy of it."

He started to say something, turned, and went out the door.

Jennifer spent the rest of the day finishing up the typing. Then she swept and dusted and made supper—a ham-and-egg casserole, biscuits, and cabbage. Supper sat on the table, however, and began to congeal. Eventually, she warmed up a little of it for herself, ate it, put the rest in the refrigerator, and went to bed. She had a feeling it was an omen for the future. He'd mentioned something that first day about rarely being home before bedtime. But couldn't he have warned her at lunch?

She woke up on time her second morning at the ranch. By 6:15 she was moving gracefully around the spacious kitchen in jeans and a green T-shirt. Apparently, Everett didn't mind what she wore, so she might as well be comfortable. She cooked a huge breakfast of fresh sausage, eggs, and biscuits, and made a pot of coffee.

Everything was piping hot and on the table when Everett came into the kitchen in nothing but his undershorts. Barefooted and bare-chested, he was enough to hold any woman's eyes. Jennifer, who'd seen her share of almost-bare men on the beaches, stood against the counter and stared like a starstruck girl. There wasn't an ounce of fat anywhere on that big body and he was covered with thick black hair—all over his chest, his flat stomach, his broad thighs. He was as sensuously male as any leading man on television, and she couldn't drag her fascinated eyes away.

He cocked an eyebrow at her, his eyes faintly amused at what he recognized as shocked fascination. "I thought I heard something moving around down here. It's just as well I took time to climb into my shorts." And he turned away to leave her standing there, gaping after him.

A minute later he was back, whipping a belt around the faded blue denims he'd stepped into. He was still barefooted and bare-chested as he sat down at the table across from her.

"I thought I told you to stay in bed," he said as he reached for a biscuit.

"I was afraid you'd keel over out on the plains and your horse wouldn't be able to toss you onto his back and bring you home." She grinned at his puzzled expression. "Well, that's what Texas horses do in western movies."

He chuckled. "Not my horse. He's barely smart enough to find the barn when he's hungry." He buttered the biscuit. "My aunt used to cook like this," he remarked. "Biscuits as light as air."

"Sometimes they bounce," she warned him. "I got lucky."

He gave her a wary glance. "If these biscuits are any indication, so did I," he murmured.

"I saw a henhouse out back. Do I gather the eggs every day?"

"Yes, but watch where you put your hand," he cautioned. "Snakes have been known to get in there."

She shuddered delicately, nodding.

They ate in silence for several minutes before he spoke again. "You're a good cook, Jenny."

She grinned. "My mother taught me. She was terrific."

"Are your parents still alive?"

She shook her head, feeling a twinge of nostalgia. "No. They died several months ago, in a plane crash."

"I'm sorry. Were you close?"

"Very." She glanced at him. "Are your parents dead?"

His face closed up. "Yes," he said curtly, and in a tone that didn't encourage further questions.

She looked up again, her eyes involuntarily lingering on his bare chest. She felt his gaze, and abruptly averted her own eyes back to her empty plate.

He got up after a minute and went back to his bedroom. When he came out, he was tucking in a buttoned khaki shirt, and wearing boots as well. "Thanks for breakfast," he said. "Now, how about taking it easy for the rest of the day? I want to be sure you're up to house-work before you pitch in with both hands."

"I won't do anything I'm not able to do," she promised.

"I've got some rope in the barn," he said with soft menace, while his eyes measured her for it.

She stared at him thoughtfully. "I'll be sure to carry a pair of scissors on me."

He was trying not to grin. "My God, you're stubborn."

"Look who's talking."

"I've had lots of practice working cattle," he replied. He picked up his coffee cup and drained it. "From now on, I'll come to the table dressed. Even at six o'clock in the morning."

She looked up, smiling. "You're a nice man, Mr. Culhane," she said. "I'm not a prude, honestly I'm not. It's just that I'm not accustomed to sitting down to break-fast with men. Dressed or undressed."

His dark eyes studied her. "Not liberated, Miss King?" he asked.

She sensed a deeper intent behind that question, but she took it at face value. "I was never unliberated. I'm just old-fashioned."

"So am I, honey. You stick to your guns." He reached for his hat and walked off, whistling.

She was never sure quite how to take what he said. As the days went by, he puzzled her more and more. She noticed him watching her occasionally, when he was in the house and not working with his cattle. But it wasn't a leering kind of look. It was faintly curious and a little protective. She had the odd feeling that he didn't think of her as a woman at all. Not that she found the thought surprising. Her mirror gave her inescapable proof that she had little to attract a man's eyes these days. She was still frail and washed out.

Eddie was the elder of the ranchhands, and Jenny liked him on sight. He was a lot like the boss. He hardly ever smiled, he worked like two men, and he almost never sat down. But Jenny coaxed him into the kitchen with a cold glass of tea at the end of the week, when he brought her the eggs before she could go looking for them.

"Thank you, ma'am. I can sure use this." He sighed, and drained almost the whole glass in a few swallows. "Boss had me fixing fences. Nothing I hate worse than fixing fences," he added with a hard stare.

She tried not to grin. With his jutting chin and short graying whiskers and half-bald head, he did look fierce.

"I appreciate your bringing in the eggs for me," she replied. "I got busy mending curtains and forgot about them."

He shrugged. "It wasn't much," he murmured. He narrowed one eye as he studied her. "You ain't the kind I'd expect the boss to hire."

Her eyebrows arched and she did grin this time. "What would you expect?"

He cleared his throat. "Well, the boss being the way he is...an older lady with a mean temper." He moved restlessly in the chair he was straddling. "Well, it takes a mean temper to deal with him. I know, I been doin' it for nigh on twenty years."

"Has he owned the Circle C for that long?" she asked.

"He ain't old enough," he reminded her. "I mean, I knowed him that long. He used to hang around here with his Uncle Ben when he was just a tadpole. His parents never had much use for him. His mama run off with some man when he was ten and his daddy drank hisself to death."

It was like having the pins knocked out from under her. She could imagine Everett at ten, with no mother and an alcoholic father. Her eyes mirrored the horror she felt. "His brother must have been just a baby," she burst out.

"He was. Old Ben and Miss Emma took him in. But Everett weren't so lucky. He had to stay with his daddy."

She studied him quietly, and filled the tea glass again. "Why doesn't he like city women?"

"He got mixed up with some social-climbing lady from Houston," he said curtly. "Anybody could have seen she wouldn't fit in here, except Everett. He'd just inherited the place and had these big dreams of making a fortune in cattle. The fool woman listened to the dreams and came harking out here with him one summer." He laughed bitterly. "Took her all of five minutes to give Everett back his ring and tell him what she thought of his plans. Everett got drunk that night, first time I ever knew him to take a drink of anything stronger than beer. And that was the last time he brought a woman here. Until you come along, at least."

She sat back down, all too aware of the faded yellow shirt and casual jeans she was wearing. The shirt was Everett's. She'd borrowed it while she washed her own in the ancient chugging washing machine. "Don't look at me like a contender," she laughed, tossing back her long dark-blond hair. "I'm just a hanger-on myself, not a chic city woman."

"For a hanger-on," he observed, indicating the scrubbed floors and clean, pressed curtains at the windows and the food cooking on the stove, "you do get through a power of work."

"I like housework," she told him. She sipped her own tea. "I used to fix up houses for a living, until it got too much for me. I got frail during the winter and I haven't quite picked back up yet."

"That accent of yours throws me," he muttered. "Sounds like a lot of Southern mixed up with Yankee."

She laughed again. "I'm from Georgia. Smart man, aren't you?"

"Not so smart, lady, or I'd be rich, too," he said with a rare grin. He got up. "Well, I better get back to work. The boss don't hold with us lollygagging on his time, and Bib's waiting for me to help him move cattle."

"Thanks again for bringing my eggs," she said.

He nodded. "No trouble."

She watched him go, sipping her own tea. There were a lot of things about Everett Culhane that were beginning to make sense. She felt that she understood him a lot better now, right down to the black moods that made him walk around brooding sometimes in the evening.

It was just after dark when Everett came in, and Jenny put the cornbread in the oven to warm the minute she heard the old pickup coming up the driveway. She'd learned that Everett Culhane didn't work banker's hours. He went out at dawn and might not come home until bedtime. But he had yet to find himself without a meal. Jenny prided herself in keeping not only his office, but his home, in order.

He tugged off his hat as he came in the back door. He looked even more weary than usual, covered in dust, his eyes dark-shadowed, his face needing a shave.

She glanced up from the pot of chili she was just taking off the stove and smiled. "Hi, boss. How about some chili and Mexican cornbread?"

"I'm hungry enough to even eat one of those damned salads," he said, glancing toward the stove. He was still wearing his chaps and the leather had a fine layer of dust over it. So did his arms and his dark face.

"If you'll sit down, I'll feed you."

"I need a bath first, honey," he remarked.

"You could rinse off your face and hands in the sink," she suggested, gesturing toward it. "There's a hand towel there, and some soap. You look like you might go to sleep in the shower."

He lifted an eyebrow. "I can just see you pulling me out."

She turned away. "I'd call Eddie or Bib."

"And if you couldn't find them?" he persisted, shedding the chaps on the floor.

"In that case," she said dryly, "I reckon you'd drown, tall man."

"Sassy lady," he accused. He moved behind her and suddenly caught her by the waist with his lean, dark hands. He held her in front of him while he bent over her shoulder to smell the chili. She tried to breathe normally and failed. He was warm and strong at her back, and he smelled of the whole outdoors. She wanted to reach up and kiss that hard, masculine face, and her heart leaped at the uncharacteristic longing.

"What did you put in there?" he asked.

"One armadillo, two rattlers, a quart of beans, some tomatoes, and a hatful of jalapeño peppers."

His hands contracted, making her jump. "A hatful of jalapeño peppers would take the rust off my truck."

"Probably the tires, too," she commented, trying to keep her voice steady. "But Bib told me you Texans like your chili hot."

He turned her around to face him. He searched her eyes for a long, taut moment, and she felt her feet melting into the floor as she looked back. Something seemed to link them for that tiny space of time, joining them soul to soul for one explosive second. She heard him catch his breath and then she was free, all too soon.

"Would…would you like a glass of milk with this?" she asked after she'd served the chili into bowls and put it on the table, along with the sliced cornbread and some canned fruit.

"Didn't you make coffee?" he asked, glancing up.

"Sure. I just thought…"

"I don't need anything to put out the fire," he told her with a wicked smile. "I'm not a tenderfoot from *Jawja*."

She moved to the coffeepot and poured two cups. She set his in front of him and sat down. "For your information, suh," she drawled, "we Georgians have been known to eat rattlesnakes while they were still wiggling. And an aunt of mine makes a barbecued sparerib dish that makes Texas chili taste like oatmeal by comparison."

"Is that so? Let's see." He dipped into his chili, savored it, put the spoon down, and glared at her. "You call this hot?" he asked.

She tasted hers and went into coughing spasms. While she was fanning her mouth wildly, he got up with a weary sigh, went to the cupboard, got a glass, and filled it with cold milk.

He handed it to her and sat back down, with a bottle of Tabasco sauce in his free hand. While she gulped milk, he poured half the contents of the bottle into his chili and then tasted it again.

"Just right." He grinned. "But next time, honey, it wouldn't hurt to add another handful of those peppers."

She made a sound between a moan and a gasp and drained the milk glass.

"Now, what were you saying about barbecued spareribs making chili taste like oatmeal?" he asked politely. "I especially liked the part about the rattlers..."

"Would you pass the cornbread, please?" she asked proudly.

"Don't you want the rest of your chili?" he returned.

"I'll eat it later," she said. "I made an apple pie for dessert."

He stifled a smile as he dug into his own chili. It got bigger when she shifted her chair so that she didn't have to watch him eat it.

CHAPTER FOUR

IT HAD BEEN a long time since Jennifer had been on a horse, but once Everett decided that she was going riding with him one morning, it was useless to argue.

"I'll fall off," she grumbled as she stared up at the palomino gelding he'd chosen for her. "Besides, I've got work to do."

"You've ironed every curtain in the house, washed everything that isn't tied down, scrubbed all the floors, and finished my paperwork. What's left?" he asked, hands low on his hips, his eyes mocking.

"I haven't started supper," she said victoriously.

"So we'll eat late," he replied. "Now, get on."

With a hard glare, she let him put her into the saddle. She was still weak, but her hair had begun to regain its earlier luster and her spirit was returning with a vengeance.

"Were you always so domineering, or did you take lessons?" she asked.

"It sort of comes naturally out here, honey," he told her with a hard laugh. "You either get tough or you go broke."

His eyes ran over her, from her short-sleeved button-up blue print blouse down to the legs of her worn jeans, and he frowned. "You could use some more clothes," he observed.

"I used to have a closetful," she sighed. "But in recent months my clothing budget has been pretty small. Anyway, I don't need to dress up around here, do I?"

"You could use a pair of new jeans, at least," he said. His lean hand slid along her thigh gently, where the material was almost see-through, and the touch quickened her pulse.

"Yours aren't much better," she protested, glancing down from his denim shirt to the jeans that outlined his powerful legs.

"I wear mine out fast," he reminded her. "Ranching is tough on clothes."

She knew that, having had to get four layers of mud off his several times. "Well, I don't put mine to the same use. I don't fix fences and pull calves and vet cattle."

He lifted an eyebrow. His hand was still resting absently on her thin leg. "You work hard enough. If I didn't already know it, I'd be told twice a day by Eddie or Bib."

"I like your men," she said.

"They like you. So do I," he added on a smile. "You brighten up the place."

But not as a woman, she thought, watching him. He was completely unaware of her sexually. Even when his eyes did wander over her, it was in an indifferent way. It disturbed her, oddly enough, that he didn't see her as a woman. Because she sure did see him as a man. That sensuous physique was playing on her nerves even now as she glanced down at it with a helpless appreciation.

"All we need is a violin," she murmured, grinning.

He stared up at her, but he didn't smile. "Your hair seems lighter," he remarked.

The oddest kind of pleasure swept through her. He'd noticed. She'd just washed it, and the dullness was leaving it. It shimmered with silvery lights where it peeked out from under her hat.

"I just washed it," she remarked.

He shook his head. "It never looked that way before."

"I wasn't healthy before," she returned. "I feel so much better out here," she remarked, sighing as she looked around, with happiness shining out of her like a beacon. "Oh, what a marvelous view! Poor city people."

He turned away and mounted his buckskin gelding. "Come on. I'll show you the bottoms. That's where I've got my new stock."

"Does it flood when it rains?" she asked. It was hard getting into the rhythm of the horse, but somehow she managed it.

"Yes, ma'am, it does," he assured her in a grim tone. "Uncle Ben lost thirty head in a flood when I was a boy. I watched them wash away. Incredible, the force of the water when it's unleashed."

"It used to flood back home sometimes," she observed.

"Yes, but not like it does out here," he commented. "Wait until you've seen a Texas rainstorm, and you'll know what I mean."

"I grew up reading Zane Grey," she informed him. "I know all about dry washes and flash floods and stampeding."

"Zane Grey?" he asked, staring at her. "Well, I'll be."

"I told you I loved Texas," she said with a quick smile. She closed her eyes, letting the horse pick its own way beside his. "Just breathe that air," she said lazily. "Rett, I'll bet if you bottled it, you could get rich overnight!"

"I could get rich overnight by selling off oil leases if I wanted to," he said curtly. He lit a cigarette, without looking at her.

She felt as if she'd offended him. "Sorry," she murmured. "Did I hit a nerve?"

"A raw one," he agreed, glancing at her. "Bobby was forever after me about those leases."

"He never won," she said, grinning. "Did he?"

His broad shoulders shifted. "I thought about it once or twice, when times got hard. But it's like a cop-out. I want to make this place pay with cattle, not oil. I don't want my land tied up in oil rigs and pumps cluttering up my landscape." He gestured toward the horizon. "Not too far out there, Apaches used to camp. Santa Ana's troops cut through part of this property on their way to the Alamo. After that, the local cattlemen pooled their cattle here to start them up the Chisolm Trail. During the Civil War, Confederates passed through on their way to Mexico. There's one hell of a lot of history here, and I don't want to spoil it."

She was watching him when he spoke, and her eyes involuntarily lingered on his strong jaw, his sensuous mouth. "Yes," she said softly, "I can understand that."

He glanced at her over his cigarette and smiled. "Where did you grow up?" he asked curiously.

"In a small town in south Georgia," she recalled. "Edison, by name. It wasn't a big place, but it had a big heart. Open fields and lots of pines and a flat horizon like this out beyond it. It's mostly agricultural land there, with huge farms. My grandfather's was very small. Back in his day, it was cotton. Now it's peanuts and soybeans."

"How long did you live there?"

"Until I was around ten," she recalled. "Dad got a job in Atlanta, and we moved there. We lived better, but I never liked it as much as home."

"What did your father do?"

"He was an architect," she said, smiling. "A very good one, too. He added a lot to the city's skyline in his day." She glanced at him. "Your father…"

"I don't discuss him," he said matter-of-factly, with a level stare.

"Why?"

He drew in an impatient breath and reined in his horse to light another cigarette. He was chain smoking, something he rarely did. "I said, I don't discuss him."

"Sorry, boss," she replied, pulling her hat down over her eyes in an excellent imitation of tall, lean Bib as she mimicked his drawl. "I shore didn't mean to rile you."

His lips tugged up. He blew out a cloud of smoke and flexed his broad shoulders, rippling the fabric that covered them. "My father was an alcoholic, Jenny."

She knew that already, but she wasn't about to give Eddie away. Everett wouldn't like being gossiped about by his employees. "It must have been a rough childhood for you and Robert," she said innocently.

"Bobby was raised by Uncle Ben and Aunt Emma," he said. "Bobby and I inherited this place from them. They were fine people. Ben spent his life fighting to hold this property. It was a struggle for him to pay taxes. I helped him get into breeding Herefords when I moved in with them. I was just a green kid," he recalled, "all big ears and feet and gigantic ideas. Fifteen, and I had all the answers." He sighed, blowing out another cloud of smoke. "Now I'm almost thirty-five, and every day I come up short of new answers."

"Don't we all?" Jennifer said with a smile. "I was lucky, I suppose. My parents loved each other, and me, and we were well-off. I didn't appreciate it at the time. When I lost them it was a staggering blow." She leaned forward in the saddle to gaze at the horizon. "How about your mother?"

"A desperate woman, completely undomesticated," he said quietly. "She ran off with the first man who offered her an alternative to starvation. An insurance salesman," he scoffed. "Bobby was just a baby. She walked out the door and never looked back."

"I can't imagine a woman that callous," she said, glancing at him. "Do you ever hear from her now? Is she still alive?"

"I don't know. I don't care." He lifted the cigarette to his chiseled lips. His eyes cut around to meet hers, and they were cold with memory and pain. "I don't much like women."

She felt the impact of the statement to her toes. She knew why he didn't like women, that was the problem, but she was too intelligent to think that she could pry that far, to mention the city woman who'd dumped him because he was poor.

"It would have left scars, I imagine," she agreed.

"Let's ride." He stuck the cigarette between his lips and urged his mount into a gallop.

Riding beside him without difficulty now, Jennifer felt alive and vital. He was such a devastating man, she thought, glancing at him, so sensuous even in faded jeans and shirt. He was powerfully built, like an athlete, and she didn't imagine many men could compete with him.

"Have you ever ridden in rodeo competition?" she asked suddenly without meaning to.

He glanced at her and slowed his mount. "Have I what?"

"Ridden in rodeos?"

He chuckled. "What brought that on?"

"You're so big…"

He stopped his horse and stared at her, his wrists crossed over the pommel of his saddle. "Too big," he returned. "The best riders are lean and wiry."

"Oh."

"But in my younger days, I did some bareback riding and bulldogging. It was fun until I broke my arm in two places."

"I'll bet that slowed you down," she murmured dryly.

"It's about the only thing that ever did." He glanced at her rapt face. Live oaks and feathery mesquite trees and prickly pear cactus and wildflowers filled the long space to the horizon and Jennifer was staring at the landscape as if she'd landed in heaven. There were fences everywhere, enclosing pastures where Everett's white-faced Herefords grazed. The fences were old, graying and knotty and more like posts than neatly cut wood, with barbed wire stretched between them.

"Like what you see?" Everett mused.

"Oh, yes," she sighed. "I can almost see it the way it would have been a hundred and more years ago, when settlers and drovers and cattlemen and gunfighters came through here." She glanced at him. "Did you know that Dr. John Henry Holliday, better known as Doc, hailed from Valdosta, Georgia?" she added. "Or that he went west because the doctors said he'd die of tuberculosis if he didn't find a drier climate quick? Or that he and his cousin were supposed to be married, and when they found out about the TB, he went west and she joined a nunnery in Atlanta? And that he once backed down a gang of cowboys in Dodge City and saved Wyatt Earp's life?"

He burst out laughing. "My God, you do know your history, don't you?"

"There was this fantastic biography of Holliday by John Myers Myers," she told him. "It was the most exciting book I ever read. I wish I had a copy. I tried to get one once, but it was out of print."

"Isn't Holliday buried out West somewhere?" he asked.

"In Glenwood Springs, Colorado," she volunteered. "He had a standing bet that a bullet would get him before the TB did, but he lost. He died in a sanitarium out there. He always said he had the edge in gunfights, because he didn't care if he died—and most men did."

She smiled. "He was a frail little man, not at all the way he's portrayed in films most of the time. He was blond and blue-eyed and most likely had a slow Southern drawl. Gunfighter, gambler, and heavy drinker he might have been, but he had some fine qualities, too, like loyalty and courage."

"We had a few brave men in Texas, too," he said, smoking his cigarette with a grin. "Some of them fought a little battle with a few thousand Mexicans in a Spanish mission in San Antonio."

"Yes, in the Alamo," she said, grinning. "In 1836, and some of those men were from Georgia."

He burst out laughing. "I can't catch you out on anything, can I?"

"I'm proud of my state," she told him. "Even though Texas does feel like home, too. If my grandfather hadn't come back, I might have been born here."

"Why did he go back?" he asked, curious.

"I never knew," she said. "But I expect he got into trouble. He was something of a hell-raiser even when I knew him." She recalled the little old man sitting astride a chair in her mother's kitchen, relating hair-raising escapes from the Germans during World War I while he smoked his pipe. He'd died when she was fourteen, and she still remembered going to Edison for the funeral, to a cemetery near Fort Gaines where Spanish moss fell from the trees. It had been a quiet place, a fitting place for the old gentleman to be laid to rest. In his home country. Under spreading oak trees.

"You miss him," Everett said quietly.

"Yes."

"My Uncle Ben was something like that," he murmured, lifting his eyes to the horizon. "He had a big heart and a black temper. Sometimes it was hard to see the one for the other," he added with a short laugh. "I idolized him. He had nothing, but he bowed to no man. He'd have approved of what I'm doing with this place. He'd have fought the quick money, too. He liked a challenge."

And so, she would have bet, did his nephew. She couldn't picture Everett Culhane liking anything that came too easily. He would have loved living in the nineteenth century, when a man could build an empire.

"You'd have been right at home here in the middle eighteen hundreds," she remarked, putting the thought into words. "Like John Chisum, you'd have built an empire of your own."

"Think so?" he mused. He glanced at her. "What do you think I'm trying to do now?"

"The same thing," she murmured. "And I'd bet you'll succeed."

He looked her over. "Would you?" His eyes caught hers and held them for a long moment before he tossed his cigarette onto the ground and stepped down out of the saddle to grind it under his boot.

A sudden sizzling sound nearby shocked Jennifer, but it did something far worse to the horse she was riding. The gelding suddenly reared up, and when it came back down again it was running wild.

She pulled back feverishly on the reins, but the horse wouldn't break its speed at all. "Whoa!" she yelled into its ear. "Whoa, you stupid animal!"

Finally, she leaned forward and hung on to the reins and the horse's mane at the same time, holding on with her knees as well. It was a wild ride, and she didn't have time to worry about whether or not she was going to survive it. In the back of her mind she recalled Everett's sudden shout, but nothing registered after that.

The wind bit into her face, her hair came loose from its neat bun. She closed her eyes and began to pray. The jolting pressure was hurting, actually jarring her bones. If only she could keep from falling off!

She heard a second horse gaining on them, then, and she knew that everything would be all right. All she had to do was hold on until Everett could get to her.

But at that moment, the runaway gelding came to a fence and suddenly began to slow down. He balked at the fence, but Jennifer didn't. She sailed right over the animal's head to land roughly on her back in the pasture on the other side of the barbed wire.

The breath was completely knocked out of her. She lay there staring up at leaves and blue sky, feeling as if she'd never get a lungful of air again.

Nearby, Everett was cursing steadily, using words she'd never heard before, even from angry clients back in New York City. She saw his face come slowly into focus above her and was fascinated by its paleness. His eyes were colorful enough, though, like brown flames glittering at her.

"Not…my…fault," she managed to protest in a thin voice.

"I know that," he growled. "It was mine. Damned rattler, and me without my gun…"

"It didn't…bite you?" she asked apprehensively, her eyes widening with fear.

He blew out a short breath and chuckled. "No, it didn't. Sweet Jenny. Half dead in a fall, and you're worried about me. You're one in a million, honey."

He bent down beside her. "Hurt anywhere?" he asked gently.

"All over," she said. "Can't get…my breath."

"I'm not surprised. Damned horse. We'll put him in your next batch of chili, I promise," he said on a faint smile. "Let's see how much damage you did."

His lean, hard hands ran up and down her legs and arms, feeling for breaks. "How about your back?" he asked, busy with his task.

"Can't…feel it yet."

"You will," he promised ruefully.

She was still just trying to breathe. She'd heard of people having the breath knocked out of them, but never knew what it was until now. Her eyes searched Everett's quietly.

"Am I dead?" she asked politely.

"Not quite." He brushed the hair away from her cheeks. "Feel like sitting up?"

"If you'll give me a hand, I'll try," she said huskily.

He raised her up and that was when she noticed that her blouse had lost several buttons, leaving her chest quite exposed. And today of all days she hadn't worn a bra.

Her hands went protectively to the white curves of her breasts, which were barely covered.

"None of that," he chided. "We don't have that kind

of relationship. I'm not going to embarrass you by staring. Now get up."

That was almost the final blow. Even half dressed, he still couldn't accept her as a woman. She wanted to sit down on the grass and bawl. It wouldn't have done any good, but it might have eased the sudden ache in her heart.

She let him help her to her feet and staggered unsteadily on them. Her pale eyes glanced toward the gelding, now happily grazing in the pasture across the fence.

"First," she sputtered, "I'm going to dig a deep pit. Then I'm going to fill it with six-foot rattlesnakes. Then I'm going to get a backhoe and shove that stupid horse in there!"

"Wouldn't you rather eat him?" he offered.

"On second thought, I'll gain weight," she muttered. "Lots of it. And I'll ride him two hours every morning."

"You could use a few pounds," he observed, studying her thinness. "You're almost frail."

"I'm not," she argued. "I'm just puny, remember? I'll get better."

"I guess you already have," he murmured dryly. "You sure do get through the housework."

"Slowly but surely," she agreed. She tugged her blouse together and tied the bottom edges together.

When she looked back up, his eyes were watching her hands with a strange, intent stare. He looked up and met her puzzled gaze.

"Are you okay now?" he asked.

"Just a little shaky," she murmured with a slight grin.

"Come here." He bent and lifted her easily into his

arms, shifting her weight as he turned, and walked toward the nearby gate in the fence.

She was shocked by her reaction to being carried by him. She felt ripples of pleasure washing over her body like fire, burning where his chest touched her soft breasts. Even through two layers of fabric, the contact was wildly arousing, exciting. She clamped her teeth together hard to keep from giving in to the urge to grind her body against his. He was a man, after all, and not invulnerable. She could start something that she couldn't stop.

"I'm too heavy," she protested once.

"No," he said gently, glancing down into her eyes unsmilingly. "You're like feathers. Much too light."

"Most women would seem light to you," she murmured, lowering her eyes to his shirt. Where the top buttons were undone, she saw the white of his T-shirt and the curl of dark, thick hair. He smelled of leather and wind and tobacco and she wanted so desperately to curl up next to him and kiss that hard, chiseled mouth...

"Open the gate," he said, nodding toward the latch.

She reached out and unfastened it, and pushed until it came free of the post. He went through and let her fasten it again. When she finished, she noticed that his gaze had fallen to her body. She followed it, embarrassed to find that the edges of her blouse gapped so much, that one creamy pink breast was completely bare to his eyes.

Her hand went slowly to the fabric, tugging it into place. "Sorry," she whispered self-consciously.

"So am I. I didn't mean to stare," he said quietly,

shifting her closer to his chest. "Don't be embarrassed, Jenny."

She drew in a slow breath, burying her red face in his throat. He stiffened before he drew her even closer, his arms tautening until she was crushed to his broad, warm chest.

He didn't say a word as he walked, and neither did she. But she could feel the hard beat of his heart, the ragged sigh of his breath, the stiffening of his body against her taut breasts. In ways she'd never expected, her body sang to her, exquisite songs of unknown pleasure, of soft touches and wild contact. Her hands clung to Everett's neck, her eyes closed. She wanted this to last forever.

All too soon, they reached the horses. Everett let her slide down his body in a much too arousing way, so that she could feel the impact of every single inch of him on the way to the ground. And then, his arms contracted, holding her, bringing her into the length of him, while his cheek rested on her hair and the wind blew softly around them.

She clung, feeling the muscles of his back tense under her hands, loving the strength and warmth and scent of him. She'd never wanted anything so much as she wanted this closeness. It was sweet and heady and satisfying in a wild new way.

Seconds later, he let her go, just as she imagined she felt a fine tremor in his arms.

"Are you all right?" he asked softly.

"Yes," she said, trying to smile, but she couldn't look up at him. It had been intimate, that embrace. As intimate as a kiss in some ways, and it had caused an un-expected shift in their relationship.

"We'd better get back," he said. "I've got work to do."

"So have I," she said quickly, mounting the gelding with more apprehension than courage. "All right, you ugly horse," she told it. "You do that to me again, and I'll back the pickup truck over you!"

The horse's ears perked up and it moved its head slightly to one side. She burst into laughter. "See, Rett, he heard me!"

But Everett wasn't looking her way. He'd already turned his mount and was smoking another cigarette. And all the way back to the house, he didn't say a word.

As they reached the yard she felt uncomfortably tense. To break the silence, she broached a subject she'd had on her mind all day.

"Rett, could I have a bucket of paint?"

He stared at her. "What?"

"Can I have a bucket of paint?" she asked. "Just one. I want to paint the kitchen."

"Now, look, lady," he said, "I hired you to cook and do housework and type." His eyes narrowed and she fought not to let her fallen spirits show. "I like my house the way it is, with no changes."

"Just one little bucket of paint," she murmured.

"No."

She glared at him, but he glared back just as hard. "If you want to spend money," he said curtly, "I'll buy you a new pair of jeans. But we aren't throwing money away on decorating." He made the word sound insulting.

"Decorating is an art," she returned, defending her

professional integrity. She was about to tell him what she'd done for a living, but as she opened her mouth, he was speaking again.

"It's a high-class con game," he returned hotly. "And even if I had the money, I wouldn't turn one of those fools loose on my house. Imagine paying out good money to let some tasteless idiot wreck your home and charge you a fortune to do it!" He leaned forward in the saddle with a belligerent stare. "No paint. Do we understand each other, Miss King?"

Do we ever, she thought furiously. Her head lifted. "You'd be lucky to get a real decorator in here, anyway," she flung back. "One who wouldn't faint at the way you combine beautiful old oriental rugs with ashtrays made of old dead rattlesnakes!"

His dark eyes glittered dangerously. "It's my house," he said coldly.

"Thank God!" she threw back.

"If you don't like it, close your eyes!" he said. "Or pack your damned bag and go back to Atlanta and turn your nose up..."

"I'm not turning my nose up!" she shouted. "I just wanted a bucket of paint!"

"You know when you'll get it, too, don't you?" he taunted. He tipped his hat and rode off, leaving her fuming on the steps.

Yes, she knew. His eyes had told her, graphically. When hell froze over. She remembered in the back of her mind that there was a place called Hell, and once it did freeze over and made national headlines. She only wished she'd saved the newspaper clipping. She'd shove it under his arrogant nose, and maybe then she'd get her paint!

She turned to go into the house, stunned to find Eddie coming out the front door.

He looked red-faced, but he doffed his hat. "Mornin', ma'am," he murmured. "I was just putting the mail on the table."

"Thanks, Eddie," she said with a wan smile.

He stared at her. "Boss lost his temper, I see."

"Yep," she agreed.

"Been a number of days before when he's done that."

"Yep."

"You going to keep it all to yourself, too, ain't you?"

"Yep."

He chuckled, tipped his hat, and went on down the steps. She walked into the house and burst out laughing. She was getting the hang of speaking Texan at last.

CHAPTER FIVE

JENNIFER SPENT THE rest of the day feverishly washing down the kitchen walls. So decorators were con artists, were they? And he wouldn't turn one loose in his home, huh? She was so enraged that the mammoth job took hardly any time at all. Fortunately, the walls had been done with oil-based paint, so the dirt and grease came off without taking the paint along with them. When she was through, she stood back, worn out and damp with sweat, to survey her handiwork. She had the fan going full blast, but it was still hot and sticky, and she felt the same way herself. The pale yellow walls looked new, making the effort worthwhile.

Now, she thought wistfully, if she only had a few dollars' worth of fabric and some thread, and the use of the aging sewing machine upstairs, she could make curtains for the windows. She could even buy that out of her own pocket, and the interior-decorator-hating Mr. Everett Donald Culhane could just keep his nasty opinions to himself. She laughed, wondering what he'd have said if she'd used his full name while they were riding. Bib had told her his middle name. She wondered if anyone ever called him Donald.

She fixed a light supper of creamed beef and broccoli, remembering that he'd told her he hated both of those dishes. She deliberately made weak coffee. Then she sat down in the kitchen and pared apples while she waited for him to come home. Con artist, huh?

It was getting dark when he walked in the door. He was muddy and tired-looking, and in his lean, dark hand was a small bouquet of slightly wilted wildflowers.

"Here," he said gruffly, tossing them onto the kitchen table beside her coffee cup. The mad profusion of bluebonnets and Indian paintbrush and Mexican hat made blue and orange and red swirls of color on the white tablecloth. "And you can have your damned bucket of paint."

He strode past her toward the staircase, his face hard and unyielding, without looking back. She burst into tears, her fingers trembling as they touched the unexpected gift.

Never in her life had she moved so fast. She dried her tears and ran to pour out the pot of weak coffee. She put on a pot of strong, black coffee and dragged out bacon and eggs and flour, then put the broccoli and chipped beef, covered, into the refrigerator.

By the time Everett came back down, showered and in clean denims, she had bacon and eggs and biscuits on the table.

"I thought you might like something fresh and hot for supper," she said quickly.

He glanced at her as he sat down. "I'm surprised. I was expecting liver and onions or broccoli tonight."

She flushed and turned her back. "Were you? How strange." She got the coffeepot and calmly filled his cup and her own. "Thank you for my flowers," she said without looking at him.

"Don't start getting ideas, Miss King," he said curtly, reaching for a biscuit. "Just because I backed down on the paint, don't expect it to become a habit around here."

She lowered her eyes demurely to the platter of eggs she was dishing up. "Oh, no, sir," she said.

He glanced around the room and his eyes darkened, glittered. They came back to her. He laid down his knife. "Did you go ahead and buy paint?" he asked in a softly menacing tone.

"No, I did not," she replied curtly. "I washed down the walls."

He blinked. "Washed down the walls?" He looked around again, scowling. "In this heat?"

"Look good, don't they?" she asked fiercely, smiling. "I don't need the paint, but thank you anyway."

He picked up his fork, lifting a mouthful of eggs slowly to his mouth. He finished his supper before he spoke again. "Why did it matter so much about the walls?" he asked. "The house is old. It needs thousands of dollars' worth of things I can't afford to have done. Painting one room is only going to make the others look worse."

She shrugged. "Old habits," she murmured with a faint smile. "I've been fixing up houses for a long time."

That went right past him. He looked preoccupied. Dark and brooding.

"Is something wrong?" she asked suddenly.

He sighed and pulled an envelope from his pocket

and tossed it onto the table. "I found that on the hall table on my way upstairs."

She frowned. "What is it?"

"A notice that the first payment is due on the note I signed at the bank for my new bull." He laughed shortly. "I can't meet it. My tractor broke down and I had to use the money for the payment to fix it. Can't plant without the tractor. Can't feed livestock without growing feed. Ironically, I may have to sell the bull to pay back the money."

Her heart went out to him. Here she sat giving him the devil over a bucket of paint, and he was in serious trouble. She felt terrible.

"I ought to be shot," she murmured quietly. "I'm sorry I made such a fuss about the paint, Rett."

He laughed without humor. "You didn't know. I told you times were hard."

"Yes. But I didn't realize how hard until now." She sipped her coffee. "How much do you need...can I ask?" she asked softly.

He sighed. "Six hundred dollars." He shook his head. "I thought I could swing it, I really did. I wanted to pay it off fast."

"I've got last week's salary," she said. "I haven't spent any of it. That would help a little. And you could hold back this week's..."

He stared into her wide, soft eyes and smiled. "You're quite a girl, Jenny."

"I want to help."

"I know. I appreciate it. But spend your money on yourself. At any rate, honey, it would hardly be a drop in the bucket. I've got a few days to work it out. I'll turn up something."

He got up and left the table and Jennifer stared after him, frowning. Well, she could help. There had to be an interior-design firm in Houston, which was closer than San Antonio or Austin. She'd go into town and offer her services. With any luck at all, they'd be glad of her expert help. She could make enough on one job to buy Everett's blessed bull outright. She was strong enough now to take on the challenge of a single job. And she would!

As luck would have it, the next morning Eddie mentioned that his wife, Libby, was going to drive into the city to buy a party dress for his daughter. Jennifer hitched a ride with her after Everett went to work.

Libby was a talker, a blond bearcat of a woman with a fine sense of humor. She was good company, and Jennifer took to her immediately.

"I'm so glad Everett's got you to help around the house," she said as they drove up the long highway to Houston. "I offered, but he wouldn't hear of it. Said I had enough to do, what with raising four kids. He even looks better since you've been around. And he doesn't cuss as much." She grinned.

"I was so delighted to have the job," Jennifer sighed, smiling. She brushed back a stray wisp of blond hair. She was wearing her best blue camisole with a simple navy blue skirt and her polished white sling pumps with a white purse. She looked elegant, and Libby remarked on it.

"Where are you going, all dressed up?" she asked.

"To get a second job," Jennifer confessed. "But you mustn't tell Everett. I want to surprise him."

Libby looked worried. "You're not leaving?"

"Oh, no! Not until he makes me! This is only a temporary thing," she promised.

"Doing what?"

"Decorating."

"That takes a lot of schooling, doesn't it?" Libby asked, frowning.

"Quite a lot. I graduated from interior-design school in New York," Jennifer explained. "And I worked in the field for two years. My health gave out and I had to give it up for a while." She sighed. "There was so much pressure, you see. So much competition. My nerves got raw and my resistance got low, and I wound up flat on my back in a hospital with pneumonia. I went home to Atlanta to recuperate, got a job with a temporary talent agency, and met Robert Culhane on an assignment. He offered me a job, and I grabbed it. Getting to work in Texas was pretty close to heaven, for me."

Libby shook her head. "Imagine that."

"I was sorry about Robert," Jennifer said quietly. "I only knew him slightly, but I did like him. Everett still broods about it. He doesn't say much, but I know he misses his brother."

"He was forever looking out for Bobby," Libby confirmed. "Protecting him and such. A lot of the time, Bobby didn't appreciate that. And Bobby didn't like living low. He wanted Everett to sell off those oil rights and get rich. Everett wouldn't."

"I don't blame him," Jennifer said. "If it was my land, I'd feel the same way."

Libby looked surprised. "My goodness, another one."

"I don't like strip-mining, either," Jennifer offered. "Or killing baby seals for their fur or polluting the rivers."

Libby burst out laughing. "You and Everett were made for each other. He's just that way himself." She glanced at Jennifer as the Houston skyline came into view. "Did Bobby tell you what Everett did the day the oil man came out here to make him that offer, after the geologists found what they believed was oil-bearing land?"

"No."

"The little oil man wanted to argue about it, and Everett had just been thrown by a horse he was trying to saddle-break and was in a mean temper. He told the man to cut it off, and he wouldn't. So Everett picked him up," she said, grinning, "carried him out to his car, put him in, and walked away. We haven't seen any oil men at the ranch since."

Jennifer laughed. It sounded like Everett, all right. She sat back, sighing, and wondered how she was going to make him take the money she hoped to earn. Well, that worry could wait in line. First, she had to find a job.

While Libby went into the store, Jennifer found a telephone directory and looked up the addresses of two design shops. The first one was nearby, so she stopped to arrange a time and place to rendezvous with Libby that afternoon, and walked the two blocks.

She waited for fifteen minutes to see the man who

owned the shop. He listened politely, but impatiently, while she gave her background. She mentioned the name of the firm she'd worked with in New York, and saw his assistant's eyebrows jump up. But the manager was obviously not impressed. He told her he was sorry but he was overstaffed already.

Crestfallen, she walked out and called a taxi to take her to the next company. This time, she had better luck. The owner was a woman, a veritable Amazon, thin and dark and personable. She gave Jennifer a cup of coffee, listened to her credentials, and grinned.

"Lucky me." She laughed. "To find you just when I was desperate for one more designer!"

"You mean, you can give me work?" Jennifer burst out, delighted.

"Just this one job, right now, but it could work into a full-time position," she promised.

"Part-time would be great. You see, I already have a job I'd rather not leave," Jennifer replied.

"Perfect. You can do this one in days. It's only one room. I'll give you the address, and you can go and see the lady yourself. Where are you staying?"

"Just north of Victoria," Jennifer said. "In Big Spur."

"How lovely!" the lady said. "The job's in Victoria! No transportation problem?"

She thought of asking Libby, and smiled. "I have a conspirator," she murmured. "I think I can manage." She glanced up. "Can you estimate my commission?"

Her new employer did, and Jennifer grinned. It would be more than enough for Everett to pay off his note. "Okay!"

"The client, Mrs. Whitehall, doesn't mind paying for quality work," came the lilting reply. "And she'll be tickled when she hears the background of her designer. I'll give her a ring now, if you like."

"Would I! Miss… Mrs… Ms…?"

"Ms. Sally Ward," the owner volunteered. "I'm glad to meet you, Jennifer King. Now, let's get busy."

Libby was overjoyed when she heard what Jennifer was plotting, and volunteered to drive her back and forth to the home she'd be working on. She even agreed to pinch-hit in the house, so that Everett wouldn't know what was going on. It would be risky, but Jennifer felt it would be very much worth the risk.

As it turned out, Mrs. Whitehall was an elderly lady with an unlimited budget and a garage full of cars. She was more than happy to lend one to Jennifer so that she could drive back and forth to Victoria to get fabric and wallcoverings and to make appointments with painters and carpet-layers.

Jennifer made preliminary drawings after an interview with Mrs. Whitehall, who lived on an enormous estate called Casa Verde.

"My son Jason and his wife, Amanda, used to live with me," Mrs. Whitehall volunteered. "But since their marriage, they've built a house of their own farther down the road. They're expecting their first child. Jason wants a boy and Amanda a girl." She grinned. "From the size of her, I'm expecting twins!"

"When is she due?" Jennifer asked.

"Any day," came the answer. "Jason spends part of the time pacing the floor and the other part dar-

ing Amanda to lift, move, walk, or breathe hard." She
laughed delightedly. "You'd have to know my son, Miss
King, to realize how out of character that is for him.
Jason was always such a calm person until Amanda
got pregnant. I think it's been harder on him than it
has on her."

"Have they been married long?"

"Six years," Mrs. Whitehall said. "So happily. They
wanted a child very much, but it took a long time for
Amanda to become pregnant. It's been all the world to
them, this baby." She stared around the room at the fad-
ing wallpaper and the worn carpet. "I've just put this
room off for so long. Now I don't feel I can wait any
longer to have it done. Once the baby comes, I'll have
so many other things to think of. What do you suggest, my dear?"

"I have some sketches," Jennifer said, drawing out
her portfolio.

Mrs. Whitehall looked over them, sighing. "Just
what I wanted. Just exactly what I wanted." She nodded. "Begin whenever you like, Jennifer. I'll find somewhere else to sit while the workmen are busy."

And so it began. Jennifer spent her mornings at Casa
Verde, supervising the work. Afternoons she worked at
Everett's ranch. And amazingly, she never got caught.

It only took a few days to complete the work. Luckily, she found workmen who were between jobs and
could take on a small project. By the end of the week,
it was finished.

"I can't tell you how impressed I am." Mrs. Whitehall

sighed as she studied the delightful new decor, done in soft green and white and dark green.

"It will be even lovelier when the furniture is delivered tomorrow." Jennifer grinned. "I'm so proud of it. I hope you like it half as much as I do."

"I do, indeed," Mrs. Whitehall said. "I…"

The ringing of the phone halted her. She picked up the extension at her side. "Hello?" She sat up straight. "Yes, Jason! When?" She laughed, covering the receiver. "It's a boy!" She moved her hand. "What are you going to name him? Oh, yes, I like that very much. Joshua Brand Whitehall. Yes, I do. How is Amanda? Yes, she's tough, all right. Dear, I'll be there in thirty minutes. Now you calm down, dear. Yes, I know it isn't every day a man has a son. I'll seen you soon. Yes, dear."

She hung up. "Jason's beside himself," she said, smiling. "He wanted a boy so much. And they can have others. Amanda will get her girl yet. I must rush."

Jennifer stood up. "Congratulations on that new grandbaby," she said. "And I've enjoyed working with you very much."

"I'll drop you off at the ranch on my way," Mrs. Whitehall offered.

"It's a good little way," Jennifer began, wondering how she'd explain it to Everett. Mrs. Whitehall drove a Mercedes-Benz.

"Nonsense." Mrs. Whitehall laughed. "It's no trouble at all. Anyway, I want to talk to you about doing some more rooms. This is delightful. Very creative. I never enjoyed redecorating before, but you make it exciting."

After that, how could Jennifer refuse? She got in the car.

Luckily enough, Everett wasn't in sight when she reached the ranch. Mrs. Whitehall let her out at the steps and Jennifer rushed inside, nervous and wild-eyed. But the house was empty. She almost collapsed with relief. And best of all, on the hall table was an envelope addressed to her from Houston, from the interior-design agency. She tore it open and found a check and a nice letter offering more work. The check was for the amount Everett needed, plus a little. Jennifer endorsed it, grinning, and went in to fix supper.

CHAPTER SIX

EVERETT CAME HOME just before dark, but he didn't come into the house. Jennifer had a light supper ready, just cold cuts and bread so there wouldn't be anything to reheat. When he didn't appear after she heard the truck stop, she went out to look for him.

He was standing by the fence, staring at the big Hereford bull he'd wanted so badly. Jennifer stood on the porch and watched him, her heart aching for him. She'd decided already to cash her check first thing in the morning and give it to him at breakfast. But she wondered if she should mention it now. He looked so alone…

She moved out into the yard, the skirt of her blue shirtwaist dress blowing in the soft, warm breeze.

"Rett?" she called.

He glanced at her briefly. "Waiting supper on me again?" he asked quietly.

"No. I've only made cold cuts." She moved to the fence beside him and stared at the big, burly bull. "He sure is big."

"Yep." He took out a cigarette and lit it, blowing out a cloud of smoke. He looked very western in his worn jeans, batwing chaps, and close-fitting denim shirt, which was open halfway down his chest. He was a sensuous man, and she loved looking at him. Her eyes went up to his hard mouth and she wondered for what seemed the twentieth time how it would feel on her own. That made her burn with embarrassment, and she turned away.

"Suppose I offered you what I've saved?" she asked.

"We've been through all that. No. Thank you," he added. "I can't go deeper in debt, not even to save my bull. I'll just pay off the note and start over. The price of beef is expected to start going up in a few months. I'll stand pat until it does."

"Did anyone ever tell you that you have a double dose of pride?" she asked, exasperated.

He looked down at her, his eyes shadowed in the dusk by the brim of his hat. "Look who's talking about pride, for God's sake," he returned. "Don't I remember that you tried to walk back to town carrying a suitcase and a typewriter in the blazing sun with no hat? I had to threaten to tie you in the truck to get you inside it."

"I knew you didn't want me here," she said simply. "I didn't want to become a nuisance."

"I don't think I can imagine that. You being a nuisance, I mean." He took another draw from the cigarette and crushed it out. "I've had a good offer for the bull from one of my neighbors. He's coming over tomorrow to talk to me about it."

Well, that gave her time to cash the check and make one last effort to convince him, she thought.

"Why are you wearing a dress?" he asked, staring down at her. "Trying to catch my eye, by any chance?"

"Who, me?" she laughed. "As you told me the other day, we don't have that kind of relationship."

"You were holding me pretty hard that day the rattlesnake spooked your horse," he said unexpectedly, and he didn't smile. "And you didn't seem to mind too much that I saw you without your shirt."

She felt the color work its way into her hairline. "I'd better put supper on the...oh!"

He caught her before she could move away and brought her gently against the length of his body. His hand snaked around her waist, holding her there, and the other one spread against her throat, arching it.

"Just stand still," he said gently. "And don't start anything. I know damned good and well you're a virgin. I'm not going to try to seduce you."

Her breath was trapped somewhere below her windpipe. She felt her knees go wobbly as she saw the narrowness of his eyes, the hard lines of his face. She'd wanted it so much, but now that it was happening, she was afraid.

She stilled and let her fingers rest over his shirt, but breathing had become difficult. He felt strong and warm and she wanted to touch his hair-roughened skin. It looked so tantalizing to her innocent eyes.

He was breathing slowly, steadily. His thumb nudged her chin up so that he could look into her eyes. "You let me look at you," he said under his breath. "I've gone half mad remembering that, wondering how many other men have seen you that way."

"No one has," she replied quietly. She couldn't drag her eyes from his. She could feel his breath, taste the smokiness of it, smell the leather and tobacco smells of his big, hard body so close to hers. "Only you."

His chest rose heavily. "Only me?"

"I was career-minded," she said hesitantly. "I didn't want commitment, so I didn't get involved. Everett…"

"No. I don't want to fight." He took her hands and slid them up and down over the hard muscles of his chest. His breathing changed suddenly.

He bent and drew her lower lip down with the soft pressure of his thumb. He fit his own mouth to it with exquisite patience, opening it slowly, tempting it, until she stood very still and closed her eyes.

His free hand brought her body close against his. The other one slowly undid the top two buttons of her dress and moved inside to her throat, her shoulder, her collarbone. His mouth increased its ardent pressure as his fingers spread, and his breathing became suddenly ragged as he arched her body and found the soft rise of her breast with his whole hand.

She gasped and instinctively caught his wrist. But he lifted his mouth and looked into her eyes and slowly shook his head. "You're old enough to be taught this," he said quietly. "I know how delicate you are here," he breathed, brushing his fingers over the thin lace. "I'm going to be very gentle, and you're going to enjoy what I do to you. I promise. Close your eyes, honey."

His mouth found hers again, even as he stopped speaking. It moved tenderly on her trembling lips, nibbling, demanding, in a silence bursting with new sensations and promise.

She clung to his shirtfront, shocked to find that her

legs were trembling against his, that her breath was coming quick enough to be audible. She tried to pull away, but his fingers slid quietly under the bra and found bare, vulnerable skin, and she moaned aloud.

Her nails bit into his chest. "Rett!" she gasped, on fire with hunger and frightened and embarrassed that he could see and feel her reaction to him.

"Shh," he whispered at her mouth, gentling her. "It's all right. It's all right to let me see. You're so sweet, Jenny Wren. Like a bright new penny without a single fingerprint except mine." His mouth touched her closed eyelids, her forehead. His fingers contracted gently, his palm feeling the exquisite tautening of her body as she clung to him and shuddered. "Yes, you like that, don't you?" he breathed. His mouth brushed her eyelids again, her nose, her mouth. "Jenny, put your hand inside my shirt."

His voice was deep and low and tender. She obeyed him blindly, on fire with reckless hunger, needing to touch and taste and feel him. Her hands slid under his shirt and flattened on hair and warm muscle, and he tautened.

"Does that…make you feel the way… I feel?" she whispered shakily, looking up at him.

"Exactly," he whispered back. He moved his hand from her breast to her neck and pressed her face slowly against his bare chest.

She seemed to sense what he wanted. Her mouth touched him there tentatively, shyly, and he moaned. He smelled of faint cologne and tobacco, and she liked the way his hard muscles contracted where she touched them with her hands and her lips. He was all man. All man. And her world was suddenly narrowed to her senses, and Everett.

He took her face in his hands and tilted it, bending to kiss her with a hungry ferocity that would have frightened her minutes before. But she went on tiptoe and linked her arms around his neck and gave him back the kiss, opening her mouth under his to incite him to further intimacy, shivering wildly when he accepted the invitation and his tongue went into the sweet darkness in a slow, hungry tasting.

When he finally released her, he was shaking too. His eyes burned with frustrated desire, his hands framed her face, hot and hard.

"We have to stop. Now."

She took a slow, steadying breath. "Yes."

He took his hands away and moved toward the house, lighting a cigarette eventually after two fumbles.

She followed him, drunk on sensual pleasure, awed by what she'd felt with him, by what she'd let him do. She felt shy when they got into the house, into the light, and she couldn't quite meet his eyes.

"I'll get supper on the table," she said.

He didn't even reply. He followed her into the kitchen, and with brooding dark eyes watched her move around.

She poured coffee and he sat down, still watching her.

Her hands trembled as she put the cream pitcher beside his cup. He caught her fingers, looking up at her with a dark, unsmiling stare.

"Don't start getting self-conscious with me," he said quietly. "I know you've never let another man touch you like that. I'm proud that you let me."

She stared at him, eyes widening. Of all the things she'd expected he might say, that wasn't one of them.

His nostrils flared and his hand contracted. "After supper," he said slowly, holding her eyes, "I'm going to carry you into the living room and lay you down on the sofa. And I'm going to make love to you, in every way I know. And when I get through, you'll shudder at the thought of another man's hands on you."

His eyes were blazing, and her own kindled. Her lips parted. "Rett, I can't…you know."

He nodded. "We won't go that far." His fingers caressed her wrist and his face hardened. "How hungry are you?" he asked under his breath.

Her heart was beating wildly. She looked at him and it was suicide. She felt shaky to her toes.

"Make love to me," she whispered blindly as she reached for him.

He twisted her down across his lap and found her mouth in a single motion. He groaned as he kissed her, his breath sighing out raggedly.

"Oh, God, I need you," he ground out, standing with her in his arms. "I need you so much!"

He turned, still kissing her, and carried her through into the living room, putting her gently down on the worn couch. After giving her a hot stare, he turned and methodically drew all the curtains and closed and locked the door. Then he came back, sitting down so that he was facing her.

"Now," he whispered, bending with trembling hands to the bodice of her dress. "Now, let's see how much damage we can do to each other's self-control, Jenny Wren. I want to look at you until I ache to my toes!"

He unbuttoned it and she sank back against the pillows, watching unprotestingly. He half lifted her and slipped the dress down her arms. Her bra followed it. And then he leaned over her, just looking at the soft mounds he'd uncovered.

His fingers stroked one perfect breast, lingering on the tip until she cried out.

"Does that hurt?" he whispered, looking into her eyes.

She was trembling, and it was hard to talk. "No," she breathed.

He smiled slowly, in a tender, purely masculine way, and repeated the brushing caress. She arched up, and his eyes blazed like dark fires.

"Jenny!" he growled. His fingers held her breasts up to his hard mouth. He took her by surprise, and she moaned wildly as she felt the warm moistness envelop her. Her hands dug into his hair and she dragged his head closer, whimpering as if she were being tortured.

"Not so hard, baby," he whispered raggedly, lifting his head. "You're too delicate for that, Jenny."

"Rett," she moaned, her eyes wild.

"Like this, then," he whispered, bending to grind his mouth into hers. His hand swallowed her, stroking, molding, and she trembled all over as if with a fever, clinging to him, needing something more than this, something closer, something far, far more intimate....

Her hands moved against his chest, trembling as they explored the hard muscles.

"Be still now," he whispered, easing her back into the cushions. "Don't move under me. Just lie still, Jenny Wren, and let me show you…how bodies kiss."

She held her breath as his body moved completely onto hers. She felt the blatant maleness of it, the warmth, the tickle of hair against her soft breasts, the exquisite weight, and her hungry eyes looked straight into his as they joined.

"Oh," she whispered jerkily.

"Sweet, sweet Jenny," he breathed, cupping her face in his hands. "It's like moving on velvet. Do you feel me…all of me?"

"Yes." Her own hands went to his back, found their way under his shirt. "Rett, you're very heavy," she said with a shaky smile.

"Too heavy?" he whispered.

"Oh, no," she said softly. "I…like the way it feels."

"So do I." He bent and kissed her, tenderly, in a new and delicious way. "Not afraid?"

"No."

"You will be," he whispered softly. His hands moved down, sliding under her hips. He lifted his head and looked down at her just as his fingers contracted and ground her hips up into his in an intimacy that made her gasp and cry out.

He shuddered, and she buried her face in his hot throat, dizzy and drowning in deep water, burning with exquisite sensation and blinding pleasure.

"Jenny," he groaned. His hands hurt. "Jenny, Jenny,

if you weren't a virgin, I'd take you. I'd take you, here, now, in every way there is…!"

She barely heard him, she was shaking so badly. All at once, he eased himself down beside her and folded her into his arms in a strangely protective way. His hands smoothed her back, his lips brushed over her face in tiny, warm kisses. All the passion was suddenly gone, and he was comforting her.

"I never believed…what my mother used to say about…passion," Jenny whispered at his ear, still trembling. "Rett, it's exquisite…isn't it? So explosive and sweet and dangerous!"

"You've never wanted a man before?" he breathed.

"No."

"I'll tell you something, Jenny. I've never wanted a woman like this. Not ever." He kissed her ear softly. "I want you to know something. If it ever happened, even accidentally, you'd never want to forget it. I'd take you so tenderly, so slowly, that you'd never know anything about pain."

"Yes, I know that," she murmured, smiling. Her arms tightened. "You could have had me, then, lofty principles and all," she added ruefully. "I didn't realize how easy it was to throw reason to the wind."

"You're a very passionate woman." He lifted his head and searched her eyes. "I didn't expect that."

"You didn't seem much like a passionate man either," she confessed, letting her eyes wander slowly over his hard, dark face. "Oh, Rett, I did want you in the most frightening way!"

His chest expanded roughly. "Jenny, I think we'd

better get up from here. My good intentions only seem to last until I get half your clothes off."

She watched him draw away, watched how his eyes clung to her bare breasts, and she smiled and arched gently.

"Oh, God, don't do that!" he whispered, shaken, as he turned away.

She laughed delightedly and sat up, getting back into her clothes as she stared at his broad back. He was smoking a cigarette, running a restless hand through his hair. And he was the handsomest man she'd ever seen in her life. And the most... loved.

I love you, she thought dreamily. I love every line and curve and impatient gesture you make. I'd rather live here, in poverty, with you than to have the world in the bank.

"I'm decent now," she murmured, smiling when he turned hesitantly around. "My gosh, you make me feel good. I was always self-conscious about being so small."

His eyes narrowed. "You're not small, baby," he said in a gruff tone. "You're just delicate."

Her face glowed with pride. "Thank you, Rett."

"Let's see if the coffee's still warm," he said softly, holding out his hand.

She took it, and he pulled her up, pausing to bend and kiss her slowly, lingering over the soft, swollen contours of her warm mouth.

"I've bruised your lips," he whispered. "Are they sore?"

"They're delightfully sensitive," she whispered back,

going on tiptoe. "You know a lot about kissing for a cattleman."

"You know a lot for a virgin," he murmured, chuckling.

"Pat yourself on the back, I'm a fast study." She slid her hand pertly inside his shirt and stroked him. "See?"

He took her hand away and buttoned his shirt to the throat. "I'm going to have to watch you, lady," he murmured, "or you'll wrestle me down on the couch and seduce me one dark night."

"It's all right," she whispered. "I won't get you pregnant. You can trust me, honey," she added with a wicked smile.

He burst out laughing and led her into the kitchen. "Feed me," he said, "before we get in over our heads."

"Spoilsport. Just when things were getting interesting."

"Another minute, and they'd have gone past interesting to educational," he murmured dryly, with a pointed glance. "Men get hot pretty fast that way, Jenny. Don't rely on my protective instincts too far. I damned near lost my head."

"Did you, really?" she asked, all eyes. "But I don't know anything."

"That's why," he sighed. "I…haven't touched a virgin since I was one myself. Funny, isn't it, that these days it's become a stigma. Back when I was a kid, decent boys wouldn't be seen with a girl who had a reputation for being easy. Now it's the virgins who take all the taunting." He stopped, turning her, and his face was solemn. "I'm glad you're still innocent. I'm glad that I can look at you and make you blush, and watch all those first reactions that you've never shown anybody else. To hell with modern morality, Jenny. I love the fact that you're as old-fashioned as I am."

"So do I. Now," she added, studying him warmly. "Rett..." Her fingers went up and touched his hard mouth. "Rett, I think I..." She was about to say "love you" when a piece of paper on the floor caught his eye.

"Hey, what's this?" he asked, bending to pick it up.

Her heart stopped. It was the check she'd gotten in the mail. She'd stuck it in her pocket, but it must have fallen out. She watched him open it and read the logo at the top with a feeling of impending disaster. She hadn't meant to tell him where it came from just yet...

His lean hand closed around the check, crumpling it. "Where did you get this kind of money, and what for?" he demanded.

"I... I worked part-time for a design house in Houston, decorating a lady's living room," she blurted out. "It's for you. To pay off your bull," she said, her face bright, her eyes shining. "I went to Houston and got a part-time job decorating a living room. That's my commission. Surprise! Now you won't have to sell that mangy old Hereford bull!"

He looked odd. As if he'd tried to swallow a watermelon and couldn't get it down. He stood up, still staring at the crumpled check, and turned away. He walked to the sink, staring out the darkened window.

"How did you get a job decorating anything?"

"I studied for several years at an excellent school of interior design in New York," she said. "I got a job with one of the leading agencies and spent two years developing my craft. That's why I got so angry when you made the remark about interior decorators being con artists," she added. "You see, I am one."

"New York?"

"Yes. It's the best place to learn, and to work."

"And you got pneumonia…"

"And had to give it up temporarily," she agreed. She frowned. He sounded strange. "Thanks to you, I'm back on my feet now and in fine form. The lady I did the design for was really pleased with my work, too. But the reason I did it was to get you enough money to pay off your note…"

"I can't take this," he said in a strained tone. He put it gently on the table and started out the door.

"But, Everett, your supper…!" she called.

"I'm not hungry." He kept walking. A moment later, the front door slammed behind him.

She sat there at the table, alone, staring at the check for a long time, until the numbers started to blur. Her eyes burned with unshed tears. She loved him. She loved Everett Culhane. And in the space of one night, her good intentions had lost her the pleasure of being near him. She knew almost certainly that he was going to fire her now. Too late, she remembered his opinion of city women. She hadn't had time to explain that it was her parents' idea for her to study and to work in New York, not her own. Nor that the pressure had been too much. He thought it was only pneumonia. Could she convince him in time that she wasn't what he was sure she was? That she wanted to stay here forever, not just as a temporary thing. She glanced toward the door with a quiet sigh. Well, she'd just sit here and wait until the shock wore off and he came back.

She did wait. But when three o'clock in the morning came, with no sign of Everett, she went reluctantly upstairs and lay down. It didn't help that she still smelled leather and faint cologne, and that her mind replayed the fierce ardor she'd learned from him until, exhausted, she slept.

When her eyes slowly opened the next morning, she felt as if she hadn't slept at all. And the first thing she remembered was Everett's shocked face when she'd told him what she used to do for a living. She couldn't understand why he'd reacted that way. After the way it had been between them, she hadn't expected him to walk off without at least discussing it. She wondered if it was going to be that way until he fired her. Because she was sure he was going to. And she knew for a certainty that she didn't want to go. She loved him with all her heart.

CHAPTER SEVEN

IF SHE'D HOPED for a new start that morning, she was disappointed. She fixed breakfast, but Everett went out the front door without even sticking his head in the kitchen. Apparently, he'd rather have starved than eat what she'd cooked for him.

That morning set the pattern for the next two days. Jennifer cooked and wound up eating her efforts by herself. Everett came home in the early hours of the morning, arranging his schedule so that she never saw him at all.

He'd sold the bull. She found it out from Eddie, who was in a nasty temper of his own.

"I practically begged him to wait and see what happened," Eddie spat as he delivered the eggs to Jennifer the second morning. "When that neighbor didn't want the bull, Everett just loaded it up and took it to the sale without a word. He looks bad. He won't talk. Do you know what's eating him?"

She avoided that sharp look. "He's worried about money, I think," she said. "I offered him what I had. He got mad and stomped off and he hasn't spoken to me since."

"That don't sound like Everett."

"Yes, I know." She sighed, smiling at him. "I think he wants me to go away, Eddie. He's done everything but leave the ranch forever to get his point across."

"Money troubles are doing it, not you." Eddie grinned. "Don't back off now. He needs us all more than ever."

"Maybe he does," Jennifer said. "I just wish he'd taken the money I offered to lend him."

"That would be something, all right, to watch Everett take money from a lady. No offense, Miss Jenny, but he's too much man. If you know what I mean."

She did, unfortunately. She'd experienced the male in him, in ways that would haunt her forever. And worst of all was the fact that she was still hungry for him. If anything, that wild little interlude on the sofa had whetted her appetite, not satisfied it.

For lunch, she put a platter of cold cuts in the refrigerator and left a loaf of bread on the table along with a plate and cup; there was coffee warming on the stove. She pulled on a sweater and went down to visit Libby. It was like baiting a trap, she thought. Perhaps he'd enjoy eating if he didn't have to look at a city woman.

Libby didn't ask any obvious questions. She simply enjoyed the visit, since the children were in school and she could talk about clothes and television programs with the younger woman.

At one o'clock, Jennifer left the house and walked slowly back to see if Everett had eaten. It was something of a shock to find him wandering wildly around the kitchen, smoking like a furnace.

"So there you are!" he burst out, glaring at her with

menacing brown eyes. "Where in hell have you been? No note, no nothing! I didn't know if you'd left or been kidnapped, or stepped into a hole…"

"What would you care if I had?" she demanded. "You've made it obvious that you don't care for my company!"

"What did you expect?" he burst out, his eyes dangerous. "You lied to me."

"I didn't," she said in defense.

"I thought you were a poor little secretary in danger of starving if I didn't take you in," he said through his teeth. He let his eyes wander with slow insolence over the white blouse and green skirt she was wearing. "And what do I find out? That you lived and worked in New York at a job that would pay you more in one week than I can make here in two months!"

So that was it. His pride was crushed. He was poor and she wasn't, and that cut him up.

But knowing it wasn't much help. He was as unapproachable as a coiled rattler. In his dusty jeans and boots and denim shirt, he looked as wild as an outlaw.

"I had pneumonia," she began. "I had to come south…"

"Bobby didn't know?" he asked.

"No," she said. "I didn't see any reason to tell him. Everett…!"

"Why didn't you say something at the beginning?" he demanded, ramming his hand into his pocket to fish for another cigarette.

"What was there to say?" she asked impotently. She took the sweater from around her shoulders, and her green eyes pleaded with him. "Everett, I'm just the same as I always was."

"Not hardly," he said. His jaw clenched as he lit the cigarette. "You came here looking like a straggly little hen. And now…" He blew out a cloud of smoke, letting his eyes savor the difference. They lingered for a long time on her blouse, narrowing, burning. "I brought a city girl here once," he said absently. His eyes caught hers. "When she found out that I had more ideas than I had money, she turned around and ran. We were engaged," he said on a short laugh. "I do have the damndest blind spot about women."

She wrapped her arms around her chest. "Why does it make so much difference?" she asked. "I only took the designing job to help, Rett," she added. She moved closer. "I just wanted to pay you back, for giving me a job when I needed it. I knew you couldn't afford me, but I was in trouble, and you sacrificed for me." Her eyes searched his dark, hard face. "I wanted to do something for you. I wanted you to have your bull."

His face hardened and he turned away, as if he couldn't bear the sight of her. He raised the cigarette to his lips and his back was ramrod straight.

"I want you to leave," he said.

"Yes, I know," she said on a soft little sigh. "When?"

"At the end of the week."

So soon? she thought miserably. Her eyes clouded as she stared at his back, seeing the determination in every hard line of it. "Do you hate me?" she asked in a hurting tone.

He turned around slowly, the cigarette held tautly in

one hand, and his eyes slashed at her. He moved closer, with a look in his dark eyes that was disturbing.

With a smooth motion, he tossed the unfinished cigarette into an ashtray on the table and reached for her.

"I could hate you," he said harshly. "If I didn't want you so damned much." He bent his head and caught her mouth with his.

She stiffened for an instant, because there was no tenderness in this exchange. He was rough and hurting, deliberately. Even so, she loved him. If this was all he could give, then it would be enough. She inched her trapped hands up to his neck and slid them around it. Her soft mouth opened, giving him all he wanted of it. She couldn't respond, he left her no room. He was taking without any thought of giving back the pleasure.

His hard hands slid roughly over her breasts and down to her hips and ground her against him in a deep, insolent rhythm, letting her feel what she already knew—that he wanted her desperately.

"Was it all a lie?" he ground out against her mouth. "Are you really a virgin?"

Her lips felt bruised when she tried to speak. "Yes," she said shakily. He was still holding her intimately, and when she tried to pull back, he only crushed her hips closer.

"No, don't do that," he said with a cruel smile. "I like to feel you. Doesn't it give you a sense of triumph, city girl, knowing how you affect me?"

Her hands pushed futilely at his hard chest. "Everett, don't make me feel cheap," she pleaded.

"Could I?" He laughed coldly. "With your prospects?" His hands tightened, making her cry out. His mouth lowered. This time it was teasing, tantalizing. He brushed it against her own mouth in whispery motions that worked like a narcotic, hypnotizing her, weakening her. She began to follow those hard lips with her own, trying to capture them in an exchange that would satisfy the ache he was creating.

"Do you want to stay with me, Jenny?" he whispered.

"Yes," she whispered back, her whole heart in her response. She clutched at his shirtfront with trembling fingers. Her mouth begged for his. "Yes, Everett, I want to stay…!"

His breath came hard and fast at her lips. "Then come upstairs with me, now, and I'll let you," he breathed.

It took a minute for his words to register, and then she realized that his hands had moved to the very base of her spine, to touch her in ways that shocked and frightened her.

She pulled against his hands, her face red, her eyes wild. "What do you mean?" she whispered.

He laughed, his eyes as cold as winter snow. "Don't you know? Sleep with me. Or would you like to hear it in a less formal way?" he added, and put it in words that made her hand come up like a whip.

He caught it, looking down at her with contempt and desire and anger all mixed up in his hard face. "Not interested?" he asked mockingly. "You were a minute ago. You were the other night, when you let me strip you."

Her teeth clenched as she tried to hang on to her dignity and her pride. "Let me go," she whispered shakily.

"I could please you, city girl," he said with a bold,

slow gaze down her taut body. "You're going to give in to a man someday. Why not me? Or do I need to get rich first to appeal to you?"

Tears welled up in her eyes. His one hand was about to crack the delicate bone in her wrist, and the other was hurting her back. She closed her eyelids to shut off the sight of his cold face. She loved him so. How could he treat her this way? How could he be so cruel after that tenderness they'd shared!

"No comment?" he asked. He dropped his hands and retrieved his still-smoking cigarette from the ashtray. "Well, you can't blame a man for trying. You seemed willing enough the other night. I thought you might like some memories to carry away with you."

She'd had some beautiful ones, she thought miserably, until now. Her hands reached, trembling, for her sweater. She held it over her chest and wouldn't look up.

"I've got some correspondence on the desk you can type when you run out of things to do in the kitchen," he said, turning toward the door. He looked back with a grim smile on his lips. "That way you can make up some of the time you spent decorating that woman's house for her."

She still didn't speak, didn't move. The world had caved in on her. She loved him. And he could treat her like this, like some tramp he'd picked up on the street!

He drew in a sharp breath. "Don't talk, then," he said coldly. "I don't give a damn. I never did. I wanted you, that's all. But if I had the money, I could have you and a dozen like you, couldn't I?"

She managed to raise her ravaged face. He seemed

almost to flinch at the sight of it, but he was only a blur through the tears in her eyes, and she might have been mistaken.

"Say something!" he ground out.

She lifted her chin. Her pale, swollen eyes just stared at him accusingly, and not one single word left her lips. Even if he threw her against the wall, she wouldn't give him the satisfaction of even one syllable!

He drew in a furious breath and whirled on his heel, slamming out the door.

She went upstairs like a zombie, hardly aware of her surroundings at all. She went into her room and took the uncashed checks that he'd signed for her salary and put them neatly on her dresser. She packed very quickly and searched in her purse. She had just enough pocket money left to pay a cab. She could cash the design firm's check in town when she got there. She called the cab company and then lifted her case and went downstairs to wait for it.

Everett was nowhere in sight, neither were Eddie and Bib, when the taxi came winding up the driveway. She walked down the steps, her eyes dry now, her face resolved, and got inside.

"Take me into town, please," she said quietly.

The cab pulled away from the steps, and she scanned the ranchhouse and the corrals one last time. Then she turned away and closed her eyes. She didn't look back, not once.

FORTUNATELY, JENNIFER HAD no trouble landing a job. Sally Wade had been so impressed with the work that she'd done for Mrs. Whitehall that she practically created a position for Jennifer in her small, and still struggling, design firm. Jennifer loved the work, but several weeks had passed before she was able to think about Everett without crying.

THE CUP OF coffee at Jennifer's elbow was getting cold. She frowned at it as her hand stilled on the sketch she was doing for a new client.

"Want some fresh?" Sally Wade asked from the doorway, holding her own cup aloft. "I'm just going to the pot."

"Bless you," Jennifer laughed.

"That's the first time you've really looked happy in the three months since you've been here," Sally remarked, cocking her head. "Getting over him?"

"Over whom?" came the shocked reply.

"That man, whoever he was, who had you in tears your first week here. I didn't pry, but I wondered," the older woman confessed. "I kept waiting for the phone to ring, or a letter to come. But nothing did. I kind of thought that he had to care, because you cared so much."

"He wanted a mistress," Jennifer said, putting it into words. "And I wanted a husband. We just got our signals crossed. Besides," she added with a wan smile, "I'm feeling worlds better. I've got a great job, a lovely boss, and even a part-time boyfriend. If you can call Drew a boy."

"He's delightful." Sally sighed. "Just what you need. A live wire."

"And not a bad architect, either. You must be pleased

he's working with us." She grinned. "He did a great job on that office project last month."

"So did you," Sally said, smiling. She leaned against the doorjamb. "I thought it a marvelous idea, locating a group of offices in a renovated mansion. It only needed the right team, and you and Drew work wonderfully well together."

"In business, yes." Jennifer twirled her pencil around in her slender fingers. "I just don't want him getting serious about me. If it's possible for him to get serious about anyone." She laughed.

"Don't try to bury yourself."

"Oh, I'm not. It's just…" She shrugged. "I'm only now getting over… I don't want any more risks. Not for a long time. Maybe not ever."

"Some men are kind-hearted," Sally ventured.

"So why are you single?" came the sharp reply.

"I'm picky," Sally informed her with a sly smile. "Very, very picky. I want Rhett Butler or nobody."

"Wrong century, wrong state."

"You're from Georgia. Help me out!"

"Sorry," Jennifer murmured. "If I could find one, do you think I'd tell anybody?"

"Point taken. Give me that cup and I'll fill it for you."

"Thanks, boss."

"Oh, boy, coffee!" a tall, redheaded man called from the doorway as he closed the door behind him. "I'll have mine black, with two doughnuts, a fried egg…"

"The breakfast bar is closed, Mr. Peterson," Jennifer told him.

"Sorry, Drew," Sally added. "You'll just have to catch your own chicken and do it the hard way."

"I could starve," he grumbled, ramming his hands in his pockets. He had blue eyes, and right now they were glaring at both women. "I don't have a wife or a mother. I live alone. My cook hates me…"

"You're breaking my heart," Sally offered.

"You can have the other half of my doughnut," Jennifer said, holding up a chunk of doughnut with chocolate clinging to it.

"Never mind." Drew sighed. "Thanks all the same, but I'll just wither away."

"That wouldn't be difficult," Jennifer told him. "You're nothing but skin and bones."

"I gained two pounds this week," he said, affronted.

"Where is it," Sally asked with a sweeping glance, "in your big toe?"

"Ha, ha," he laughed as she turned to go to the coffeepot.

"You *are* thin," Jennifer remarked.

He glared at her. "I'm still a growing boy." He stretched lazily. "Want to ride out to the new office building with me this morning?"

"No, thanks. I've got to finish these drawings. What do you think?"

She held one up, and he studied them with an architect's trained eye. "Nice. Just remember that this," he said, pointing to the vestibule, "is going to be a heavy-traffic area, and plan accordingly."

"There goes my white carpet," she teased.

"I'll white carpet you," he muttered. He pursed his lips as he studied her. "Wow, lady, what a change."

She blinked up at him. "What?"

"You. When you walked in here three months ago, you looked like a drowned kitten. And now..." He only sighed.

She was wearing a beige suit with a pink candy-striped blouse and a pink silk scarf. Her blond hair was almost platinum with its new body and sheen, and she'd had it trimmed so that it hung in wispy waves all around her shoulders. Her face was creamy and soft and she was wearing makeup again. She looked nice, and his eyes told her so.

"Thanks."

He pursed his lips. "What for?"

"The flattery," she told him. "My ego's been even with my ankles for quite a while."

"Stick with me, kid, I'll get it all the way up to your ears," he promised with an evil leer.

"Sally, he's trying to seduce me!" she called toward the front of the office.

She expected some kind of bantering reply, but none was forthcoming. She looked up at Drew contemplatively. "Reckon she's left?"

"No. She's answered the phone. You still aren't used to the musical tone, are you?"

No, she wasn't. There were quite a lot of things she wasn't used to, and the worst of them was being without Everett. She had a good job, a nice apartment, and some new clothes. But without him, none of that mattered. She was going through the motions, and little more. His contempt still stung her pride when she recalled that last horrible scene. But she couldn't get him out of her mind, no matter how she tried.

"Well!" Sally said, catching her breath as she rejoined them. "If the rest of him looks like this voice, I may get back into the active part of the business. That was a potential client, and I think he may be the Rhett Butler I've always dreamed of. What a silky, sexy voice!"

"Dream on," Jennifer teased.

"He's coming by in the morning to talk to us. Wants his whole house done!" the older woman exclaimed.

"He must have a sizeable wallet, then," Drew remarked.

Sally nodded. "He didn't say where the house was, but I assume it's nearby. It didn't sound like a long-distance call." She glanced at Jennifer with a smile. "Apparently your reputation has gotten around, too," she laughed. "He asked if you'd be doing the project. I had the idea he wouldn't have agreed otherwise." She danced around with her coffee cup in her hand. "What a godsend. With the office building and this job, we'll be out of the red, kids! What a break!"

"And you were groaning about the bills just yesterday," Jennifer laughed. "I told you something would turn up, didn't I?"

"You're my lucky charm," Sally told her. "If I hadn't hired you, I shudder to think what would have happened."

"You know how much I appreciated getting this job," Jennifer murmured. "I was in pretty desperate circumstances."

"So I noticed. Well, we did each other a lot of good. We still are," Sally said warmly. "Hey, let's celebrate. Come on. I'll treat you two to lunch."

"Lovely!" Jennifer got up and grabbed her purse. "Come on, Drew, let's hurry before she changes her mind!"

She rushed out the door, with Drew in full pursuit, just ahead of Sally. And not one of them noticed the man sitting quietly in the luxury car across the street, his fingers idly caressing a car phone in the backseat as he stared intently after them.

CHAPTER EIGHT

DREW HAD ASKED Jennifer to go out with him that night, but she begged off with a smile. She didn't care for the nightlife anymore. She went to company functions with Sally when it was necessary to attract clients or discuss new projects, but that was about the extent of her social consciousness. She spent most of her time alone, in her modest apartment, going over drawings and planning rooms.

She enjoyed working for Sally. Houston was a big city, but much smaller than New York. And while there was competition, it wasn't as fierce. The pressure was less. And best of all, Jennifer was allowed a lot of latitude in her projects. She had a free hand to incorporate her own ideas as long as they complemented the client's requirements. She loved what she did, and in loving it, she blossomed into the woman she'd once been. But this time she didn't allow herself to fall into the trap of overspending. She budgeted, right down to the pretty clothes she loved—she bought them on sale, a few at a time, and concentrated on mix-and-match outfits.

It was a good life. But part of her was still mourning Everett. Not a day went by when she couldn't see him, tall and unnerving, somewhere in her memory. They'd been so good for each other. She'd never experienced such tenderness in a man.

She got up from the sofa and looked out at the sky-line of Houston. The city was bright and beautiful, but she remembered the ranch on starry nights. Dogs would howl far in the distance, crickets would sing at the steps. And all around would be open land and stars and the silhouettes of Everett's cattle.

She wrapped her arms around her body and sighed. Perhaps someday the pain would stop and she could really forget him. Perhaps someday she could remember his harsh accusations and not be wounded all over again. But right now, it hurt terribly. He'd been willing to let her stay as his mistress, as a possession to be used when he wanted her. But he wouldn't let her be part of his life. He couldn't have told her more graphically how little he thought of her. That had hurt the most. That even after all the caring, all the tenderness, she hadn't reached him at all. He hadn't seen past the shape of her body and his need of it. He hadn't loved her. And he'd made sure she knew it.

There were a lot of nights, like this one, when she paced and paced and wondered if he thought of her at all, if he regretted what had happened. Somehow, she doubted it. Everett had a wall like steel around him. He wouldn't let anyone inside it. Especially not a city woman with an income that could top his.

She laughed bitterly. It was unfortunate that she had fallen in love for the first time with such a cynical man. It had warped the way she looked at the world. She felt as if she, too, were impregnable now. Her emotions were carefully wrapped away, where they couldn't be touched. Nobody could reach her now. She felt safe in her warm cocoon. Of course, she was as incapable of caring now as he'd been. And in a way, that was a blessing. Because she couldn't be hurt anymore. She could laugh and carry on with Drew, and it didn't mean a thing. There was no risk in dating these days. Her heart was safely tucked away.

With a last uncaring look at the skyline, she turned off the lights and went to bed. Just as she drifted off, she wondered who the new client was going to be, and grinned at the memory of Sally's remark about his sexy voice.

She overslept the next morning for the first time in months. With a shriek as she saw the time, she dressed hastily in a silky beige dress and high heels. She moaned over her unruly hair that would curl and feather all around her shoulders instead of going into a neat bun. She touched up her face, stepped into her shoes, and rushed out into the chill autumn morning without a jacket or a sweater. Oh, well, maybe she wouldn't freeze, she told herself as she jumped into the cab she'd called and headed for the office.

"So there you are," Drew said with mock anger as she rushed breathlessly in the door, her cheeks flushed, her eyes sparkling, her hair disheveled and sexy around her face. "I ought to fire you."

"Go ahead. I dare you." She laughed up at him. "And I'll tell Sally all about that last expense voucher you faked."

"Blackmailer!" he growled. He reached out and lifted her up in the air, laughing at her.

"Put me down, you male chauvinist." She laughed gaily. Her face was a study in beauty, her body lusciously displayed in the pose, her hands on his shoulders, her hair swirling gracefully as she looked down at him. "Come on, put me down," she coaxed. "Put me down, Drew, and I'll take you to lunch."

"In that case," he murmured dryly.

"Jennifer! Drew!" Sally exclaimed, entering the room with a nervous laugh. "Stop clowning. We've got business to discuss, and you're making a horrible first impression."

"Oops," Drew murmured. He turned his head just as Jennifer turned hers, and all the laughter and brightness drained out of her like air out of a balloon. She stared down at the newcomer with strained features and eyes that went from shock to extreme anger.

Drew set her down on her feet and turned, hand extended, grinning. "Sorry about that. Just chastising the staff for tardiness." He chuckled. "I'm Andrew Peterson, resident architect. This is my associate, Jennifer King."

"I know her name," Everett Culhane said quietly. His dark eyes held no offer of peace, no hint of truce. They were angry and cold, and he smiled mockingly as his eyes went from Jennifer to Drew. "We've met."

Sally looked poleaxed. It had just dawned on her who Everett was, when she got a look at Jennifer's white face.

"Uh, Mr. Culhane is our new client," Sally said hesitantly. Jennifer looked as if she might faint. "You remember, Jenny, I mentioned yesterday that he'd called."

"You didn't mention his name," Jennifer said in a

cool voice that shook with rage. "Excuse me, I have a phone call to make."

"Not so fast," Everett said quietly. "First we talk."

Her eyes glittered at him, her body trembled with suppressed tension. "I have nothing to say to you, Mr. Culhane," she managed. "And you have nothing to say to me that I care to hear."

"Jennifer..." Sally began nervously.

"If my job depends on working for Mr. Culhane, you can have my resignation on the spot," Jennifer said unsteadily. "I will not speak to him, much less work with him. I'm sorry."

She turned and went on wobbly legs to her office, closing the door behind her. She couldn't even sit down. She was shaking like a leaf all over and tears were burning her eyes. She heard voices outside, but ignored them. She stared at an abstract painting on the wall until she thought she'd go blind.

The sound of the door opening barely registered. Then it closed with a firm snap, and she glanced over her shoulder to find Everett inside.

It was only then that she noticed he was wearing a suit. A very expensive gray one that made his darkness even more formidable; his powerful body was streamlined and elegant in its new garments. He was holding a silverbelly Stetson in one lean hand and staring at her quietly, calculatingly.

"Please go away," she said with as much conviction as she could muster.

"Why?" he asked carelessly, tossing his hat onto her desk. He dropped into an armchair and crossed one

long leg over the other. He lit a cigarette and pulled the
ashtray on her desk closer, but his eyes never left her
ravaged face.

"If you want your house redone, there are other
firms," she told him, turning bravely, although her legs
were still trembling.

He saw that, and his eyes narrowed, his jaw tautened.
"Are you afraid of me?" he asked quietly.

"I'm outraged," she replied in a voice that was little
more than a whisper. Her hand brushed back a long,
unruly strand of hair. "You might as well have taken
a bullwhip to me, just before I left the ranch. What do
you want now? To show me how prosperous you are?
I've noticed the cut of your suit. And the fact that you
can afford to hire this firm to redo the house does indi-
cate a lot of money." She smiled unsteadily. "Congratulations. I hope your sudden wealth makes you happy."

He didn't speak for a long minute. His eyes wandered
over her slowly, without any insult, as if he'd forgotten
what she looked like and needed to stare at her, to fill
his eyes. "Aren't you going to ask me how I came by
it?" he demanded finally.

"No. Because I don't care," she said.

One corner of his mouth twitched a little. He took
a draw from the cigarette and flicked an ash into the
ashtray. "I sold off the oil rights."

So much for sticking to your principles, she wanted
to say. But she didn't have the strength. She went behind her desk and sat down carefully.

"No comment?" he asked.

She blanched, remembering with staggering clarity the last time he'd said that. He seemed to remember it, too, because his jaw tautened and he drew in a harsh breath.

"I want my house done," he said curtly. "I want you to do it. Nobody else. And I want you to stay with me while you work on the place."

"Hell will freeze over first," she said quietly.

"I was under the impression that the firm wasn't operating in the black," he said with an insolent appraisal of her office. "The commission on this project will be pretty large."

"I told you once that you couldn't buy me," she said on a shuddering breath. "I'd jump off a cliff before I'd stay under the same roof with you!"

His eyes closed. When they opened again, he was staring down at his boot. "Is it that redheaded clown outside?" he asked suddenly, jerking his gaze up to catch hers.

Her lips trembled. "That's none of your business."

His eyes wandered slowly over her face. "You looked different with him," he said deeply. "Alive, vibrant, happy. And then, the minute you spotted me, every bit of life went out of you. It was like watching water drain from a glass."

"What did you expect, for God's sake!" she burst out, her eyes wild. "You cut me up!"

He drew in a slow breath. "Yes. I know."

"Then why are you here?" she asked wearily. "What do you want from me?"

He stared at the cigarette with eyes that barely saw it. "I told you. I want my house done." He looked up. "I can afford the best, and that's what I want. You."

There was an odd inflection in his voice, but she was too upset to hear it. She blinked her eyes, trying to get herself under control. "I won't do it. Sally will just have to fire me."

He got to his feet and loomed over the desk, crushing out the cigarette before he rammed his hands into his pockets and glared at her. "There are less pleasant ways to do this," he said. "I could make things very difficult for your new employer." His eyes challenged her. "Call my bluff. See if you can skip town with that on your conscience."

She couldn't, and he knew it. Her pride felt lacerated. "What do you think you'll accomplish by forcing me to come back?" she asked. "I'd put a knife in you if I could. I won't sleep with you, no matter what you do. So what will you get out of it?"

"My house decorated, of course," he said lazily. His eyes wandered over her. "I've got over the other. Out of sight, out of mind, don't they say?" He shrugged and turned away with a calculating look on his face. "And one body's pretty much like another in the dark," he added, reaching for his Stetson. His eyes caught the flutter of her lashes and he smiled to himself as he reached for the doorknob. "Well, Miss King, which is it? Do you come back to Big Spur with me or do I give Ms. Wade the sad news that you're leaving her in the lurch?"

Her eyes flashed green sparks at him. What choice was there? But he'd pay for this. Somehow, she'd make him. "I'll go," she bit off.

He didn't say another word. He left her office as

though he were doing her a favor by letting her redecorate his house!

Sally came in the door minutes later, looking troubled and apologetic.

"I had no idea," she told Jennifer. "Honest to God, I had no idea who he was."

"Now you know," Jennifer said on a shaky laugh.

"You don't have to do it," the older woman said curtly.

"Yes, I'm afraid I do. Everett doesn't make idle threats," she said, rising. "You've been too good to me, Sally. I can't let him cause trouble for you on my account. I'll go with him. After all, it's just another job."

"You look like death warmed over. I'll send Drew with you. We'll do something to justify him…"

"Everett would eat him alive," she told Sally with a level stare. "And don't pretend you don't know it. Drew's a nice man but he isn't up to Everett's weight or his temper. This is a private war."

"Unarmed combat?" Sally asked sadly.

"Exactly. He has this thing about city women, and I wasn't completely honest with him. He wants to get even."

"I thought revenge went out with the Borgias," Sally muttered.

"Not quite. Wish me luck. I'm going to need it."

"If it gets too rough, call for reinforcements," Sally said. "I'll pack a bag and move in with you, Everett or no Everett."

"You're a pal," Jennifer said warmly.

"I'm a rat," came the dry reply. "I wish I hadn't done this to you. If I'd known who he was, I'd never have told him you worked here."

JENNIFER HAD HOPED to go down to Big Spur alone, but
Everett went back to her apartment with her, his eyes
daring her to refuse his company.

He waited in the living room while she packed, and
not one corner escaped his scrutiny.

"Looking for dust?" she asked politely, case in hand.

He turned, cigarette in hand, studying her. "This
place must cost you an arm," he remarked.

"It does," she said with deliberate sarcasm. "But I can
afford it. I make a lot of money, as you reminded me."

"I said a lot of cruel things, didn't I, Jenny Wren?"
he asked quietly, searching her shocked eyes. "Did I
leave deep scars?"

She lifted her chin. "Can we go? The sooner we get
there, the sooner I can get the job done and come home."

"Didn't you ever think of the ranch as home?" he
asked, watching her. "You seemed to love it at first."

"Things were different then," she said noncommit-
tally, and started for the door.

He took her case, his fingers brushing hers in the
process, and producing electric results.

"Eddie and Bib gave me hell when they found out
you'd gone," he said as he opened the door for her.

"I imagine you were too busy celebrating to notice."

He laughed shortly. "Celebrating? You damned little
fool, I…!" He closed his mouth with a rough sigh. "Never
mind. You might have left a nasty note or something."

"Why, so you'd know where I went?" she demanded.
"That was the last thing I wanted."

"So I noticed," he agreed. He locked the door, handed
her the key, and started down the hall toward the eleva-

tor. "Libby told me the name of the firm you'd worked for. It wasn't hard to guess you'd get a job with them."

She tossed her hair. "So that was how you found me."

"We've got some unfinished business," he replied as they waited for the elevator. His dark eyes held hers and she had to clench her fists to keep from kicking him. He had a power over her that all her anger couldn't stop. Deep beneath the layer of ice was a blazing inferno of hunger and love, but she'd die before she'd show it to him.

"I hate you," she breathed.

"Yes, I know you do," he said with an odd satisfaction.

"Mr. Culhane..."

"You used to call me Rett," he recalled, studying her. "Especially," he added quietly, "when we made love."

Her face began to color and she aimed a kick at his shins. He jumped back just as the elevator door opened.

"Pig!" she ground out.

"Now, honey, think of the kids," he drawled, aiming a glance at the elevator full of fascinated spectators. "If you knock me down, how can I support the ten of you?"

Red-faced, she got in ahead of him and wished with all her heart that the elevator doors would close right dead center on him. They didn't.

He sighed loudly, glancing down at her. "I begged you not to run off with that salesman," he said in a sad drawl. "I told you he'd lead you into a life of sin!"

There were murmured exclamations all around and a buzz of conversation. She glared up at him. Two could play that game.

"Well, what did you expect me to do, sit at home and

knit while you ran around with that black-eyed hussy?" she drawled back. "And me in my delicate condition…"

"Delicate condition…?" he murmured, shocked at her unexpected remark.

"And it's your baby, too, you animal," she said with a mock sob, glaring up at him.

"Darling!" he burst out. "You didn't tell me!"

And he grabbed her and kissed her hungrily right there in front of the whole crowd while she gasped and counted to ten and tried not to let him see that she was melting into the floor from the delicious contact with his mouth.

The elevator doors opened and he lifted his head as the other occupants filed out. He was breathing unsteadily and his eyes held hers. "No," he whispered when she tried to move away. His arm caught her and his head bent. "I need you," he whispered shakily. "Need you so…!"

That brought it all back. Need. He needed her. He just needed a body, that was all, and she knew it! She jerked herself out of his arms and stomped off the elevator.

"You try that again and I'll vanish!" she threatened, glaring up at him when they were outside the building. Her face was flushed, her breath shuddering. "I mean it! I'll disappear and you won't find me this time!"

He shrugged. "Suit yourself." He walked alongside her, all the brief humor gone out of his face. She wondered minutes later if it had been there at all.

CHAPTER NINE

HE HAD A LINCOLN NOW. Not only the car, but a driver to go with it. He handed her bag to the uniformed driver and put Jennifer in the backseat beside him.

"Aren't we coming up in the world, though?" she asked with cool sarcasm.

"Don't you like it?" he replied mockingly. He leaned back against the seat facing her and lit a cigarette. "I didn't think a woman alive could resist flashy money."

She remembered reluctantly how he'd already been thrown over once for the lack of wealth. Part of her tender heart felt sorry for him. But not any part that was going to show, she told herself.

"You could buy your share now, I imagine," she said, glancing out the window at the traffic.

He blew out a thin cloud of smoke. The driver climbed in under the wheel and, starting the powerful car, pulled out into the street.

"I imagine so."

She stared at the purse in her lap. "They really did find oil out there?" she asked.

"Sure did. Barrels and barrels." He glanced at her over his cigarette. "The whole damned skyline's cluttered with rigs these days. Metal grasshoppers." He sighed. "The cattle don't even seem to mind them. They just graze right on."

Wouldn't it be something if a geyser blew out under one of his prize Herefords one day, she mused. She almost told him, and then remembered the animosity between them. It had been a good kind of relationship that they'd had. If only Everett hadn't ruined it.

"It's a little late to go into it now," he said quietly. "But I didn't mean to hurt you that much. Once I cooled down, I would have apologized."

"The apology wouldn't have meant much after what you said to me!" she said through her teeth, flushing at the memory of the crude phrase.

He looked away. For a long minute he just sat and smoked. "You're almost twenty-four years old, Jenny," he said finally. "If you haven't heard words like that before, you're overdue."

"I didn't expect to hear them from you," she shot back, glaring at him. "Much less have you treat me with less respect than a woman you might have picked up on the streets with a twenty-dollar bill!"

"One way or another, I'd have touched you like that eventually!" he growled, glaring at her. "And don't sit there like lily-white purity and pretend you don't know what I'm talking about. We were on the verge of becoming lovers that night on the sofa."

"You wouldn't have made me feel ashamed if it had happened that night," she said fiercely. "You wouldn't have made me feel cheap!"

He seemed about to explode. Then he caught himself

and took a calming draw from the cigarette. His dark eyes studied the lean hand holding it. "You hurt me."

It was a shock to hear him admit it. "What?"

"You hurt me." His dark eyes lifted. "I thought we were being totally honest with each other. I trusted you. I let you closer than any other woman ever got. And then out of the blue, you hit me with everything at once. That you were a professional woman, a career woman. Worse," he added quietly, "a city woman, used to city men and city life and city ways. I couldn't take it. I'd been paying you scant wages, and you handed me that check…" He sighed wearily. "My God, I can't even tell you how I felt. My pride took one hell of a blow. I had nothing, and you were showing me graphically that you could outdo me on every front."

"I only wanted to help," she said curtly. "I wanted to buy you the damned bull. Sorry. If I had it to do all over again, I wouldn't offer you a dime."

"Yes, it shows." He sighed. He finished the cigarette and crushed it out. "Who's the redhead?"

"Drew? Sally told you. He's our architect. He has his own firm, of course, but he collaborates with us on big projects."

"Not on mine," he said menacingly, and his eyes darkened. "Not in my house."

She glared back. "That will depend on how much renovation the project calls for, I imagine."

"I won't have him on my place," he said softly.

"Why?"

"I don't like the way he looks at you," he said coldly. "Much less the way he makes free with his hands."

"I'm twenty-three years old," she reminded him. "And I like Drew, and the way he looks at me! He's a nice man."

"And I'm not," he agreed. "Nice is the last thing I am. If he ever touches you that way again when I'm in the same room, I'll break his fingers for him."

"Everett Donald Culhane!" she burst out.

His eyebrows arched. "Who told you my whole name?"

She looked away. "Never mind," she said, embarrassed.

His hand brushed against her hair, caressing it. "God, your hair is glorious," he said quietly. "It was nothing like this at the ranch."

She tried not to feel his touch. "I'd been ill," she managed.

"And now you aren't. Now you're...fuller and softer-looking. Even your breasts..."

"Stop it!" she cried, red-faced.

He let go of her hair reluctantly, but his eyes didn't leave her. "I'll have you, Jenny," he said quietly, his tone as soft as it had been that night when he was loving her.

"Only if you shoot me in the leg first!" she told him.

"Not a chance," he murmured, studying her. "I'll want you healthy and strong, so that you can keep up with me."

Her face did a slow burn again. She could have kicked him, but they were sitting down. "I don't want you!"

"You did. You will. I've got a whole campaign mapped out, Miss Jenny," he told her with amazing arrogance. "You're under siege. You just haven't realized it yet."

She looked him straight in the eye. "My grandfather held off a whole German company during World War I rather than surrender."

His eyebrows went up. "Is that supposed to impress me?"

"I won't be your mistress," she told him levelly. "No matter how many campaigns you map out or what kind of bribes or threats you try to use. I came with you to save Sally's business. But all this is to me is a job. I am not going to sleep with you."

His dark, quiet eyes searched over her face. "Why?"

Her lips opened and closed, opened again. "Because I can't do it without love," she said finally.

"Love isn't always possible," he said softly. "Sometimes, other things have to come first. Mutual respect, caring, companionship…"

"Can we talk about something else?" she asked tautly. Her fingers twisted the purse out of shape.

He chuckled softly. "Talking about sex won't get you pregnant."

"You've got money now. You can buy women," she ground out. "You said so."

"Honey, would you want a man you had to buy?" he asked quietly, studying her face.

Her lips parted. "Would I…" She searched his eyes. "Well, no."

"I wouldn't want a woman I had to buy," he said simply. "I'm too proud, Jenny. I said and did some harsh things to you," he remarked. "I can understand why you're angry and hurt about it. Someday I'll try to explain why I behaved that way. Right now, I'll settle for regaining even a shadow of the friendship we had. Nothing more. Despite all this wild talk, I'd never deliberately try to seduce you."

"Wouldn't you?" she asked bitterly. "Isn't that the whole point of getting me down here?"

"No." He lit another cigarette.

"You said you were going to…" she faltered.

"I want to," he admitted quietly. "God, I want to! But I can't quite take a virgin in my stride. Once, I thought I might," he confessed, his eyes searching her face. "That night… You were so eager, and I damned near lost my head when I realized that I could have you." He stared at the tip of his cigarette with blank eyes. "Would you have hated me if I hadn't been able to stop?"

Her eyes drilled into her purse. "There's just no point in going over it," she said in a studiously polite tone. "The past is gone."

"Like hell it's gone," he ground out. "I look at you and start aching," he said harshly.

Her lower lip trembled as she glared at him. "Then stop looking. Or take cold showers! Just don't expect me to do anything about it. I'm here to work, period!"

His eyebrows arched, and he was watching her with a faintly amused expression. "Where did you learn about cold showers?"

"From watching movies!"

"Is that how you learned about sex, from the movies?" he taunted.

"No, I learned in school! Sex education," she bit off.

"In my day, we had to learn it the hard way," he murmured. "It wasn't part of the core curriculum."

She glanced at him. "I can see you, doing extracurricular work in somebody's backseat."

He reached out and caught her hair again, tugging on it experimentally. "In a haystall, actually," he said, his voice low and soft and dark. Her head turned and he held her eyes. "She was two years older than I was, and she taught me the difference between sex and making love."

Her face flushed. He affected her in ways nobody else could. She was trembling from the bare touch of his fingers on her hair; her heart was beating wildly. How was she going to survive being in the same house with him?

"Everett…" she began.

"I'm sorry about what I said to you that last day, Jenny," he said quietly. "I'm sorry I made it into something cheap and sordid between us. Because that's the last thing it would have been if you'd given yourself to me."

She pulled away from him with a dry little laugh. "Oh, really?" she said shakenly, turning her eyes to the window. They were out of Houston now, heading south. "The minute you'd finished with me, you'd have kicked me out the door, and you know it, Everett Culhane. I'd have been no different from all the other women you've held in contempt for giving in to you."

"It isn't like that with you."

"And how many times have you told that story?" she asked sadly.

"Once. Just now."

He sounded irritated, probably because she wasn't falling for his practiced line. She closed her eyes and leaned her head against the cool window pane.

"I'd rather stay in a motel," she said, "if you don't mind."

"No way, lady," he said curtly. "The same lock's still on your door, if you can't trust me that far. But staying at Big Spur was part of the deal you and I negotiated."

She turned her head to glance at his hard, set profile. He looked formidable again, all dark, flashing eyes and coldness. He was like the man she'd met that first day at the screen door.

"What would you have done, if I'd given in?" she asked suddenly, watching him closely. "What if I'd gotten pregnant?"

His head turned and his eyes glittered strangely. "I'd have gotten down on my knees and thanked God for it," he said harshly. "What did you think I'd do?"

Her lips parted. "I hadn't really thought about it."

"I want children. A yardful."

That was surprising. Her eyes dropped to his broad chest, to the muscles that his gray suit barely contained, and she remembered how it was to be held against him in passion.

"Libby said you loved the ranch," he remarked.

"I did. When I was welcome."

"You still are."

"Do tell?" She cocked her head. "I'm a career woman, remember? And I'm a city girl."

His mouth tugged up. "I think city girls are sexy."

His dark eyes traveled down to her slender legs encased in pink hose. "I didn't know you had legs, Jenny Wren. You always kept them in jeans."

"I didn't want you leering at me."

"Ha!" he shot back. "You knew that damned blouse was torn, the day you fell off your horse." His eyes dared her to dispute him. "You wanted my eyes on you. I'll never forget the way you looked when you saw me staring at you."

Her chest rose and fell quickly. "I was shocked."

"Shocked, hell. Delighted." He lifted the cigarette to his mouth. "I didn't realize you were a woman until then. I'd seen you as a kid. A little helpless thing I needed to protect." His eyes cut sideways and he smiled mockingly. "And then that blouse came open and I saw a body I'd have killed for. After that, the whole situation started getting impossible."

"So did you."

"I know," he admitted. "My brain was telling me to keep away, but my body wouldn't listen. You didn't help a hell of a lot, lying there on that couch with your mouth begging for mine."

"Well, I'm human!" she burst out furiously. "And I never asked you to start kissing me."

"You didn't fight me."

She turned away. "Can't we get off this subject?"

"Just when it's getting interesting?" he mused. "Why? Don't you like remembering it?"

"No, I don't!"

"Does he kiss you the way I did?" he asked shortly,

jerking her around by the arm, his lean hand hurting. "That redhead, have you let him touch you like I did?"

"No!" she whispered, shocking herself with the disgust she put into that one, telling syllable.

His nostrils flared and his dark eyes traveled to the bodice of her dress, to her slender legs, her rounded hips, and all the way back up again to her eyes. "Why not?" he breathed unsteadily.

"Maybe I'm terrified of men now," she muttered.

"Maybe you're just terrified of other men," he whispered. "It was so good, when we touched each other. So good, so sweet… I rocked you under me and felt you respond, here…" His fingers brushed lightly against the bodice of her dress.

Coming to her senses all at once, she caught his fingers and pushed them away.

"No!" she burst out.

His fingers curled around her hand. He brought her fingers to his mouth and nibbled at them softly, staring into her eyes. "I can't even get in the mood with other women," he said quietly. "Three long months and I still can't sleep for thinking how you felt in my arms."

"Don't," she ground out, bending her head. "You won't make me feel guilty."

"That isn't what I want from you. Not guilt."

Her eyes came up. "You just want sex, don't you? You want me because I haven't been with anyone else!"

He caught her face in his warm hands and searched it while the forgotten cigarette between his fingers sent up curls of smoke beside her head.

"Someday, I'll tell you what I really want," he said,

his voice quiet and soft and dark. "When you've forgotten, and forgiven what happened. Until then, I'll just go on as I have before." His mouth twisted. "Taking cold showers and working myself into exhaustion."

She wouldn't weaken; she wouldn't! But his hands were warm and rough, and his breath was smoky against her parted lips. And her mouth wanted his.

He bent closer, just close enough to torment her. His eyes closed. His nose touched hers.

She felt reckless and hungry, and all her willpower wasn't proof against him.

"Jenny," he groaned against her lips.

"Isn't…fair," she whispered shakily.

"I know." His hands were trembling. They touched her face as if it were some priceless treasure. His mouth trembled, too, while it brushed softly over hers. "Oh, God, I'll die if I don't kiss you…!" he whispered achingly.

"No…" But it was only a breath, and he took it from her with the cool, moist pressure of his hard lips.

She hadn't dreamed of kisses this tender, this soft. He nudged her mouth with his until it opened. She shuddered with quickly drawn breaths. Her eyes slid open and looked into his slitted ones.

"Oh," she moaned in a sharp whisper.

"Oh," he whispered back. His thumbs brushed her cheeks. "I want you. I want to live with you and touch you and let you touch me. I want to make love with you and to you."

"Everett…you mustn't," she managed in a husky

whisper as his mouth tortured hers. "Please, don't do this…to me. The driver…"

"I closed the curtain, didn't you notice?" he whispered.

She looked past him, her breath jerky and quick, her face flushed, her eyes wild.

"You see?" he asked quietly.

She swallowed, struggling for control. Her eyes closed and she pulled carefully away from his warm hands.

"No," she said then.

"All right." He moved back and finished his cigarette in silence.

She glanced at him warily, tucking back a loose strand of hair.

"There's nothing to be afraid of," he said, as if he sensed all her hidden fears. "I want nothing from you that you don't want to give freely."

She clasped her hands together. Her tongue touched her dry lips, and she could still taste him on them. It was so intimate that she caught her breath.

"I can't go with you," she burst out, all at once.

"Your door has a lock," he reminded her. "And I'll even give you my word that I won't force you."

Her troubled eyes sought his and he smiled reassuringly.

"Let me rephrase that," he said after a minute. "I won't take advantage of any…lapses. Is that better?"

She clutched her purse hard enough to wrinkle the soft leather wallet inside. "I hate being vulnerable!"

"Do you think I don't?" he growled, his eyes flashing. He crushed out his cigarette. "I'm thirty-five, and it's never happened to me before." He glared at her. "And it had to be with a damned virgin!"

"Don't you curse at me!"

"I wasn't cursing," he said harshly. He reached for another cigarette.

"Will you please stop that?" she pleaded. "I'm choking on the smoke as it is."

He made a rough sound and repocketed the cigarette. "That's it! I quit. You'll be carrying a noose around with you next."

"I'm glad you're quitting smoking, but I won't be throwing a rope around your neck," she promised him with a sweet smile. "Confirmed bachelors aren't my cup of tea."

"Career women aren't mine."

She turned her eyes out the window. And for the rest of the drive to the ranch she didn't say another word.

The room he gave her was the one she'd had before. But she was surprised to see that the linen hadn't been changed. And the checks he'd written for her were just where she'd left them, on the dresser.

She stared at him as he set her bag down. "It's...you haven't torn them up," she faltered.

He straightened, taking off his hat to run a hand through his thick, dark hair. "So what?" he growled, challenge in his very posture. He towered over her.

"Well, I don't want them!" she burst out.

"Of course not," he replied. "You've got a good paying job, now, don't you?"

Her chin lifted. "Yes, I do."

He tossed his hat onto the dresser and moved toward her.

"You promised!" she burst out.

"Sure I did," he replied. He reached out and jerked her up into his arms, staring into her eyes. "What if I lied?" he whispered gruffly. "What if I meant to throw you on that bed, and strip you, and make love to you until dawn?"

He was testing her. So that was how it was going to be. She stared back at him fearlessly. "Try it," she invited.

His mouth curled up. "No hysterics?"

"I stopped having hysterics the day that horse threw me and you got an anatomy lesson," she tossed back. "Go ahead, take me."

His face darkened. "It wouldn't be like that. Not between you and me. Honey," he said softly, "you want me. Desperately."

She did. The feel of him, the clean smell of his body, the coiled strength in his powerful muscles were all working on her like drugs. But she was too afraid of the future to slide backwards now. He wanted her. But nothing more. And without love, she wanted nothing he had to offer.

"You promised," she said again.

He sighed. "So I did. Damned fool." He set her down on her feet and moved away with a long sigh to pick up his hat. His eyes studied her from the doorway. "Well, come on down when you're rested, and I'll have Consuelo fix something to eat."

"Consuelo?"

"My housekeeper." His eyes watched the expressions that washed over her face. "She's forty-eight, nicely plump, and happily married to one of my new hands. All right?"

"Did you hope I might be jealous?" she asked.

His broad chest rose and fell swiftly. "I've got a lot of high hopes about you. Care to hear a few of them?"

"Not particularly."

"That's what I was afraid of." He went out and closed the door behind him with an odd laugh.

CHAPTER TEN

CONSUELO WAS A TREASURE. Small, dark, very quick around the kitchen, and Jennifer liked her on sight.

"It is good that you are here, señorita," the older woman said as she put food on the new and very elegant dining room table. "So nice to see the señor do something besides growl and pace."

Jennifer laughed as she put out the silverware. "Yes, now he's cursing at the top of his lungs," she mused, cocking her ear toward the window. "Hear him?"

It would have been impossible not to. He was giving somebody hell about an open gate, and Jennifer was glad it wasn't her.

"Such a strange man," Consuelo sighed, shaking her head. "The room he has given you, señorita, he would not let me touch it. Not to dust, not even to change the linen."

"Did he say why?" Jennifer asked with studied carelessness.

"No. But sometimes at night…" She hesitated.

"Yes?"

Consuelo shrugged at the penetrating look she got from the younger woman. "Sometimes at night, the señor, he would go up there and just sit. For a long time. I wonder, you see, but the only time I mention this strange habit, he says to mind my own business. So I do not question it."

How illuminating that was. Jennifer pondered on it long and hard. It was almost as if he'd missed her. But then, if he'd missed her, he'd have to care. And he didn't. He just wanted her because she was something different, a virgin. And perhaps because she was the only woman who'd been close to him for a long time. Under the same circumstances, it could very well have been any young, reasonably attractive woman.

He came in from the corral looking dusty and tired and out of humor. Consuelo glanced at him and he glared at her as he removed his wide-brimmed hat and sat down at the table with his chaps still on.

"Any comments?" he growled.

"Not from me, señor," Consuelo assured him. "As far as I am concerned, you can sit there in your overcoat. Lunch is on the table. Call if you need me."

Jennifer put a hand over her mouth to keep from laughing. Everett glared at her.

"My, you're in a nasty mood," she observed as she poured him a cup of coffee from the carafe. She filled her own cup, too.

"Pat yourself on the back," he returned.

She raised her eyebrows. "Me?"

"You." He picked up a roll and buttered it.

"I can leave?" she suggested.

"Go ahead."

She sat back in her chair, watching him. "What's wrong?" she asked quietly. "Something is."

"Bull died."

She caught her breath. "The big Hereford?"

He nodded. "The one I sold and then bought back when I leased the oil rights." He stared at his roll blankly. "The vet's going to do an autopsy. I want to know why. He was healthy."

"I'm sorry," she said gently. "You were very proud of him."

His jaw tautened. "Well, maybe some of those heifers I bred to him will throw a good bull."

She dished up some mashed potatoes and steak and gravy. "I thought heifers were cows that hadn't grown up," she murmured. "Isn't that what you told me?"

"Heifers are heifers until they're two years old and bred for the first time. Which these just were."

"Oh."

He glanced at her. "I'm surprised you'd remember that."

"I remember a lot about the ranch," she murmured as she ate. "Are you selling off stock before winter?"

"Not a lot of it," he said. "Now that I can afford to feed the herd."

"It's an art, isn't it?" she asked, lifting her eyes to his. "Cattle-raising, I mean. It's very methodical."

"Like decorating?" he muttered.

"That reminds me." She got up, fetched her sketch pad, and put it down beside his plate. "I did those before I came down. They're just the living room and kitchen, but I'd like to see what you think."

"You're the decorator," he said without opening it. "Do what you please."

She glared at him and put down her fork. "Everett, it's your house. I'd at least like you to approve the suggestions I'm making."

He sighed and opened the sketch pad. He frowned. His head came up suddenly. "I didn't know you could draw like this."

"It kind of goes with the job," she said, embarrassed.

"Well, you're good. Damned good. Is this what it will look like when you're finished?" he asked.

"Something like it. I'll do more detailed drawings if you like the basic plan."

"Yes, I like it," he said with a slow smile. He ran a finger over her depiction of the sofa and she remembered suddenly that instead of drawing in a new one, she'd sketched the old one. The one they'd lain on that night....

She cleared her throat. "The kitchen sketch is just under that one."

He looked up. "Was that a Freudian slip, drawing that particular sofa?" he asked.

Her face went hot. "I'm human!" she grumbled.

His eyes searched hers. "No need to overheat, Miss King. I was just asking a question. I enjoyed what we did, too. I'm not throwing stones." He turned the page and pursed his lips. "I don't like the breakfast bar."

Probably because it would require the services of an architect, she thought evilly.

"Why?" she asked anyway, trying to sound interested.

He smiled mockingly. "Because, as I told you already, I won't have that redhead in my house."

She sighed angrily. "As you wish." She studied his hard face. "Will you have a few minutes to go over some ideas with me tonight? Or are you still trying to work yourself into an early grave?"

"Would you mind if I did, Jenny?" he mused.

"Yes. I wouldn't get paid," she said venomously.

He chuckled softly. "Hardhearted little thing. Yes, I'll have some free time tonight." He finished his coffee. "But not now." He got up from the table.

"I'm sorry about your bull."

He stopped by her chair and tilted her chin up. "It will all work out," he said enigmatically. His thumb brushed over her soft mouth slowly, with electrifying results. She stared up with an expression that seemed to incite violence in him.

"Jenny," he breathed gruffly, and started to bend.

"Señor," Consuelo called, coming through the door in time to break the spell holding them, "do you want dessert now?"

"I'd have had it but for you, woman," he growled. And with that he stomped out the door, rattling the furniture as he went.

Consuelo stared after him, and Jennifer tried not to look guilty and frustrated all at once.

For the rest of the day, Jennifer went from room to room, making preliminary sketches. It was like a dream come true. For a long time, ever since she'd first seen the big house, she'd wondered what it would be like to redo it. Now she was getting the chance, and she was overjoyed. The only sad part was that Everett wouldn't let her get Drew in to do an appraisal of the place. It would be a shame to redo it if there were basic structural problems.

That evening after a quiet supper she went into the study with him and watched him build a fire in the fireplace. It was late autumn and getting cold at night. The fire crackled and burned in orange and yellow glory and smelled of oak and pine and the whole outdoors.

"How lovely," she sighed, leaning back in the armchair facing it with her eyes closed. She was wearing jeans again, with a button-down brown patterned shirt, and she felt at home.

"Yes," he said.

She opened her eyes lazily to find him standing in front of her, staring quietly at her face.

"Sorry, I drifted off," she said quickly, and started to rise.

"Don't get up. Here." He handed her the sketch pad and perched himself on the arm of the chair, just close enough to drive her crazy with the scent and warmth and threat of his big body. "Show me."

She went through the sketches with him, showing the changes she wanted to make. When they came to his big bedroom, her voice faltered as she suggested new Mediterranean furnishings and a king-size bed.

"You're very big," she said, trying not to look at him. "And the room is large enough to accommodate it."

"By all means," he murmured, watching her. "I like a lot of room."

It was the way he said it. She cleared her throat. "And I thought a narrow chocolate-and-vanilla-stripe wallpaper would be nice. With a thick cream carpet and chocolate-colored drapes."

"Am I going to live in the room, or eat it?"

"Hush. And you could have a small sitting area if you like. A desk and a chair, a lounge chair..."

"All I want in my bedroom is a bed," he grumbled. "I can work down here."

"All right." She flipped the page, glad to be on to the next room, which was a guest bedroom. "This..."

"No."

She glanced up. "What?"

"No. I don't want another guest room there." He looked down into her eyes. "Make it into a nursery."

She felt her body go cold. "A nursery?"

"Well, I've got to have someplace to put the kids," he said reasonably.

"Where are they going to come from?" she asked blankly.

He sighed with exaggerated patience. "First you have a man. Then you have a woman. They sleep together and—"

"I know that!"

"Then why did you ask me?"

"Forgive me if I sound dull, but didn't you swear that you'd rather be dead than married?" she grumbled.

"Sure. But being rich has changed my ideas around. I've decided that I'll need somebody to leave all this to." He pulled out a cigarette and lit it.

She stared at her designs with unseeing eyes. "Do you have a candidate already?" she asked with a forced laugh.

"No, not yet. But there are plenty of women around."
His eyes narrowed as he studied her profile. "As a matter of fact, I had a phone call last week. From the woman I used to be engaged to. Seems her marriage didn't work out. She's divorced now."

That hurt. She hadn't expected that it would, but it went through her like a dagger. "Oh?" she said. Her pencil moved restlessly on the page as she darkened a line. "Were you surprised?"

"Not really," he said with cynicism. "Women like that are pretty predictable. I told you how I felt about buying them."

"Yes." She drew in a slow breath. "Well, Houston is full of debutantes. You shouldn't have much trouble picking out one."

"I don't want a child."

She glanced up. "Picky, aren't you?"

His mouth curled. "Yep."

She laughed despite herself, despite the cold that was numbing her heart. "Well, I wish you luck. Now, about the nursery, do you want it done in blue?"

"No. I like girls, too. Make it pink and blue. Or maybe yellow. Something unisex." He got up, stretching lazily, and yawned. "God, I'm tired. Honey, do you mind if we cut this short? I'd dearly love a few extra hours' sleep."

"Of course not. Do you mind if I go ahead with the rooms we've discussed?" she asked. "I could go ahead and order the materials tomorrow. I've already arranged to have the wallpaper in the living room stripped."

"Go right ahead." He glanced at her. "How long do you think it will take, doing the whole house?"

"A few weeks, that's all."

He nodded. "Sleep well, Jenny. Good night."

"Good night."

He went upstairs, and she sat by the fire until it went out, trying to reconcile herself to the fact that Everett was going to get married and have children. It would be to somebody like Libby, she thought. Some nice, sweet country girl who had no ambition to be anything but a wife and mother. Tears dripped down her cheeks and burned her cool flesh. What a pity it wouldn't be Jennifer.

She decided that perhaps Everett had had the right idea in the first place. Exhaustion was the best way in the world to keep one's mind off one's troubles. So she got up at dawn to oversee the workmen who were tearing down wallpaper and repairing plaster. Fortunately the plasterwork was in good condition and wouldn't have to be redone. By the time they were finished with the walls, the carpet people had a free day and invaded the house. She escaped to the corral and watched Eddie saddlebreak one of the new horses Everett had bought.

Perched on the corral fence in her jeans and blue sweatshirt, with her hair in a ponytail, she looked as outdoorsy as he did.

"How about if I yell 'ride 'em, cowboy,' and cheer you on, Eddie?" she drawled.

He lifted a hand. "Go ahead, Miss Jenny!"

"Ride 'em, cowboy!" she hollered.

He chuckled, bouncing around on the horse. She was

so busy watching him that she didn't even hear Everett ride up behind her. He reached out a long arm and suddenly jerked her off the fence and into the saddle in front of him.

"Sorry to steal your audience, Eddie," he yelled toward the older man, "but she's needed!"

Eddie waved. Everett's hard arm tightened around her waist, tugging her stiff body into the curve of his, as he urged the horse into a canter.

"Where am I needed?" she asked, peeking over her shoulder at his hard face.

"I've got a new calf. Thought you might like to pet it."

She laughed. "I'm too busy to pet calves."

"Sure. Sitting around on fences like a rodeo girl." His arm tightened. "Eddie doesn't need an audience to break horses."

"Well, it was interesting."

"So are calves."

She sighed and let her body slump back against his. She felt him stiffen at the contact, felt his breath quicken. She could smell him, and feel him, and her body sang at the contact. It had been such a long time since those things had disturbed her.

"Where are we going?" she murmured contentedly.

"Down to the creek. Tired?"

"Mmm," she murmured. "My arms ache."

"I've got an ache of my own, but it isn't in my arms," he mused.

She cleared her throat and sat up straight. "Uh, what kind of calf is it?"

He laughed softly. "I've got an ache in my back from lifting equipment," he said, watching her face burn. "What did you think I meant?"

"Everett," she groaned, embarrassed.

"You babe in the woods," he murmured. His fingers spread on her waist, so long that they trespassed onto her flat stomach as well. "Hold on."

He put the horse into a gallop and she caught her breath, turning in the saddle to cling to his neck and hide her face in his shoulder.

He laughed softly, coiling his arm around her. "I won't let you fall," he chided.

"Do we have to go so fast?"

"I thought you were in a hurry to get there." He slowed the horse as they reached a stand of trees beside the creek. Beyond it was a barbed-wire fence. Inside it was a cow and a calf, both Herefords.

He dismounted and lifted Jenny down. "She's gentle," he said, taking her hand to pull her along toward the horned cow. "I raised this one myself, from a calf. Her mama died of snakebite and I nursed her with a bottle. She's been a good breeder. This is her sixth calf."

The furry little thing fascinated Jenny. It had pink eyes and a pink nose and pink ears, and the rest of it was reddish-brown and white.

She laughed softly and rubbed it between the eyes. "How pretty," she murmured. "She has pink eyes!"

"He," he corrected. "It will be a steer."

She frowned. "Not a bull?"

He glowered down at her. "Don't you ever listen to me? A steer is a bull that's been converted for beef. A bull has…" He searched for the words. "A bull is still able to father calves."

She grinned up at him. "Not embarrassed, are you?" she taunted.

He cocked an eyebrow. "You're the one who gets embarrassed every time I talk straight," he said curtly.

She remembered then, and her smile faded. She touched the calf gently, concentrating on it instead of him.

His lean hands caught her waist and she gasped, stiffening. His breath came hard and fast at her back.

"There's a party in Victoria tomorrow night. One of the oil men's giving it. He asked me to come." His fingers bit into her soft flesh. "How about going with me and holding my hand? I don't know much about social events."

"You don't really want to go, do you?" she asked, looking over her shoulder at him knowingly.

He shook his head. "But it's expected. One of the penalties of being well-off. Socializing."

"Yes, I'll be very proud to go with you."

"Need a dress? I'll buy you one, since it was my idea."

She lowered her eyes. "No, thank you. I… I have one at my apartment, if you'll have someone drive me up there."

"Give Ted the key. He'll pick it up for you," he said, naming his chauffeur, who was also the new yardman.

"All right."

"Is it white?" he asked suddenly.

She glared at him. "No. It's black. Listen here, Everett Culhane, just because I've never—"

He put a finger over her lips, silencing her. "I like you in white," he said simply. "It keeps me in line," he added with a wicked, slow smile.

"You just remember the nice new wife you'll have and the kids running around the house, and that will work very well," she said with a nip in her voice. "Shouldn't we go back? The carpet-layers may have some questions for me."

"Don't you like kids, Jenny?" he asked softly.

"Well, yes."

"Could you manage to have them and a career at the same time?" he asked with apparent indifference.

Her lips pouted softly. "Lots of women do," she said. "It's not the dark ages."

He searched her eyes. "I know that. But there are men who wouldn't want a working wife."

"Cavemen," she agreed.

He chuckled. "A woman like you might make a man nervous in that respect. You're pretty. Suppose some other man snapped you up while you were decorating his house? That would be hell on your husband's nerves."

"I don't want to get married," she informed him.

His eyebrows lifted. "You'd have children out of wedlock?"

"I didn't say that!"

"Yes, you did."

"Everett!" Her hands pushed at his chest. He caught

them and lifted them slowly around his neck, tugging so that her body rested against his.

"Ummmm," he murmured on a smile, looking down at the softness of her body. "That feels nice. What were you saying, about children?"

"If…if I wanted them, then I guess I'd get married. But I'd still work. I mean… Everett, don't…" she muttered when he slid his hands down to her waist and urged her closer.

"Okay. You'd still work?"

His hands weren't pushing, but they were doing something crazy to her nerves. They caressed her back lazily, moving up to her hair to untie the ribbon that held it back.

"I'd work when the children started school. That was what I meant… Will you stop that?" she grumbled, reaching back to halt his fingers.

He caught her hands, arching her so that he could look down and see the vivid tautness of her breasts against the thin fabric of her blouse.

"No bra?" he murmured, and the smile got bigger. "My, my, another Freudian slip?"

"Will you stop talking about bras and slips and let go of my hands, Mr. Culhane?" she asked curtly.

"I don't think you really want me to do that, Jenny," he murmured dryly.

"Why?"

"Because if I let go of your hands, I have to put mine somewhere else." He looked down pointedly at her blouse. "And there's really only one place I want to put them right now."

Her chest rose and fell quickly, unsteadily. His closeness and the long abstinence and the sun and warmth of the day were all working on her. Her eyes met his suddenly and the contact was like an electric jolt. All the memories came rushing back, all the old hungers.

"Do you remember that day you fell off the horse?" he asked in a soft, low tone, while bees buzzed somewhere nearby. "And your blouse came open, and I looked down and you arched your back so that I could see you even better."

Her lips parted and she shook her head nervously.

"Oh, but you did," he breathed. "I'd seen you, watching my mouth, wondering…and that day, it all came to a head. I looked at you and I wanted you. So simply. So hungrily. I barely came to my senses in time, and before I did, I was hugging the life out of you. And you were letting me."

She remembered that, too. It had been so glorious, being held that way.

He let go of her hands all at once and slid his arms around her, half lifting her off her feet. "Hard, Jenny," he whispered, drawing her slowly to him, so that she could feel her breasts flattening against his warm chest. It was like being naked against him.

She caught her breath and moaned. His cheek slid against hers and he buried his face in her throat. His arms tightened convulsively. And he rocked her, and rocked her, and she clung to him while all around them the wind blew and the sun burned, and the world seemed to disappear.

His breath came roughly and his arms trembled. "I

don't feel this with other women," he said after a while. "You make me hungry."

"As you keep reminding me," she whispered back, "I'm not on the menu."

"Yes, I know." He brushed his mouth against her throat and then lifted his head and slowly released her. "No more of that," he said on a rueful sigh, "unless you'd like to try making love on horseback. I've got a man coming to see me about a new bull."

Her eyes widened. "Can people really make..." She turned away, shaking her head.

"I don't know," he murmured, chuckling at her shyness. "I've never tried it. But there's always a first time."

"You just keep your hands to yourself," she cautioned as he put her into the saddle and climbed up behind her.

"I'm doing my best, honey," he said dryly. He reached around her to catch the reins and his arm moved lazily across her breasts, feeling the hardened tips. "Oh, Jenny," he breathed shakily, "next time you'd better wear an overcoat."

She wanted to stop him, she really did. But the feel of that muscular forearm was doing terribly exciting things to her. She felt her muscles tauten in a dead giveaway.

She knew it was going to happen even as he let go of the reins and his hands slid around her to lift and cup her breasts. She let him, turning her cheek against his chest with a tiny cry.

"The sweetest torture on earth," he whispered unsteadily. His hands were so tender, so gentle. He made no move to open the blouse, although he must have known that he could, that she would have let him. His lips moved warmly at her temple. "Jenny, you shouldn't let me touch you like this."

"Yes, I know," she whispered huskily. Her hands moved over his to pull them away, but they lingered on his warm brown fingers. Her head moved against his chest weakly.

"Do you want to lie down on the grass with me and make love?" he asked softly. "We could, just for a few minutes. We could kiss and touch each other, and nothing more."

She wanted to. She wanted it more than she wanted to breathe. But it was too soon. She wasn't sure of him. She only knew that he wanted her desperately and that she didn't dare pave the way for him. It was just a game to him. It kept him from getting bored while he found himself a wife. She loved him, but love on one side would never be enough.

"No, Rett," she said, although the words were torn from her. She moved his hands gently down, to her waist, and pressed them there. "No."

He drew away in a long, steady breath. "Levelheaded Jenny," he said finally. "Did you know?"

"Know what?"

"That if I'd gotten you on the grass, nothing would have saved you?"

She smiled ruefully. "It was kind of the other way around." She felt him shudder, and she turned and pressed herself into his arms. "I want you, too. Please don't do this to me. I can't be what you want. Please, let me decorate your house and go away. Don't hurt me anymore, Rett."

He lifted and turned her so that she was lying across the saddle in his arms. He held her close and took the reins in his hand. "I'm going to have to rethink my strategy, I'm afraid." He sighed. "It isn't working."

She looked up. "What do you mean?"

He searched her eyes and bent and kissed her forehead softly. "Never mind, kitten. You're safe now. Just relax. I'll take you home."

She snuggled close and closed her eyes. This was a memory she'd keep as long as she lived, of riding across the meadow in Everett's arms on a lovely autumn morning. His wife would have other memories. But this one would always be her own, in the long, lonely years ahead. Her hand touched his chest lightly, and her heart ached for him. If only he could love her back. But love wasn't a word he trusted anymore, and she couldn't really blame him. He'd been hurt too much. Even by her, when she hadn't meant to. She sighed bitterly. It was all too late. If only it had been different. Tears welled up in her eyes. If only.

CHAPTER ELEVEN

JENNIFER WISHED FOR the tenth time that she'd refused Everett's invitation to the exclusive party in Victoria. It seemed that every single, beautiful woman in the world had decided to converge on the spot just to cast her eyes at Everett.

He did look good, Jennifer had to admit. There just wasn't anybody around who came close to matching him. Dressed in an elegant dinner jacket, he looked dark and debonair and very sophisticated. Not to mention sexy. The way the jacket and slacks fit, every muscle in that big body was emphasized in the most masculine way. It was anguish just to look at him; it was even worse to remember how it was to be held and touched by him. Jennifer felt her body tingle from head to toe and the memory of the day before, of his hands smoothing over her body, his voice husky and deep in her ear. And now there he stood making eyes at a gorgeous brunette.

She turned away and tossed down the entire contents of her brandy glass. If she hadn't been so tired from overworking herself, the brandy might not have been as potent. But it was her second glass and, despite the filling buffet, she was feeling the alcohol to a frightening degree. She kept telling herself that she didn't look bad herself, with her blond hair hanging long and loose around the shoulders of her low-cut clinging black dress. She was popular enough. So why didn't Everett dance one dance with her?

By the time she was danced around the room a couple of times by left-footed oilmen and dashing middle-aged married men, she felt like leaping over the balcony. How odd that at any party there were never any handsome, available bachelors.

"Sorry to cut in, but I have to take Jenny home," Everett said suddenly, cutting out a balding man in his fifties who was going over and over the latest political crisis with maddening intricacy.

Jennifer almost threw herself on Everett in gratitude. She mumbled something polite and completely untrue to the stranger, smiled, and stumbled into Everett's arms.

"Careful, honey, or we'll both wind up on the floor." He laughed softly. "Are you all right?"

"I'm just fine." She sighed, snuggling close. Her arms slid around him. "Everett, can I go to sleep now?"

He frowned and pulled her head up. "How much have you had to drink?"

"I lost count." She grinned. Her eyes searched his face blearily. "Gosh, Rett, you're so sexy."

A red stain highlighted his cheekbones. "You're drunk, all right. Come on."

"Where are we going?" she protested. "I want to dance."

"We'll dance in the car."

She frowned. "We can't stand up in there," she said reasonably.

He held her hand, tugging her along. They said good night to a couple she vaguely recognized as their hosts; then he got their coats from the maid and hustled her out into the night.

"Cold out here," she muttered. She nudged herself under his arm and pressed against his side with a sigh. "Better."

"For whom?" he ground out. His chest rose and fell heavily. "I wish I'd let Ted drive us."

"Why?" she murmured, giggling. "Are you afraid to be alone with me? You can trust me, honey," she said, nudging him. "I wouldn't seduce you, honest."

A couple passed them going down the steps, and the elderly woman gave Jennifer a curious look.

"He's afraid of me," Jennifer whispered. "He isn't on the pill, you see…"

"Jenny!" he growled, jerking her close.

"Not here, Rett!" she exclaimed. "My goodness, talk about impatience…!"

He was muttering something about a gag as he half-led, half-dragged her to the car.

"You old stick-in-the-mud, you." She laughed after he'd put her inside and climbed in next to her. "Did I embarrass you?"

He only glanced at her as he started the Lincoln. "You're going to hate yourself in the morning when I remind you what you've been saying. And I will," he promised darkly. "Ten times a day."

"You look gorgeous when you're mad," she observed. She moved across the seat and nuzzled close again. "I'll sleep with you tonight, if you like," she said gaily.

He stiffened and muttered something under his breath.

"Well, you've been trying to get me into bed with you, haven't you?" she asked. "Propositioning me that last day at the ranch, and then coming after me, and making all sorts of improper remarks...so now I agree, and what do you do? You get all red in the face and start cussing. Just like a man. The minute you catch a girl, you're already in pursuit of someone else, like that brunette you were dancing with," she added, glaring up at him. "Well, just don't expect that what you see is what you get, because I was in the ladies' room with her, and it's padded! I saw!"

He was wavering between anger and laughter. Laughter won. He started, and couldn't seem to stop.

"You won't think it's very funny if you take her out," she kept on, digging her own grave. Everything was fuzzy and pink and very pleasant. She felt so relaxed! "She's even smaller than I am," she muttered. "And her legs are just awful. She pulled up her skirt to fix her stockings...she hardly has any legs, they're so skinny!"

"Meow," he taunted.

She tossed back her long hair, and leaned her head back against the seat. Her coat had come open, revealing the deep neckline of the black dress. "Why won't you make love to me?"

"Because if I did, you'd scream your head off," he said reasonably. "Here, put your tired little head on my shoulder and close your eyes. You're soaked, honey."

She blinked. "I am not. It isn't raining."

He reached out an arm and pulled her against him.

"Close your eyes, sweet," he said in a soft, tender tone. "I'll take good care of you."

"Will you sleep with me?" she murmured, resting her head on his shoulder.

"If you want me to."

She smiled and closed her eyes with a long sigh. "That would be lovely," she whispered. And it was the last thing she said.

MORNING CAME WITH blinding light and some confounded bird twittering his feathered head off outside the window.

"Oh, go away!" she whispered, and held her head. "An axe," she groaned. "There's an axe between my eyes. Bird, shut up!"

Soft laughter rustled her hair. She opened her eyes. Laughter?

Her head turned on the pillow and Everett's eyes looked back into her own. She gasped and tried to sit up, then groaned with the pain and fell back down again.

"Head hurt? Poor baby."

"You slept with me?" she burst out. She turned her head slowly to look at him. He was fully dressed, except for his shoes and jacket. He even had his shirt on. He was lying on top of the coverlet, and she was under it.

Slowly, carefully, she lifted the cover and looked. Her face flamed scarlet. She was dressed in nothing but a tiny pair of briefs. The rest of her was pink and tingling.

"Rett!" she burst out, horrified.

"I only undressed you," he said, leaning on an elbow to watch her. "Be reasonable, honey. You couldn't sleep in your evening gown. And," he added with a faint grin, "it wasn't my fault that you didn't have anything on under it. You can't imagine how shocked I was."

"That's right, I can't," she agreed, and her eyes accused him.

"I confess I did stare a little," he murmured. His hand brushed the unruly blond hair out of her eyes. "A lot," he corrected. "My God, Jenny," he said on a slow breath, "you are the most glorious sight undressed that I ever saw in my life. I nearly fainted."

"Shame on you!" she said, trying to feel outraged. It was difficult, because she was still tingling from the compliment.

"For what? For appreciating something beautiful?" He touched her nose with a long, lean finger. "Shame on you, for being embarrassed. I was a perfect gentleman. I didn't even touch you, except to put you under the covers."

"Oh."

"I thought I'd wait until you woke up, and do it then," he added with a grin.

Her fingers grabbed the covers tightly. "Oh, no, you don't!"

He moved closer, his fingers tangling in her blond hair as he loomed above her. "You had a lot to say about that brunette. Or don't you remember?"

She blinked. Brunette? Vaguely she remembered saying something insulting about the woman's body. Then she remembered vividly. Her face flamed.

"Something about how little she was, if I recall," he murmured dryly.

She bit her lower lip and her eyes met his uneasily. "Did I? How strange. Was she short?"

"That wasn't what you meant," he said. One lean hand moved down her shoulder and over the covers below her collarbone. "You meant, here, she was small."

If she looked up, she'd be finished. But she couldn't help it. Her eyes met his and the world seemed to narrow down to the two of them. She loved him so. Would it be wrong to kiss him just once more, to feel that hard, wonderful mouth on her own?

He seemed to read that thought, because his jaw tautened and his breathing became suddenly ragged. "The hell with being patient," he growled, reaching for the covers. "Come here."

He stripped them away and jerked her into his arms, rolling over with her, so that she was lying on him. Where his shirt was undone, her body pressed nakedly into his hairy chest.

His eyes were blazing as they looked up into hers. He deliberately reached down to yank his shirt away, his eyes on the point where her soft breasts were crushed against his body. Dark and light, she thought shakily, looking at the contrast between his dark skin and her pale flesh.

But still he didn't touch her. His hands moved up into her hair, oddly tender, at variance with the tension she could feel in his body.

"Don't you want…to touch me?" she whispered nervously.

"More than my own life," he confessed. "But I'm not going to. Come down here and kiss me."

"Why not?" she whispered, bending to give him her mouth.

"Because Consuelo's on her way up the stairs with coffee and toast," he breathed. "And she never knocks."

She sat up with a gasp. "Why didn't you say so!"

He laughed softly, triumphantly, his eyes eating her soft body as she climbed out of the bed and searched wildly for a robe.

"Here," he murmured, throwing his long legs over the bed. He reached under her pillow and got her nightgown. "Come here and I'll stuff you in it."

She didn't even question the impulse that made her obey him instantly. She lifted her arms as he held the nightgown over her head and gasped as he bent first and kissed her rosy breasts briefly, but with a tangible hunger. While she was getting over the shock, he tugged the long cotton gown over her head, lifted her, tossed her into the bed, and pulled the covers over her with a knowing smile.

And Consuelo opened the door before she could get out a word.

"Good morning!" The older woman laughed, handing the tray to Everett. "Also is hair of the dog, in the glass," she added with a wry glance at Jennifer. "To make the señorita's head a little better."

And she was gone as quickly as she'd come. Everett put the tray down beside Jennifer on the bed and poured cream into her coffee.

"Why did you do that?" she whispered, still shaking from the wild little caress.

"I couldn't help myself," he murmured, smiling at her. "I've wanted to, for a long time."

She took the coffee in trembling hands. He steadied them, watching her shaken features.

"It's part of lovemaking," he said softly. "Nothing sordid or shameful. When we make love, that's how I'll rouse you before I take you."

She shuddered, and the coffee cup began to rock again. Her eyes, meeting his, were wild with mingled fear and hunger.

"Except," he added quietly, "that I won't stop at the waist."

Coffee went everywhere. She cursed and muttered and grumbled and moped. But when she raised her glittering eyes to his the pupils dilated until they were almost black.

He laughed softly, menacingly. "Almost," he said enigmatically. "Almost there." He got up. "I'll get Consuelo to come and help you mop up." He turned with one hand on the doorknob, impossibly attractive, wildly sensuous with his hair ruffled and his shirt open and his bare, muscular chest showing. "The brunette was Jeb Doyle's daughter," he added. "She's looking for a husband. She rides like a man, she loves cattle and kids, she's twenty-eight and she lives about five miles south of here. She may be small, but she's got nice, full hips. Just right for having children. Her name's Sandy."

She was getting madder by the second. He was baiting her! She picked up the coffee cup and, without even thinking, threw it at him.

It shattered against the closed door. He went down

the hall laughing like a banshee and she screamed after him. By the time Consuelo got to her, the rest of the coffee and the headache remedy had turned the bedspread a strange shade of tan.

For the next week, she gave Everett the coldest shoulder she could manage. He was gone from the ranch frequently, and she noticed it and remembered what he'd said about the brunette, and wanted desperately to kill him. No, not just kill him. Torture him. Slowly. Over an open fire.

It got worse. He started having supper with Jennifer every night, and the whole time he'd sit there and watch her and make infrequent but agonizing remarks about the brunette.

"Sandy's getting a new colt tomorrow," he mentioned one evening, smiling wistfully. "She asked if I'd come over and look at it for her."

"Can't she see it by herself?" she asked sweetly.

"Conformation is very important in a horse," he said. "I used to breed them years ago, before I got interested in cattle."

"Oh." She concentrated on her food.

"How's the decorating coming?"

"Fine," she said through her teeth. "We're getting the paper up in your bedroom tomorrow. Then there'll only be the other bedrooms to go. You never said how you liked the way the living room and the study came out."

"They're okay," he said. He lifted a forkful of dessert to his mouth and she wanted to jump up and stab him in the lip. Okay! And she'd spent days on the projects, working well into the night alongside the men!

He glanced up at her flushed face. "Wasn't that enthusiastic enough?" He took a sip of coffee. "Damn, Jenny, what a hell of a great job you're doing on the house!" he said with a big, artificial smile. "I'm pleased as punch!"

"I'd like to punch you," she muttered. She slammed down her napkin, slid out of the chair, and stomped out of the room.

Watching her, Everett's eyes narrowed and a faint, predatory smile curved his lips.

The next day, she concentrated on his bedroom. It was difficult to work in there, thinking about whose territory it was. Her eyes kept drifting to the bed where he slept, to the pillow where he laid his dark head. Once she paused beside it and ran her hand lovingly over the cover. Besotted, she told herself curtly. She was besotted, and it was no use. He was going to marry that skinny, flat-chested brunette!

She didn't even stop for lunch, much less supper. The workmen had left long before, and she was working on the last wall, when Everett came into the room and stood watching her with a cup of coffee in his hand.

"Have you given up eating?" he asked.

"Yep."

He cocked an eyebrow. "Want some coffee?"

"Nope."

He chuckled softly. "Bad imitation. You don't even look like Gary Cooper. You're too short."

She glared down at him. Her jeans were covered with glue. So were her fingers, her bare arms, and the front of her white T-shirt. "Did you want something?"

"Yes. To go to bed. I've got to get an early start in the morning. I'm taking Sandy fishing."

She stared into the bucket of glue and wondered how he'd look plastered to the wall. It was tempting, but dangerous.

"I'd like to finish this one wall," she murmured quietly.

"Go ahead. I'm going to have a shower." He stripped off his shirt. She glanced at him, fascinated by the dark perfection of him, by the ripple of muscle, the way the light played on his skin as he started to take off his... *trousers!*

Her eyes jerked back to the glue and her hands trembled. "Everett?" she said in a squeaky voice.

"Well, don't look," he said reasonably. "I can't very well take a bath in my clothes."

"I could have left the room," she said.

"Why? Aren't you curious?" he taunted.

She gritted her teeth. "No!"

"Coward."

She put glue and more glue on a strip of wallpaper until the glue was three times as thick as the paper it was spread on. Not until she heard the shower running did she relax. She put the wallpaper in place and started scrambling down the ladder.

Unfortunately, just because the shower was running, it didn't mean that Everett was in it. She got down and started for the door, and there he stood, with a towel wrapped around his narrow hips and not another stitch on.

"Going somewhere?" he asked.

"Yes. Out of here!" she exclaimed, starting past him.

She never knew exactly how it happened. One minute she was walking toward the door, and the next she was lying flat on the bed with Everett's hard body crushing her into the mattress.

His chest rose and fell slowly, his eyes burned down into hers. Holding her gaze, he eased the towel away and bent to her mouth.

She trembled with kindling passion. It was so incredibly sweet to let her hands run over his hard, warm body, to feel the muscles of his back and arms and shoulders and hips. To let him kiss her softly, with growing intimacy. To know the crush of his body, the blatant force of his hunger for her. To love him with her hands and her mouth.

He lifted his head a minute later and looked into her awed eyes. "You're not so squeaky clean yourself," he said softly. "Why don't you come and take a bath with me?"

Her hands touched his hard arms gently, lovingly. "Because we'd do more than bathe, and you know it," she replied on a soft sigh. "All you have to do is touch me, and you can have anything you want. It's always been like that. The only reason I'm still a virgin is that you haven't insisted."

"Why do you think I haven't?" he prodded.

She shifted. "I don't know. Conscience, maybe?"

He bent and brushed his mouth softly over hers. "Go and put on something soft and pretty. Have a shower. Then come downstairs to the living room and we'll talk."

She swallowed. "I thought you had to get to bed early. To take Sandy fishing," she murmured resentfully.

"Did it ever occur to you that you might be formidable competition for her, if you cared to make the effort?" he asked, watching her. "Or didn't you know how easy it would be to seduce me? And once you did that," he murmured, touching her soft mouth, "I'd probably feel obliged to marry you. Not being on the pill and all," his eyes went back to hers with blazing intensity, "you could get pregnant."

Her breath caught in her throat. She never knew when he was teasing, when he was serious. And now, her mind was whirling.

While she worried over his intentions, he moved away from her and got to his feet, and she stared at him in helpless fascination.

"You see?" he said, his voice deep and full of secrets, "it isn't so shocking, is it?"

She lifted her eyes to his. "You're...very..." She tried to find words.

"So are you, honey," he said. "Take your bath and I'll see you downstairs."

And he walked off, oblivious to her intent stare.

Minutes later, she went nervously down the staircase in a white dress, her hair freshly washed and dried, loose around her shoulders. Something that had been brewing between them for a long time was coming abruptly to a head, and she wasn't quite sure how to face it. She had a terrible feeling that he was going to proposition her again, and that she was going to be stupid enough to accept. She loved him madly, wanted him madly. That Sandy person was after him, and Jennifer was afraid. She couldn't quite accept the idea that he might marry someone else. Despite the pain he'd caused her, she dwelled on the fear of losing him.

He was waiting for her. In beige trousers and a patterned beige shirt, he looked larger than life. All man. Sensual and incredibly attractive, especially when she got close enough to catch the scent of his big body.

"Here," he said, offering her a small brandy.

"Thank you," she said politely. She took it, touching his fingers, looking up into dark, quiet eyes. Her lips parted helplessly.

"Now sit down. I want to ask you something."

She sat on the edge of the sofa, but instead of taking the seat beside her, he knelt on the carpet just in front of her. Because of his height, that put her on an unnerving level with his eyes.

"Afraid of me, even now?" he asked softly.

"Especially now," she whispered, trembling. She put the snifter to one side and her trembling fingers reached out and touched the hard lines of his face. "Everett, I'm…so very much in love with you," she said, her voice breaking. "If you want me to be your mistress… oh!"

She was on the carpet, in his arms, being kissed so hungrily that she couldn't even respond to him. His mouth devoured hers, hurting, bruising, and he trembled all over as if with a fever. His hands trembled as they touched, with expert sureness, every line and curve of her body.

"Say it again," he said roughly, lifting his head just enough to look at her.

Her body ached for his. She leaned toward him helplessly. "I love you," she whispered, pride gone to ashes. "I love you, I love you!"

His head moved down to her bodice, his mouth nudged at the buttons, his hands bit into her back. She reached down blindly to get the fabric out of his way, to give him anything, everything he wanted. There were no more secrets. She belonged to him.

His mouth taught her sensations she'd never dreamed her body would feel. She breathed in gasps as his lips and teeth explored her like some precious delicacy. Her hands held him there, caressed his dark head, loved what he was doing to her.

He raised his head to look at her, smiling faintly at her rapt face, her wide, dark green eyes, her flushed cheeks, the glorious disarray of her hair and her dress.

"I'll remember you like this for the rest of our lives," he said. "The way you look right now, in the first sweet seconds of passion. Do you want me badly?"

"Yes," she confessed. She brought his hand to her body and held it against her taut flesh, brushing his knuckles lazily across it. "Feel?"

His nostrils flared and there was something reckless and unbridled in the eyes that held hers. "For a virgin," he murmured, "you're pretty damned exciting to make love to."

She smiled wildly, hotly. "Teach me."

"Not yet."

"Please."

He shook his head. He sat up, leaning back against the sofa with his long legs stretched out, and looked down at her with a wicked smile. "Fasten your dress. You make me crazy like that."

"I thought that was the whole point of the thing?" she asked unsteadily.

"It was, until you started making declarations of love. I was going to seduce you on the sofa. But now I suppose we'd better do it right."

Her eyes widened in confusion. "I don't understand."

He pulled her up and across his lap. "Oh, the hell with it," he murmured, and opened the top button of her bodice again. "God, I love to look at you!"

She swallowed hard. "Don't you want me?"

"Jenny." He laughed. He turned and brought her hips very gently against his. "See?" he whispered.

She buried her face in his throat and he rocked her softly, tenderly.

"Then, why?" she asked on a moan.

"Because we have to do things in the right order, honey. First we get married, then we have sex, then we make babies."

She stiffened. "What?"

"Didn't you hear me?" He eased her head down on his arm so that he could see her face.

"But, Sandy…" she faltered.

"Sandy is a nice girl," he murmured. "I danced one dance with her, and she went back to her fiancé. He's a nice boy. You'll like him."

"Fiancé!"

He jerked her close and held her hard, roughly. "I love you," he said in a voice that paralyzed her. His eyes blazed with it, burned with it. "Oh, God, I love you, Jenny. Love you, want you, need you, in every single damned way there is! If you want me to get on my knees, I'll do it, I'll do anything to make you forget what I said and did to you that last day you were here." He bent and kissed her hungrily, softly, and lifted his head again, breathing hard. "I knew I loved you then," he said, "when you handed me that check to pay for my bull, and told me the truth. And all I could think of was that I loved you, and that you were out of my reach forever. A career woman, a woman with some money of her own, and I had nothing to offer you, no way to keep you. And I chased you away, because it was torture to look at you and feel that way and have no hope at all."

"Rett!" she burst out. Tears welled up in her eyes and she clung to him. "Oh, Rett, why didn't you tell me? I loved you so much!"

"I didn't know that," he said. His voice shook a little. His arms contracted. "I thought you were playing me along. It wasn't until you left that I realized that you must have cared one hell of a lot, to have done what you did for me." He shifted restlessly, and ground her against him. "Don't you know? Haven't you worked it out yet, why I sold the oil rights? I did it so that I'd have enough money to bring you back."

She caught her breath, and the tears overflowed onto his shirt, his throat.

"I didn't even have the price of a bus ticket." He laughed huskily, his voice tormented with memory. "And I knew that without you, the land wouldn't matter, because I couldn't live. I couldn't stay alive. So I sold the oil rights and I bought a car and I called Sally

Wade. And then, I parked across the street to watch for you. And you came out," he said roughly, "laughing and looking so beautiful…holding on to that redheaded ass's arm! I could have broken your neck!"

"He was my friend. Nothing more." She nuzzled her face against him. "I thought you wanted revenge. I didn't realize…!"

"I wouldn't let Consuelo touch your room, did she tell you?" he whispered. "I left it the way it was. For the first week or so… I could still catch the scent of you on the pillow…" His voice broke, and she searched blindly for his mouth, and gave him comfort in the only way she could.

Her fingers touched his face, loved it; her lips told him things, secrets, that even words wouldn't. Gently, tenderly, she drew him up onto the sofa with her, and eased down beside him on it. And with her mouth and her hands and her body, she told him in the sweetest possible way that he'd never be alone as long as she lived.

"We can't," he whispered, trembling.

"Why?" she moaned softly.

"Because I want you in church, Jenny Wren," he whispered, easing her onto her side, soothing her with his hands and his mouth. "I want it all to be just right. I want to hear the words and watch your face when you say them, and tell the whole world that you're my woman. And then," he breathed softly, "then we'll make love and celebrate in the sweetest, most complete way there is. But not like this, darling. Not on a sofa, with-out the rings or the words or the beauty of taking our vows together." He drew back and looked into her damp eyes. "You'll want that, when you look back on our first time. You'll want it when the children are old enough to be told how we met, how we married. You won't want a tarnished memory to put in your scrapbook."

She kissed him softly. "Thank you."

"I love you," he said, smiling. "I can wait. If," he added with a lift of his eyebrow, "you'll put your clothes back on and stop trying to lead me into a life of sin."

"I haven't taken them off," she protested.

"You have." He got up and looked down at her, with the dress around her waist.

"Well, look at you," she grumbled. His shirt was open and out of his trousers, and his belt was unbuckled.

"You did it," he accused.

She burst out laughing as she buttoned buttons. "I suppose I did. Imagine me, actually trying to seduce you. And after all the times I accused you of it!"

"I don't remember complaining," he remarked.

She got to her feet and went into his arms with a warm sigh. "Me, either. How soon can we get married?"

"How about Friday?"

"Three days?" she groaned.

"You can take cold showers," he promised her. "And finish decorating the house. You're not going to have a lot of time for decorating after we're married."

"I'm not, huh?" she murmured. "What will I be doing?"

"I hoped you might ask," he returned with a smile. He bent his head, lifting her gently in his arms. "This is what you'll be doing." And he kissed her with such tenderness that she felt tears running down her warm cheeks. Since it seemed like such a lovely occupation, she didn't even protest. After all, she'd have plenty of time for decorating when the children started school. Meanwhile, Everett showed promise of being a full-time job.

* * * * *

If you love

DIANA PALMER

then you'll love...

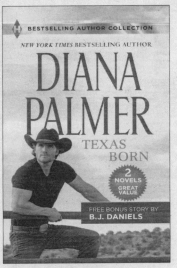

Available March 2021

**ROMANCE WHEN
YOU NEED IT**

HARLEQUIN
SPECIAL EDITION

**Believe in love. Overcome obstacles.
Find happiness.**

Save **$1.00**

off the purchase of ANY
Harlequin Special Edition book.

Available wherever books are sold,
including most bookstores, supermarkets,
drugstores and discount stores.

- ✂

Save $1.00

off the purchase of ANY Harlequin Special Edition book.

Coupon valid until July 31, 2021.
Redeemable at participating outlets in the U.S. and Canada only.
Limit one coupon per customer.

52616990

5 65373 00076 2 (8100)0 12490

DPCOUP0221

HARLEQUIN

Heartfelt or thrilling, passionate or uplifting—Harlequin is more than just happily-ever-after.

With twelve different series to choose from and new books available every month, you are sure to find stories that will move you, uplift you, inspire and delight you.

Love Harlequin romance?

DISCOVER.

Be the first to find out about promotions, news and exclusive content!

f Facebook.com/HarlequinBooks

y Twitter.com/HarlequinBooks

⊙ Instagram.com/HarlequinBooks

p Pinterest.com/HarlequinBooks

You Tube YouTube.com/HarlequinBooks

ReaderService.com

EXPLORE.

Sign up for the Harlequin e-newsletter and download a free book from any series at **TryHarlequin.com**

CONNECT.

Join our Harlequin community to share your thoughts and connect with other romance readers!
Facebook.com/groups/HarlequinConnection